W9-BJF-759

Praise for Lynn Hanna's extraordinary debut, *The Starry Child*

When it is discovered that her eight-year-old daughter, Sasha, is speaking ancient Gaelic, Rainey Nielson and linguist Matt Macinnes uncover the mystical Celtic power in Sasha's soul— and discover their own extraordinary destiny. . . .

"A richly imagined tale full of twists and turns that will keep you guessing to the last page. I couldn't put it down. Lynn Hanna weaves a wonderful timeless tale of love and legends and characters that will steal your heart away!"
—Barbara Freethy

"Hot new author Lynn Hanna makes a spectacular debut with a book that is both magical and magnetic. *The Starry Child* is remarkable, and the great news is that a sequel is on the way."
—*Romantic Times*

"*The Starry Child* is a delightful novel—intense, passionate and full of the magic of Celtic lore. Hanna is a superb storyteller." —*Contra Costa Times* (CA)

"Delightful. . . . A voyage of discovery that includes elements of romance, mystery, suspense, and fantasy. Written in a fluid poetic style, it will make readers long for a Highland getaway . . . enchanting." —*Gothic Journal*

"Imaginative. . . . The mixing of mystical myths . . . is brilliantly designed . . . unique . . . Lynn Hanna has a long-time destiny of her own as a very successful writer."
—*Under the Covers Book Review*

"Charming. . . . [A] spirited yet tender romance."
—*The Romance Reader*

CIRCLE OF TIME

Lynn Hanna

AN ONYX BOOK

ONYX
Published by New American Library, a division of
Penguin Putnam Inc., 375 Hudson Street,
New York, New York 10014, U.S.A.
Penguin Books Ltd, 27 Wrights Lane, London W8 5TZ, England
Penguin Books Australia Ltd, Ringwood, Victoria, Australia
Penguin Books Canada Ltd, 10 Alcorn Avenue,
Toronto, Ontario, Canada M4V 3B2
Penguin Books (N.Z.) Ltd, 182–190 Wairau Road,
Auckland 10, New Zealand

Penguin Books Ltd, Registered Offices:
Harmondsworth, Middlesex, England

First published by Onyx, an imprint of New American Library,
a division of Penguin Putnam Inc.

First Printing, September 1999
10 9 8 7 6 5 4 3 2 1

 REGISTERED TRADEMARK — MARCA REGISTRADA

Printed in the United States of America

PUBLISHER'S NOTE
This is a work of fiction. Names, characters, places, and incidents either are the product of
the author's imagination or are used fictitiously, and any resemblance to actual persons, living or dead, events, or locales is entirely coincidental.

BOOKS ARE AVAILABLE AT QUANTITY DISCOUNTS WHEN USED TO PROMOTE PRODUCTS OR
SERVICES. FOR INFORMATION PLEASE WRITE TO PREMIUM MARKETING DIVISION, PENGUIN
PUTNAM INC., 375 HUDSON STREET, NEW YORK, NEW YORK 10014.

To my parents, Buzz and Barbara Matthews, to my sister, Jill Zanella, and to my own "wee bairns," Noah and Sierrah. And in loving memory of my grandmother, Mary Ina Quigley, a dedicated mentor of hearing-challenged children who was well ahead of her time.

ACKNOWLEDGMENTS

This book would not have been possible without the ongoing faith and support of my literary agent and guide, Susan Ginsburg, and the intuitive and courageous editing skills of my editor, Audrey LaFehr. I would also like to acknowledge the wise and generous contributions of my friend and Scottish Gaelic teacher extraordinaire, Tris King.

Chapter 1

Visibility was zero.

Matt tried to find a more comfortable position in the plane's narrow seat. The big jet was being buffeted around like a balsa wood toy, and more than one passenger in his immediate vicinity had grabbed for the airsickness bags.

He noticed the disheveled state of the flight attendant nearest him as she tried to reassure an elderly man. Her blond hair had fallen loose from her very smooth, professional French twist so that the holder swung back and forth comically. She had not been able to use a steadying hand long enough to put it all back into place. Even though she was being very calm and efficient in the performance of her duties, her makeup was smeared, quite possibly from tears of worry she had not had the time to hide.

They had been delayed on the ground for hours in an effort to wait out the storm. But apparently, economics had won out, and someone in authority somewhere along the line had given the flight the go-ahead. As the plane took another hard pounding to the midsection, Matt had to wonder at the wisdom of the decision.

If he hadn't been so eager to get home, he would have delayed flying till the following day. But his ladies were calling to him. His beloved Rainey was calling to him. They wanted him home as much as he wanted to be there for them. So, he had gotten on board this brutal flight from hell.

He looked down the aisle a bit enviously toward the first-class section, where a colleague of his from the university, Professor Wallace Cameron, was riding. Cameron was thirty years his senior, very old school, a bit stuffy and rigid in his approach to history and life in general. But the man had a wry sense of humor when he chose to show it, and he had an astounding wealth of knowledge about the Iron Age. They had attended several overseas conferences together.

But Cameron refused to fly coach, and Matt had never been able to justify flying first class. As a result, the opportunity they might have had to pass the time comparing notes on the conference was removed. Matt had been tempted to go forward earlier to see if he could sneak in a few moments of camaraderie before the flight attendants kicked him out as a social interloper. But the weather conditions had been adverse from the start, so he had been glued to his seat for the whole miserable flight.

The plane took a hard bank to the right, which sent drinks sliding. The flight attendants were hard pressed to keep their balance as they tried to aid in the countless cleanups. A middle-aged woman two rows ahead of him loudly threatened to sue the airline over the orange juice stains on her white silk blouse.

Matt sighed. Perhaps there was something to be said for first class. Here, everyone was packed together like pencils in a box. Of course, no one had anticipated that the journey would be this rugged.

He had been on a lot of rough flights. They were an inconvenience, certainly, but they seldom really bothered him. It was just another aspect of what he did for a living. And since the day he had lost his parents to a ship disaster in the North Sea, he had preferred air travel.

The plane hit a pocket of turbulence that dropped them hundreds of feet in a matter of seconds. There were shouts of alarm from the passengers, and the lecture notes he had been studying spilled to the floor. He was about to undo his seat belt to pick them up, when he felt a restraining hand on his arm.

The woman seated beside him, an older woman dressed in a conservative gray tweed suit, pressed her lips together and shook her head at him in a maternal warning. She had been asleep up until this latest atmospheric insult. But apparently even she couldn't rest through what they were experiencing now. There was a touch of auburn to her hair still. She reminded him of a dear family friend, Emma Macpherson.

"Don't be foolhardy, young man," the woman warned, inclining her head toward the scattered paperwork.

Matt pushed his wire-rimmed glasses a bit further up the bridge of his nose as he looked down at three weeks' worth of hard work about to be trampled underfoot.

"I suppose yer right," he conceded as he turned his attention back to her. He extended his hand to her in introduction. "Matthew Macinnes."

She took his hand and shook it firmly. "Hattie MacTavish of Dormach."

The plane lurched back to the left, and the two of them exchanged a worried look. Matt decided conversation might be their best defense.

"Ah, Dormach, just to the north of Inverness, right on the water," he said, trying to keep his voice as level as possible despite the jolting they were getting. "Lovely spot. I've been there once or twice. Even took the family one time."

There was a flash outside the windows. Then another. Lightning. They gave it their attention, but when Hattie turned back to Matt, her light-blue eyes were steady, and she appeared to be unruffled by their situation.

"Old Thor's givin' us a tumble, is he not?" she said with a stoic smile.

"Aye." Matt watched as his research papers fluttered further and further down the aisle in random directions. This wasn't good.

"I'm the mayor, ye ken," Hattie continued.

"Sorry?" Matt pulled his attention back to their conversation as the cabin started to vibrate loudly. He had a very bad feeling about all of this. "Ye were sayin', Mrs. MacTavish?"

She had to raise her voice to be heard over the sounds of metal in distress and human beings in even more distress. "I was sayin', I'm the mayor of Dormach, Mr. Macinnes. And where might yer people be from?"

"The Highlands, near Glomach," he shouted back at her over the din. "Do ye get the feelin' we're in a wee bit of trouble, Madam Mayor?"

Hattie glanced around them. Some passengers were already gripping pillows in their laps in preparation for the worst.

"Are ye a religious man, Mr. Macinnes?" she asked. Her hands were steady as she rummaged through her handbag.

He hadn't been asked that question for a very long time. "I am, after a fashion," he provided. The fact that his religious beliefs would probably never fit her definitions was beside the point at the moment.

"Well, I for one, am not a religious woman," she surprised him by saying. She withdrew a small black leather-bound Bible from the depths of her bag. "My daughter-in-law always insists that I carry this whenever I travel. It has a great deal more meanin' to her than it ever has for me. But it makes the poor girl happy to think of me havin' it, so I lug it about, wherever I go, like a lucky rabbit's foot.

"It's all in Gaelic, ye ken, Mr. Macinnes? I've got a few

words of the old tongue, mind, but we're far from the islands in Dormach. Do ye have the language upon ye?"

"I do."

The lights in the cabin began to flicker, and the oxygen masks snapped down in front of their faces. A new wave of panic swept through the other passengers as everyone struggled to press the masks to their faces. Matt put his on, then took the little Bible from Hattie's hand. He opened it at random and felt very much at home with the familiar sight of Gaelic. The passage before him was one he knew by heart from his childhood.

Hattie laid her hand on his sleeve, not in terror, but in a calm request as the lights threatened to give out. She raised her mask long enough to say, "Will ye read me somethin' to distract my mind from all of this, Mr. Macinnes?"

"Of course, Mrs. MacTavish. It may be a bit tough to hear through these breathing contraptions, but I'll do my best. And please, call me Matt, if ye will." She nodded her agreement as Matt began, " 'The Lord is my shepherd . . .' "

"Och, Matt, must it be one about sheep? Save yer breath, man. Is there nothin' practical in there about how the Lord can help ye if yer luggage is spilled across the great North Sea?"

Matt smiled to the best of his ability, but Hattie's eyes were bright with unshed tears, and he had to look away for both their sakes. He turned his attention to a little girl and her mother across the way. The girl had reddish curls, not unlike his young daughter, Carrie's, but this girl was younger than Carrie, probably no more than six. Her life had barely begun.

She had been very diligent at her crayon pictures until this latest onslaught. Now she just held on to her beloved stack of pictures for dear life and looked up to her mother for reassurance that everything was going to be all right. Her mother smiled down at her. But they hit another pocket of turbulence, and the mother had to reach for the airsickness bag. The little girl began to sob softly.

Her eyes met Matt's. She was asking him for the comfort her mother could not give. He wanted to give her a hug as he would have done for his own children, but that wasn't possible. If there had been a way for him to promise her that she was going to be home in her own bed, with her own blanket and teddy bears when all of this was over, he would have done it.

But he had never believed in lying to children, even to dry their tears. It was always an injustice in the end, and the fact of the matter was, he was no airline mechanic, but from the ungodly noises the aircraft was making, it was a safe bet that everything was *not* going to be all right. So, he lifted his oxygen mask and shouted to her as best he could over the din, "You are a wonderful artist!"

The little girl smiled beneath her mask, her heart lifted. He had given her the truth.

In the instant before the lights went out for good, for Matt, everything around him seemed to go into slow motion. They all became like a tableau of themselves, a still photo pasted into some macabre scrapbook that no one else would ever see.

He wanted to turn back time, to warn each and every one of them not to get on this plane, that to do so would change not only their lives but the lives of every person they knew or cared about on earth. He wanted to give each of them another Christmas, another birthday, another chance to hug a loved one. He felt profoundly sorry for them. Then, with the suddenness of an arrow through the heart, he realized that these were things he was not even going to be able to give himself.

Somewhere in the background, he heard the flight attendants shouting out instructions in preparation to ditch. It all had an absurd ring to it. He didn't know how many thousand feet up they were at the moment, but it was ludicrous to think that a pillow beneath your head was going to save your life. But he did as he was told. It gave you something to hang on to while you kissed your backside good-bye.

Would there be pain or simply oblivion? The lights went out and didn't come on again. Only the double row of tiny lights marking the aisle remained, like a thin runway down which no one could go. In a way, the darkness was a blessing. The coughing, the cries of terror, the mumbled prayers no longer had faces attached to them. In some small way, it made it easier.

There was a faint hint of acrid, metallic smoke as the nose of the plane dropped severely. The ventilation systems closed down, and the smoke thickened with alarming speed.

They would all be dead from smoke inhalation long before they hit the water, Matt decided in some detached and logical portion of his mind. It would be a more merciful way to go, quicker than being torn to bits by the horrific impact.

He hoped Rainey would realize that his suffering had been brief. It was the kind of thing that would matter to her. A hard knot of emotion rose in his throat as visions of her flooded his mind's eye. Her dark curls, long and wild as the Highlands themselves, her eyes, the deep blue color of the loch in summer. The vision of her was so clear that all else melted away, and he felt as if he could almost reach out and caress the smoothness of her fair skin, feel the warmth of her breath against his cheek.

She was with him to the last, but, thanks be to God, only in his mind and heart, not in reality. He knew she would mourn. But he also knew she would survive the pain, not only for herself but for the sake of their daughters, Sasha and Carrie.

Strangely, he saw Sasha as he had first seen her, eight years old and unwilling to speak to a soul since the death of her biological father. Christ! How would she ever adjust to losing two fathers under almost identical conditions? How would she ever forgive him for letting this happen in her life a second time? He wouldn't be there to watch her graduate from the university or to dance at her wedding.

And Carrie, his wee Highland beauty . . . he would only be a vague childhood memory to her. A happy one, he hoped. It wasn't enough, not nearly enough!

"Matt?"

The vibration of the fuselage was shaking the plane apart, and the ugly grinding of buckling metal foretold of the hell to come. It took a moment for it to register in Matt's brain that Hattie had said his name. "Aye, Madam Mayor?"

"If it happens I don't get the chance personally, I'd appreciate it if ye would tell my family and the town that I loved them all." Her voice never quaked as she made her request, but the smoke sent her into a fit of coughing.

"Ye have my promise, Hattie," he said over the raw ache in his throat. "If ye would do me the same kindness."

"Aye."

It was the last word he ever heard from her. When he tried to pass the Bible back to her, she pushed it back into his hand. He gripped the little book for both of them in the choking darkness and started to recite the Twenty-third Psalm to himself in Gaelic. The words stopped making any sense, but there was a kind of comfort to them anyway. Hattie gasped and choked beside him, a twisted, gut-wrenching sound out of a horror movie. He heard himself doing the same, along with everyone else around him. When he reached out for Hattie's hand beside him, it was lifeless. Only seconds ago, she had still been there.

He wanted to weep for her and for all the souls succumbing to death around him, one by one. He wanted to mourn for the loss of Rainey and the girls, for poor old Cameron up in first class. Old Wallie's money hadn't spared him this inconvenience. And if there was any strength left in him, he wanted to cry for himself, for all the research he would never do, for that one small scrap of information about the Pictish tribes that he had never been able to find, for those countless thoughts and questions he would never be able to share with his daughters. And for all the nights snuggled beneath the quilts with his wife that would never happen. But there wasn't time for any of it. In fact, there was no time at all.

The blackness was a thick, stinking thing that wrapped around him like a smothering shroud. The air was poisonous, and his every instinct sent up red flags not to breathe it. Breathing meant death. Not breathing meant death of another sort. In truth, there was no choice to be made. As consciousness hung by a thread, his lungs made the choice for him, an involuntary act bred of pure animal logic.

But those burning, plastic, metallic breaths taken in spite of himself were also the enemy. The air ripped through his respiratory system like metal shavings. He wanted to puke himself inside-out to be rid of it. Drawing breath hurt like nothing in his experience and kept him distracted from the inviting images behind his eyes of pure, quiet light that signaled the end of his journey in this life. Had it not been for the pain, he could have joined the peaceful migration of souls leaving this burning hulk of crumpled metal. It would have all been so easy. A relief beyond the human imagination to simply let go.

When he coughed up the contents of his stomach into the breathing apparatus, he tore off the device, which made him gasp all the harder. Some tiny, distant part of him wanted to apologize to Hattie MacTavish for his soiling of her lovely tweeds. Absurd. Lunacy.

He had the strength to say a single word. It was the word he wanted on his lips as life left him.

"Rainey."

He heard no more voices now. Only the sound of metal ripping itself to shreds and flying apart, giving way to the inevitable. He could bear this plane no more, and his prayers became a plea for the water. The unforgiving depths of the ocean were something he understood, something he had fought before. And if the North Sea still wanted him this badly, so be it.

Chapter 2

The wind took a hard spin to the north. Rainey Macinnes felt the Highland weather go from lamb to lion in the time it took to hang another sheet on the backyard clothesline. She glanced down the long parade of freshly hung linens. It was going to have to come down with all haste. They had all awakened well before dawn this morning, and the sun was just clearing the heather-covered hills as Rainey set about the undoing of her hard work.

Her dear friend Emma Macpherson sensed the promise of a storm as well. Emma was Highland born and bred. It was not in her nature to stand by and watch others work. But as she stooped to pluck a pillowcase from the laundry basket, she gave a small groan at the ache of dirty weather in her old bones.

"Och, we're in for it, Rainey," she said as she set the pillowcase back in the basket.

"Wouldn't you know it? I really wanted the good linens ready for Matt's homecoming," Rainey said in disappointment, pulling the damp sheet off the line.

Emma gave her a teasing wink. "Oh, and it's to be one of *those* sorts of homecomin's, eh? 'Course, then, aren't they all?"

"Be nice, Emma. I'm an old married woman, remember?"

Despite her words, Rainey blushed like a schoolgirl with a crush at the merest thought of Matt, an uncharacteristic habit she had never gotten past.

Emma snorted at Rainey's ridiculous disclaimer. "Face it, love, ye fair dote on the man's every word, and he worships the sod betwixt yer wee toes. The pair of ye are forever at the come hithers. It's no as if I haven't seen ye sneak down by the loch to be at yer sparkin' games like a coupla raw teenagers." She tsked loudly.

"I miss him, I admit it," Rainey replied, neatly hiding her grin behind a flowered pillowcase. The years had only strengthened her bonds of friendship with Emma. Emma and her husband, Malcolm, saw her through the times when Matt had to be away on lecture tours. It was Matt's calling, this gift he had for the ancient languages of the Celts, and she had never begrudged him the fact that the world was always demanding his presence. Not to his face, at least.

Her heart was another matter. She hated it when he was gone. But the fact that marriage to Matthew Macinnes was still something of a honeymoon, even after nine years, was a blessing she was thankful for every day of her life.

This perpetual honeymoon state had not escaped Emma's attention. In many ways, Emma was the mother figure in Rainey's life. Fortunately, her old friend thrived on the role.

"Put yer wrap on, Rainey, there's a good lass," Emma instructed in fine maternal fashion.

The wind sent rose petals fluttering to the ground in the garden. It brought with it the scent of wet heather and the chill knowledge that they had better hurry taking in the laundry. There was a feel to the air that made Rainey's muscles knot and her blood more hesitant to run its course. It called for shelter and enough fuel to keep a warming fire burning. She shuddered and grabbed for her gray woolen sweater.

Emma buttoned up her own sweater securely. "The wind is always of a meaner persuasion when it whistles down out of the north. It's cuttin' through to the skin. We'd best get everybody in before it hits us proper."

Rainey took down the last of the pillowcases and looked to where her eighteen-year-old daughter, Sasha, sat in the rose garden, reading a worn copy of *Wuthering Heights* from the family library. It was summer break from school, a quiet reprieve from the hectic academic schedule.

But the free time only intensified the restlessness Rainey sensed in Sasha. There would come a time when the Scottish Highlands could not hold her any longer, and she would be off to the university in Edinburgh to try her wings in the big, wide world. Rainey was going to miss her company terribly.

Sasha's dark curls lifted off her shoulders in the rising wind, and her brilliant blue eyes were intent upon the story. It was almost like seeing herself at the same age, Rainey mused, a young woman ready to take on anything life had to offer. Of course, Sasha's childhood had been quite different from her own.

Rainey picked up the wicker laundry basket, her thoughts on Matt. "God, I miss him, Emma. I don't think I'll ever get used to these trips of his. Every time he starts to pack his bag, I want to tie him to the kitchen table so he can't leave. I know I'm being selfish, but I miss him even before he's out the door."

Emma took one handle of the basket as they started back to the house. "Aye, I understand what yer sayin', love. Matty Mac most definitely has a way about him." She laughed to herself. "It seems now like we've known him all our lives, does it no? But I'll never forget how he marched into yer wee house in California that first night. Just as bold as brass, he was. Why, ye pulled a kitchen knife on the poor man, thinkin' by the look of him he was some layabout creepin' up from the Boardwalk.

How were we to know little Sasha'd let him in like she'd known him since Wallace was a pup?"

Rainey had to smile to herself at the memory of her first encounter with Matthew Macinnes, Professor of Linguistics and the Antiquities. She had loved him that very first day, although she would have been perfectly willing to swear to the contrary in a court of law.

Now, she had to worry about him twenty-four hours a day while he was on all these journeys to the far reaches of the world. And what was more, she was going to tell him so in no uncertain terms. The family needed him here. *She* needed him here.

Though he was due in from Oslo in three hours, it suddenly seemed like far too long to wait. She needed to talk to him about Sasha, about the future. She wanted to see his face, to let herself be folded into the strength of his arms. She longed for the sight, the scent, and the sound of him next to her beneath the covers.

"You know what, Sash?" she called over her shoulder. "Let's go surprise your father at the airport. I have the flight number. If we go now, we should be able to make it in time. We may even beat the storm."

She glanced along the side of the house toward the loch. There she saw her nine-year-old daughter, Carrie, tossing stones at the water's edge. Carrie's auburn curls, so like Matt's, were tucked under a bright red Stanford University cap as she skipped stones, to the delight of Angus, the grizzled little Scottie dog at her side. Carrie and Angus were inseparable.

"Go get your sister, if you will, Sash. She's playing with Angus down by the water."

Sasha looked up from her reading. She didn't respond quickly to her mother's request. Instead, she turned to the north as if someone had called her name from that direction.

"Thor's Hammer," she said in quiet awe. "It's going to hit us hard."

Rainey turned to the north. The tiny hairs at the nape of her neck stood on end, and a shiver slid down her back as she watched the storm's progress. The air prickled and grew thick around them as a barrage of thunder cracked off the heathered hillsides like approaching cannon fire.

Sasha's instincts about storms were never wrong. The weather changed a dozen times a day in the Highlands. They were used to it. In a way, it had a certain Highland charm. But right now, things were going to get very nasty.

Rainey walked over to Sasha. "It's just a storm, Sash. In an hour, it'll be forgotten."

Sasha estimated the oncoming storm warily. "When does Papa get in to Inverness?"

"A couple of hours."

"I wish he were here right now." Sasha hugged her book to her chest, as if to protect the stormy lovers within its pages from the real-life storm skimming over the tops of the hills.

Rainey gave Sasha's hand a squeeze. They had lost Sasha's biological father to a storm when Sasha was very young. She and Sasha were the same height now, equals in many ways. But the bonds of shared loss between them and the subsequent recovery from tragedy would forever bring them back to the stark emotions of Sasha's early childhood.

"Let's just get everybody inside, Sash. It's going to pour. Go get Carrie, and we'll make for Inverness." She shrugged. "So I can't hang out the wash. Big deal. The garden could do with a little moisture. It's time to plant Matt's favorite greens."

As she started down the stone steps to get Carrie, Sasha turned and gave Rainey a look her mother had not seen for many happy, fleeting years. It was a look that warned of loss.

"Don't let Carrie talk you into a rock-throwing contest, Sash. There isn't time," Rainey cautioned with a smile that failed to reach her eyes.

Sasha's mood was dark and unreadable.

Rainey squared her shoulders. "He's coming back to us safely, just like he always does. He knows the nature of these storms better than we do."

Sasha nodded solemnly and ran down the path to the loch.

Emma muttered to herself as she stuffed the last of the wash into the basket. "She's that worried, love."

"She's being melodramatic," Rainey replied as she pushed the wash into the basket with a vengeance. "It's those raging teenage hormones and all that Cathy and Heathcliff on the brain. Just wait. I'll get a call from Matt to say he's staying an extra day in Oslo just to lock horns with some old Norwegian fuddy-duddy. He's probably sipping the best Scotch in the world and gobbling up some musty dean's private reserve of caviar while he waits for the weather to break." Though she gave a little laugh, there was no humor to it.

In her rush to get to the house, she tripped over the tail of one of the sheets and went sprawling on the walkway. It knocked the wind out of her. Hard as she struggled, she couldn't get any air. It was frightening, and it had the unnerving feel of premonition. The wash spilled across the newly turned garden soil, adding insult to injury. By the time Emma got to her, Rainey was swearing under her breath as she snatched up the linen.

"Here, now, lass, it's no worth all this fuss," Emma said as she settled a muddy pillowcase into the basket. "We'll toss the lot into the machine. It'll be done in a jiffy. The modern age has reached us here, ye ken?"

Rainey wadded a dirty sheet on top of the load, mashing it down among its kin. "This isn't about the wash, Emma. It's about Matt. I don't want to share him with the world for a while. Enough is enough! Look at me. I'm a nervous wreck, worrying for his safety simply because it might rain. I can't adjust to it. I've tried to be the proper university wife, sending him off to

God knows where with a cheery smile and a wave. But it's a lie. And I'm not going to lie anymore. I don't care who else needs him, we need him more.

"He's worked so many miracles to help revive interest in the old languages, and I would never want to take that away from him. But I know what it feels like to be a widow, Emma, and sometimes that's just what it's like when he goes on these trips." She surveyed the threatening skies. "I want him home so badly, I almost hope he risks those black skies."

"We'll all say a wee prayer for his safety, love," Emma said kindly. "When he gets home, the two of ye can talk it out. Things will right themselves. But ye must tell him how ye really feel, Rainey. Talk to the man straight out."

Rainey sighed from the depths of her soul. "I know. The academic world has already decided I'm not politically correct because I never attend any of those stale cocktail parties they're all so fond of. Well, they better start stacking fresh stones to throw at me because I intend to deprive them of one of their favorite play friends for a while."

Emma laid her hand on Rainey's arm. "I'm with ye, love. It's only fair for ye to want Matty here. It's a spoiled woman I've been, havin' my dear Malcolm at my side so steady these past years." She shaded her eyes as she looked to the north. The winds caught her rose-gray hair and pulled some of it loose from her customary bun. As she surveyed the worsening skies, there was the same grim thoroughness about her as she had employed watching for Nazi aircraft during the war. She cupped her hands around her mouth and called through the kitchen door.

"Malcolm! Be a love and come down here a tick."

A white-haired gentleman with extraordinarily bushy eyebrows stuck his head out of a third-story window, looking down on them in obvious impatience over being interrupted. His shirtsleeves were rolled up to the elbows, and his red trouser braces hung down around his plentiful waist. Though he and Emma had a dear little home of their own on the estate, they spent much of their time helping Rainey and the girls around the house, especially when Matt was gone.

"I'm after perfectin' the plumbin' up here, Em," Malcolm called down gruffly.

Emma leaned over and whispered in Rainey's ear, "Cloggin' it, more like."

But Rainey's usually keen sense of humor was lost to her as she watched for the girls to come back from the loch.

"Say, Malcolm, my love," Emma called sweetly, "will ye do us the kindness of goin' down by the loch and fetchin' the girls and Angus in? The Viking Storm is hard from the north, and it's a hazard for the bairns to be abroad, ye ken?" She shot him a look to let him know all was not well.

Malcolm slapped his braces into place and rolled down his sleeves as he cast a wary eye toward the rolling clouds on the horizon.

"Aye, well, not to worry, ladies. 'Tis an easy enough task, then. I'll be at it straight 'way."

He disappeared from the window, and only a moment later, Emma and Rainey heard the front door close behind him as he headed for the water.

Emma took the laundry basket from Rainey's hands and shooed her into the kitchen like a mother hen. She sat her down at the kitchen table and soon set a cup of strong tea in front of her. Rainey made a study of the steam rising from the cup.

"Remember how storms used to affect Sasha when she was little, Emma? At the first sign of thunder, she would climb on top of the highest thing in the room. It nearly gave me a heart attack sometimes. Most kids would run and hide under a chair during a thunderstorm. But Sasha always wanted to be nearer to the heart of it."

"Aye, that was a time, love. But that's no what's worryin' ye now."

Rainey raised her troubled eyes. "Something doesn't feel right."

"Can ye tell me the nature of the problem, then?"

The first isolated splatters of rain hit the kitchen windows like bird shot.

"Sasha is so tuned in to Matt, Emma. She would never be this worried without just cause."

Emma gave this information some careful consideration. She was accustomed to Rainey and Sasha's extraordinary abilities to communicate with one another. It was a skill born from a time when communication between them had been at a premium. Little Carrie showed signs of the ability as well. It was a gift the family shared. But at times it was also misery. She took a healthy sip of her tea, then got up and turned on the radio to see if they could pick up the latest weather report. The news was on commercial.

"Chances are, Rainey, what with the weather bein' dirty as all this, his flight's been grounded, and he's still at the hotel, chalkin' up room service. Ye must call him, love." She went to get the phone and set it in front of Rainey along with the square of notepaper that had the phone number of Matt's hotel in Oslo.

"You're right. It's ridiculous to sit and fret over nothing. If he hasn't checked out, my worries are over."

There was static on the line to Oslo. The reception was terrible, and she could barely make out the information from the other end. She hung up the receiver slowly.

"He's gone. The desk clerk said she thinks he had airline tickets in his hand when he checked out."

Emma refilled her teacup. "Och, well, then, he's most likely sittin' in some Norwegian airline terminal, cursin' the fact he can't get back to ye sooner."

"Right. He probably never got off the ground. And if he did, they always find ways to fly around the big storms. I'm sure he's fine."

She got the phone book from the top of the refrigerator and thumbed through the pages, looking for airline information. Despite her calm words, her fingers trembled slightly. This was a nightmare she had lived through before.

The line was busy. She slammed the receiver down, only to pick it up immediately and dial the number again. Still busy. She tried a third time, and it rang. The pen in her hand was poised to write down any morsel of information. There was nothing to write. She hung up.

"What did they say?" Emma asked, noting that Rainey had gone very pale.

"It was a recording. The flight's been delayed. They didn't say where. They say to call back in half an hour for another update." She wrapped her fingers around the gold locket she always wore around her neck. It had been in the Macinnes family for generations, and it had been Matt's wedding gift to her. She stood very still in the middle of the room as thunder roared from beyond the loch.

The weather report came on the radio. The storm was being billed as the worst in half a century, stretching from the northernmost tip of Norway to Great Britain. Fishing boats all up and down the North Sea had gone missing. Villages along the coast had been blown to bits, with reports of heavy casualties. All unnecessary travel was being curtailed, and the airports were in the process of being closed down until the storm passed.

Emma laid her hand on Rainey's shoulder. "There, now, ye see? They're not permittin' any flights to take off, from here to the North Pole. He's under shelter, love. Ye've nothin' to fret about. Do ye suppose we should close the upstairs shutters?"

Rainey stared hard at the phone, mindless of Emma's question about the shutters. If Matt was indeed grounded by the storm, he would call to let them know he was safe and running late. He wouldn't let them worry. She had gotten a call through to Oslo. The connection had been pitiful, but she had accomplished it. He would call. In fact, he should have called by now.

It felt as though she might melt the phone with her eyes as she willed it to ring.

"Come along now, ladies, there's a nasty bit o' weather rollin' down the valley," Malcolm instructed Sasha and Carrie. A former military man, Malcolm brooked no insubordination when it came to moving his charges from one place to another.

But Sasha was captivated by the storm as it drew near. She sat on a flat rock next to the water's edge and watched the clouds gather, as if she were a seasoned general calculating the fighting strength of a formidable enemy.

Little Carrie gave Malcolm an unmistakable look of friendly challenge from beneath the brim of her red baseball cap. Her cheeks glowed from sunshine and exercise, and there was a definite promise of mischief in her blue-gray eyes.

"I'll bet you can't skip a stone eleven times, Malcolm," she tossed at him boldly. "I can. Angus saw me do it."

Malcolm gave Emma's beloved Scottie a look of skepticism as Angus, his tongue lolling out and his stubby tail wagging madly, gave Carrie what could only be termed a conspiring wink. Malcolm knew he was about to be had. He just wasn't sure exactly how.

"None of that now," he said with mock sternness. "Everyone's to get into the house this instant. I'll no be responsible for the consequences if one of ye lights up like a Christmas tree from bein' out in the weather's to come. Besides, lass, I taught yer father how to skip stones across this water when he was but a wee bairn. 'Twould hardly seem fair." He folded his arms and puffed up his chest with pride.

Carrie grabbed his sleeve. "Just one stone, Malcolm. I promise, just one. And the loser has to carry the shovel behind Angus for . . . two weeks."

Malcolm rubbed his chin and narrowed his eyes at the far side of the loch as the first drops of rain splashed off his shoulders and the top of his head.

"Verra well, lassie, one toss each. Then you and yer sister are to march straight for the house. No games, no tomfoolery, ye ken? Is it a bargain, then?" He spat into his palm and extended it to her. She did likewise and they shook on it.

Malcolm was the first to throw. For the sake of time, he chose a stone quickly and gave it a hefty heave. His arthritis was a factor, but he managed to skip it nine times.

Carrie gave him a sideward glance of grudging respect as she stepped up to the line they had drawn in the sand. But her expression turned a bit smug, and she produced from her pocket a stone of such perfect smoothness and proportion, it was obvious she had been saving it for just such an occasion. It was aerodynamically perfect for skipping, and she rubbed her fingers across it lovingly, a grin of triumph already warming on her freckled face.

Malcolm pressed his lips together. "Just toss the t'ing, lassie," he said as visions of two weeks' worth of dog droppings came to mind.

Carrie pulled back her arm, fully prepared for sweet victory, when something peculiar in the water caught her eye. She dropped her perfect stone, its grand purpose forgotten, and waded into the water, shoes and all, to scoop up the black object. It was a bird, a dead raven. Carrie cradled it defensively in her arms as if it were a favorite doll someone had carelessly broken. Its folded wings still shone iridescent, and its eyes, though void of life, still gazed toward the heavens as if death had taken it by surprise.

Malcolm was about to tell Carrie to put it down, that it was probably diseased. But Sasha shot him a glance, silently asking him to leave well enough alone. He realized that Carrie was looking beyond him, toward the trail that led to the house.

"How long till Papa gets home?" she asked. Though the words were said softly, there was an edge of demand to them.

Malcolm looked over his shoulder to find Rainey standing at the top of the path. Her face was expressionless, but she flinched almost imperceptibly when she saw the raven in Carrie's arms. The rains began to fall with a vengeance.

"Come in for your coats now, girls," she said evenly. "We're going to the airport."

Chapter 3

By the time Rainey and the family made it to the airport at Inverness, Matt's flight number had been removed from the arrival and departure board, and signs had been posted saying anyone with an inquiry should see a Mrs. Renfrew at the main courtesy desk. They had made the drive quickly and in virtual silence, no one daring to bring up the subject of Matt's flight out of fear of the Pandora's Box it might open.

Rainey stared hard at the empty board, trying to sort this experience from the day her first husband had gone down. It was a different airport. In some very important ways, she was a different person. And yet the similarities sent pinpricks of both memory and premonition down her spine.

She didn't want any part of this. She wanted to go home, because if the news was bad, she didn't want to hear about it in this place. There had been enough recurring nightmares in her life, and this just added to her bone-deep hatred of airports.

Carrie tugged at her sleeve as they all walked toward the main desk. "Why are we here, Mama?" she asked as she stared at all the different people with their coats and baggage.

Rainey barely heard her question. "We're here to meet Papa,

Care. Only it looks like . . . it looks like it might be a while before he catches up to us."

Carrie tugged again, and Rainey nearly snapped at her. Her
nerves were wound very tight, and if she didn't get some straight
information fast, someone was going to be shouted down to their
knees. She reminded herself that Carrie had not been through
any of this before, and out of reflex she glanced at Sasha.

Sasha took Carrie's hand and drew her over to a set of plastic
chairs against the wall. Rainey tucked her hair behind her ear
out of nervous habit and paced back and forth. There wasn't
time for delays. And yet she knew that for Carrie's sake, what
was happening had to be addressed.

Sasha tousled Carrie's auburn curls affectionately. Sad memories flooded her mind as she remembered the last time something like this had happened. She had been younger than Carrie,
and she had stopped talking completely, a reaction to the loss
of her father and the promises she had made in answer to his
death.

That same mechanism was still in place, buried somewhere
deep in her heart. With Matt's help, she had overcome it years
ago when they had resolved the problems that had been at the
heart of it. Ever since, she had been the first one to speak her
mind without hesitation. But she couldn't help thinking how
much simpler it would be now to simply fall back into that utter
silence, to spare herself the pain of having to talk to Carrie as
she knew she must. When Carrie smiled up into her eyes so
very innocently, far from wanting to be silent, Sasha wanted to
cry out from the anguish of having to tell Carrie her Papa might
be lost to her forever.

Emma laid a reassuring hand on Rainey's shoulder. "Malcolm and I are goin' to go on ahead, love. We'll meet ye at the
main desk."

Rainey waved them on numbly. She went down on her knees in front of Carrie and took her hand. The hallway gave her the same disconnected feeling as an intensive care unit. She was there. She was doing everything she could. And yet, somewhere, beyond where they were right now, she couldn't help feeling that Matt was fighting for his life. Every second was absolutely of the essence.

Carrie frowned at the looks of concern on the faces of the other two. "I said, why are we here? This isn't where we're supposed to be. Papa isn't in this dumb place, and he needs us to come and help him."

Rainey and Sasha glanced at each other. With any other child the question on their minds would have seemed ludicrous. But with this family, it was only natural to ask.

"Do you know where Papa is?" Sasha asked kindly.

Carrie nodded so vigorously her curls bounced comically. "He's with the selkies, of course," she said matter-of-factly.

"With the selkies, sweetheart?" Rainey replied. She prayed it wasn't a euphemism for death. "So you think your Papa is somewhere where there are seals?"

"Not just any old seals, Mama. Selkies."

Selkies were said to be seals blessed with a touch of magic. Certainly they could all use a bit of help from the supernatural at the moment. Rainey was about to ask for a more specific location when Emma and Malcolm came hurrying toward them.

"What is it?" Rainey called. "Is he okay? Have they come in?"

Malcolm shook his head. "Och, lassie, the news is not so good."

Emma gave a worried glance at Sasha and Carrie. She pulled Rainey to one side. "They've got a whole room full of sad folks set apart, just waitin', Rainey. I saw their faces. They're not gettin' any good news, I can tell ye that. That fancy airline lady is tryin' to be of comfort to them, but it looks as though there's little to be done."

Rainey pulled away. "Well, they can count us out. I'm not going through that airline-lounge hell again, Emma, and I certainly won't subject the girls to it. It's like waiting to be sentenced for a crime you didn't commit."

"Aye, I understand, Rainey, and I don't blame ye one bit," Emma agreed. "But I'm that sorry to tell ye the waitin' room's not the worst of it. Ye must come have a look at the telly, I'm afraid, love."

Rainey didn't want to go. As long as there was nothing concrete, nothing visual, she could handle it, she could be strong. But she knew in her heart that Emma was going to show her something she wouldn't be able to dismiss as someone else's nightmare, someone else's loss. If she didn't see the proof, it would mean nothing had happened. It was that simple.

She wasn't a coward. It was just that whatever was on the screen didn't have anything to do with her or with Matt. As long as she didn't look, all of this madness didn't apply to her.

But Emma was already leading her toward a little hole-in-the-wall snack bar. Her feet were moving in spite of her best resolve to turn them the other way. If she didn't stop, if she just kept walking, the truth couldn't catch up to her. And once she was done walking, she would start running until it was all over, until she could think about processing all the implications of what life without Matt would mean.

The breath caught in her throat at the thought of never seeing his face again, never hearing his laugh, never hearing him rave with that absolute passion of his about some obscure piece of broken pottery he had found in the north country. She started to twist the wedding ring on her finger.

No, she wasn't ready. There had to be more time to ground

herself, to gather her strength so that whatever was about to flash before her eyes wouldn't cut too deeply, wouldn't dig a massive hole in her heart.

She had to put on a show of courage for the rest. It was owed to them and to Matt. But it was too much to ask of her right now. Right now, she wanted to get out of this *Twilight Zone* airport. Perhaps if she could sleep a bit first. Then, maybe tomorrow she could be the trooper everyone expected her to be. Maybe next week. But not today. Today was no good. In fact, she wanted it wiped off the face of the calendar.

The news was being broadcast on a small television screen in the snack bar. The sound was bad and the color wasn't adjusted very well, but the coverage showed churning waves the size of mountains covered with the floating wreckage of a horrendous crash.

The news commentator was carrying on with a perverse sort of pride about its being the worst European air disaster in a decade. So thorough was the devastation that the possibility of explosives and other forms of sabotage had not been ruled out. Search and Rescue had been combing the waters, but they had produced no evidence of survivors, and any further efforts had to be postponed because of high winds and approaching darkness.

There was some speculation by the home office, the commentator said, as to whether it was going to be worth risking the living to pursue what was quietly being acknowledged to be a useless search. The impact had been far too great, the waters far too rough and frigid to allow any hope for human survival.

Rainey stared at the fingerprint-smeared screen as if she half expected to spy Matt signaling his miraculous survival to her from the midst of the pounding seas. But there was nothing. Nothing but broken and twisted rubble for as far as the eye could see. It was like a Hollywood film sadly lacking in plot as the waves pulled down more debris while she watched. Only this was no product of movie magic. This was like the aftermath of war.

Emma took Rainey's hand and sat her down out of sight of the TV. The girls sat down on either side of her.

Sasha touched the velvet pouch she wore around her neck. It contained a brooch Matt had given her long ago. She always wore it when there was a chance she would need a bit of spiritual solace.

Each of them had a treasure trove of memories. But none of them was ready to say good-bye to Matthew Macinnes—most of all, Rainey. She took each girl by the hand as they sat together, unwilling and unable to take whatever must be their next logical step. Rainey closed her eyes and tried to force her thinking processes past the hard ache in her heart.

Matt was still there, so very much alive in her soul. Was it an illusion, like the sensation left behind when a limb was removed? Or was it real? There was a tug on her sleeve, and she opened her eyes. Little Carrie's smile of optimism was so genuine, it nearly broke her heart.

"Don't worry, Mama," she said with a consoling pat to her mother's arm. "Papa's okay. But why are we all sitting around here? He's waiting."

A change came over Sasha's face, a realization. "Carrie's right, Mama," she said with utmost conviction. "He's out there somewhere, waiting for us to find him. We have to go look for him."

Emma nodded. "Our Matty Mac has no left us, I'm that certain of it. I say we find him our own selves. He'll be watchin' for us."

Malcolm had never been one to sit still in times of trouble. He had come away from the airline counter with a handful of tickets in his hand. "They're gettin' all their information thirdhand out of Edinburgh, Rainey. If we want the real news, we're best to go there. They've all but closed down the search for now, so there's nothin' more to be done here for the night. The weather has eased, and local flights are back in operation. They had the good sense not to charge us for the tickets. And what's more, I've got it in writin' we're to ride free of charge and be provided with decent hotel accommodations, the lot of us, wherever we must go in connection with this nasty business."

Rainey took the tickets, her mind racing. The images of horror were still so fresh that the thought of putting them all onto an airplane made her physically ill. But with all those expectant faces looking to her for their marching orders, she had to make the decision.

"Thank you, Malcolm. It sounds like they're not going to pursue the search much longer. But that's not going to stop us. We can't count on anyone but those of us standing right here." She gave them a smile that had a haunted quality to it. "Luckily, there's no one on earth I trust more. If the authorities are planning to give out on us, we'll have to take matters into our own hands. I've got no problem with that. Matt is out there somewhere, counting on us to find him. If . . . if he's hurt, it's all the more reason why we have to hurry."

She looked at each of them in turn. "Maybe someone at the university will be willing to help us. We'll give it a try once we reach Edinburgh. There'll be more flights to the crash site from there, anyway. But one way or another, from here on out, we're in motion."

"And which fine Edinburgh hotel might it be for ye this evenin', folks? I've been directed to convey ye to the Balmoral or the Caledonian, whatever is yer preference."

Their overly cheery cabbie had been waiting for them at the

Edinburgh airport, holding a sign with the name "Macinnes" on it. He had been hired for their use by the airline, but apparently he had no clue about the tragic nature of their problem, since he was determined to make tourists of them as he drove away from the terminal.

The lights of the city gave the old thoroughfares and buildings a glow that spoke of centuries of history. But when they drove past the woolens shop where Matt had bought Rainey the shawl she was now wearing around her shoulders, any hint of renewed interest at being in the city evaporated. They all knew that shop and the sentimental importance it held for Rainey and Matt. It just brought the magnitude of the day's developments into sharper focus, and Emma patted Rainey's hand in support.

"Steady, love," Emma said softly. "We're workin' to fix things. Keep the faith."

Rainey smiled her thanks, but she had to turn her eyes toward the scenery outside the window as she wrapped the shawl around herself more securely.

The cabbie's gray muttonchop whiskers had all but taken over his ruddy face, and it was obvious that he prided himself as a landmark not to be missed.

"Now, I for one highly recommend the 'Bal' if it's a view of the castle yer after," he expounded to them with a theatrical flair. "They'll be lightin' the towers before the hour's out. But if the ladies are keen on plunderin' the shops come mornin', mind ye, ye'd be best to camp at the Caledonian. Lovely establishment, that. Shop til ye drop, eh, lassies?"

The frigid looks he got in the rearview mirror from the women—and the dog, for that matter—warned him his attempt at tour guide was losing him his tip instead of fattening it. He wiped the commercial grin off his face and glued his eyes to the traffic.

Malcolm had positioned himself in the front seat, to keep the cabbie honest for the drive through town. He cleared his throat with proper military authority and pointed the driver in the right direction.

"We'll no be goin' to any hotel just yet, man," he said in a businesslike tone. "We wish to go to the university by the most direct route, if ye would. We've no need of the scenic tour nor the roundabout." The cabbie nodded curtly, clearly disappointed that he had misjudged this group. Malcolm folded his arms across his chest and frowned in concentration on the road before them.

Carrie leaned her head against her mother's shoulder. "Why are we going to Papa's office, Mama?" she asked over a yawn. "How many times do I have to say it? Papa isn't there."

Rainey smoothed Carrie's curls and exchanged a look of concern with Sasha. "We know, sweetheart. But the authorities have very strict rules about how and when they can search for people. They don't want to make things worse by putting the rescue people in danger. So, it might take a day or two for them to start looking for your papa. We have to keep checking with the airline to find out what the latest news is.

"But we aren't going to wait. We can't go north until morning, so we're going to see if there's anybody at the university who might be willing to help us make a search of our own. Then, we're going to take the earliest flight we can to where they think survivors might be, so we can get a good head start on a search of our own."

Carrie pressed a hand over her yawn. "But we *know* where he is, Mama. I told you, he's with the selkies."

Rainey smoothed Carrie's curls. "I know, Care. But there are so many places where the selkies like to go. We'll have to get some maps to help us see where their favorite spots are." She hadn't been able to stop shaking since they left the Inverness airport, and she hoped Carrie wouldn't pick up on it.

"He's by the big wall, Mama. We just have to go to the big wall." Carrie muttered something unintelligible and nestled down into the instant sleep of the young.

"What was that last thing she said, Mama?" Sasha asked as she wrapped her arm around Carrie protectively. "It sounded strange, almost like a foreign language."

Rainey smiled down at Carrie. "I think she was just already half in her dreams. This has been so hard on us all. I wish to God there had been any kind of sign of survivors. How in the world are we going to find some big wall where selkies live?"

"I don't know, but it all seems very clear to Carrie. Where do you suppose she means? It sounds like she's going to walk us right up to the place if we give her the chance."

Emma pressed her lips together in thought. "I say we make straightaway for Orkney. The very name of the place means 'seal islands.' And given the prevailin' currents from out of the north, it's most likely where a man might drift. Of course, the fact they've got sixty-seven islands in the group could be a detriment."

"Orkney." Rainey let the word settle in her mind. It felt right. "And they have a lot of seals there?"

Malcolm turned in his seat. "Oh, aye, Rainey, no lodgin's to speak of, but the place is fair crawlin' with the creatures. Though I'd be hard-pressed to tell ye which of the bunch was seal and which selkie. It's a bit beyond me ken."

The cabbie gave him a frown, though it was hard to tell if it was a demonstration of skepticism over the subject matter or disapproval at Malcolm's inability to identify an enchanted creature on sight who was at times a human, at times a seal.

Malcolm made a grumbling noise deep in his throat and pointed toward a turnoff.

"Mind the road, man," he said curtly. "It's what yer paid to do, is it no?"

The cabbie lifted one eyebrow. "Aye, it's my job, true enough."

Rainey settled Carrie against Sasha's shoulder and leaned forward in her seat. She glanced at the cabbie's registration card, which was posted to the backseat.

"Mr. Mackay," she began.

"It's Olie, mum," he said to her reflection in the rearview mirror. "Have ye decided where yer spendin' the night, then?" He chanced catching Rainey's eye in the rearview again, and she smiled through her worry.

"If you had your choice of hotels, Olie, and someone else, an airline company, say, was going to pick up the tab, where would you stay?"

He gave it some serious thought. "If it was no out of me own pocket, mind, I'd grab the Balmoral. They'll feel it in their livers, that airline company, if ye go for the works at that place. Set the lot of 'em back on their heels." He smiled to himself.

Rainey sat back. "Then that's where you can take us, Olie. But first, we have some errands to take care of at the university. When we're done, if you're at liberty, we'll have you show us the fine points of the Balmoral Hotel."

"Oh, I'll be at liberty, mum. The airline has put me at yer disposal, ye might say. If ye'd like, I could curl meself up outside yer door and be yer watchdog for the night."

Malcolm's backbone stiffened. "That'll no be necessary, sir. These ladies are quite well protected by such as myself. And we already have a proper watchdog in our midst."

Olie eyed Angus as the little Scottie snored on Emma's lap.

"A dog at the Balmoral," he said in wonder. "That airline must have done a wee bit more than lose yer luggage."

Rainey settled Carrie back in her arms. Carrie stirred in her sleep, and Rainey patted her back as if she were still a babe in arms. "They did indeed, Olie. They lost my husband."

Chapter 4

The corridors of the university were quiet as they made their way to Matt's office on the second floor of the Language Studies Building. Matt seldom used the office, so it came as something of a surprise when the old brass doorknob turned easily. The wood-paneled walls were shelved from floor to ceiling with reference material, some modern, some obscure, but the massive oak desk was absolutely neat and tidy, added testimony to the room's normal slumber.

Rainey wasn't sure what clues she expected to find in this room. There were no cryptic notes or ancient maps secreted away somewhere to give her the answers she needed. She knew for a fact that Matt had gone to Norway, and she knew he had been trying to get home to them. These things had been a given from the start.

And although it was compelling to see and touch the material things that spoke so clearly of the man she loved, it also stripped away small bits of her heart each time her eyes came to rest on a favorite book of Gaelic poetry or a pen that had been given to him by the girls years before as a Christmas gift. These were the things of solid reality, the things that would have to be inventoried and removed if . . . If they were wrong.

Emma folded her arms across her chest and looked to Rainey. "Verra well, love, we're all here. So where would ye have us start? Should we be goin' up and down the halls bangin' on doors in a search for volunteers, then? Or is there a phone list of some kind, maybe?"

They all waited for Rainey to give them their orders, their faces bright with hope, their energies tapped in to hers. But in Rainey's soul, there was a surge of panic. She had done her job. She had kept them all going and never doubted for an instant that their instincts about Matt were correct, despite the mounting evidence to the contrary. But now, standing amid the tokens and trappings of his life, she was excruciatingly tired, as if she hadn't slept for a thousand years.

But there was another part of her that demanded they leave for the north this instant, on foot if necessary. There were no flights to where they needed to go until the early morning, not even a charter to be had. She had double-checked. They were stuck here for the night, and the wasting of so many precious hours was unbearable. The only saving grace might be if they could recruit some help while they waited out the night.

She had intentionally avoided Edinburgh and the university in the past, preferring to keep to the sanctuary of their home in the remote Highlands. Her years in the advertising industry had given her more than enough opportunity to deal with the public. And she and Matt had been of one mind about keeping the girls in the country for their formative years. She was a stranger within these walls. There wasn't a soul here who owed her even the tiniest favor.

She sat down behind Matt's pristine desk and started to pull open drawers. They, too, were uncharacteristically tidy. But in one drawer, she came across a directory of university personnel.

"What have we here?" she said, as the others clustered around her. "It looks like this thing has hardly been touched, but here and there, a star has been drawn beside someone's name. Of course, it isn't impossible that the stars mean these people are to be avoided. But it's a place to start. One's in the history department, one's in communications, two are in archaeology, and the remaining two are here in the language department. Let's see if anyone's still around."

She tried the numbers with little success.

"The history guy is on sabbatical. The man in communications is out of his office until Wednesday. The two in archaeology are leading a research expedition to Greece for their graduate students. And of the language profs, one is away on sick leave, and the other's phone is out of order." She cradled her head in her hands. "What made me think we'd find any help here? I'm really sorry, everybody."

Sasha laid her hand on her mother's shoulder comfortingly. "That last one, Mama, the language department one with the broken phone, it's here in this building, isn't it?"

Rainey nodded. "Professor Cameron? It should be down at the far end of the hall as nearly as I can tell. But I don't think there's much point, Sasha. Everybody's gone home for the night by now, and it won't do any good to leave messages, since we'll be up and gone in the morning before anybody even gets to work. Although I do seem to remember your father mentioning this Professor Cameron before he left."

Sasha glanced at Emma, who gestured toward the door with a tilt of her head.

"Just stay here for a minute, everybody," Sasha said. "I'll run down to the room and see if anybody's home. I won't be a minute. It's got to be worth a try."

Rainey looked up at Sasha. "All right, sweetheart, go ahead. Do you want one of us to come with you?"

"That's okay, Mama, why don't you use the time to double-check if there are any more names to try in the directory. You've always been pretty good with stars."

Her mother's smile was a tentative one, but it was a smile all the same. Sasha wrote the room number on her palm and headed through the door purposefully. Once in the hall, however, she had to get her bearings. She had visited Matt here once or twice, but only as a very young child. The place had seemed enormous to her then. It was still pretty intimidating. But she would be attending classes here in the not too distant future. She decided to attack the problem of finding Professor Cameron's office as if she would one day own the place.

Halfway down the hall, the sequence of the numbers changed in a totally illogical fashion. She was looking for Room 364, but the numbers jumped from 358 to 372. Obviously, there was another section of the floor that she had somehow missed.

But the halls were rigidly straight, and the only side halls she found had rooms with numbers that didn't help her in the least. There wasn't time for a game of hide-and-seek, and she was tempted to just go back, rather than make everyone wait while she went on what was probably a wild goose chase.

If she could find a human being, chances were the answer to finding the missing room would be a simple one. But all the doors were locked and the rooms behind the glass squares in the doors were either dark or empty of people. She was starting to feel like Alice at the Mad Hatter's Tea Party in some peculiar academic Wonderland.

She came to one room that had no number on its door, only a small rectangle of brighter paint and two nail holes where the number had once been. There was a small window she could peer through, but when she tried the door, it wouldn't budge. She knocked. No answer. And yet, she could see a tall, broadshouldered young man with sandy red hair and a ridiculous handlebar moustache strolling the length of the room, his nose buried in an ancient-looking volume. She knocked louder this time, but he acted as if he didn't hear a thing.

"Rude academic snob!" There was no time for this. She took off one of her heavy, all-weather boots and smacked the heel against the door until she noticed it was starting to leave a mark on the wood. No response. What was more, the man was apparently trying to hide from her—she couldn't see him anymore.

"Fine. Forget it!" she huffed as she hopped around, trying to get her boot back on without having to take the time to sit down. She lost her balance, and as she grabbed for a cart full of textbooks parked against the wall, the whole thing overturned with a crash. The next thing she knew, she was on her backside, glaring up at Mr. Handlebar Moustache.

He looked to be in his early twenties, and there was definitely a hint of mischief in his dark brown eyes. Fortunately for the future of his skull, he had the decency not to laugh at her as she sat sprawled on the floor. She wanted to deck him, just to give him a hint of how it felt to hit the ground hard. So when he offered her his hand, she declined it, preferring to get up on her own. She glanced down the hall to where her family was waiting.

"Freshman?" he asked simply.

"No."

"Cat burglar? Because if indeed that is the case, ye'd be best to take to task another vocation, how shall I put it, to fall back on?" He tsked to himself theatrically as he looked down at the scattered books.

Sasha picked them up hastily and stacked them back on the righted cart. There was an odd quality about his speech, as if some of the corners had been shaved off the words. She supposed he was talking that way to make fun of her further. "Look, I know this is all a big joke to you," she said bitterly, "but I don't have time. I need you to point out Room 364 to me. It's very important."

He folded his arms and tapped his chin with his forefinger in careful thought. "Three-sixty-four, ye say? Well, let's see now." He turned dramatically and pointed to the room he had just vacated.

"You're kidding."

He shook his head in the negative and shrugged. "Wrong number?"

"I'll say."

"Ye were lookin' for Professor Cameron, then?" he asked, taking particular interest in the green-velvet pouch she wore around her neck.

Sasha narrowed her eyes at him. "I sincerely hope you aren't going to tell me you're Cameron."

He snorted at the notion. "Hardly. Although I have high hopes of bein' seventy-five years of age one day, I'm in no particular hurry to get there today. I'm Kyle Maclennan, Professor Cameron's assistant. Ye'll be kind enough not to stare at the bloody shackles of my indenturment, if ye please. And you, mystery lady. . . . We've established yer not a freshman nor a cat burglar. So a man can only assume yer the Queen of the Woodland Fairies."

The breath caught in Sasha's throat. The blood drained from her head, and she gripped the book cart for support. It was a term of endearment her biological father had used to describe her. And Matt, in his turn, with no previous knowledge of the tradition, had called her the same. Now, here was a third man calling her Queen of the Woodland Fairies. It took her completely by surprise, and her knees started to buckle.

"Here, now, miss, yer about to dent our hallowed halls again. This sort of behavior will never do." He lifted her lightly into his arms. "Bein' a Yank, I suppose ye'll have me nicked for sexual harassment at this juncture. Ah, well, it's a dirty job, but someone's got to do it, now, haven't they?" He set her down on the leather wing chair behind Cameron's ostentatious antique desk, then went down on his haunches in front of her to rub the backs of her hands. "Are ye still with us, then, miss?"

She frowned in concentration, unwilling to look him in the eye. "Cameron? Where is he?"

"Old Wallie? Why, I suspect he's on his way back from the conference in Oslo even as we speak." He moved away from her and sat down on the edge of the desk.

"Oslo?" She met his eyes at last, and he read the sorrow there.

"Whatever is it's got ye so dug up, lass?"

She straightened in the chair. "I'm Sasha Macinnes."

"Macinnes? Professor Mac's elder?"

Sasha nodded.

Kyle rose and started to pace the book-lined office. "He talks of ye endlessly, Professor Mac—you and yer mother and wee Carrie. It's like I've known ye since . . ." He looked at her out of the corner of his eye, trying to reconcile his former image of her with what sat before him now. "He gave the impression ye were but a wee child, not a woman in full flower." Their cheeks stained simultaneously.

"Forgive me, Miss Macinnes, I have the habit of speakin' my thoughts aloud at the most inopportune moments. Believe me, I was on a first-names basis with the willow switch for the majority of my youth. And would be still, were it not for Old Wallie's arthritis." He cleared his throat. "But ye must know more about Cameron's comin's and goin's than I do. They were travelin' together, Cameron and yer father." He stopped and turned to her, a look of genuine concern on his face. "What's this really about?"

"Don't you ever watch the news?"

He dismissed the notion with a wave of his hand. "I've little use for current events, as a rule."

Sasha walked over to the ceiling-high set of windows. Night was falling, and the lights of the city were beginning to blink on. How dark it must be where her father was tonight. She turned to Kyle and twisted a loose button on her jacket.

"There's been a plane crash. The flight from Oslo went down in the North Sea. The news says there are no survivors so far."

"Sweet Christ." Kyle ran his hand through his hair and sat down heavily on the desk. "I heard talk of the storm, of course. But I had no idea . . . Cameron isn't fit for that sort of trauma. He's a heart condition, for godsakes. His doctors advised him against traveling. The changes in cabin pressure, the stress of a change of diet. The poor old bastard couldn't even sleep away from his own humidifier." The words choked in his throat as he thought about the possible loss of his friend and mentor. Only then did it occur to him that another person in the room was experiencing the same anguish.

"I'm so sorry, Miss Macinnes," he said in all sincerity. "Please believe me, I had no idea ye were suffering under such difficult news. I pray ye will not think me insensitive to your situation. Your father is a very dear friend and colleague. I will forever be in awe of his knowledge and his extraordinary skills as a teacher. Please, is there any way I may be of service to ye and yer dear family? Ye have only to ask."

It was hard for Sasha to listen to Kyle's words. They smacked of condolence. Although they were sincere, they were inappropriate as far as she was concerned, and she didn't want to hear any more.

"My family and I are going to Orkney to find my father, Mr. Maclennan. Despite what they're saying on the news, he isn't dead. Please don't ask me how I know it. I just do. Carrie says he's with the selkies. And I believe her. I don't know about Professor Cameron. I'm sure he's a good man, and I hope he survived the crash. But I do know my father is very much alive.

"The Search and Rescue people aren't going to help much longer. We can't count on them. The weather is too rough, and the crash was too bad. We're on our own. And if you truly want to help us, you'll come to Orkney. We need all the help we can get."

"Orkney. Yes, it would be Orkney," he said. Thoughts of the place distracted him.

His dark eyes touched a dangerous and vulnerable place inside Sasha. It took her by surprise, but for some reason it didn't strike her as an intrusive touch. It made her ache to her soul, and she had to turn her attention back to the lights of Edinburgh out of self-protection. The lights blurred before her sight, and she wanted nothing more desperately than to go home to the security of her own bedroom. She was being smothered here, and she couldn't stay any longer for his answer.

"My family is waiting," she said as she tried to breeze past him. His shoulder brushed her arm, and she froze. He moved aside, and she raised her eyes to his.

"I'll go with ye to Orkney, Miss Macinnes," he said, his words rough with emotion held firmly in check. "It's a duty owed."

"I'm sure my father would understand if your responsibilities here took precedence, in light of Professor Cameron's absence." She was careful to train her sight over his shoulder, but she caught his grim smile.

"Who's to say but what we may discover Old Wallie out there cavortin' among the selkies as well?"

Sasha walked to the door with an air of regal dignity. "If you're serious about helping us, come to the lobby of the Balmoral Hotel tomorrow morning at five o'clock sharp. We won't wait for you."

"No, I don't expect ye will, Miss Macinnes," he conceded as he opened the door for her and bowed formally. "Until tomorrow, then, may sleep take ye without a struggle." She gave him a quizzical look and hurried through the door.

Kyle sat back down on Cameron's desk and absently started to put things in order. The impact of loss hit him squarely as he straightened a stack of handwritten notes Cameron had left to direct him in his next lecture series. He was the only one on campus who could make heads or tails of Cameron's handwriting. In his heart, it felt to Kyle like Old Wallie was in fact gone, and he sighed from deep in his soul. It was hardly the first time he had lost someone dear to him.

But the notion of Matthew Macinnes's passing was quite another matter. The life force of the man had pulsed in the room through his adopted daughter. He believed Matt was alive, thanks to Sasha. Could she possibly be unaware of what an incredibly powerful force she was, this woman who bore herself like a queen with such ease? She had ambushed him good and proper.

He reached to the back of the middle drawer of Cameron's desk and withdrew a key. With it, he unlocked one of the lower drawers and pulled out a half-empty bottle of fine, single malt Scotch and a small glass that looked like it would be put to better service with a toothbrush in it. With two fingers of rich, amber whiskey in his glass, Kyle raised a solitary toast.

"Gu sla `n fallain. A' cur dhinn a' chainalais!"* he declared to the empty room, meaning, "Safe and sound. Banishing melancholy." He put the glass to his lips, then paused and raised it again. "And to Orkney, by God, *'ionad falaich nan ro `n slapach.'" The hiding place of the seals.

"I think we better look for help somewhere else, Mama," Sasha said with a frown as she sat down with the others. "There was a guy there, but I don't think we should take him with us."

Rainey exchanged a look with Emma. "You mean someone

actually volunteered to help, sweetheart? What's wrong with him? Is he too old?"

Sasha shook her head, hoping fervently that her cheeks weren't burning as she remembered the amused look in Kyle Maclennan's eyes as she lay sprawled on the floor. "He's just some teaching assistant. Kyle something-or-other. But I don't think he's very reliable. He's too full of himself—you know?"

"I see." Rainey saw the blush in Sasha's cheeks. There was something else going on here, but she doubted that she would get anything more out of Sasha for the moment. "Well, then, I guess we're officially on our own for now."

Sasha seemed extremely interested in that loose button on her jacket. "I told that Kyle person that if he wanted to come with us, he'd have to be in the lobby by five o'clock tomorrow morning. But I'll be pretty surprised if he shows up."

Rainey stood up slowly. "Well, we'll check when the time comes. For now, let's find out if Olie and his cab are still waiting to take us to the hotel. I told him to phone ahead and secure our rooms at the Balmoral. The way things are going, we may still end up sleeping in the park."

As they all made their way toward the stairs, they had to walk by Cameron's office. Sasha dreaded the idea that Kyle might stick his head out to say good-bye or embarrass her in some way. But as they filed past, the window in the door was dark, and there was a note taped to it saying the office was closed until further notice. Sasha stared down at the button she had just twisted loose into her hand. There was no way sleep was going to take her "without a struggle" tonight.

When they reached the Balmoral, there was a phone message waiting for them on the answering machine in Rainey's room. Carrie crawled across the bed to peek over her mother's shoulder as Rainey pushed the replay button.

"Is it from Papa?" she asked excitedly.

"No, sweetheart. It's from the airlines. They're saying the company's search efforts are going to hinge on whether the government authorities decide to pursue the job. For now, all rescue attempts are on hold until weather conditions improve to the north. It could take days. If too much time goes by, they'll scrub the mission and just wait to see if anybody shows up on the beaches."

Emma had Angus in her arms. She scratched the little Scottie's ear and snorted in disgust. "I wonder what they'd do if the president of the company had been on that plane," she said with a derisive snort.

Rainey gave her a look of request. "Would you mind taking everybody downstairs for supper, Emma? I think I need a few minutes alone to catch my breath."

Malcolm stepped forward and wrapped his arm around Emma's shoulder. He gave Rainey a look of paternal concern. "Not to worry, Rainey. Emma and I will take the girls to supper. And ye can bet we'll no be lookin' at the a la carte section of the menu, ye ken, seein' it's to be on the airline's tab. There's nothin' more to be done tonight, lass. When we come back to the room, we'll give those maps ye got the once-over. See if it's of any help."

"Right. I think I'll lose my mind if we don't do something toward the search tonight. Thank you. Both of you."

Emma set Angus down for a turn at watch at the foot of the bed and took Rainey's hand into her own. Rainey's fingers were cold. "What can we bring ye, then, love? Some soup to warm ye, perhaps?"

It was a simple question. And yet, Rainey couldn't seem to find an answer to it as she stared down at their hands. Emma tucked her finger under Rainey's chin, raising her eyes.

"Seas do cho `irichean,* Rainey, *dh 'amais e air deagh bhuathal a-nocht, agus tha e la `idir mar na daragaibh," she

said kindly, meaning, "Nail your colors to the mast, Rainey. He has found a snug harbor tonight, and he is strong as the oaks."

"You're right, as always, Emma. It's silly of me to worry about him. But I can't help wishing we had more help." She glanced at the message button on the phone. It was dark.

Emma tsked at her like a mother hen. "Now, now, why don't ye prop yer legs up and close yer eyes for a minute or two while the room is quiet, love. We won't be long, but we'll give ye a chance for a wee bit of privacy. If ye have need of us, just ring down to the restaurant, and we'll be back at yer side quick as a flash."

Rainey gave her most of a smile. "You're my guardian angel, Emma. You're always saving my life."

"Aye, well, I hope ye won't mind, love, but I've set me wings on another soul for the time bein'," she said with a wink.

"That's the first good news I've heard all day."

Rainey slipped off her shoes and swung her legs up onto the bed. When she closed her eyes, she heard the others tiptoe out of the room. She missed them the instant the door shut behind them, and yet dream images immediately demanded her full attention.

In the dream, she was poised on the edge of an enormous sea cliff. The sheer heights were covered with gray-and-white gulls, and as she hazarded a glance to the jagged beach below, she wanted to turn away, to cover her eyes.

Matt lay on the rocks, his eyes closed, whether in sleep or something far worse, she couldn't tell. He opened his eyes slowly, and she could see herself reflected in them. He was so real to her, she was tempted to dive headlong down the cliff to his side with no regard for the consequences. But her feet were leaden. They refused to move, and as she watched, a group of gray seals came up on the rocks, surrounding Matt. Only one of them was aware of her presence at the top of the cliff. That seal turned and gave her a look of wisdom and recognition.

Waiting for you, the look said. *We are both waiting for you.*

Matt's name was warm on Rainey's lips as she startled into wakefulness. Angus jumped up on the bed and buried his black nose under her trembling hand. She stroked his wiry fur absently.

"The selkies, Angus," she said, her words still haunted by her dreams. "We have to find the selkies."

As they made their way across the lobby toward the restaurant for their supper, Sasha smothered a gasp and grabbed Emma's sleeve. "I don't believe it," she said in a harsh whisper. "What's *he* doing here?"

"Whatever is the matter, Sasha?" Emma asked with alarm.

Sasha inclined her head toward an overstuffed leather chair that was partially hidden by a potted palm. All Emma could see was a worn backpack and a long-legged young man with sandy red hair and a rather outrageous moustache who was sleeping soundly where he sat. He didn't appear to pose any immediate threat to life or limb, as far as she could see.

"Do ye know the man, Sasha?"

Malcolm came up beside them, hiking his trousers a bit higher. "What seems to be the problem, ladies?"

"I'm no quite certain, Malcolm," Emma said as she took in Sasha's agitated state.

Carrie tugged at Sasha's sleeve. Sasha had no patience for her, and when Carrie looked to where the man slept, a mischievous grin lit her freckled face.

"That one's yours, big sister," she said with total confidence.

Sasha looked down at Carrie, her expression somewhere between disbelief and dismay.

"What do you mean he's mine, Carrie?" she demanded.

Carrie pulled her baseball cap firmly over her brow and set her hands on her hips.

"I mean, he's like your Sleeping Beauty, Sash." She clapped

her hands over her heart theatrically. "The only way to wake him up is with a big smooch." She puckered her lips and made ridiculous kissing noises. Sasha groaned in humiliation and tried to grab Carrie as she ducked behind Emma for protection. Emma separated them to arm's length.

"That'll do, the pair of ye." She turned to Sasha. "Now, if ye don't mind, lassie, tell what this is all about."

Sasha tried to worry her loose button, but it was no longer there. "He's from the university," she said miserably. "His name is Kyle Maclennan. He's the one from Cameron's office. I thought he wouldn't show up when I told him he'd have to be here at five o'clock tomorrow morning."

Malcolm considered Kyle from a distance. "Well, the lad's here and long before the appointed hour. I'd say we're hardly in a position to leave him behind. Go and wake him, Sasha. We're best to put one decent meal in the man before we sally forth into the wilds."

Sasha desperately wanted to refuse to go and wake him. She wanted nothing more than to let him hibernate for a hundred years. Maybe if she hadn't reacted to his being there, he might have slept through till noon, and they would have been long gone. But it was too late for such thoughts, and the truth was, they needed him. One look at Carrie told her that the more fuss she made, the more she was going to suffer unending embarrassment for it.

"Fine!" She stalked over to Kyle and glowered down at him. If only looks could kill, just this once, she would be a happy person.

"Wake up, Maclennan," she ordered without charity. He didn't stir. "Come on, rise and shine, Edinburgh! I don't have all night." Nothing.

Maybe she *had* managed to do him in with a look. But, no, she could see he was still breathing the deep, even rhythms of sleep. Talk about your sound sleepers! She kicked the heel of his hiking boot with her toe, and he leapt to his feet, instantly wide awake and apparently ready for battle.

When he saw her, he blinked as if she had been in his dreams and had now somehow crossed over into the waking world.

Sasha was taken by surprise, and as she took a step back, she stumbled over his backpack. For the second time in one evening, she found herself looking up at him from the ground. She opened her mouth with every intention of giving him a piece of her mind, but he raised his index finger in a gesture that told her to wait. The move made her hunger for blood.

He withdrew a small object from the pocket of his plaid flannel shirt and tucked it in his ear. This done to his satisfaction, he folded his arms across his chest and waited patiently as she struggled to her feet. When she stood before him, he pointed to his ear.

"I didn't want to miss a single lick of yer scold, ye ken," he said casually. "The left one's dead to the world, but the right one functions quite well with the help of modern technology."

Sasha dusted off her backside and tried to absorb this new revelation. To her disappointment, it took quite a bit of the steam out of her anger. If he was deaf and in the habit of removing his hearing aid while he studied, it would explain why he hadn't answered her knock at the university.

"But you're in the language department. How do you get away with it?" she nearly shouted, articulating each word with painful care.

He pressed his finger to his lips. "Ye needn't deafen the good ear, Miss Macinnes. The device is doin' its job royally at the moment. And as I believe I told ye, the one ear works fine with a wee bit of help. It only means I have to pay closer attention to what's bein' said. I suppose it makes me a better student of language in a way, more attentive to detail."

She chewed on the notion. A small twinge of sympathy began to nudge at her conscience, but she did her best to steel herself to it as she frowned down at the backpack that had so recently lain in wait for her.

"We're going to go eat in the restaurant," she said, without much invitation in her voice. "If you want to come with us, you have to come right now."

He looked over her shoulder to where the others were waiting with curious looks on their faces. They appeared to be a very tightly knit group. There was visible unrest in the ranks over one of their precious lambs straying so far from the fold.

"I thank ye for yer kind invitation," he said politely. "But if it's all the same, I'll take my rest here and leave ye to yer family. I suspect we'll be seein' quite a bit of each other over the next few days. So perhaps it's for the best if we keep to a distance at present."

She brightened. "Good. I mean, we can bring you something if you haven't eaten, I guess."

"No need."

"Okay, well, good-bye, then." Sasha turned to go, but for some reason, she was only mildly relieved that he wasn't coming to the restaurant. She paused when she thought she heard him say something peculiar. "Excuse me, did you say something?" He shrugged, and she felt the urge to deck him again. At least he had the decency to look uncomfortable over the fact she had heard him.

"I said, *'Hvor lang tid vil det ta?'* It's Norwegian. It means 'How long will it take?' "

"How long will what take?"

"A small matter. It's not important just now. I speak my thoughts out loud sometimes, remember? It's to do with the hearing loss, I imagine." He sat down in the chair and propped his legs up on his backpack as Sasha continued to frown at him.

"Yer party is waitin', Miss Macinnes. *Gus an a-ma `ireach*. Until tomorrow."

"Gus an a-ma `ireach," she replied, grateful that he had switched to Gaelic, a language she knew extremely well. She preferred to be on common ground with him. What it hadn't done, however, was cure the trembling in her knees as she walked away from him.

Chapter 5

Rainey felt a sense of awe at the desolate beauty of Orkney. The stark, almost treeless terrain of the island of Eday offered no protection from the harsh gales that scoured the rolling, heathered hills.

The wind crept up under her jacket, and she shivered to think what hardships Matt must have endured through the night. She couldn't let herself dwell on it, she told herself firmly. There was far too much to be done. She walked over to the boulder where Malcolm and Kyle were poring over the collection of maps they had brought along.

Her reaction to Kyle Maclennan was a mixed one. On his own merits, she liked the man. He was polite, intelligent, and appeared to be absolutely dedicated to their cause. On the other hand, once Sasha had explained to her who he was in the hotel lobby, she had refrained from saying another word to anyone for the entire trip. Sasha's campaigns of silence were never something to be taken lightly.

There was definitely something going on between Sasha and Kyle. How there could have been time enough for Sasha to develop a dislike for him was a puzzle. Sasha wasn't normally the kind of person to condemn someone without just cause. As a child, she had suffered too much from the snap judgments and wrong assumptions of people who should have known better than to impose such prejudices on others. So there had to be a concrete reason.

Sasha's welfare would always take precedence over the concerns of an outsider. There was no question. But she would feel far more comfortable in this enforced isolation of theirs if she knew what was going on in Sasha's mind.

Kyle himself appeared to be a bit confused by Sasha's behavior. During the flight, he had brought it up to her conversationally that they would be landing on Eday at the only airport in Great Britain actually called London Airport. An innocuous bit of trivia, but Sasha had answered his statement with a scowl, then slumped down in her seat and pretended to fall asleep.

It had been unquestionably rude, and Rainey had been prepared to say as much. But Emma had laid a hand on her arm and warned her silently against making an issue of it. Everyone's nerves were on edge, and Emma's move reminded her that it would be wise to pick her battles carefully if they were going to make this mission work. She would have to wait for the clues to Sasha's behavior to reveal themselves.

As she looked over Malcolm's shoulder at the map, she could see that their route was being plotted straight for the cliffs at the northernmost tip of the island. To try to search everywhere would be impossible. And they had decided collectively that they should concentrate their efforts on the areas that best matched her dream of where Matt was. It was what they could manage for now.

All the official searches were still on hold. And since they had had to impose on the generosity of the local constable in order to borrow the ancient English Ford they were using for transportation, it was in everyone's best interest for them to use their time well.

Malcolm cleared his throat, his sensibilities somewhat out of joint. "Two minutes, Rainey. Then we'll be off. Just as soon as I persuade this young dirk here of the most efficient method of gettin' to our destination. He fancies himself somethin' of an expert in the matter."

Kyle shook his head and smiled. "Hardly an expert, Malcolm. I only mentioned that I'm somewhat familiar with the region because for the past four years I've spent my summers workin' on the university digs up here. I have a certain amount of familiarity with these islands. They're a passion of mine. And I happen to know for a fact that the road this map shows has been replaced with an equally bad but shorter one just to the west of it. It'll cost us two hours if we try to go by the old one."

Rainey was beginning to understand the problem with Kyle Maclennan. This business of stubbornly speaking your mind without thought for the honey was a trait she had run into before. In fact, it was something of a strange bedfellow of hers, since Matt was famous for it. Matt had mellowed some over the years, but every now and then, the gentle, poetic side of his nature was tossed to the backseat in favor of the crusading knight, the stalwart defender of justice and truth, no matter whose toes he flattened in the process. The problem they were having with Kyle was that he displayed the same characteristics as the man they all loved and missed. Of course, understanding the problem didn't necessarily solve it.

"Let me have a look at the map, please, gentlemen," she offered.

She checked the copyright date on the map—1979. Kyle Maclennan would have been a small boy barely starting grammar school in 1979. Still, Malcolm was in a huff over the status of his authority, so the situation had to be handled tactfully, or this one minor incident might well taint the rest of the expedition. She traced the old road with the tip of her finger. There was a tiny notation to one side of it. She smiled secretly as she read it.

"Malcolm," she said sweetly, "it says something here next to the road, but I can't quite make it out. You're the map expert. Can you make heads or tails of what it says?"

Kyle started to take a step forward to take care of it for her, but Emma had the good sense to grab his arm to hold him back. He gave her a puzzled look, and she shook her head slowly to warn him off. He shrugged and folded his arms across his chest as Malcolm squinted at the fine print held at arm's length.

"Hmm, it looks to say there's a new road to be built startin' in 1980. 1980?" He shifted the map to read the copyright date. "Och, but this t'ing is as old as decent whiskey. See here, Rainey? We'd be best to look at a newer map to get the proper information. Would ye no agree, young Maclennan?"

There was a volume of reply in Kyle's expression, but he had the good grace to say, "Aye, right ye are, Malcolm."

"Right, well, then, hop to it, man, and find us a newer map. We've wasted enough precious time as 'tis."

"Whatever is yer pleasure, Malcolm," Kyle replied evenly. Out of reflex, his eyes slid to Sasha to see if she had witnessed the injustice done to him. She turned her head away quickly, but not fast enough to hide her grin. Clearly to her satisfaction, figuratively speaking, he had just landed on his backside.

The new road was such a misery, there was some question in everybody's mind whether the old road could have been any worse. By the time they reached the cliffs, a chilly mist had closed in along the coast, soaking everything with a heavy blanket of dampness.

Visibility was almost nonexistent, and the cliffs, known to the world as Red Head, were so treacherous, no one could be allowed to venture far from the old Ford. Despite the danger, it took a lot of serious persuasion to keep Rainey from going out. Emma had to pull her aside.

"If ye were to get lost out there, Rainey, there'd be more of us in jeopardy tryin' to run ye to ground," she insisted. "You and I both know it's Sasha would be leadin' the search and wee Carrie not far behind. And if ye were to injure yerself, what choice would we have but leave off the search altogether in order to see to yer health?"

Rainey chewed her lip out of restlessness and frustration. "But what if he's just on the other side of the cliffs, Emma? What if he's within shouting distance, but he's unable to speak? How can we expect him to spend another night in this hostile place if there's anything in the world we can do to help him right now? It's driving me up the wall."

Emma drew a wool beret from her coat pocket and settled it over Rainey's dark curls. "I know what yer feelin', love. We're all sufferin' from it. But cooler heads must prevail. There's far too much at stake here to go runnin' off into the mists. It's nearly dark already. No a one of us is expendable for that kind of madness, ye ken? 'Twould do us all a disservice, includin' dear Matty."

Rainey glanced over her shoulder at the girls. She turned her back to them so they wouldn't hear her. "I felt his presence so strongly at first, Emma. I was so sure he was all right. And yet, now, theoretically, we're closer to him in terms of geography, but I'm having a hard time getting a read on him, I guess you might say. It scares the hell out of me. I don't know what's changed." She shuddered and wrapped her jacket more snugly against the cold.

Emma handed her a pair of woolen gloves. "Ye've got yerself all in knots, love. Ye canna think in a straight line when yer head's so full of the worst that could happen. We'll make camp and put some water to boil. Things'll look more promisin' to ye after ye've had a good hot cuppa tea."

"I'm afraid I'm not going to feel any better until we're out there searching those cliffs. It's the only thing that's going to help me right now."

"Understood, love. But do an old woman a favor and try the tea for the meantime, eh?"

Rainey nodded her grudging consent, but her heart was clearly not in it.

"What'll I do if I never hear him in my heart again, Emma?" she whispered with a sense of desperation.

Emma laid her hand on Rainey's arm. "Ye know that old radio of Malcolm's in our livin' room at home, the wooden one that came through the war?"

"The one you keep on the mantel?"

"Aye, the same. Well, that wee radio is old-fashioned and totally out of style these days. We could've chucked it long ago or sold it for an antique."

Rainey sighed and toyed with the damp soil at her feet. "Your point being?"

Emma tucked her finger under Rainey's chin and raised her eyes. "That old radio of Malcolm's pulls in the Edinburgh and Glasgow stations just fine once ye give it a proper tunin' to the right channel. It takes a wee bit of patience and finesse, ye ken? And to anybody else not familiar with how to set the thing, it would seem a worthless hunk of junk. But it's all in the fine-tunin', ye see? Minor adjustments to the system. With all that's gone on, ye've just lost the frequency, love, that's all. It's still there, broadcastin' away loud and clear as ye please. Ye just have to tune back in to the right station, Rainey. It'll happen."

"I pray you're right," she said as she gave Emma a hug of thanks.

"The girls still hear him," Emma whispered in Rainey's ear. "Ye can see it in their eyes."

Rainey turned to Sasha and Carrie. The girls were helping with the unpacking, but they looked up from their tasks at their mother's silent call. They each gave her a small smile of reassurance and went back about their work. It was enough for now.

They made camp for the night with the army surplus equipment the island's constable had crammed into the trunk of the car for them. The stuff reeked of mothballs and creosote. But it was still sturdy, according to its provider. The constable had claimed to want to come and help with the expedition, but he had been forced to decline, purportedly because he was the only arm of the law on the island and therefore shouldn't stray too far from his kitchen "command center," and because in point of fact, it was his youngest's birthday. He was careful to mention more than once, however, that he was the island's official coroner, "Shouldsuchservicesberequiredgodforbid." The consensus had been that his absence was hardly a loss.

Malcolm sighed nostalgically at the sight of all the old familiar army gear. The tents were a torture to put together for a novice, so everyone was content to follow his orders when it came to getting the stubborn canvas into an upright position. Once this much was done, Emma and Rainey tried to persuade the vintage camp stove into service. It was pitiful at best. But they were able to get a pan of water hot enough for tea and to partially melt the bland dried soup they had brought along.

Carrie stared down at her meager supper in disappointment. "Could I have a peanut butter sandwich instead, Mama, please?" she asked. "This soup's crunching my teeth, and I don't think it's supposed to. Why can't we cook the real food in Emma's backpack? She showed me. She's got makings for biscuits and shepherd's pie. I'm sorry. I know you tried really hard to cook this stuff."

Rainey took the bowl from Carrie's hand and tried to stir it a bit more. Not only was it crunchy, it was already cold. "We just don't have a good enough fire to cook very well, Care. If this were a vacation trip instead of a rescue mission, we could have planned everything better. As it is, we have to make the best of things. If we manage to find your father tomorrow, we'll all be home, eating at the kitchen table in no time. As ugly as this food is, I wish we could be sharing it with him. I'll try to heat up some more water, sweetheart. I think I saw some cocoa among Emma's supplies."

"Thanks, Mama," Carrie said apologetically. "But it's okay, I'll just work on my soup a little more."

Emma patted Carrie's shoulder. "There's the sturdy trooper, lass."

Carrie forced down another crunchy bite. "Mama?"

"Yes, sweetheart?"

"About Papa . . ." She furrowed her brow over what she had to say. "I thought you and Sasha knew."

Rainey knelt down and took Carrie's hand. She didn't like the sound of this. "Knew what, Care?"

"You should have asked me. This isn't Papa's island. There's no castle here. That's how come I wondered why we came to this one. Papa's on the island with the castle."

Kyle overheard their conversation. He came over to them and went down on his haunches beside Carrie.

She offered him her bowl. *"Har De suppe?"* she asked. Have you any soup?

"Takk, jeg er forsynt," he replied without a second thought, meaning, "Thanks, nothing more."

Rainey intervened at this point. "Excuse me, I seem to be missing something very important here."

Kyle took the bowl from Carrie's hand and offered it to Rainey. "I'm sorry, Mrs. Macinnes, did ye not get any soup?"

Rainey pushed the bowl away. "No, thank you. I mean, I don't understand what the two of you are saying."

Kyle raised one eyebrow and turned to Carrie. She gave him a teasing smile of satisfaction, and as he looked back at Rainey, he expelled a long breath, realizing he was a man in trouble again.

"I beg your pardon, Mrs. Macinnes," he said humbly. "Your daughter started it. That is to say, when I heard Norwegian spoken, I automatically responded in kind." The waters were getting deeper. "I assumed because the language was used that Carrie was versed in it."

Rainey pulled back Carrie's baseball cap so she could see her better. "Norwegian, Care?"

Carrie shrugged, her freckled face all innocence. "I don't know, Mama. It's just kind of there."

Emma was sitting on a rock across from them with Angus on her lap. Rainey gave her a telling look. This was not the first time one of her children had started speaking a foreign language having never had a lesson. It was how Sasha had first come to know Gaelic.

"We're in for it proper, now that the wee one is speakin' somethin' new," Emma said as she rubbed Angus's ears. Angus closed his eyes in sheer bliss.

Malcolm cleared his throat gruffly. "Och, my bones were too old for all this the first go-round."

Kyle considered the unreadable looks on the faces of everyone else in the group and decided it would be prudent to continue in English.

"Tell me, Carrie," he said with such formality that Carrie sat up very straight. "Is this castle you spoke of one we might discover on our maps? Or is it of another variety?"

He wasn't sure why he had asked the question in such a peculiar way. But in light of their recent Norwegian exchange, it didn't seem too far out of alignment. All the women in Matthew Macinnes's life were entirely extraordinary, Kyle had concluded, and he was convinced he was far beyond his depth with each and every one of them. But there was no turning back now, and Rainey seemed to have no sticking points about his rather odd question.

Carrie glanced at him out of the corner of her eye. "It's still there, mostly. It's pretty new compared to the real ones."

Kyle felt his head start to spin. But somehow, it felt like an amazing opportunity. He wondered if Professor Macinnes had ever found himself in a similar situation.

"Do you think you could point the castle out on one of Malcolm's maps?" he asked.

"Maybe." Carrie gave a small shiver and smiled at Sasha, who sat silently watching from between two of the tents. "Kyle, don't you think we need a nice fire to keep us warm?"

"I do."

Carrie broke into a laugh of pure delight. "Did you hear that, Sasha? He said 'I do' to me first, so that means he's mine to keep."

"You're asking for it, little sister," Sasha replied in embarrassed misery.

Kyle looked from one sister to the other as Malcolm handed him a map of the islands and clapped him on the shoulder.

"Dunna let the females grind ye down, man. It's a vicious club they're in, the lot of them, bent on keepin' a man on his knees." He caught Emma's look of disapproval. "That is to say, their brand of bonnie wisdom sometimes eludes the likes of you and me, lad. Have a care. Do ye ken what I'm sayin' to ye?"

"I do."

Tears filled Carrie's eyes, she laughed so hard. "He said it again!"

Kyle blushed to his toes and Malcolm grumbled in disgust as

he walked over to sit beside Emma. "Och, the younger generation! Hopeless, the lot of them."

Rainey grabbed the stack of maps. "Please, everyone, we have to figure this out. We've wasted too much time already."

Kyle unfolded the map of Orkney quickly. "Aye, mum. Sorry." He pointed a flashlight at the northernmost islands, then settled the light on where they were now. "Have at it, Carrie, show us the way," he offered, as he handed the light to her.

Carrie took the flashlight, and for a moment she didn't move it from where they already were. Then, she trailed the light further north.

"It should be this one, don't you think?" she said with a gleam in her eye. "I mean, it has his name on it and everything." They all clustered around Carrie as she pointed to the small, narrow island called Papa Westray.

Kyle tapped his chin with his finger and gave Carrie a look of mock academic sternness. "Its name is the result of bein' a home to the holy fathers of the ancient Celtic Church, Carrie, and not as a tribute to yer father, I'm afraid."

Carrie raised one eyebrow in a show of pride. "Everybody knows that. I only said it *should* be that island, didn't I?"

"Aye, I'll give ye that."

She seemed satisfied for the moment as she frowned in concentration at the map. Slowly, the flashlight's beam traveled to the left until it shone on Papa Westray's larger sister, the Isle of Westray. Not only did the map show the presence of Noltland Castle, it also showed a peninsula of substantial cliffs bordering the northwest corner of the island. Carrie looked to her mother, all playfulness gone.

"It's where the selkies are, Mama. I promise. It's where Papa is."

Rainey traced the cliffs with her fingertip. For the first time all day, something felt right.

Sasha touched the cliffs on the map as well, her expression distant. "He's waiting for us there, Mama. I feel it, too."

Rainey picked up the map and hugged it. "If we drove back to the constable's right now, do you think there's any way we could get closer to Westray before morning? Maybe we should find a way to get in touch with Search and Rescue to give them this new information. If they knew just where to look . . ."

Malcolm studied another map of the same area. "It'll do us no good, I'm afraid, lass. Aside from the wicked mists closin' in and the roads bein' so bad, there are no ferries runnin' out there in the dark, and none of the pros are goin' to be allowed to risk it in these conditions. We must wait till the dawn."

Her eyes filled with tears, but she blinked them back. "We could have been to him by now. We're on the wrong damn island. Mistakes like this may cost him his life. How can I sit here till morning, knowing he's lost, knowing he's hurt? How can I make it through this night?"

Emma wrapped her arm around Rainey's shoulders. "We're doin' our best, love. None of us thought to ask Carrie if this was the right island. We must be more in tune with that wee pixie, that's all. She'll lead us to where we need to be. We'll make it through this night together and send Matty Mac our love and strength to bide him till the mornin'."

"What if it's not good enough, Emma?" Rainey said, barely above a whisper.

Emma squared her shoulders. "It's more than good enough, love, I promise ye."

Kyle stared at the map. "Are ye sure it's wise to make yer decisions based on the guesses of the girls, ma'am? I mean, I'm sure they're that close to her father, but I'm not sure this is the most sensible way to conduct a search of this kind."

Rainey met Kyle's look of skepticism head-on, her smile a cool one. "I know how difficult it must be for you to accept this,

Mr. Maclennan, but all the high-tech equipment and manpower in the world can't hold a candle to my daughters' instincts about Matthew Macinnes. I don't know if I've thanked you for coming to our assistance in all of this as you have. Your help is much appreciated. And we will all certainly understand if you find our methods too unusual for your taste and choose to return home at this juncture.

"Under normal circumstances, more conventional rescue techniques might work fine. But in our case, because of the relationship my family and I share, I guarantee you, 'the girls' are our best source of accurate information. I hope you will be able to accept that fact on faith for now."

Kyle gave her a nod, but clearly, he was not thoroughly converted. A short time later, when the darkness had closed in around them with a vengeance, he walked out of the camp with a flashlight, a small shovel, and two big plastic garbage bags. He didn't give them any explanation, but said only that he would be headed to the southwest and promised to return within half an hour.

By the time he had been gone for five minutes, Sasha was pacing the periphery of the camp. Rainey walked over to her to offer her a cup of tea. Sasha looked down at the cup, hardly seeing it as Rainey pressed it into her hand.

"Okay, Sash, let's have it. What's the story with this guy? Did he say something to offend you back in Edinburgh? Because if he did, I want to know about it."

"Not exactly." Sasha's eyes were trained in the direction Kyle had taken. "I guess you could say he was kind of rude."

"How so?"

Sasha bit her fingernail. "Well, I knocked on the door to Cameron's office, and Maclennan wouldn't answer it."

Rainey wrapped her jacket around herself more securely. "So, you think he was intentionally ignoring you?"

"I was convinced of it."

"Well, that certainly qualifies as rude. But you must have gotten him to open the door somehow, or he wouldn't be here with us tonight."

Sasha started on a fresh nail. "That's just it. There was a cart full of books in the hall, and I sort of knocked it over by accident."

"You knocked it over. I see. That must have gotten his attention."

Sasha groaned in exasperation. "Don't you see, Mama?" she said in a frantic whisper. "He's deaf!"

"What?"

"Please, Mama, don't *you* start with me. I said it took my knocking over all those books for him to hear that I was there at all. He had his hearing aid shut off so he could study. He honestly hadn't known I was there. And when he did figure it out, there I was sprawled out on the floor with a million books scattered all over the place. It was totally humiliating. And then, on top of everything else, he asked me if I was a freshman. A *freshman*. . . . Like it was a joke or an insult. What was I supposed to tell him? That I hadn't even achieved *that* level of incompetence yet?" She looked up at the dark mists rolling over them as if she hoped for guidance from above.

"I think you're making too much of it, Sasha," Rainey said kindly. Inwardly, she breathed a sigh of relief that the problem hadn't been anything more serious. This was manageable.

"There's more, Mama."

"More?"

"He called me the Queen of the Woodland Fairies."

"The name both Matt and Alan called you?" she said in surprise.

"That's right, Mama. Both of them. Even though they never knew each other."

"Kyle must have overheard Matt use the term to refer to you

at some point," Rainey reasoned. "It's certainly not a common term to call someone. It probably just stuck in his mind, and it was a spontaneous response once he knew who you were."

"That's the problem. When he said it, I was a stranger to him. He didn't have any idea who I was."

Malcolm called to them in a voice booming enough to be heard on the distant shores of the Mainland. "Edinburgh's back. Of course, he shouldna have gone off runnin' amuck in the night in the first place. If the man has whiskey, 'tis only right he should share it with his fellow travelers on a night like this and no hoard it to himself behind a rock."

Rainey and Sasha turned as one to see the thin beam from Kyle's flashlight cutting through the mists. The sound of the two plastic bags being dragged behind him made them both wonder if he had perhaps "dug up" some local wildlife for their supper. He hauled the bags to the center of the camp and dumped the contents out in a pile.

Kyle flashed the light on it. "Peat, my friends. Now the trick will be to see if we can get it to catch in this weather. If we're clever, we may get a wee bit more food and warmth into ourselves before bed."

Rainey was gratified to see he had the good sense not to look at Sasha at the mention of the word "bed." A wise move on his part. It dawned on her that she was fast becoming a rabidly protective mother. Was there just cause, she wondered, other than what Sasha had already told her?

She didn't have the stamina right now to be Sasha's nursemaid on top of everything else. But she made a mental note to keep a close watch over things, and if the opportunity arose, she would find out how Kyle Maclennan had taken it into his head to use the expression "Queen of the Woodland Fairies."

Emma, Malcolm, and Kyle all had experience with peat fires, and before long, a warm glow was emanating from the stacked squares of sod. It was hardly a roaring blaze, but in time, a pot of water was bubbling merrily within it, and everyone could warm their hands and feet. A round of hot tea and cocoa renewed everyone's outlook on life.

The mists lifted, revealing a staggering field of stars twinkling above them, and as tired as they all were, no one wanted to give up on such a sky too soon. Sasha was the astronomer of the group, and she rattled off the names of more than a dozen constellations for them with ease.

But the quiet of the place had a roar all its own. Not far below them, the waves crashed against the sandstone cliffs of Red Head with timeless determination. But once the winds died down, there was little more to break the breathless silence of all the ages except what could only be termed the infinite hum of the stars above them. With no trees or rocks for shelter, the expanse of Creation all around them was an almost crushing thing, so they all chose to focus on the little fire for comfort. It was real, of immediate use, and of a manageable size for the eye to take in and understand.

Emma refilled everyone's cup, then snuggled up next to Malcolm beneath a motheaten army blanket. There was a pall on the group as each person's thoughts went out to Matt, somewhere to the far north. If their good wishes for him were to be of any use, their spirits were going to have to be lifted substantially.

"I'm of the opinion we're all in need of a story," she said, stifling a yawn. "But most of mine have been told till they're frayed at the corners. I'm thinkin' this group could use a wee bit of fresh blood." She gave Kyle a wink. "What do ye say, young Maclennan, is there an adventure tale upon ye at the moment?"

Kyle rolled his tin cup between his hands to warm them, his dark eyes trained on the steam rising from the tea. "New or old, livin' or dead?" he asked.

"Old!" Carrie said before anyone else could voice a vote.

His eyes rose to Rainey.

"Living," she said simply, her eyes still on the fire.

He smiled at her choice. "Och, an old tale of a living soul. A proper challenge. But as it happens, I know of such a thing. Some choose to call it a fairy tale. I, personally, prefer the term 'legend.' That is to say, as far-fetched as it may seem, I sincerely believe it to be based on fact."

Sasha gave him the first smile she had ever bestowed upon him. "A legend?"

"Aye, it's all that."

Rainey looked to Emma and mouthed the word "legend."

Emma blew a stray strand of hair out of her eyes, then pressed her lips together at Kyle's use of the word that had become so important in their lives, thanks to Matt. It appeared that Kyle Maclennan was also a believer in such things. Whether that would make it go harder or easier on him had yet to be seen.

Chapter 6

Kyle breathed in the pungent smoke from the peat fire. The scent of the earthy heat struck him as familiar, not just from this one night but from the distant memory of scores of nights he felt sure dwelled in the primal soul of each human being. That was a somewhat controversial notion for a university man, but the lowing fire triggered a sense of the past and the love of storytelling in his heart as no other sight or smell could.

He hugged the scant warmth of his tin teacup between his hands and smiled to himself as he stared into the red-orange caves of fire that smoldered between the rough chunks of peat. It wasn't difficult to lose himself in the hypnotic pulse of organic matter succumbing to flame.

Malcolm stifled a yawn. "Be at yer story, man, or the lot of us'll be snorin' in our seats. It's no as if we have all night."

"But we do," Sasha said simply. She wrapped her jacket around herself protectively and glanced down at her watch. "I mean, I know I'm not looking forward to crawling into those smelly old army sleeping bags."

Carrie flicked a few drops of her cocoa into the fire to hear them sizzle. "I think we should bury those old sleeping bags." She turned up her freckled nose and pulled the army blanket around her shoulders against the chill in the air. "I want to sleep with the selkies like Papa."

Kyle saw the look of worry flicker across Rainey's face. She was a good lady, Matthew Macinnes's wife, and he didn't fancy watching her fight her emotions so. "Ah, the selkies," he said quickly. "But they're a subject of my story."

Carrie gave him a winning smile. "Then I like it already."

Malcolm groaned. "And I for one would prefer to judge it for myself, assumin' I'm to hear the t'ing before I freeze where I sit."

Emma gave Malcolm a scolding look, and he grumbled to himself in Gaelic.

"Just be about yer story, if ye please, Kyle," she said encouragingly.

"Aye, well, in point of fact, the tale has to do with that island we're aimin' for on the morrow. Westray. And it's to do with the neighborhood where all of ye live as well." He was gratified to see he had their attention. "This is a story I heard told in a library when I was naught but a wee lad. And perhaps because I was told it at such a tender age, I've never for one moment doubted the truth of it." He hunkered down on his small folding camp stool and settled his gaze back on the fire.

"It seems in the olden times when the Vikings were makin' all of Scotland tremble with their warlike, plunderin' ways, in the forests not far from the munroes known as the Five Sisters, there lived a Celtic king and queen. Their domain centered around a great waterfall so tall it was said to scrub the skies clean after a decent rain."

"Glomach," Sasha said softly, her eyes still attentive to the fire.

"Aye, right you are," Kyle responded in surprise. "Ye know the tale, then."

Sasha's attention remained where it was. "My mother and I

know a story or two about the falls. As you say, they're in our neighborhood. This one has a familiar ring to it." She exchanged an unreadable glance with Rainey. "But, by all means, continue."

Kyle looked from Sasha to Rainey, wondering at the complexity of the two women.

"Please feel free to correct me, ladies, if my recountin' goes astray."

Sasha shrugged. "It's your story, Edinburgh."

He raised one eyebrow, thoroughly aware that her simple statement was a challenge. His hands had suddenly gone cold, and he rubbed them for warmth.

"Right, then. The king was a great warrior and a fair-minded man who was much beloved by his people, while the queen was said to be possessed of extraordinary beauty and a gift for healing and for song. It was also said that for countless generations, the women of the queen's family had held the power to summon the stars out of the sky and that they could change rainbows into mountains of precious jewels. The king and queen had but one daughter, and although she was very young, she was said to have her mother's gift as well."

Malcolm coughed on his cocoa, and Kyle took this as a gesture of skepticism.

"Now, ye must consider, Malcolm, this is but a local fairy tale," Kyle said in explanation.

"Legend," Rainey interjected.

"All right," Kyle conceded. "I'm always up for a good battle of semantics. But I'd have to say, my understandin' of the term 'legend' most often implies there's a thread of truth to the story."

Rainey gave him what could only be termed a sly smile. "I think we understand each other perfectly, Kyle."

"What were the people's names?" Carrie insisted with genuine interest before he had time to digest Rainey's last statement. She sat next to Kyle to ensure she wouldn't miss any of his story.

Kyle frowned in concentration. "Ye know, I don't recall ever hearin' their names, lass. But it's hard to say if it's because it's been so long or because I was never told. Perhaps your mother or your sister has knowledge of the names."

Carrie didn't wait. "I'll bet my papa would know their names. He knows the names of all the ones who ever lived in the woods."

Kyle gave her a grin. "Then it will be the first order of business to ask your papa about it on the ride home tomorrow. I'm that certain he'll set me straight on it in no time."

Carrie nodded with satisfaction.

But Malcolm heaved a sigh. "The story, man. The story."

"Oh, aye. Well, there came a day when the Viking hordes stormed down out of the north. They were a fierce and merciless lot, all with their red beards and horned helmets. There were far too many of them to hold back, and although the Celtic king put up a valiant defense, his warriors were no match for the Norsemen.

"The women of the clan fought side by side with their men, givin' a brave accountin' of themselves against the overwhelmin' odds. Many died for their trouble. And some of the more comely were stolen away to the icy shores of the far north. The bonnie Celtic queen was one such victim. She was captured in battle by a mighty Viking warlord.

"Because of her courage and her beauty, the warlord decided to keep her for his own. In her homeland she was a queen, but in the Vikings' domain, she was little more than a slave to the cruel demands of her captor. She had with her only one tangible reminder of her old life, a necklace of purest silver, hand-fashioned as a weddin' gift by her husband. On it was a pendant in the shape of three circles joined at the middle, an ancient symbol for nature's most powerful elements, water, wind, and fire. This the warlord tore from the queen's throat and placed around his own neck as a reminder of his dominance over her."

As Rainey looked up from the fire, she found Sasha staring at her intently. The story had touched a chord for them both. There was a woman much like Kyle described in their family history.

"There are some who say the queen bore the warlord a dozen handsome sons in her servitude," Kyle continued, "but that she refused to nurse them or nurture them in any way. There are some who say she was beaten daily for her refusal to bow before the warlord and that her burnin' hatred for him gave her the power to train her body against the conception of any children.

"In either event, the queen's coldness only made the Viking want her all the more. It was probably the one thing that kept him from killin' her outright for her rebellious ways. That and the fact she had a glorious singin' voice. She was said to have the voice of an angel, and even when she was forced to sing against her will, the sad, hypnotic beauty of her songs made the most battle-seasoned of those Viking brutes weep at her feet.

"For her own part, the queen thought of nothin' but escape. She didn't know what had become of her husband and her daughter. If they were alive, she had a life to return to. If they were dead . . . in another sense, they still needed her close by."

Emma rubbed Angus's ears to warm them as he sat curled in her lap. "Och, but it's a sad thing to be separated from yer own family," she said with a sigh.

Malcolm wrapped his arm around her shoulders. "Now, Em, we'll be goin' to California to see yer Robbie come fall. He's a grown man with a life of his own."

Emma nestled into his arms. "Och, I know that. But he's my only son, and I purely miss him."

"Aye, love." Malcolm nodded for Kyle to continue his story.

"The queen was careful not to make any foolish, premature attempts at escape," Kyle explained. "To do so would only have resulted in her recapture and an increase in the security around her. So, as hard as it was for her, she bided her time for eight long winters. And while many a Scot withered and died in captivity, the queen only grew more beautiful and serene for her sufferin'.

"Every night she sang of her sorrows and dreamt of her beloved home and the family she might never see again. She wished her loved ones happiness and health and prayed for their safety above her own. It was all she could do. Her faith that they would all be reunited one day was what kept her going.

"Then the time came when she could at last put her simple plan for escape into action. She had managed to secrete a small boat beneath a blanket of branches in a cove not far from the warlord's stronghold. She had lived among them long enough that no one gave much thought to the idea of her escape. The warlord seldom let her wander far from his side when he was at home, so taken was he with her songs and her beauty. And when he set sail to ravage foreign shores, she was restricted to a very small area at the center of his compound.

"But over the years, the number of guards trailing behind her had been reduced to a single man. And to the queen's advantage, this one burly, war-hardened bear of a Viking was madly in love with her. He himself was the slave, in thrall to the queen's sweet, melancholy songs. He lumbered about after her like a besotted schoolboy, hangin' on her every word, jealous of every other man in the camp.

"The queen wouldn't give him the time of day, mind ye. But

it only made him want her all the more. And most dangerous of all was the guard's jealousy toward the warlord himself."

Rainey smiled into the fire. "A lovesick Viking—that makes for quite an image."

"Aye, testimony to the advantages of shackles and a cell for yer prisoners, I suppose."

Sasha raised one eyebrow at his comment. "It sounds to me like you're not that far from Viking mentality yourself, Mr. Maclennan."

Kyle leaned his hands on his knees and gave Carrie a wink of conspiracy. "Right, then, as I was sayin', there came a day when the Viking warlord called the queen before him. As always, her faithful guard was at her side. The warlord decreed that when he returned from his next raids on the lands to the south, if the queen did not consent to become his willing and passionate bride, he would have her buried in the sand up to her neck as was the custom with weakhearted children, whereupon she would be left to die for her ungrateful arrogance."

Rainey shuddered. "A regular Mahatma Gandhi."

Kyle rubbed his chin in thought. "Aye, well, it was a different time, ye must understand. And as cruel and inhumane as it seems to us today, there were far worse things bein' done on a much larger scale in those days, and in the name of organized religion as well, mind ye."

Sasha sat up at this. "So you're defending the practice of burying a human being alive?"

"Hardly, Miss Macinnes. I'm only suggestin' that ye would do well to be a wee bit more open-minded and learn the facts before ye run off to the holy mount to set yer prejudices in stone."

"Prejudices? My revulsion at the senseless destruction of human life is a prejudice?"

"Of a kind."

Carrie sighed. "They're starting again, Mama."

"I know, sweetheart." Rainey held up her hand to interrupt the train of conversation. "I'd really like to hear how the story turns out," she said calmly.

Kyle cleared his throat. "Of course, Mrs. Macinnes. I shall do my level best to give it to ye, despite the odds against my success."

Sasha rose from her seat and without another word, walked off toward the tents. Kyle's eyes never left her until she had melted into the darkness. And when he returned his attention to the fire, he had no patience for its meager light. It was beginning to die down, so he stood up and kicked the burning peat into a more efficient stack with the toe of his boot, using it for an excuse to vent his frustration over Sasha's antagonistic treatment of him.

"I seem to have crossed the lines of diplomacy," he said to no one in particular.

"The queen, Kyle," Carrie insisted. "Did the evil Viking bury her in the sand? Did the selkies save her?"

Kyle smiled at her impatience, but his eyes still wandered toward the tents. "I suppose I must credit myself for bein' quite the brilliant storyteller to have ye be so anxious to hear more."

Carrie gave him a shrug. "You're pretty good, I guess. Just tell me what happens!"

He rubbed his chin in thought and sat down again. "Aye, well, the Viking warlord made off for the south with his ugly horde of marauders, just as he said he would. And the Celtic queen knew it would be her only chance for escape. She wasn't about to give herself over to the warlord, mind, so it was down to a real hardknock case of do or die. She had only her wits and her courage to save herself."

Rainey wrapped her jacket more securely against the damp blackness that closed in around them like so many faceless strangers bent on eavesdropping. The sea air had an icy sting to it, and the incessant crashing of the waves against the cliffs nearby made her think of battering rams pounding down a protective castle gate.

"How very alone the queen must have felt," she said sadly. "I mean, to be stolen away from the people and the country you love and thrown into slavery in a place where everything and everyone is foreign to you."

Kyle nodded. "Aye, it's a hard thing to be the outsider. Sometimes, if too many years go by, a person comes to doubt the existence of that original life. Perhaps it was nothin' but a dream, ye ken, a fantasy concocted to fill the dark holes. If there's nothin' to go back to, and the present is impossible to bear, a person may be pushed to extraordinary lengths to make things better."

"Like the queen," Carrie interjected.

Kyle cleared his throat. "Aye, like the queen. With the warlord gone, she turned her energies toward freein' herself quickly. If she left her bodyguard behind, he would be put to the ax for failin' at his duty. So she persuaded him to come with her for the promise of a single song. They waited until the camp was asleep, and under the cover of darkness, they stole away to the wee boat she had hidden to make their escape.

"The plan was workin' brilliantly, by the look of things. There was only one problem. Before he left, the warlord, who was a mistrustful blackguard by nature, assigned a second person to secretly keep a watch over the queen. This second guard was a lad nearly grown but too young to go with the raidin' parties. He had yet to prove to the warlord that he was worthy of the duties of a man, so he was very anxious for an opportunity to demonstrate his loyalty.

"I suppose ye could say he was a wee bit trigger-happy. And there was one more added feature to the situation. The secret guard was the first guard's younger brother. The older guard had been both father and mother to the lad, teachin' him not only the ways of the world but the fine points of Viking warfare as well. Thus they were tied not only by blood kinship but by the kinship of the sword. The two men had argued often about the older guard's obsession with the queen."

Emma tsked at this news. "I don't like the sound of this."

"Yer instincts are good, Mrs. Macpherson. For no sooner had the friendly guard helped the queen into their boat, than out of the darkness dashed the young lad, his sword drawn, his head set on changin' his older brother's mind for good and all.

"Now, as devoted as the two men were to one another, there was no easy solution to their problem. Had these been men of another heritage, perhaps they would have tossed a coin or thrown the dice to see which of them should prevail. But these were Viking men, and as bound as the young lad was to challenge his brother's treason, so was the older man bound to answer the challenge in kind, with no holds barred."

Carrie was in awe of all of this. "It would be like Sasha and me fighting. They were really trying to hurt each other?"

Kyle shook his head. "I'm afraid it was far worse than that, Carrie. They were actually bent on killin' one another. And as the queen's boat drifted away from shore, the moon rose. She saw the fightin' grow worse. The rocky shore was icy, and when the older guard hazarded a glance for the queen's safety, the tide of battle turned.

"The young lad had been trained too well to make the mistake of overlookin' his advantage when his opponent was distracted. He lunged forward and his sword struck home. The older guard reeled from his wound, and before both men could absorb what it meant, the wounded guard reacted out of instinct, and slid his sword between his brother's ribs. As they both lay bleedin' their lives into the sand, they heard the plaintive song the queen sang as she drifted away into the cold, black waters. She kept her promise to her faithful guard."

He saw Carrie start to open her mouth in protest if this was the end of his tale.

"Wait for it, if ye please, lass. For ye see, there are some who say that the faithful guard's spirit turned into a selkie right on the spot. Most times, selkies are said to be female, mind ye. But they say at the sound of her sweet song, he dove straight into those frigid northern waters and swam beside the queen's boat all the way to these islands where we are now, guidin' her to safety, keepin' watch over her."

Carrie's eyes were wide with wonder. "He turned into a selkie? But what happened to the queen?"

"Aye, well, the Vikings were hard on her heels. They combed these islands, looking for her for all they were worth because the warlord might kill them if they failed to bring her home to him. But she had hidden herself away in the ruins of an ancient burial cairn, a long tunnel used by the island dwellers thousands of years ago.

"As they searched, the Vikings marked each of the empty side paths in the cairn with their runic writin', a kind of stick alphabet. That writin' remains there to this day. I've seen it."

"Amazing," Rainey said for them all. "Did they ever find her?"

Kyle stood up, stretched, and set about reorganizing the fire. "They found bits of wreckage on the Isle of Westray. They were convinced, and rightly so, that the queen was on that island, so a group of them stayed there to keep searchin' for her. And one night, the queen heard the Vikings talkin' amongst themselves. She had an excellent knowledge of their language by now, and she came to understand that the warlord had decreed to them all that if she ever escaped and returned to her home and family, all of Scotland would be punished for it. There would be no mercy for her countrymen."

Rainey looked up at the stars, those same stars the queen had come to know so well long ago. "How utterly sad and isolated she must have felt to realize she was so near her home, but to go there would mean only death to everyone she held dear. In a way, it was worse than slavery because the decisions were in her own hands."

"True enough," Kyle agreed as he, too, looked up at the stars. "She had only her loyal selkie to keep her company. Each night he would come up onto the shore where the queen's wee boat had crashed on the rocks and wait patiently to see if she would come to him with her lovely songs. As often as she dared, she did come to him when the seas pounded in the throes of a storm. Against the roar of the sea, she would sing to him softly, melancholy songs of her home and her family.

"The warlord came to the island himself, half mad with rage and loss. He was unable to sleep and was often seen to stand stock-still in the middle of the camp, listenin' for any hint of her songs. At last, he shouted for all to hear that he would slaughter every man, woman, and child in Scotland in retaliation for the queen's escape. He would bring Thor's Hammer down upon the land, bringin' all Creation to its knees.

"The queen heard his black promise. She knew her own freedom was no longer a consideration. So she walked boldly into the warlord's encampment, her head held high. At first, the warlord threw himself at her feet, kissin' the hem of her torn and muddied gown. But then, a change came over him, and he ordered her taken to his tent and tethered to a pole. He ordered three days of celebration in honor of his triumph over the queen."

Carrie frowned. "But he didn't really win. I mean, he couldn't find her, so in a way, the queen beat him. She let him find her."

"Right ye are, lass. But of course the warlord didn't see it that way. His warriors built a fire so ridiculously huge, it could be seen from the Scottish mainland, so the Scots were warned of the Vikings' presence.

"The warlord's men were hungry for more than festivity. They had come for blood. So as the queen was bein' led away, the warlord proclaimed that at the end of the three days of celebration, they would follow through with their original plan and all of Scotland would be laid to waste."

Malcolm groaned. "So yer tellin' us the queen let herself get captured for nothin', man?"

"It seemed so. But when the warlord fell asleep in a drunken stupor beside her, the queen took the warlord's own knife and put an end to him. She took back her beloved silver necklace that he had taken from her and slipped away into the night while the camp snored.

"In the mornin', when they found the warlord dead, in true Viking fashion, they all fell to fightin' with one another. The warlord's cousin prevailed, but the attack of the south was put off for the time bein'. However, the cousin vowed to return in search of the murderous queen as a tribute to the dead warlord. Which is why, every eight years, all of Scotland suffers beneath the killin' storm known as Thor's Hammer.

"It's said the queen ran to her beach, where she changed into a selkie on the spot and swam away with her selkie guardian, for she was never seen again. But, if ever a person is lucky enough to find the queen's silver weddin' necklace and return it to its rightful home in the Highlands after all these centuries, such an event might well put an end to Thor's Hammer for good and all, so the legend says."

A brilliant meteor shower burst forth overhead, scattering the sky with trails of sparkling light. They all watched in awe.

Emma and Malcolm thanked Kyle for his story, then took themselves off to bed, leaving just three next to the fire.

"Thor's Hammer," Rainey said softly. She touched the gold locket at her throat.

"Aye, yer acquainted with the term, then, Mrs. Macinnes?"

Rainey nodded. "I've had two husbands in this life. Thor's Hammer has robbed me of them both."

Kyle took Rainey's hand into his own. "Please forgive me, Mrs. Macinnes. It was never my intention to bring such pain to mind. It was only a tale of the selkies to please yer wee daughter."

"It's all right, Kyle. It actually helped in a way. Maybe in some sense I understand the nature of that horrible storm now."

"It's only a story, mum," Kyle said kindly.

"Oh, it's far more than that," she assured him as she got Carrie to her feet. "Thank you for sharing it with us."

"My pleasure."

As he looked at Rainey and Carrie, Kyle had the strangest sensation that there was a man standing behind the two of them, his arms wrapped around them protectively. He almost addressed the man before he realized the newcomer was lacking one very important quality—substance. By the time he recognized it was an image of Matthew Macinnes, it had faded. But in the fire's dim light, he saw that Rainey's face radiated a timeless strength and energy that went far beyond the Rainey Macinnes he knew. At this moment, she was larger than life, and he wasn't quite sure what to say to her.

"Oidhche mhath, Kyle," she said with a sad smile, bidding him a good night in Gaelic.

"Oidhche mhath," he replied out of reflex.

He could think of nothing else to add, under the circumstances, so he headed for the tents. There were only three of them, so while Emma and the little Scottie shared with Sasha, and Rainey shared with Carrie, he was assigned to share sleeping quarters with Malcolm. Malcolm's gusty snores greeted him as he pulled back the tent flap. And in that moment of hesitation, something teased the corner of his eye, something in the mists a short distance away.

He saw Sasha sitting on a flat rock, her dark curls lifting on the cold breezes, her back to him. The only reason he could see her silhouette at all was because there was something glowing in front of her. His first instinct was that it was a candle. The light was soft and somewhat erratic, as if it were somehow floating in motion. But, even so far away, there was an unusual golden sparkle to it, unlike any candle he had ever seen.

In a heartbeat of shock and recognition, he saw what his imagination had had the gall to promise him. At the center of the halolike glow, there was a tiny, winged being. He was sure of it! It saw him instantly, and as Sasha started to whirl in his direction, everything plunged into total blackness.

He could not have seen it, he assured himself firmly. It was the stuff of a child's dream. And yet the image was burned into his brain. It would not go away.

"Sasha?" Her name came out of his throat as a kind of rasping croak. He hadn't meant to say it at all. The far-off waves pounding against the rocks were the only reply, and once again he had to question what he had seen. He was tired and disoriented.

He turned his sight back toward the northern stars. "Professor Mac," he whispered urgently, "I know ye've troubles of yer own, sir. But if it's true ye can hear things beyond the ken of regular folk, and if it's all the same to ye, I could really use yer words of wisdom right now." He started to climb into the tent but ducked out long enough to add, "And while yer at it, man, if it's not too much of a bother to reveal the information, where the hell are ye when yer body's about ye?"

He climbed into the musty tent and lay awake, hoping for a sensible solution to the question of why, on top of everything else, he now had fairies in his life. If the answer came, his ears weren't strong enough to hear it.

Chapter 7

It was the shiny object that first caught the kittiwake's attention. The stalwart little gull had always been partial to things that glinted in the light. She preened her gray wings in the first pale light of dawn, pretending to ignore the object's pull on her curiosity.

Her life was a hard one. She was diligent about her responsibilities, as were most of her kind. But this one weakness had gotten her into trouble on a number of occasions.

A bright fishing lure had washed up on the rocks once, before she was old enough to tend a nest of her own. The lure was covered with sharp barbs that had left her bright-yellow bill scarred to this day. And then, of course, there was the aluminum foil incident that had disturbed her bowels for most of a week. It dehydrated her and robbed her of her appetite. That foolish bit of indulgence had nearly cost her her life. But even now, she couldn't resist the shiny things. Her nature simply wouldn't permit her to ignore them.

She caught the updraft off the sheer sandstone cliff that was her home and drifted down toward the jagged rocks of the narrow cove below. After all, this was her domain, which she shared with several thousand other winged tenants, of course, and she had every right to investigate any suspicious changes in the neighborhood.

The storm that had torn down out of the north two nights before had left the cove a battlefield of broken debris. Among the wreckage, the kittiwake spotted a small pile of twigs, feathers, and guano. Tiny bits of shell were still stuck to it, probably all that was left of the beautiful nest she had built for chicks who would never see her.

She felt a sense of interruption at the sight, not sorrow so much as a lack of completion, as if she had failed to fulfill a vital task assigned to her. But there were countless other battered nests strewn across the rocks and floating in tatters on the tide, casualties of the brutal winds and the driving rain. She was not alone in her misfortune. The survival of each egg was always a gamble. But even now, some of her offspring from other years flew above her through the broken mists of dawn.

Loss was a basic part of the equation. There was no time to dwell upon it. Nor was there reason to. She had to be on about her business.

The shiny object was larger than the fishing lure had been, closer in size to the notorious aluminum foil. She maintained a healthy suspicion of it as she made swooping passes in its vicinity to see if it would respond to the threat of a predator. There was no visible life to it. Its surface was not as polished as the similar objects of her experience. And it had appendages, dispelling the notion that it might be a fish with bright scales. Its legs looked unworthy of conveying the thing's weight around, even with the help of the tide. Still, it caught a hint of light now and then, just enough to hold her fast to her curiosity.

But there was another peculiarity about the object. It was tangled in the talons of a large, dead animal. She had seen the ugly carcass yesterday. It was badly damaged. Parts of it were clearly broken. It had washed up onto the rocks the night of the storm.

But because of its size and distasteful shape, nothing had gone near it—with one exception.

The night before, as the icy mists locked in around the cliff, she had seen a herd of seals come up onto the rocks and cluster around the carcass. She had fully expected to see the thing taken down to its bones this morning. But such was not the case. The seals had departed with the coming of first light, and the carcass was none the worse for wear. Now it possessed the Shiny Thing. The object's call was utterly irresistible.

She wasn't happy about that carcass. It didn't smell right.

Scavenging was as basic to her as salt air. Every kind of dead thing in the world had washed up on the rocks of her cove at one time or another. As far as she was concerned, she had seen it all. Each of them had its own life smell, those trespassers. But more particularly, each had its own death smell. Blood and crushed bone, rotting fish, decay, parasite larvae—none of it put her off. More to the point, each one gave off its own kind of dinner invitation. But there was something very wrong about this new carcass. She dearly wished it were not clutching the Shiny Thing. It was a problem.

As she hovered above the carcass, her eyes locked on the dull shine of the object. She had to learn everything there was to know about it before one of her neighbors beat her to it. Her concentration was so absolute that she didn't see the carcass move. That first time was little more than a twitch at the far end. But it was followed by an unexpected growl from the carcass's mouth—not at all a proper thing for a carcass to do.

She shot upward and circled tightly, surprised and bewildered as she watched the Creature close its talons slowly around the Shiny Thing. This would help to explain why the beast's death smell had been so disturbing. It was giving off a foreign kind of *life* smell instead.

Her circles grew more bold. If this ugly, half-dead beast

wanted to challenge her to a contest for possession of the Shiny Thing, so be it. She knew what she wanted, and the Creature was hardly in any shape to put up a fight. It was on her turf. She was strong, healthy, and her belly was warm with a tasty herring breakfast. She was ready.

As she swooped down to test the beast's defensive skills, though, something triggered inside her. With great effort, the Creature opened and closed its mouth. No growls or squawks came out. The gesture was one of utter helplessness, a silent plea for mercy. It should have buoyed her hopes of victory against her monstrous opponent. But it only threw her instincts into a state of confusion.

The Creature needed her.

Before the storm, her nest had needed her. She had had a job to perform, a task basic to the survival of her kind. Her precious mission had ended abruptly and without apology. She had been prepared to take that development in stride. But now, as she blinked down at the sorry state of the Creature, there was something on her mind other than the Shiny Thing. Without another thought, she swooped low, flying the length of the beast before she sped toward open waters.

Within minutes, she returned, her scarred bill loaded down with the wiggling tails of fresh herring. Whatever else was wrong with the Creature, it still had to eat. Being a provider was one of her favorite things, because she was extremely good at it. She perched on a nearby rock and watched her new charge with a wary eye. Its eyes were open now, though they were clouded, the distraction of its pain most likely. Some living things were more adept than others at putting physical misery aside. She supposed this one wasn't very good at it.

There was fresh blood above one of its eyes, and a portion of one of its lower parts was not all pointing in the same direction. She had seen ones of her own kind survive for a time with such afflictions. But they never lasted very long. No more than she expected the Creature to live through another night on the bare rocks without the benefit of fur or feathers. There was every chance it had a hide disease of some kind on top of its other problems, since all that was left to protect it from the bite of the elements was a few torn bits of thin, colored stuff like nothing she had ever seen before. It couldn't be of much use, a heredi- tary defect most likely. Such a strange skin malady might help to explain the beast's unfamiliar smell.

For a moment, it gave her a feeling of usefulness to tend the Creature. She was willing to be generous. But the instant she sensed it was truly dead, the Shiny Thing would be her reward for her services. It was not up for negotiation.

She hopped down off her rock and waddled cautiously toward her charge. It had taken her by surprise when she dis- covered it was still alive. There weren't going to be any more surprises as far as she was concerned. If it growled again, or tried to grab for her, their silent agreement would be summarily revoked.

The Creature watched her approach. Its eyes were a bit clearer now, as if concentrating on her movements gave it something to focus on other than its pain. That was a good sign of sorts. If the beast was able to control its pain, it might be able to prolong its future. Of course, that might work against her designs on the Shiny Thing, she reminded herself. But she wouldn't begrudge the beast whatever time it had in this life.

She stood next to the Creature's broken part for a while, watching for any dilation of its eyes that would signal her it was about to make an abrupt move toward her. Foolishly, it tried to roll itself over onto its less damaged side. If she had been able, she would have warned it that such an action was most proba- bly a mistake. As it was, she could only give the whole idea a kind of shrug in her mind and take a step or two back as the

Creature's face took on a strange shade. It barked like a seal over the flood of seawater and bits of half-digested matter that dumped out of its cracked mouth.

She considered the contents of the mess and decided there was nothing there worthy of her attention. Pathetic. The Creature should have taken care of these matters yesterday. Of course, she had been convinced it was dead yesterday because of its closed eyes and lack of motion. This was probably its first opportunity for bodily maintenance. She darted a look at the talon that held the Shiny Thing, just in case the beast's preoccupation with its belly had prompted it to let go of the prize.

It hadn't. The belly spasms had only made it clutch the object tighter, and she was tempted to keep the herring for herself because of such inconvenient stubbornness. It would be far easier just to go on about her business for the rest of the day and snatch the object away the moment the elements put an end to the beast. She wagged her tailfeathers in a display of displeasure and frustration over the Creature's disorganized behavior, then flew back to her perching rock to wait for the thing to become more civilized.

It looked weaker at the end of its spillings, but its hide no longer had a sick tinge. Still, it was unquestionably a hideous thing, unlike the sleek, efficient residents of the sea and sky that made up her world. She wasn't sure she was actually doing anyone a favor by considering ways to keep it alive, however briefly.

She decided it was probably a male. Even females of this grotesque species were bound to be smarter than to get themselves into this kind of stupid predicament. And in the unlikely event that he survived and found a way to reproduce, the cove might be littered with such ugly, helpless offenses to nature. It was the responsibility of all the cliff dwellers to drive off threats to the cove's balance and safety. The Creature fit both criteria.

She had always been very decisive by nature. Her life demanded lightning-quick decisions. But at the moment, she could not decide whether to help the Creature or not.

It should have been a simple thing. Any young child could tell you something about the house in which he lived and some small portion of his kith and kin. Matt could remember none of it. What was more, he couldn't have said what year it was to save his life. To save his life . . .

He had been lost in a nightmare of tangled shreds of dream, hallucination, and broken memory for as long as he could remember—however long that might be. Only one set of images had brought him any degree of comfort. He had been beside a small fire somewhere in the wilderness. But the warmth he had felt from that place had come not from the glowing peat but from the two people there with him, a woman and a young girl.

The woman's beauty had taken his breath away. Her dark-blue eyes had looked at him with such open love, he had wanted to kneel at her feet and swear his life to her. And the little girl with her impish eyes and auburn curls had struck a chord deep in his heart. They had been familiar to him. And yet, he had the strangest sensation that he might have known them in a life other than his present one.

Words tumbled through his brain in tight little balls made up of half a dozen different languages, disorganized groupings of sound disconnected from their meanings. Each time he tried to slow down the whirling storm in his thought processes, his head ached with such ferocity, he was sure it would crack down the middle. It was difficult to get his eyes to focus. He had no way of recalling if his sight had ever been much good to him, and the pain in his head robbed him of any determination to find out its true limits.

His leg was in serious trouble. That much was a certainty. It was the pain of it that had brought him back to consciousness. A sad twist to revive only to experience such punishment. The tiny twitch of a torn calf muscle had sent liquid fire up his spine and pulled him up through the fog in his head to this stone-cluttered cove that now constituted his world. It offered some degree of shelter from the wicked winds off the sea. But the elements were very patient in their determination to test the tethers of his will to live.

He wanted to sink into a long and peaceful sleep. He wanted it more than anything else. Any other possibility was too overwhelming to consider. And if such a sleep could only be achieved through death, well, the journey to that destination could hardly be a long one.

And yet, that one memory of the woman and the little girl kept his black wish from being fulfilled. Each time he closed his eyes in the hope he wouldn't have to open them again, their images returned. They wouldn't let him drift away. He loved them for it, and he hated them for it.

From time to time, the wreckage of a memory floated through his mind's eye. Surrealistic sensations of floating helplessly in the frigid, storm-maddened sea sent shudders through him as surely as the cold north wind itself did. In these dark visions he was clinging to life while death stained the crest of every wave with blood and carnage. These things came as a monstrous dose of déjà vu. Yet he had no memory of how he had ended up in the water, no understanding of how he knew in his heart that he was the only survivor of some horrific disaster. His disjointed memories tied themselves to images of a ship going down. It would make sense. And yet, it wasn't right.

It didn't matter. What did matter was that in the aftermath of shock and trauma, he was freezing to his soul.

Steep cliffs of red and brown sandstone rose at his back, and the gray sea pounded against the sharp rocks in front of him.

Moving any distance was out of the question until he could master the pain. It was all too fresh, and he didn't have what it took for heroics at present. If the tide came in and overtook him, there was nothing whatever he could do to improve his lot. The adrenaline that had gotten him this far was tapped out, and the cold weighed him down with lethargy.

When he could piece together his thoughts at all, he had to question the reasons for his own survival. He had managed to save himself for his own sake, of course. But was anyone shedding tears of sorrow over him? Would anyone possess the faith in him to suppose he was still alive, despite the overwhelming evidence to the contrary?

The woman? The child? They probably didn't exist anywhere but in his hallucinations. Perhaps it would be better if he slipped back into the sea right now to become kin to the selkies who played in these cold waters. They had been in his fevered dreams as well, it struck him. To drift beneath the waves would spare him the suffering that was inevitably to come.

Had he always been a coward, he wondered?

He shivered to his bones, and his eyes blurred with tears. There was certainly enough strength left in him to dredge up a truly prizewinning case of morbid self-pity, he mused with a bitter snort.

Stark emotion knotted his stomach, a very real recognition of his own impending death. He coughed harshly and the sudden move brought bone splinter scraping against bone splinter in his leg. A roar of pain tore from him and he retched up what little was left in his belly. The cliff's startled population rose to the air as one, circling cautiously because of the trespasser's outburst. Despite the frigid air, sweat dripped down his temples.

It wasn't worth it.

And yet, through the torture of it all, one word kept flashing through his head like the searching beacon of a lighthouse, *creideamh*. He didn't know how, but he knew what it meant. Faith. He had to nail his thin energies to this word. If there was a ragged army of salvation marked for him anywhere in Creation, this fair word would be its banner.

He tried to focus on the gray skies overhead. Early morning, or late afternoon? He couldn't get his bearings well enough to know. But one way or another, night would come. He tried to think of a way to help his chances against the cold temperatures darkness would bring, but he couldn't home in on the problem long enough to solve it. If indeed there was a solution. What the sea had failed to do, the coming of night would probably accomplish.

A profusion of seabirds constantly circled the nesting cliffs above him—terns, kittiwakes, and gulls primarily. They dove and soared in a splendid display of aerial acrobatics. Each time his mind began to sink too deeply into the pain, their plaintive calls intensified, and he would be forced to return to awareness. There was a natural benevolence about them.

But the realist in him kept watch for the true carrion hunters. His thoughts were twisted indeed, it dawned on him—here he was, experiencing a bout of low self-esteem over the prospect of not being much of a meal.

A meal.

The pain had done a good job of suppressing his appetite. But now, as sparse as the prospects were, his body was demanding nourishment. He managed to control the spinning in his head long enough to see that the female kittiwake was still watching him from a few feet away. In her bill was a huge batch of fresh herring, enough to feed her young brood, he supposed.

Although he was at a loss to say where or when, he was quite certain he had had some decent meals in his life. He doubted that he had ever had to stoop to fish guts, even really fresh ones.

But after its coarse behavior of moments before, his stomach had the nerve to announce its desire to share the little kittiwake's sushi.

What he really needed desperately was fresh water. His throat was parched and raw from his hours in the salt water. But if there was even the remotest chance of persuading the gull to share her bounty, he would take on the problem of water afterward.

The kittiwake blinked her bright eyes at him as if to ask why, if this great hulking creature on the rocks was hungry, he didn't pick himself up, lumber down to the water, and go do something constructive about the problem like any other self-respecting citizen of these cliffs. She ruffled her black-tipped feathers and began to waddle closer to him, pacing first one direction, then the other, each time a little nearer. A few of the small herring in her bill still wiggled about in their captivity, and she clamped down on them to keep them still.

He wanted to say something fetching to her, to whistle to her softly and address her as he would a pet. But even in his addled brain, he recognized that she was wild and not dependent upon anyone but herself. She seemed wary of his chattering teeth and his hands, which trembled incessantly from the cold. Slowly, he started to grip one hand with the other.

For the first time, he realized he was holding something in his right hand, a silver necklace, as nearly as he could tell. He had no recollection of how he had come by it, and it did little to help establish a time frame in his mind.

The piece was elegantly simple in its design, a pendant made of three intertwining circles, suspended from a length of chain on either side. It looked old. But it might have been from fifty years ago or a thousand years ago, for all he knew. The closure was a very basic hook-and-eye device, and the most natural thing to do was to clasp it around his neck so that it wouldn't wash out to sea on its own. Whatever its source, it might eventually provide vital clues about his past, or help someone identify his body. He couldn't afford to lose it, even if he was accused of having stolen it in the end. His hands were stiff and uncooperative, but after a number of clumsy attempts, he secured it around his neck. The strange thing was, having it there had an unsettling effect on the kittiwake.

With a great flourish, she puffed up her chest boldly, showing off her pristine white underfeathers and making her displeasure very clear. Although she was careful not to make eye contact with him, her eyes darted incessantly toward the necklace. She paused now and then to be certain he wasn't trembling and his teeth weren't chattering when she wasn't looking. But he was being good, and in time, she ventured near his head.

He wasn't sure what to expect from her next, but to his surprise, she hopped squarely onto his chest. She dumped her bounty of herring onto his solar plexus and started to peck at the necklace in a way that made him think she had designs on taking it away from him. It was a temptation to drive her away, since some of her pecking pinched his skin. But it occurred to him that if she ended up leaving one meal behind at the end of her efforts, perhaps he could get another serving out of her before she completely lost interest. He stayed very still and averted his eyes for fear she might be attracted to them.

A pair of dapper young male birds circled noisily above them, making their "kitti-wak" calls. They were the female's offspring, perhaps, or just a couple of delinquents. The female hopped off of him, leaving the herring behind, and flapped her gray wings rapidly to warn the intruders off. It was unclear whether she was concerned for her safety or if she simply had no intention of sharing the cove at the moment. In either case, her point was well taken, and the males rose in a gale of disgruntled squawks to rejoin the general fray. The female settled her prim plumage with a great deal of ceremony and gave the Shiny Thing stealer a look of regal superiority. She offered no objection when he stuffed the fish into his mouth before she had the chance to change her mind. It was almost as if it had been her plan all along.

Then she did something even more surprising. Like a dowager duchess strolling her royal gardens, she walked toward the base of the cliff. He had had no opportunity or ability to investigate his surroundings, and as he tried to make the chilly fish slide down his throat, he did his best to follow her path with his eyes.

There was a narrow, recessed area in the cleft where the two sides of the cove joined. He watched as the kittiwake ducked her head inside the space. When he saw her head again, she was holding her bill vertical and swallowing. She ducked her head in a second time and repeated the procedure, being sure he saw what she was doing.

Drinking! She had her own personal source of fresh water. When she had drunk her fill, she flew back to her perching rock to preen. Though she appeared to be thoroughly engrossed in her complex grooming regimen, he could see she was keeping a careful eye on him and the necklace around his throat. It looked as if she was considering whether she was going to have to show him the water a second time because of his sluggish nature.

He wanted to pull her to him and hug her until her tailfeathers fell out. She was saving his sorry life, and it gave him an unreasoning surge of hope. Now all he had to do was drag himself to that blessed water. It would kill him to try. If he didn't try, he would die anyway.

His brain resisted the notion of organized thought. The pain behind his eyes felt like cannon fire. And each time he considered what to do about his leg, it telescoped his attention back to the pain, and he had to travel the slow, agonizing loop of gaining some small control over it again. It exhausted him and reminded him of his weakness. But water was not an optional concern. The fish tails scratching in his throat made that very clear to him.

He looked down at the shredded remnants of his clammy clothing. Not much to work with there. But if he was clever, he might be able to come up with pieces of his trousers of sufficient length to secure a splint of some kind. Common sense told him he wouldn't be able to begin to set the bones. He couldn't afford the brain cells if he lost consciousness again. But if he could immobilize his leg somehow, he might be able to endure the crawl to water. That in itself should earn him some kind of medal.

The simple act of looking at the area around him in search of usable driftwood made his head spin afresh. He had to do it more slowly, focus on one small section at a time, then move on to the next small patch. It was taking forever, and the search was producing no likely candidates.

A hint of motion caught the corner of his eye, and he realized the kittiwake was flying away. He had come to think of her as his guardian angel. If she left him now, his luck might truly be at an end. He wanted to call out to her, to summon her back. But he couldn't piece the words together to do it. Chances were, to shout at her would only frighten her. She was a bird, for godsakes. But she was *his* bird, and he missed her spartan companionship already.

He let his sight wander toward the gray horizon to see if he could still distinguish the kittiwake. But the sky was full of gray and white birds. Even on his best day, he doubted he would have been able to pick her out from among the throng. He could only hope the cove was her habitual home and that she would return.

Something else caught his eye—a slow, steady motion traversing the line of the horizon. It was a ship. He knew that much. But he longed to see it up close, not solely for the vital purpose of rescue, but because he needed to establish a time frame in his mind. It would have come as only a minor surprise to discover the vessel was of an ancient Celtic design, or perhaps Viking. The word for "ship" came to mind in four separate languages. Who the hell was he? *Where* the hell was he?

A low, roaring sound began in his ears, and he tore his sight away from such distance for fear the dizziness would return. Perhaps there was water stuck inside. That would certainly make sense. But the noise intensified, crowding his head. The birds overhead weren't overly bothered by it, reinforcing the impression that he alone heard it. Or, perhaps the birds were used to it. Either way, the noise grew louder, until it felt like his head would explode from the searing ache it caused in his head.

An unimaginably huge bird with stiff wings cleared the top of the cliffs above him, flying higher than any of the others. There were letters on its flanks, and smoke issued from its tail. The sheer immensity of it took his breath away.

"Chan eil eun, dearg amadan," he said to himself over the din. Not a bird, fool. *"Buidheann adhair."* An airplane. He drew in a ragged breath and shuddered till his bones shook as memory prickled in his brain like a thousand tiny electrical shocks.

He hadn't escaped the death of a ship. He had been aboard a plane that had gone down.

Broken images of the older woman who had been sitting next to him on the plane floated before his mind's eye—rose-gray hair, a warm smile, a melancholy face. There had been a familiarity about her. Or was it that he knew someone like her?

A drowning flood of images. A little girl across the aisle engrossed in an endless crayon masterpiece—houses, cats, stars.

There was something there as well, the fleeting hint of a memory, lost as quickly as it had come.

A withdrawn blond teenager next to the window, her knuckles white with tension at being in the air in the middle of a storm that was fast becoming the wrath of the gods. Her eyes were red from tears of what? Lost love, perhaps?

He felt the death of each of them carve a bloody scar across his soul. He cried out with the agony of it, and the cliff's dwellers rose to the air again. But self-preservation gave way to the preservation of the next generation, and the birds returned to their precarious homes as memory locked him in mortal combat.

Screams. Tearful prayers hastily whispered. Preposterous promises to God shouted into nothingness. A flash. Then another and a third. A loss of air pressure. Oxygen masks. Useless. Acrid, killing smoke. Darkness. Plunging downward for a split second, an eternity. Impact. Neck-snapping concussion. Smell of blood and human waste. Frigid water over his head. Twisted metal, tangled seat belt pulling him down. A bone breaking. Smothering salt. Choking weight of the pounding waves. Surface. The depths. Surface. The depths. Survival! Loss of his mind. Loss of the world.

He pressed his forearm over his eyes as sobs of shock and loss racked his body. Could he have saved any of them? Was he given the slimmest opportunity? Or had he seen only to his own survival? He couldn't remember. But dark suspicion began to coil inside him. The bitter taste of death tainted his mouth and he rolled sideways to lose the herring. The abrupt move brought his injured leg down hard on the rocks, and his stomach went into useless spasms again from the pain.

He begged God to keep him from remembering any more. He only wanted to be rid of the horror at any cost. But the mercy of a total loss of memory was at an end. The crash played over and over in his head. Each time he remembered impressions of another person, another haunting detail to give that person reality and dimension—a worn book of poetry, a lap full of vacation snapshots.

It crushed his meager strength, and he stared at the incoming tide with empty eyes. He welcomed the cold now. It meant the torture would last only a little while longer. A gift. But when he succumbed to sleep, shivering through his wretched dreams, the seals the kittiwake had seen the night before returned to the cove.

A sleek, gray-brown female was the first to approach the man. Her dark, expressive eyes were intent on his every move. He cried out in the midst of his nightmares, and she shuffled back, startled. But he quieted, and she decided he was probably harmless for the moment. She looked over her shoulder to where a grizzled older seal sat keeping watch over her intently. He looked unsettled at the female's boldness toward the man, but with a deft move, he dove into the water and slid right back out again to signal to the others of the herd that all was safe. The others lumbered onto the rocks and surrounded the human with their smooth warmth as if he were one of their own kind. His shivering eased, and his slumber must have sweetened, for only once more did he speak through his dreams, a single word, spoken softly.

"Rainey."

The seals had no complaint about the gentle sound of it, and the female snuggled closer to him, keeping a careful watch for a time. It was important to her that he be safe. Satisfied for now, she set her soft muzzle in his hand and let her eyes close.

Chapter 8

Kyle stood motionless, staring out toward the mists of the open sea in the pale, predawn grayness. He mouthed the name that had come to him in his dreams, the strange and exotic name—Macha. There it was, the Celtic queen's name he had been unable to remember in his telling of the story of the selkies. He could see her as clearly as if he had known her all his life, tall, slender, dark curls down to her waist, and eyes . . . eyes as deep and penetrating a blue as those of the Macinnes women.

There was an image of a younger woman, too. He knew immediately that her name was Sirona. As beautiful as Macha, the young woman could only be the daughter the Celtic queen had left behind. And yet, young Sirona looked for all the world like Rainey Macinnes. It made him dizzy.

The story of these people had haunted him since he was very small. And the fact was, although he had indeed heard it told at a library once, it had already been familiar to him. He couldn't remember where he had heard it the first time. It had always just been there, like the color of his eyes. And his inability to hear.

Macha.

But there was more. He knew with a certainty that the warlord's name had been Gunnar. The information was coming to him in flashes. He could see these people of old so clearly, it was a frightening phenomenon. The older guard's name was Olgar. He didn't know why, but he knew everything there was to know about Olgar. The man was partial to honeyed mead, reindeer meat, and spirited, dark-haired women of foreign descent.

A chill slid down his spine, and he blinked to try to clear his head of the impossible images there. He felt the worn, smooth hilt of the sword in his hand as he faced Olgar. His sight blurred with sweat and tears. He couldn't pull air into his lungs. It was all far too real. More than for his own life, he was fighting for his brother's life.

When he felt a hand clap down on his shoulder, he whirled into a battle stance, ready for combat. Malcolm stared at him as if he had lost his senses, and he struggled to justify his visions with reality.

"Roust yerself from yer daydreamin', Edinburgh," Malcolm instructed him. "The women are ready. It'll be light soon, and we're out of here."

"Aye." The word came out, but he still couldn't make himself move. Now, on top of everything else, there was a low roaring noise in his ear. He couldn't tell if it was real or another manifestation of his visions of the past. "I know I'm the last candidate for bringin' up such things, but does anyone else hear a strange noise?"

Rainey was walking toward him, and the temptation to address her as Sirona was very strong. He rubbed his eyes, trying to clear them of everything but the immediate present. They would think he was daft. And they might be right.

They all listened for Kyle's suspicious noise.

"Och, tis nothin' but the surf hittin' against the rocks, man," Malcolm concluded.

Kyle pressed his hearing aid deeper into his ear. Everything was in decent working order, as far as he could tell. But the roaring noise was definitely getting louder.

Carrie stared into the mists toward the south. "Look, Mama!" she shouted. "There's a hell thing coming!"

Sasha followed the line of Carrie's sight. She saw it, too. "Not a 'hell thing,' silly, a *helicopter*. Over there, Mama, coming up from the south." They all watched the RAF chopper's loud, methodical approach.

Rainey glanced at Emma. "If one of those monsters can manage to get up in the air, there's no reason why the official search for Matt can't resume, right?"

Emma eyed the rolling mists overhead with a wary eye. "I don't know, Rainey. I have to wonder about this. The weather's still strong against tryin' to fly. I don't think this is part of Search and Rescue. Somethin' else is afoot."

Malcolm started to walk forward. "Pilot's goin' to set her down. Maybe they've already found our Matty Mac for us. Give us a wee prayer, then, Em."

"Aye, will do," Emma said as they all ventured toward the spot where the helicopter had touched down.

The pilot didn't shut down the engines, but the constable who had loaned them their camping equipment stumbled out of the chopper clumsily. His uniform cap caught in the backwash and went flying, leaving his bald head to the mercy of the elements.

It took an uncomfortable moment for him to chase the hat down. His hefty girth testified to the fact that there was little else for his wife to do on the island but cook to please her husband, and he puffed up to them quite red in the face with exertion.

"Mrs. Macinnes, I'm that glad we found ye, ma'am," he shouted over the helicopter's roar.

Rainey was careful to keep her hopes on a very tight rein. "Has my husband been found, constable?"

The constable suddenly found his boots of great interest. "Well, no, ma'am," he said, with a tight little laugh that implied her question had been rather nonsensical, to his way of thinking. "I had to move heaven and earth to get the borrow of the chopper here to come and fetch ye all back to safety."

He hiked up his trousers and turned to give the chopper pilot a smart salute. The pilot wore an RAF jumpsuit, and despite the fact that the sun was still hiding beneath the horizon, he had on dark glasses. Something in his demeanor said that *Top Gun* had made it this far north. He jutted his thumb upward repeatedly to indicate that it was time to go.

The constable turned back to Rainey impatiently. "Ye see, missus, they had themselves a press conference on the telly," he told her, as if he were confiding a state secret. "I've no wish to be harsh with ye, ma'am, but there's nothin' left of that plane yer husband was on. The sad truth is it sank to the bottom like a stone, it did. And the weather bein' so raw like it is, I have to see to yer well-bein', even if you don't have a mind to. It's what I get paid to do, make sure the lot of ye ain't a danger to yerselves."

Malcolm stepped between Rainey and the constable. "Now, see here, man, let's get to the heart of the matter. We told ye from the start we didn't care what they were sayin' on the telly. This search is our own. Matthew Macinnes is alive, ye wee badger, and if it's all the same, you and yer ugly dragonfly over there are keepin' us from bein' about our job."

Rainey raised her hand to calm Malcolm. She looked the constable squarely in the eye. "Why are you *really* here, constable?"

The constable kept a watchful eye on Malcolm. "Well, the fact of the matter is, ma'am, my missus needs the car back. She's that put out I let ye take it on such a harebrained—that's to say, yer mission of mercy. We need the car, Mrs. Macinnes. I got Jerry, the chopper pilot there, to help me come after ye, but he's got his assigned duties to tend to, ye know. There's supposed to be a full crew in that thing before it flies. The whole Northern Quadrant is grounded till further notice. But seein' he's me brother-in-law ... well, I'm just sorry things didn't work out for ye, ma'am. Ye seem like a nice enough person, but I can be of no further help to ye. If ye want Jerry to give ye and the others a lift back to town, I'll take care of the car and the equipment. Ye'll miss the ferry, I expect, but it'll go easier on the old folks to go by chopper."

He raised one eyebrow at Malcolm in challenge, and it was clear that Malcolm was going to be perfectly willing to take the bait. So Rainey was quick to intervene.

"Thank you, constable," she said with utmost calmness, even as she gave Emma a covert wink. "We would appreciate that helicopter ride." She turned to Sasha and Carrie with a carefully disciplined smile on her face. "It would be an adventure, wouldn't it, girls? Just imagine, flying in a helicopter. Maybe it would take our minds off our worries."

Carrie wasn't convinced. "I don't want to go in that noisy old thing," she protested with a pout.

Sasha took her hand and gave it a quick squeeze. "But you know what, Care? Flying up that high, we might even be able to see some selkies. What would you think about that?"

Kyle caught the spirit of the conspiracy. "That's right, Carrie, if we go by helicopter, it will be easier to find the selkies." Carrie began to brighten to the idea.

The constable raised his cap and scratched his bare head. "Well, now, I doubt ye'll see much sea life. The ride back's over land."

Rainey raised her finger to her lips to quiet the constable's discouraging speech. "You never know, constable," she said, as if she were talking to a five-year-old child. "Selkies are magical creatures. They might surprise us."

He settled his cap back on his head and looked down at Carrie's upturned face. "Oh, right, I got ye. Ye got to keep up appearances for the wee one. I got kids of my own, ye know. They're not much for magic and such like. Not enough room in the day, ye know what I mean?"

"Of course," Rainey said graciously, "I'm sure your life is a hectic one."

The constable puffed up his chest again. "I got to uphold the law, missus. It's like a callin' with me."

The chopper pilot yelled for them to hurry up, and everyone raced for their belongings as the constable explained to Jerry that he would have a larger passenger load for the ride back. After a flurry of very animated negotiations, Jerry seemed resigned to the task of bus driver. The only real sticking point was that Rainey insisted on riding up front, claiming she was prone to airsickness, which only sitting forward would remedy. Fortunately, Jerry was so anxious to get the chopper back to the base before it was discovered missing that he grudgingly consented to let her up front for the sake of expediency.

Once they were safely in the air, Rainey tried to strike up a conversation with Jerry. This was going to go a lot easier if they could get him to cooperate.

"So, Jerry," she shouted over the racket of the engines, "how far can one of these babies go when the occasion arises?"

He gave her a look that revealed nothing. "When the tank's full, she could take ye to London if ye'd a mind to go."

She reacted with appropriate awe. "No kidding? All that way?"

"Aye, no problem. The way she's tanked up at the moment from all the down time, she could still make it most of the way."

Rainey gave him a dazzling smile. "Amazing. So, hypothetically, if I wanted to go somewhere, like Westray, for example, do you suppose she could handle it?"

Jerry gave it careful consideration. "Sure, she'd make it easy." He regarded Rainey through his aviator glasses. "Only nobody's goin' to Westray today. It's socked in solid. Even the ferries are huggin' the shore."

"Fairies?" Carrie asked from the backseat.

Sasha hushed her. "Big boats, not the other kind!" she whispered.

"Oh."

Rainey didn't break her train of thought. "So, as I say, hypothetically, Jerry, if a pilot was good, I mean, a real professional at his job, and there was enough money to be made to pay for his exceptional skills—let's say three hundred pounds cash right here, right now, no questions asked—do you think that pilot could baby-sit a bunch of harmless family folk to Westray? No one but his banker would ever be the wiser."

She couldn't read Jerry's eyes under those damnable dark glasses. Nothing else had been easy. There was no reason to believe this would be. After all, he was already out on a limb having the chopper out of the hangar at all. This would very definitely add to the risk. She had to hope he had gambling debts or a dozen kids who needed new shoes.

Jerry slowed the chopper down. Whether it was sign of his softening to their cause or simply in preparation to throw them all out, she didn't know. But she could see the muscles working along his jawline as he struggled with his decision.

"And if that pilot were to say no to such a proposition, what then?" he asked with a grim smile.

Rainey sat back and folded her arms across her chest. "Well, Jerry, then I guess that pilot would be up for some flying lessons without the aid of his chopper."

Jerry gave her a grin of disbelief. "What, ye'd toss me over the side, ye wee slip of a thing?"

She tucked her hair behind her ear. "Let me point out to you that the young man sitting directly behind you has a black belt in the martial arts."

Jerry glanced at Kyle over his shoulder. Kyle did his best to appear inscrutable and unconquerable.

"Right, so then it's one against one," Jerry concluded. "I think I'll take my chances, since none of the rest of that lot back there is likely to know how to fly one of these birds."

"One against one," Rainey said. She pressed her fingers to her lips in thought. "Actually, Jerry, that's not quite correct."

Kyle leaned forward. "Actually, Mrs. Mac, there, is the one who taught me, friend. Studied in Japan, that one. She's a Yank, ye ken? A man cannot trust 'em. They're all daft and dangerous."

Everyone was silent as Jerry digested this information.

"Four hundred pounds cash, and if anythin' comes of this other than a medal of honor, ye'll swear in a court of law ye were all wearin' vests made out of dynamite. Agreed?"

Rainey wrapped her jacket more securely around her middle. She gave Jerry a wicked smile. "They're just little sticks of dynamite, Jerry. The big ones always make me look overweight. Feel better now?"

"Christ, no, missus! The fact is, I'm feelin' worse."

Rainey watched the flat green expanses of Westray speed past beneath her feet. The helicopter had brought them this far. It had to be right. She checked her map and looked ahead into the rolling mists.

It was extremely dangerous to fly under such conditions. And if the terrain hadn't been so barren, she would have been tempted to call off the flight herself for the sake of everyone's safety. But since reaching the northern half of the island, they had seen few signs of life other than ancient stone fences, a single farmhouse distant from its neighbors in the extreme, the occasional wild rabbit, and seabirds of a dozen varieties.

The precious light of day wouldn't last very long. They no longer had their camping equipment or their ground transportation. And the very thought of Matt having to spend another night in the elements was more than she could handle right now. It simply wasn't going to happen.

But Jerry was at his limits. She had already tried to coerce him into flying them along the jagged cliffs on the island's corner. He had flatly refused, contending that as badly as he needed her bribe money, the bottom line was that he was an RAF pilot, and he wouldn't risk government machinery or their lives any further for the sake of "some daft Yank's lost cause." She hadn't pushed him any more. It was a blessing to have gotten here at all. Now, all they needed was half a dozen miracles before nightfall.

"Where is he, Carrie? Where is your papa?" she said, as much to herself as to Carrie as she saw a tumbledown group of standing stones slip past beneath them.

Carrie hugged Angus in the backseat, and the Scottie licked her face as if she were made of sugar. "We have to go to the castle, Mama. I know Papa isn't far from it."

Jerry had been very quiet for the last ten minutes. Rainey knew he was getting cold feet about landing too near civilization, what little of it there was on the island. No matter what happened from here on out, it was going to be risky for everyone. She checked the map again.

With a military-sounding clearing of his throat, Jerry announced that they would be in the town of Pierwall in five minutes. It was apparent from his tone that he didn't expect any conversation on the matter.

Rainey folded her map and slipped it into her purse. "Do you have enough fuel to make it back to your home base without getting more, Jerry?"

He turned to her suspiciously. "Why do ye ask, missus?"

"Because according to the map, Noltland Castle is only a few more miles to the west, and that's where we need to go."

Jerry returned his sight to the skies before them. "Can't happen."

Emma leaned forward in her seat behind Jerry. "It makes no real difference to ye, now, does it, Jerry?"

Malcolm chimed in. "Aye, for that matter, there'd be fewer folk to see ye this far from home if ye were to land us near the castle. It's a bargain to be considered, lad."

"There's nothin' there this time of year, no lodgin's or car rentals," Jerry insisted without much conviction. "Ye'd have no way of gettin' back to town, and I for one cannot be baby-sittin' ye any longer."

Rainey laid her hand on his arm. She saw him glance down at it nervously. Jerry wasn't a bad sort. He just didn't like not being in control of the situation. "We understand that you have to go, Jerry. We know we'll be on our own. But look at it this way, we'll be out of your hair once and for all. Noltland is the only castle shown on the map, and it's near the cliffs where my husband is."

Jerry gave her a doubtful snort. "And how can ye know that, missus?"

"We just know, Jerry. You'll have to trust me on this one."

"Daft to the bone, the lot of ye." He turned the chopper toward the west.

They watched with mixed emotions as Jerry's helicopter disappeared into the dense mists. He had set them down in an open field near the castle ruins, his conscience only permitting him to accept half of the promised bribe at leaving them, in essence, stranded.

The massive, stone-walled fortress before them showed signs

of renovation, but for now, the weather was still too unseasonable for any work to be in progress. There was a single farmhouse near the base of the castle, but the windows were shuttered and the note on the door said simply SUPPLIES. There was nothing to indicate if that meant an absence of a day or a month.

Emma tapped Rainey's shoulder. "If it's no too much trouble, love, I'd like to have a basic outline of yer plan, if I may."

Malcolm buttoned up his tweed jacket against the cold. "Aye, lass, there's some us didn't get their oatmeal this mornin', and lunch is lookin' to be a bit of a bleak prospect as well."

Rainey wrapped her fingers around the locket at her throat in hopes it would lend her wisdom. "We're at the castle. That's the main thing," she said with as much resolve as she could muster.

Carrie tugged at her sleeve. "Not this dumb castle, Mama. The old one," she said with the face of an angel. They all turned to her as one.

Rainey knelt down beside her. "Not again, Care. What do you mean, 'not this castle'? It's the only castle on this island. We came here because you said we had to go to this castle to find your papa."

A hint of worry began to show on Carrie's face. "No, Mama, *you* said we had to come to this castle. I never did."

"But it's the *only* castle, Carrie," Sasha said in exasperation. "Now what are we going to do? I can't believe you, Carrie!" She picked up a rock and tossed it at the stone fence not far away. It made a satisfying *clack* as it hit its mark.

Kyle went down on his haunches next to Carrie. He chose to overlook Sasha's glare at his interference. Carrie gave him a half smile before she remembered that everyone was upset with her.

"All right, then, Creideamh, my friend," he said kindly. She gave him the rest of that smile. "We've established that large hunk of gray stone over there is not the castle in question."

"Right." Carrie lifted her chin proudly and regarded the rest of the onlookers.

"So, what we have to do now is figure out exactly where the proper castle might be. I've been to this island before. Maybe once you remind me about it, I'll remember where it is, too." He cleared a patch of wet soil with his boot, and with a small stick, he drew a square in the lower righthand corner. He touched the center of the square with the stick. "This is the castle we're seeing right now, where we're standing." He handed her the stick. "So where is your castle from here?"

She furrowed her brow at his question. "My castle?"

Sasha began to pace. "This is never going to work. Next she'll send us all to Balmoral."

Rainey squeezed Carrie's hand to reassure her. "Just do your best to tell us where the castle is that will lead us to Papa."

Carrie shrugged. "Okay." She drew a ruffled line along the far side of the cleared patch, then, after careful consideration, near a large curve, she drew not a square, but a rectangle. Satisfied, she handed the stick back to Kyle.

"Alv Befestning," she said to him with total confidence.

He stared at the rectangle. *"Alv Befestning.* There's a twist."

Malcolm whispered in Emma's ear, "Are the pair of them at speakin' in tongues, now, love?"

"I don't know, Malcolm. And it appears to be a mystery to Rainey and Sasha as well."

"What does it mean?" Sasha insisted.

Kyle turned to her slowly. "It's Norwegian. It means Fairy Stronghold. The lass is no talkin' about some sixteenth-century youngster like Noltland. We're talkin' hard-core archaeology here. I know of no such place on the maps. But I'd be willin' to bet it's there, right where Carrie says it is."

Carrie gave a little laugh. "The selkies can see it, can't they, Kyle?"

Kyle considered her question. He answered it with a question of his own. Putting the rest of the group out of his thoughts for the moment, he looked at Carrie squarely, his eyes warm and encouraging.

"When I asked ye before where yer castle was from here, lassie, ye seemed a bit confused by my question."

"Er, I suppose." She darted a look at her mother and at Sasha. While she saw cautious interest in her mother's eyes, Sasha's eyes flashed her a warning. She wasn't sure what she should do. She leaned over and whispered in Kyle's ear.

"Hvor lenge har De vaert her?" she asked.

She had asked him how long he had been here in Norwegian. On the surface, the question was a simple one. Yet he was suddenly at loss to answer her. He sensed she was asking far more of him than how long it had been since the helicopter had dropped them off.

It left him in turmoil because the instant she had asked the question, an impossible answer had sprung to the tip of his tongue, a number that would have made his memories of Macha seem like current events by comparison. He couldn't remember that ridiculous number now. His brain had convinced his subconscious of the absurdity of it and it had vanished in a flash. Now, he was utterly speechless as he looked into the dancing blue eyes of a nine-year-old who knew more of the past than he would ever know. He replied the only way he could.

"Jeg forstar ikke, elskling." I don't understand, sweetheart.

She gave him a world-weary smile that held a touch of sorrow and patted him on the head. *"Noe dag,"* she assured him. Someday.

Malcolm cleared his throat gruffly. "If it's all the same, I say we'd best find some form of transportation for ourselves if we're to get to this wee box in the mud before the sun goes down. Now, we've traveled all this way, and we have no accommodations for the night. I believe the question has been put upon the table. What is the plan, Rainey?"

The question was one more of paternal concern than censure, Rainey knew, but it stung all the same. Everyone was relying on her. She prayed she would hear Matt's guiding voice somewhere in the middle of it. Instead, she heard Sasha calling to her from the side of the farmhouse.

They all trouped around to the back of the structure. There was a large double garage there. Its windows were also shuttered, but Sasha had found a crack in the boards that afforded a peek inside. It was dark, but they could still make out the shapes of building equipment, ropes, ladders, tarps, and tools. One other thing stood out. A bright-red cross could be clearly seen. It was painted on the canvas side of a World War II ambulance truck. It had huge, all-terrain tires on it, and from what they could see, it was in good working order. Of course, that was no guarantee it would start. And finding out would require your basic breaking and entering.

Emma leaned over Rainey's shoulder. "No too bad a plan, love. The Allies used the islands a lot durin' the war. Most of what they left behind was never in such good shape as that thing. But which of us is to be the one to do the hard time if we get caught in the act of gettin' at that beauty?"

Kyle stepped forward. "It may not be as difficult as ye think, Emma. The residents of these islands are a trusting sort. They have very little reason not to be, as isolated as they are. I'd be willin' to bet . . ."

He trotted around to the garage doors. They were closed, but there were no signs of alarms or padlocks of any kind. When he turned the door handle, it unlatched easily. He raised the door and walked inside as if he owned the place. As he opened the truck cab's door, he smiled. The key was under the floor mat.

Everything was in immaculate shape. This wasn't just a utility vehicle. It was somebody's beloved hobby, a collector's precious keepsake, no longer intended for the field. He climbed into the driver's seat and turned the ignition. It had a full tank of gas, and the engine roared into action.

Rainey walked up beside Kyle. "I suppose we'd better leave a note for the owner. I mean, this thing is obviously somebody's pride and joy. I only hope we won't be too hard on it."

Kyle smiled down at her from his perch in the driver's seat like a small boy with a new Christmas present. "Not to worry, missus. This fine old nurse has just been waitin' for another chance to do what she was built to do—save lives." He jumped out as the motor warmed and tossed ropes, tarps, and large pieces of plywood into the back. "I'm afraid there'll be no such things as seat belts, so we'd best do what we can to make things safe and secure in the back. It's bound to be a rugged ride to the sea."

Rainey looked at the truck with loving eyes. As Matt would say, it was a gift. She scribbled off a note to the owner, promising faithfully that they would return everything within twenty-four hours and that they were on a genuine mission of mercy. She left her home address and phone number for good measure. Their only hope was that the owners would be understanding, or that the local constabulary would be. It didn't matter to her. What mattered was that they were going to be in motion again, one step closer to Matt.

She felt a familiar tug at her sleeve. Carrie looked up at her, her eyes clouded with tears, and Rainey felt a surge of adrenaline shoot up her spine.

"Mama, we have to hurry now," she said with profound simplicity.

Rainey, too, sensed that something was changing. Matt's life was in immediate jeopardy, and as she watched the others casually investigate the diverse paraphernalia inside the garage, she had a moment of panic.

"Get in the truck, everybody!" she shouted. They all turned to her with looks of surprise at her sudden outburst. "There's no more time, damn it! Get in!"

They all clambered into the truck, with Kyle in the driver's seat and Rainey and Carrie as his copilots. Rainey held the map on her knees so that Carrie could point them in the right direction. The roads were little better than matching ruts, made worse by a hard winter. It was tough going in the front and total misery in the back. But the truck was a stalwart veteran, willing to tackle anything in front of it.

A tear slid down Carrie's cheek as she touched her mother's sleeve. She kept her eyes lowered as she spoke.

"We have to send him help right now, Mama. He can't wait anymore. It has to be right now."

Rainey exchanged a glance with Kyle.

"I can't push this thing any harder, missus. If we break an axle, the truck will be of no help to anyone."

She knew it was true. They were going as fast as they could. But there was no telling how long it would take them to find Matt once they reached the cliffs, and Carrie's warning was a very real one. Something had to be done immediately. She sensed Sasha leaning over her shoulder from the back of the truck. Sasha closed her eyes and whispered a single name into her ear.

"Mar a' Ghealach."

With a guarded glance at Kyle, Rainey nodded and closed her eyes. There was no time for secrecy or explanations. She took Sasha's hand, and the two of them sat motionless and silent, save for the jolting of the truck. Carrie smiled as she watched the two women summon help for her father. It would be better now. The selkies would help him, but now he would have added guardians as well. She looked up at Kyle with a grin full of mischief.

"Furtachd is fo `ir an glaic a la `imhe," she said with confidence.

Kyle glanced down at her and raised one eyebrow. "So, it's Gaelic now, is it, ye wee scamp? 'Help and deliverance in the hollow of his hand.' And what precisely does that mean, if I may be so bold as to ask?"

Carrie wiped the tears from her cheeks and tapped the side of his head. "Why should I tell you what you already know?" she said teasingly.

He kept his eyes on the puddled ruts in front of them. "What I already know, ye say?"

Carrie folded her arms across her chest and nodded.

An image flashed in front of his mind's eye, an image of Sasha sitting in the dark, her long hair lifting on the night breeze, her eyes dancing with mystery and challenge as she held a tiny glowing being in the palm of her hand.

Impossible.

He shot a glance at Rainey and Sasha as they went about their meditation. They looked more like sisters than mother and daughter. And in that brief look, he saw a rapture shared between them. Whatever it was they were conjuring up, he envied the bond that could create such unity of heart and purpose.

If only Sasha would share that kind of magic with him, and not out of necessity, but out of desire. Perhaps, if she could read his thoughts, she would know how dear she was to him, though they had hardly spoken a civil word to each other. He couldn't explain his attraction to her, even to himself. It made his head hurt to try. She was all thorns. And yet, at times, he glimpsed the rose. Those brief glimpses were enough to keep him hooked, enough to keep him playing the fool.

Without warning, she appeared to him in his mind's eye dressed only in wisps of sheer gossamer, a dazzling forest sprite dancing unhindered among the oaks, herself aglow as the tiny being had been. The Queen of the Woodland Fairies. The scent of her hair was lavender and rose petals, she danced so very near. If only she could read his thoughts . . . He could hear her gentle voice.

"You're about to drive us into a ditch, Edinburgh! Get your act together or give up the wheel! God, I can't believe this guy!" Sasha smacked him hard on the shoulder just as he was about to go off the road. His fantasy collapsed into ashes.

"Sorry!" He steered the truck back on course with no small jostling to the passengers in the back. Angus started to bark and Malcolm growled promises of mutiny in at least two languages. Even Rainey was giving him disgruntled looks.

He didn't dare turn his eyes toward the heavens, but he did say a silent prayer that if there were spare protectors of any random sort left wherever such things came from, he would appreciate the loan of a seasoned veteran for the next ten minutes.

Chapter 9

Claustrophobia was an absurd complaint in light of his circumstances, Matt told himself. After all, the open ocean stretched out in front of him in endless supply. But that same ocean wasn't content with its wealth of space. It also wanted to claim the rocks where he sat. There was nothing he could do to curb its greed, and as his small patch of safety grew tighter and tighter, he had a strong urge to scratch at the sandstone cliff at his back, like a man trapped in solitary confinement felt the need to dig away at the walls of his cell.

He couldn't climb it. He couldn't even sit up properly. All that was left to him was to try and carve out another inch of sanctuary to delay the inevitable. He didn't have the heart.

A mental picture of himself doing such a thing invaded his mind's eye, and he burst into half-mad laughter at the ridiculousness of it. It was a laughter that hurt to his soul, but he couldn't seem to stop. He sounded like a man who belonged in a straitjacket. He knew that, and the lunatic sound degenerated into a kind of keening, grieving howl, a cry for all he had lost, though he could put a name to none of it. His bitter tears of sorrow were cold as they traced paths through the dried blood on his face. Helplessness cut through his resolve to endure more than the pain of all his wounds. He wanted to live, by God! But it was all too hard.

It had surprised him to wake up at all. He supposed it must be the same day, though he had no guess as to the time. Chances were good that he had missed lunch as well as breakfast by now, if the grumblings of his belly were any indication. He had been doubly surprised that he had been relatively warm when he awakened. He couldn't explain it. And now he was trembling so fiercely, it hardly seemed to matter why he had once been warm. He had managed to bind his leg well enough to bear the pain of dragging himself to the kittiwake's fresh water supply against the cliff. It was the last traveling he would do in this life, he imagined, and it had cost him dearly.

The lethargy of injury and cold kept him from trying to think of a way to expedite his own rescue. Fire would have been a lifesaver in any number of ways. But everything around him was wet, including his legs where the waves lapped at his ankles. Even if he had had the absurd good luck to produce a spark by striking two rocks together, there was nothing dry enough to burn.

In a way, it was a perverse kind of blessing, this stark and useless terrain. If the potential had been there, in however meager a form, and if he had had the presence of mind, he would have been duty-bound to apply himself to try whatever method was open to him to save himself. As it was, he had no options. It was easier that way. And easy had a lot of appeal just now.

His dear little kittiwake had abandoned him. He supposed her sensibilities were out of joint over his invasion of her water source, although he had been convinced at first that she wanted him to make use of it. Certainly, it was her privilege to change her mind, but a slippery bite or two of herring right now would have done him a world of good.

He watched the aerial ballet circling the cliffs above him,

hoping to catch sight of his sometimes provider with the scarred bill. It occurred to him that as free as they all seemed, the birds were tied to the cliff, too. Each food pass they made into the waves ended in a prompt return to nest. For all their worldwide migratory skills, for the duration of the nesting season they were obliged never to lose sight of this cliff. It made for a strange kind of captivity all its own. He watched in fascination as each bird went about its appointed rounds. Despite the cramped accommodations, no one seemed to make any serious social errors that would offend a close neighbor. It amazed him. It also made his head spin.

There was another problem. He was becoming given to hallucination. In a way, it was a gift, this propensity he was developing for creating things in his mind that couldn't exist in the real world. It was a peculiar sort of entertainment. There was nothing inviting about his real world, but there was everything inviting about this other world that visited him from time to time. It was populated with magical beings, winged things. He supposed they must be angels. There was some frame of reference in his head for such phenomena. But strangely, the word for them that kept coming to mind was *bean-si`th,* which he was quite sure meant something other than "angel."

His first experience with his world of escape had been the incident with the woman and the little girl beside the peat fire. He had enjoyed that one and wished he could relive it a hundred times. But it had ended a short distance from the fire. A third female, somewhere in between the ages of the other two, had been sitting alone on a flat rock in the dark. And in her hands had been a small, winged being surrounded by a glowing light. He had been fascinated by the pair of them. But they had been startled by something, and the scene had gone to blackness. He had wanted to see more.

The second incident was different. It had involved a seal who had communicated to him that her name was Macha. It seemed extremely urgent to her that he understand her name. He had discounted this encounter until he remembered that the seal had changed shape briefly during their meeting in order to speak her name. For the blinking of an eye, the animal had taken on the form of a woman. It had all happened so quickly, he had decided it was a product of his head injury and nothing more.

But now, as these happenings began to stack up, he wondered if there was more to it. Especially in light of the fact that he was seeing a small, winged creature at the moment who was in no way relative to the bird population. He could only pray that it was an angel come to take him to heaven because even though he knew daylight still clung to the cliffs, his sight was growing dark. Whether it meant he was going to lose consciousness or lose his life, he had no way of knowing. But he knew that either possibility might prove permanent. It was nearly over.

"A bhean-sithe, thoir an aire air do mhac. Fo`ir is tro`cair orm," he whispered. He knew what it meant now. It was Gaelic for "Fairy, keep watch over your son. Mercifully save me."

A strange thing to say . . . But somehow pertinent in light of the tiny visitor now perched on his chest. He could barely see her through the growing fog in his head. She was most certainly a hallucination, he told himself. And yet, he knew she was real, believed it with every fiber of his being.

She was dressed in the dark-green leaves of a summer rose, and settled within the red-gold clouds of her hair was a crown of forest violets and forget-me-nots. With each flutter of her gossamer wings, a veil of sparkling dust floated in the air. Her bright green eyes misted with tears over his misery as she smiled at him with utter compassion. She could easily fit in the palm of his hand, and she weighed no more than a butterfly.

He blinked, trying to get his eyes to function as he watched her rise. It came as no surprise to him when she kissed him lightly on the cheek. That tiny blessing was somehow familiar. She stroked his cheek comfortingly, and his spirits began to return. Her voice was like honey against his skin, and he forgot about the cold.

"Hallo, a Mhata, de` dh'e`irich dhut, mo dhlu`th charaid?" she said, meaning, "Hello, Matt, what has happened to you, my dear friend?"

He raised his trembling hand, and she flew to the tip of his index finger to seat herself there. As he drew her closer, he smiled.

"A Mhata." His voice rasped over the word. It was a revelation. "My name! My name is Matt." The little fairy nodded and looked up at him shyly from beneath her long lashes. "And you, my bonnie, bonnie wee savior, are Mar a' Ghealach, whose name means 'Like the Moon,' a name as glowin' as its owner. I saw ye in the dark, did I not?" She smiled and blushed becomingly. And though she spoke to him only in Gaelic, he understood her every word.

"You are far from your home, my friend." She kept a careful watch on his state of mind to be certain she wasn't losing him. The pulse of life beating inside him was very fragile.

He exhaled in a rush, and the dust from her wings rose in a shining burst. There seemed to be a limitless supply of it. "Aye, and I can only suppose that ye are far from home as well, love."

She smoothed some of the dirt from the top of his fingernail. "And for that reason, I cannot remain with you."

He could no longer hold his hand up, so he set it down on his chest. "So this is by way of a last farewell, I imagine," he said as evenly as he could. Here was his one tie to the past, and she was about to write him off as a lost cause. He wanted no more of this roller coaster ride.

Mar a' Ghealach saw the despair in his eyes. He had misunderstood her intentions, and she had to make things right. But it was true that her time with him was limited. If she stayed much longer, she would lose the strength to return to the sacred oak that was her home. She rose on the air and hovered very near his eyes. He could no longer look at her.

"A Mhata, is beag fios a tha agad-sa ciod e a tha a-muigh ort fhe`in," she said kindly—or "Little do you know what destiny has in store for you." She touched the silver necklace around his throat. Still, he would not look at her.

"Ah, but I know precisely what destiny has in store for me, lass," he replied with a bitter twist. "I came to this place alone, and I shall leave it alone. I don't know what led me here, but I am certain there is no one who can lead me back." The cannon fire in his head started afresh, and the bones in his leg began a new campaign of terror.

The little fairy saw his pain and saw his faith begin to waver. It was dangerous for them both. She no longer had the strength to ease his physical pain. She was losing him, and far too much depended on his survival.

"I must go, Matt," she whispered sadly against his cheek. "But others are coming. They are being guided by their hearts, and you must remain strong. Give them a beacon to follow, my dearest friend. You must show them the way. It is your faith in them that will bring them to you. You must not fail them."

She saw it in his eyes now. He wanted to believe her. He knew she was telling him the truth. But once she left, all that might change.

"I have gifts for you, Matt," she called to him as she rose on the mists. "I lock these gifts inside your heart, where they can never be lost again. Hold them fast, my friend, and we shall all rejoice at your homecoming."

She was gone from his sight as surely as if she had never been there at all, and a shroud of doubt descended over him. He wasn't sure it had happened at all. And if it had, it had probably been a product of infection. Now he was more alone than ever.

"Gifts? What bloody gifts might those be, fairy?" he shouted. The bird population was startled into flight once again, but he had no patience for it. He shook his fist at them. "Go on, ye damned rats with wings! Yer no more free to go than I am. Look at that! Yer already back in yer cells, the lot of ye, glued to the rocks by yer own guano. Not a free bird among ye! I despise ye all!"

As he lowered his sight back to the horizon, he realized he was not alone. His kittiwake was perched on his good foot, her scarred bill overloaded with herring. She cocked her head to one side and shook out her pristine feathers as if to show him her distaste at his uncivilized behavior. She, for one, had not given up on him.

And beyond her, he saw the selkie. She watched him cautiously with her big, dark eyes, clearly gauging his sanity. His survival mattered to her as well. It was almost comical, this zoo harem of his. And yet, he loved the two of them desperately, as only a stranded man could. He wondered if there had ever been other "ladies" in his life, ones of the human variety. . . . The two women and the girl from his vision crowded into his head, demanding his attention.

There was a strange sensation in his chest. It started as a shudder starts, with a tensing of the muscles and the stillness of anticipation. But it grew inside him. His pulse began to pound and he couldn't force himself to breathe. He expected a killing stroke to follow. His heart was going to explode. No man's heart could withstand this phenomenon.

He looked to the kittiwake and the selkie beyond with anguish in his eyes as he tried to say good-bye to them. No words would come. He had no breath to speak, and he pressed his trembling hand to the trickle of fresh water above his head with a prayer that water would somehow save him.

The rivulets dripping down the side of the cliff were like the flow of a miniature waterfall. The sight triggered something inside of him, and he drew in a huge draught of air. His lungs ached from the saving grace of it as he gulped in another breath. His hand was still pressed against the cliff as he watched the water split and flow over his fingers.

"Glomach," he said in a hoarse whisper.

Where his mind had been blank with terror, it now held impossibly beautiful words, each one deserving of its own shrine. Here was the fairy's precious gift to him. Here was the miracle that would save him.

He laughed to himself at the simplicity of it. But this time it was not the laugh of a madman. It was the jubilant sound of a man who now had hope. And faith.

"Faith." He said the word like a prayer. "Creideamh, my dear little Carrie. And Sasha. Beautiful, magical, impossible Sasha, how I do love ye and yer sister." He shook his head as a flood of memories came to him about the antics of their childhood. These memories brought another image to his mind—a stunning woman with dark curls and deep-blue eyes that saw through him to his very soul.

"Rainey, *mo chridhe*."

A surge of possessive pride raced through his blood. More than a woman, she was wife to him and mate. His senses tingled with the memory of her, the scent of lavender and lemon, the silken texture of her skin beneath his fingertips, the sweet, soft feel of her breath as she whispered words of ecstasy against his cheek. She was the love of his life, his strength, his comfort, and his conscience. He could tell himself he had lived without her once. But the truth was he had only been going through the motions then, and he could never go back to that shadow life. There were few things he truly needed, but he needed her.

But there were still gaps in his memory. He had no recollection of anything wrong between them. Surely, he would remember it now if his journey aboard the airplane had been the result of his exile from her. He couldn't sort it out in his mind whether the flight had been toward home or toward some other destination. All he knew was that if she was looking for him with love in her heart, she would find him. And if she no longer harbored any love for him, he had no wish to be found.

The kittiwake hopped up the length of him and delivered the feast on his chest, as was her habit. She eyed the silver at his throat covetously and gave it a tentative peck. Matt let her have her way as he stuffed the cold herring into his mouth. He was tempted to give her the thing as a thank-you for the groceries. But there was the thought at the back of his mind that once she had her prize, she might abandon her maternal campaign of bribery. There was no point in working against himself when so many elements were already so busy at it.

"Hello, little nurse," he said to her, as she cocked her head from one side to the other. "Here's a development. I have a language. English, I believe."

She looked at him skeptically, unimpressed with his announcement, since he still had no proper grasp of the only language that mattered to her. She opened her bill and squawked loudly in his face to remind him of his persistent ignorance, and he had the audacity to cover his ears.

There was little hope of educating him if that was going to be his attitude, she supposed. With a final unsuccessful attempt at snatching the silver from his throat, she rose on the updraft and hovered above him, now and then casting a dubious look at him.

That her fresh droppings landed within an inch of his head

was no accident. She was a queen of such things. It gave her a sense of pride to show off her gift for accuracy, and even this miscreated beast showed a healthy respect for her skills as he looked up at her with his mouth hanging open.

Now, he was just plain *asking* for it. But she was above the crass. Leave the easy marks for the youngsters who had yet to tend a proper nest. She was a bird of the world. A bird of responsibilities. And as she dipped her right wing to catch the outbound breezes, she decided it couldn't hurt to bring the Creature another meal. It gave her pleasure to show the others that she was such an extraordinary hunter, she could keep even this strange monstrosity alive.

But as she winged her way toward the herring schools, the Shiny Thing was very much on her mind. If her charge was going to be stubborn enough to remain alive, she was going to have to find another way to get her treasure from him.

He was still weak. Perhaps when he closed his eyes in sleep, she would find a way. She would have to fill his belly before darkness fell, or she would be asleep as well, and her plan would fail. Her inspiration made her impatient, and she hurried her flight over the waves to where the silver fishes danced.

Matt knew in no uncertain terms now that it had been a mistake to stretch his aching muscles. Before, some of them had had the decency to subside into numbness. But now he had encouraged the blood back into them, and each one, large and small, screamed its individual and collective unhappiness. But the tide was rolling out, and with each passing minute, he had the tiniest bit more room. It was sheer luxury to have his feet out of the freezing waves.

At least there was no doubt in his mind that he was still alive, he realized darkly. Death might touch fire to his immortal soul, but he had to question the likelihood that hell would bother to conjure up ten thousand bodily aches for him personally. It simply wasn't practical, considering the enormity of the place's clientele.

As he shifted his weight painfully in a vain effort to find a more comfortable set of sharp edges in the rocks, he saw that the selkie was only a few yards out. And she was not alone.

A second sleek head dodged among the waves, mirroring the female's every move. A male, by the look of it, although he didn't seem bent on courting her at the moment. More specifically, he was looking to her protection. His head was grizzled and marked with countless old scars. And while the male's attention was divided between the female and the cove, he was alert to the possibility of threat from any quarter. Plainly, this was not his favorite set of circumstances, but he had no wish to displease the female. He was devoted to her, and she clearly relied on his watchful presence.

The female grew more bold, but still hesitated to come up onto the rocks. Matt could see that she needed some form of assurance, some guarantee that he was sane and wouldn't harm her. He wanted to communicate with her again.

There were no illusions in his head that she would appear to him in human form as she had before. That had been a manifestation of his fevered lunacy. But there was such intelligence, such wisdom in those large dark eyes—he longed to spend time with her on whatever terms she might invent. He was desperate to know more about her, his selkie.

"A Mhacha, teann rium, tha feum orm," he called to her in soft Gaelic, which meant, "Macha, come close to me, I am in need." It was a polite invitation, nothing more. She blinked at his words. *"Tha mi an inbhe mhath. De` tha i agad air?"* I've made considerable progress. What do you think?

He pointed to the last of the herring on his chest as proof of his prosperity and to the pitiful bindings around his leg as being worthy of her admiration. It was a temptation to hold the little herring out to her, to coax her to come to him. But it would be an insult, he decided, since she could doubtless fill her own belly far better than he ever could. So he let the fish stay where it was. The decision was hers. If he could have spoken to her escort, he probably would have been told that the decisions were always hers, and that that was as it should be.

To say she spoke to him would be misstating the case. There was no cartoon balloon superimposed over her mouth, no voice styling to remind him of some movie star or his long-passed grandmother. Instead, it was like a series of gentle breezes speaking in his head, or perhaps the sound of wind chimes waltzing in the breeze. Her messages to him were not in English or Gaelic. They came to him in a third language, a language of the far north, not as familiar to him as the other two. Still, her meaning was very clear to him.

He was not the one she was looking for. It was someone he knew, she assured him, but her time was short. He had to summon this other person to him immediately, or the future would be lost to them all. There was no need to speak his next question aloud. The selkie climbed up on the rocks beside him and pressed her cold, wet nose to his cheek.

"Hun heter Sirona," she breathed against his ear.

Immediately, she backed her way down into the safety of the waves as her companion darted in tight circles around her to wrap her in protection after so bold and foolhardy a move. She dove beneath the waves and put distance between herself and the man. Then, she raised her head to see what his reaction might be. She wasn't sure if his look of bewilderment was because he hadn't understood her message, or because he was somehow the wrong human.

The second alternative was not an option. Too much had been risked. Too much was at stake.

"She is called Sirona," Matt repeated to himself. It meant nothing to him, and he rubbed his aching temples over the puzzle of it. He tried to apply his thinking processes to the problem as he watched the selkie swim nervously from side to side in a kind of waterborne pacing. She expected something of him. But he had no clue what.

"I'm sorry," was all he could manage to say. He said it in English, in Gaelic, and in the language she had used, which he recalled as being Norwegian. But she wanted nothing to do with his apologies. She wanted something very specific from him. He had been given the gift of remembrance concerning his wife and children. But he had no knowledge of this other person—assuming it was a person at all.

He didn't want to let the selkie down. In fact, he fervently wanted to be of help to her. But aside from saying the name over and over, he had no clue how to conjure up this all-important being. By the same token, the selkie was so distraught by his ignorance, he had to do something.

He concentrated on the word. "Sirona." There was an ethereal beauty to it, like silk drawn across marble. It gave him comfort to say it. It seemed to give the selkie comfort as well to hear his rough chant of it. She danced among the waves as her beleaguered companion did his best to keep up with her. If she had known his memory of the word was hollow, it would have curbed her joy, he imagined.

As he continued his strange mantra, it struck him that the necklace around his throat felt warm against his skin. It was more than the meager stuff his body was producing. The heat was being generated by the metal itself, and in time the whole of his upper body was warmed by it.

He wished to God he had known about this phenomenon earlier. It would have come in damned handy. There was some concern in his mind about whether he could take it too far. But for now, it was a blessing he was willing to accept without question.

He smiled at the selkie with gladness in his heart. It was a simple happiness they shared, he decided. There was no reason to push any of it further.

To add to his bounty, he spotted the kittiwake coming in for a landing with a fresh load of provisions in her bill. Bonnie wee bird. Her obsession with the necklace struck him as endearing. But she had her thick feathers to keep her warm, and he had no more thoughts of parting with his new source of warmth, no matter how adorable she might be.

She looked confused by his chanting of Sirona's name. Perhaps she was offended by the interruption of this meal that had required so much of her energy, he decided. Or perhaps she suspected that he had forgotten how to feed himself, because she picked up one of the fresh herring and wagged it up and down in her beak, apparently to get his whole attention.

She seemed encouraged when he popped the rest of the fish into his mouth over the noise he was making. But he could tell she wasn't very pleased when he didn't chew his food very thoroughly. No doubt she was convinced she would have to partially digest it for him in advance. Clearly, she was regarding him as a great deal of trouble, since she herself had no teeth.

"Not to worry, little nurse," he said quickly, "your misbegotten chick is fendin' for himself rather nicely, I should think. I haven't lost my touch."

She cocked her head to give him a dubious look. She had forgotten how big he really was. It was going to take a cove full of herring to fill his belly enough to make him nod off. But the Shiny Thing was giving off a warm glow that made it even more inviting than before. She had to have it for her own, even if it meant a hundred trips to the herring schools.

Without further adieu, she spread her wings and headed out

to sea, leaving the Creature to his silly songs. There was nothing hard work couldn't cure.

Matt watched her fly off with a satisfied sigh. She really was quite a bird. The selkie raised her shoulders out of the water when he paused in his saying of Sirona's name, and he snapped back to his duties. Whatever the cause of the warmth the necklace was giving off, it was directly proportional to the number of times he said the name. He gave no thought whatsoever to the notion that his chanting might have any other effect on his life. He was content to take his small blessings as they came to him. It wasn't as if things could get much *worse*.

And the drowsiness he was experiencing felt like true and honest fatigue rather than the onset of unconsciousness or the loss of his life. It was an almost pleasant feeling. He didn't want to stop saying Sirona's name. It would probably mean a return of the cold.

But the call of potentially gentle dreams was a very strong one. It had to take him to a better place, however briefly. He would just rest his eyes for a moment or two. And when he awoke, maybe his subconscious would have supplied him with a solution to his problems. It was a possibility. It was such a little thing, sleep. Certainly not a sin by anyone's definition. It cost nothing, but could render a man whole again.

The dream was on him before he could even think of saying no to it. It was a dream like no other he had ever had. A beautiful woman stood at the top of an enormous waterfall. In the pool below her lay the broken bodies of dozens of men, women, and children. Behind her, men in ancient armor shouted at her and threatened her with swords and spears. Yet through it all, she maintained her regal bearing.

He watched in horror as the woman leapt from the top of the falls to disappear in the bloodied pool below. A battle cry tore from his throat at the injustice of what he had just witnessed. It tore at his heart, and he drew his own sword, thinking to right this terrible wrong.

But as he looked once again to the top of the falls, he saw that she was there. Her enemies were gone, and all around her, joyous birds darted and swooped, and all the flowers of spring burst forth in brilliant flower. She was so exquisite to the eye that he could hardly bear to look at her. And atop her flowing dark hair, as impossible as it was, there rested a crown made of dazzling stars. With each rainbow of mist that rose from the falls, the crown drew more sparkling light until he had to turn away out of fear it would blind him.

When he opened his eyes again within the extraordinary dream, he was kneeling at the woman's feet, the hilt of his sword held toward heaven in a pledge of love and loyalty to her. He felt the radiance of her smile upon him, and when he raised his eyes to her at last, there was but one word in his heart.

Sirona.

Chapter 10

Rainey kept Kyle company as he steered the faithful old ambulance through the dense fog. The mists were the worst they had ever been, and the roads were thick with jagged rocks and bumper-deep puddles. She was tired to the bone, but she could tell Kyle was having trouble adjusting to the fact that Carrie was the one guiding them to Matt.

She also noticed that he spent a great deal of time glancing at Sasha in the rearview mirror, which could prove to be a hazard for them all if he drove them into a ditch. The safest thing was probably going to be to keep his attention on other matters.

"Did you notice that little sign on the side of the truck that said THE RITZ, Kyle? I wonder what that's all about," she offered casually. He frowned at her question, clearly perturbed at this break in his concentration on Sasha.

"I haven't a clue, mum," he said without much thought. "I suppose it's something to do with the irony of war." He dismissed the subject with a shrug as the thick fog soaked the windshield. "Have ye any notion how much further we have to go? It feels like we've driven halfway around the world, but I cannot discount the notion that we may have been goin' in a tight circle the whole time. If only I could have a landmark or two to guide the way."

Rainey checked her watch. Timewise, they had driven long enough to be close to their goal. But Kyle was right. With no visible frames of reference to mark their progress, this was a very frustrating process.

"I have to suppose we're nearly there, Kyle, but your guess is as good as mine."

Kyle's eyes went to the rearview mirror again. He spoke so everyone would hear. "I wonder if any of the residents of the back might have access to . . . outside information."

Malcolm glanced at all the faces beside him to see if anyone else had a reply to such an inquiry. "We haven't the foggiest what yer talkin' about, Edinburgh," he said with conviction.

Carrie giggled at Malcolm's choice of words, then leaned over to whisper into Sasha's ear, "I think he's talking about the fairies!"

Sasha returned Kyle's look in the mirror at last. It took him by surprise and the color rose in his cheeks. It wasn't the kind of look he wanted.

Emma saw all of this exchange. "What sort of outside help did ye have in mind, Kyle?" she asked kindly.

He was sorry, now, that he had opened his mouth. His being sorry was a phenomenon that was becoming far too frequent.

"I beg yer pardon, all," he was quick to say. "I only meant, if anyone had any . . . instincts about how our journey was comin', I'd appreciate the input. I wasn't tryin' to imply that this family is, for want of a better term, supernatural." This time, he kept his sight locked forward.

"I promise you, Kyle, we're just an ordinary family in an extraordinary situation," Rainey said calmly.

He had the decency not to laugh in her face, but he couldn't resist voicing his reactions to all that he had experienced so far.

"I must confess to ye, Mrs. Macinnes, some of what I have seen since this journey began has struck me as nothin' short of . . . perhaps 'miraculous' would be the most pertinent term."

"That's a pretty big word," she replied. Carrie was sleeping against her shoulder, and she shifted her into a more comfortable position. Carrie seemed determined to stay in her dreams. "I suppose I should be flattered. But the fact is, words like 'miraculous' can get people into a lot of trouble. And, as you may have gathered, trouble is not something we need in any more generous supply."

"Aye, I see yer point." He strained to see the road ahead. The mists were like a damp gray blanket thrown across the windshield. In his current state of mind, he had to wonder if some of the forces of nature were intentionally working against them. He could only hope those forces weren't working against him personally.

"And let me ask you this, if I may, Kyle," Rainey persisted. "Have you had any of these so-called miraculous experiences of your own—ones concerning yourself, I mean?"

So, there was method here, Kyle realized. Either she was trying to discover a missing piece to the puzzle, something that he might be able to provide in this search for her husband, or she was trying to find out if he was going to help or hinder them if some of this "miraculous" talent was going to be necessary to carry out their rescue. At this point he wasn't certain himself.

He cranked the wheel hard to avoid a large rock in the road, and a passenger in the back threatened him with a death of a thousand cuts. He knew precisely which passenger. Sasha had been criticizing his driving for the past hour. Maybe she had invented that method of execution in a former incarnation, he mused. Nothing would surprise him.

"In point of fact," he said cautiously, "I did have one experience of my own, Mrs. Macinnes. I must suppose it was the product of fatigue and all this open air."

"Really. Would you mind sharing it with me, Kyle?"

From the utter calm of her demeanor, they might have as easily been discussing the comparative cost of buttermilk, Kyle mused. But her face was white from stress, and her fingers were trembling slightly. He had seen that much at a glance.

To reveal the incredible vision of his Viking brother might make him more the fool than he already was in her eyes. He had the names of the participants in the selkie story now. Somehow, that made it all the more real. But what Rainey Macinnes would think of his "daydreams" was quite another matter.

"Well, ye see, missus," he began, "the story of the selkies I told to you and Carrie, ye recall how I couldn't remember the characters' names?"

"Yes, you said you might never have been told their names." She started to trace something in the drops of condensation on the window. The adrenaline was pumping to her extremities. Her every instinct had homed in on what he was about to say.

"Aye, well, the truth is, I remember the names now." It felt like his throat was going to close. Even with headlights on and the windshield wipers going full tilt, he couldn't see a thing.

"So, the warlord's name was . . . ?"

"Gunnar."

She nodded her understanding. Only one name was truly going to mean anything to her. She knew now that Kyle would give it to her. She could feel the truth of it coursing through her blood. But this whole process with Kyle had a dreamlike quality, a feeling of déjà vu. It had to be lived out in a precise way.

"And the Viking guardian?" she asked as casually as she could.

"Olgar." The timber of his voice had changed slightly, as if the information were coming through the vocal cords of another. "But the Celtic queen, isn't it her name you most want to hear? Her name was . . ."

Rainey leaned back to reveal what she had been drawing on the window. There, printed in the droplets, was the word "Macha."

The truck left its track again as Kyle slammed them to a sudden stop. He ignored the shouts of protest from the back and looked at Rainey in astonishment.

"You know this name, mum? Ye were familiar with the story from before, then."

She smiled at him with a touch of melancholy as Carrie sat up and rubbed the sleep from her eyes. Carrie looked from her mother to Kyle. Kyle's expression was one of confusion, and she patted his knee comfortingly.

"We're there now," she said with confidence.

Kyle gazed down at her, his thoughts still on the name drawn on the window. "Actually, we've only stopped for a moment, love. I had to get somethin' straight. And the fact of the matter is, I haven't got it straight yet. But we can be on our way again." He started to put the truck in gear, and Carrie laid her hand over his gently on the wheel. She shook her head in the negative, and he wondered if she might be better to ride in the back.

"We should stop, Kyle," Rainey agreed. "We must be close to where we have to go."

He shrugged and put the truck into park. But as he started to climb out to stretch his legs, he froze before his foot hit the ground. Because the truth was, there was no ground beneath his foot. They were poised on the very edge of a sheer cliff. Had he started the engine and put it into drive, they might well have gone over the edge. He could hear the waves pounding a hundred and fifty feet below them, even before the mists parted enough for him to see the vast open space beneath his feet. When he clambered back into his seat, he found Carrie grinning at him impishly. She had known precisely where they were.

God would have had them all as new harp students if she hadn't chosen to awaken at that moment. But then, he was learning that very little was really left to chance in his dealings with Carrie. He tsked at her.

"Hun likner en liten engel nar hun sover," he said in Norwegian as he tried to settle his heart out of his throat. It meant, "She looks like a little angel when she sleeps."

"Tusen hilsener fra havet," she replied teasingly in the same language. It meant, "A thousand greetings from the sea," and his shudder at the thought made her laugh.

"I strongly suggest ye all check yer footin' before ye leave this vehicle," he called to the passengers in the back. It surprised him when Sasha didn't have a snappy comeback to his advice. She looked at him with no emotion whatsoever, and he had no idea what to make of it. He made a promise to himself that once this mission of mercy was over, he was going to throw himself into his work for a year to clear his palate of Sasha Macinnes.

"When everyone's on safe ground, I'll back us up a bit." He thought he heard Sasha mutter her doubts over whether he knew which of the gears was reverse, but he couldn't swear to it. And at least she hadn't barked it in his face. It was a kind of progress, he supposed. Or maybe she had at long last decided on the best method of his demise. Certainly plunging himself over a cliff in a stolen ambulance required a considerable amount of ingenuity.

When the truck was a respectable distance from the edge of the cliff, Kyle got out and joined the others. Everyone was clustered around Carrie, waiting for her next announcement. A part of him still had to wonder at the wisdom of hanging all their hopes on the whims of a nine-year-old. But Creideamh Macinnes was hardly a typical child.

He hung back a few paces to watch the changes in that adorable, freckled face. She closed her eyes and pointed toward the north. Without a moment's hesitation, they all began to walk in that direction, being very mindful of the rocky cliffs only a few feet away. Thirty paces from the truck she stopped and pointed to the ground beneath them. Though he was not in the middle of the group, when she opened her eyes, her focus was on him.

"Ikke vaer redd, det er ikke farlig," she said calmly.

"She's saying not to be afraid, that it's not dangerous," he provided.

"What's not dangerous?" Malcolm insisted. He looked all around them and saw nothing, but Emma laid a cautionary hand on his arm.

"Wait for it, love," she whispered in his ear. "She's workin' up to somethin'."

Rainey knelt down in front of Carrie and took up her hands. "Tell us about this place, Carrie."

Her eyes were still on Kyle. "Do you know this place?" she asked him.

Kyle looked around at the rocky terrain and the cliff's edge, only a few feet away. There was a general familiarity about it, he supposed. He had been to the island briefly for the university two summers ago, an anthropological tour of study. But they hadn't come this far north. The location was new to him, and as far as he could see, there was nothing significant about it.

He gave Carrie a bewildered smile. "I'm sorry, lass, the place is new to me. I hope that's not too much of a disappointment to ye."

Carrie walked over to him and took him by the hand. He let himself be led to where she had been standing. It didn't make any difference, and he looked down at her with a shrug.

"Vent et oyeblikk," she said out of the corner of her mouth.

Kyle glanced at the others, who were all watching with interest. He was going to let them down, and he hated the thought of it.

"She told me to wait a moment," he explained. "But I don't really see what good . . . hello, what's this, then?"

There was a kind of rhythmic vibration under his feet. Not a phenomenon of a mechanical variety, though. It reminded him of the sensations he got in his good ear when he turned off his hearing aid to block out music that was too loud. He could still *feel* the rhythm and the bass line through his skin, but the melody, if there indeed was one, was lost to him.

It was the kind of thing he had experienced just before Sasha had made herself known outside his classroom in Edinburgh. Without the benefit of his hearing, he had been drawn to her presence outside his door, even before all those books had hit the floor. It was a sort of magnetic attraction.

"There most definitely is something going on here," he said as he stared down at his own feet. It wouldn't have surprised him to see lightning shoot up through the ground, and for the first time, he wondered if he and Carrie were safe where they stood. He looked around with fresh eyes. There was a familiarity, a mixture of sound and scent that was exclusive to this place. It was definitely getting under his skin.

"Why has this place changed, Creideamh?" he heard himself ask.

Carrie squeezed his hand reassuringly. "It's because of the sea. The sea has taken away a lot of the cliff over the centuries."

"Over the centuries?" Why didn't it surprise him to hear her speak in such terms?

For the first time since arriving at the site, Carrie looked to her mother. "The old castle, my *real* castle, is still here, Mama. This used to be a beautiful place, a place to commune with those who had gone before us, a place of rest for those who were starting their next journey. There were four rooms and a pretty courtyard with a stone roof over it where you could sit and talk with the spirits and dream about what was on the other side of the ocean." She spread her arms and whirled about with a joyous sense of reunion. Then she stopped cold and turned back to Kyle, her young face very serious.

"Do you remember when you were last here?" she asked solemnly.

Instinctively, Kyle looked to Sasha for reinforcement. The moment he did it, he wondered if it had been a mistake. She had hardly been an ally thus far. But he saw no censure in her eyes, no hint of sarcasm. He knew she had none of the language Carrie was so familiar with, so he made his request to her in Gaelic.

"Tha mi eadar da` lionn, Sasha, agus is math an sga`than su`il caraide," meaning, "I am at a loss, Sasha, and a friend's eye makes a good mirror." In English, he added, "Will ye stand beside me? I think I can do what I'm supposed to do in all this, if ye'll lend me yer amazin' strength. What do ye say, Highland girl, are ye game?"

Rainey touched the locket at her throat. The words Kyle had used were so similar to ones Matt had said to her long ago, it might have been Matt speaking. Instead, this request had been made not of her but of Sasha. Kyle was calling to Sasha as Matt had once called to her.

The far-reaching implications of it were more than she could focus on at the moment. The one thing she knew for certain, from the look on Sasha's face, was that she was a woman who had made up her mind about this man, for good or ill. She was grateful for the feel of Emma's hand on her arm as Sasha stepped forward.

"Steady on, love," Emma whispered in her ear. "It's been comin' since they first laid eyes on each other. You and I both knew it for the truth."

"She's so very young, Emma," Rainey said softly.

"Is she, now?"

Rainey watched as Sasha approached Kyle. Sasha's walk was not that of a girl, but of a woman who was very aware that she was drawing near a man whose opinion of her mattered a great deal. It made Rainey's heart ache to see it happen. She hadn't had time to contemplate this kind of transition in Sasha's life—or her own.

A new pang of longing rose in her heart, a longing for Matt. He hadn't known Sasha as a very small child. There were so many milestones in her life he had missed—her first words, her first steps. Alan had been there for them. He had been a good husband and father.

But Sasha's relationship with Kyle was something Rainey didn't want to have to deal with alone. She wanted Matt by her side. He was near, she could feel his presence. And it was killing her to know the minutes were slipping by.

Kyle didn't know what to expect as Sasha walked up to him. Her expression was unreadable. He experienced a moment of doubt as he tried to decide whether she was going to help him or smack him a good one. It was impossible for him to tell. But when she stood squarely in front of him, she did something totally out of character. She stood on her tiptoes and yanked a handful of the hair behind his left ear. He didn't know what to make of it.

She gave it another proper tug. "This belongs to me, Edinburgh," she said firmly. "If I say cut it, you cut it. If I say keep it, you keep it, understood?"

"Not really." She gave it a third healthy tug. "Fine! It belongs to you! Christ, but this is a lunatic family."

Sasha gave him a secretive smile. "We're very much a family tied to the moon." She gave Carrie a conspiring wink, and Carrie hid a giggle behind her hand. When she raised her eyes to Kyle again, Sasha saw the mixture of joy and bewilderment on his face.

"Get on with it, Edinburgh, so we can get to the business of rescuing my father. I think we're all waiting to see what he has to say about you. All you need to know is locked up, there in your heart." She pressed her warm palm against his chest and smiled with satisfaction when he momentarily lost the ability to breathe. "Here, *mo fhear-saoraidh,* I'll give you the key. Now, you can't ever say I never gave you anything."

She slipped the velvet pouch from around her neck and laid it in his hand. She had referred to him as her "deliverer," and it had nearly sent him to his knees. Now, here was a second gift. What could he possibly give her in return? He slid the pouch's contents into the palm of his hand. It was a silver brooch about one and a half inches across and one inch high, comprising intricately woven, crisscrossed patterns.

It was stunning to the eye, and he recognized that while having a Celtic feel to its design, the piece was unmistakably Viking in origin. It felt warm in his hand from its contact with Sasha, and he was hard-pressed not to dwell on that fact.

But it provided him with other feelings as well. He knew now when it was that he had last been in this place, and it tore him in two. With the subtlety of a fever rising in his blood, he felt the presence of another inside him, sharing his skin, his heart. It was no demon taking over his soul. It was a kindred spirit. But the impact of this intrusion made him weak in the knees. He sat down hard on the edge of the cliff and took his head in his hands. For now, he was lost to those around him. There was a roughness as he spoke to the waves below.

"I am here for my brother's sake. I am here for Olgar." He drew in a sharp breath at the strange sound of his own voice. Sasha reached down to touch his shoulder kindly, a move that would have brought him close to heaven only moments before. Now, he was oblivious to her hand upon his shoulder, lost in the confusion of all that was happening to him.

Sasha turned to Rainey with a look of concern. "Is he all right, Mama?"

Rainey set her hand on Kyle's other shoulder. "We'll keep an eye on him, Sash. I've had a suspicion from the start that there was more than one reason Kyle was here for us. We'll just have to wait and see."

Carrie considered Kyle's state. "He's going to make things right, Mama," she said firmly. "Then it'll be time for him to go to heaven."

Sasha was not reassured by this revelation, and she wrapped her arm around Kyle's shoulder protectively. "Heaven, Care?"

"Sorry, not heaven, Sash. I meant to say Valhalla."

It meant the same thing.

A lone kittiwake rose on the updraft beside him. In her scarred beak was a necklace of shining silver. She seemed to be showing it off to them as she floated there, eye to eye with them. But there was a suspicious noise from below, and she became distracted. The necklace slipped from her beak and fell toward the rocks below like a stone. She dove after it as if it were her life savings about to be lost. Once she was among the fray of others of her kind, there was no distinguishing her.

Rainey had gone down on her knees to watch the little gull's downward progress. The protruding nests blocked her sight of the scant beach below, but when she rose to her feet, her eyes were bright with tears of recognition.

"Macha's necklace," she said reverently. "We're in the right place. There are seals down there. I saw them. Thank God! This has to be it!"

Chapter 11

"I cannot let ye do this, Rainey," Emma insisted as Rainey secured the end of the rope to the truck's solidly built undercarriage. "I don't know what we were thinkin', tryin' to do this on our own. It's madness—and you with yer hatred of the heights. Malcolm says it's most likely two hundred feet to the bottom, and there's no such a thing as a guarantee there's any footin' to speak of once yer down there. And on top of everythin' else, God only knows what ye may find, love. We're all prayin' for Matty's safe deliverence. But it's no the kind of thing ye should be doin' alone."

Rainey started to knot the random lengths of rope together, end to end. She didn't know how much there was of it altogether. If she got part of the way down the sheer, rocky side and ran out of rope. . . .

"I don't have time to think about it, Emma," she said firmly. "All the signs are here. Carrie brought us straight to this place. The old castle is here, and the seals. Even Macha's necklace, for godsakes, although there's no telling where it landed after that bird let go of it." She turned her attention to the seals waiting below. "Macha herself is here, Emma. I can feel Sirona's spirit calling out to me to go down there. I trust that voice. This has to

happen, for everyone's sake. If there was a single reason to believe Matt was down there, I would have to go. And the fact is,
we have a whole handful of reasons to believe."

"Och, stubborn," Emma said with very little steam. "Ye
should let one of the men do it."

Rainey leaned near her. "We both know this isn't a job for
Malcolm," she said softly. "If anything happened to him, Emma,
I would never forgive myself for letting him do it. He's going to
try to talk me into it. You and I both know it. So, you'll have to
back me on this."

"Aye, I suppose yer right. But what about young Edinburgh?"

Rainey inclined her head toward where Kyle sat like a
wounded animal brought down by a tranquilizer dart. He began
to tear pieces of dried root into bits. Rainey shook her head.

"I'm afraid our friend Kyle, there, isn't quite himself just
now. Look at him, Emma. You and I both know Kyle is in his
early twenties. But to see him now, you'd think you were looking at a man who should have been dead a long time ago. I don't
know if this is going to have any long-lasting effects on Kyle.
We both know that when these kinds of communications happen to a person, there's a very real reason for it. Something has
to be fixed in his present-day life as well as the one he's con-
nected to right now. What I do know for certain is that he's not
our man at the moment. And no way am I going to send you or
one of the girls on this little expedition. No, I have to do this on
my own, so stop mothering me, friend." She gave Emma a
smile of thanks.

"Aye, love, I hear ye," Emma said with a sigh.

Rainey saw Malcolm striding toward them with the word
"hero" written in the set of his jaw. This wasn't going to be easy.

"One crisis at a time," she said as much to herself as to Emma.

"See here, now, Rainey," Malcolm insisted with a military
clip, "I cannot allow ye to take such risks. I'm quite prepared to

go over the side for ye, if ye've a mind to see this thing through." He tried to take the rope from her hands, and they both saw that his hands were shaking. They shook from time to time now that he was along in years. No one thought it a sign of failing courage. But the climb was out of the question for him.

Rainey set her hand on his shoulder fondly. "Thank you, Malcolm," she said with all sincerity, "but the truth is, you're the only one who can manage the gears on the truck for me. Kyle is out of it, the girls don't know how, and I need for Emma to give the signals when I tug on the rope. The fact is, you're the only one who has experience with that old warhorse. I can't do it without you running things topside. Will you do that for me, Malcolm? For Matt's sake?"

Malcolm blustered and cleared his throat. His offer to make the climb had been absolutely genuine, but he had to admit to himself, however grudgingly, that he had his limitations. Rescuing one man was going to be job enough without forcing this rag-tag bunch to rescue him into the bargain. "Aye, well, when ye put it that way, I suppose there's no help for it," he grumbled. "But there's nothin' says I have to like it." He gave her a quick hug.

"I knew you wouldn't like it, Malcolm," Rainey admitted, "but you have to see the wisdom of doing it this way."

He straightened his jacket self-consciously. "I see no such a thing, lassie. But since that's the way it's to be, let's be about it." He busied himself double-checking all of the knots, and Emma gave Rainey a covert wink.

Rainey motioned to Sasha and Carrie. "Listen up, ladies, here is the plan, such as it is. It looks like there's a little cove down there. Not much to look at, but maybe enough to shelter a man, out of sight from above." She contemplated the edge of the cliff. "I don't for the life of me see how Macha got up that thing when she first arrived on the island."

Carrie considered the rope as well. "I think she probably took the steps, Mama."

Rainey turned to her slowly. "What are you telling me, Creideamh Macinnes? There are steps? You were going to let me go over the side of that monstrous thing, when all the time I could have just taken 'the steps'?"

"They may not be there anymore," Carrie said with a shrug. "And besides, Mama, you always know the best thing to do." She gave her mother a smile of the angels.

"Where are these steps, Care?" Rainey said as she planted her hands on her hips. "Do you know where they are?"

Carrie placed her hands on her own hips in imitation of her mother. "They belong to the castle. They're under your feet, Mama. The people built them so it would be easier to get water from the spring at the bottom of the cliff. They kept the water for special days because it was blessed by the spirits who visited this place. But the climb was too dangerous, so even though it took them many, many years, they cut the steps into the rock."

Rainey looked down and saw nothing but a broad mound of overgrown dirt. There were no physical distinctions to show where a stairway might be. Malcolm fetched a pair of shovels, a flashlight, and the portable first aid kit from the truck. He handed a shovel to Rainey.

"If the lassie says there's a set of stairs beneath our feet, missy, then we'd best be at our diggin'. I only hope we dunna have to create a new set of steps whilst we're lookin' for the old."

He dug his shovel into the sandy soil, and Rainey followed his lead. Before long, they had exposed an opening into the main chamber of the cairn. Except for the daylight entering from their digging, it was very dark inside. But when they shone a light against the inner walls, they saw that there was room for several people to walk about, although the roof of linteled stone would force visitors to hunch down. Whether the construction would still have its integrity after thousands of years was a question there was only one way to answer.

Carrie tugged at her mother's sleeve. "Let me go, Mama. I know where the steps are. I can lead you to them. Please?"

Rainey looked down into those very determined young eyes. "How can you be sure, Care? What if the whole thing caves in on you? I'll go first. Or I can still do the cliff. I'll be all right. I just can't let you take the risk, sweetheart."

She was relieved to see Carrie nod in compliance. But it wasn't like her to give in on a point so easily. Before she had time to react, Carrie dashed through the opening.

"I have to get to Papa! He needs me!" she shouted as she disappeared into the blackness.

"Carrie! Come back!" Visions of Carrie being crushed beneath tons of slab rock burned through Rainey's mind. "I'm going after her," she said quickly as she grabbed the rescue supplies. She glanced at Sasha as she scrambled into the narrow entrance. "Leave the rope over the side, Sash. Watch for a tug on it. I'll try to send a message up to you if we make it to the bottom." Their eyes held. "And Sasha, if you don't hear from us within the hour, don't come after us. You mustn't risk it."

She looked to Malcolm. "If we don't contact you, take the truck and go for whatever kind of help you can find. Promise them money or their pictures on the front page of a newspaper. Promise them a lawsuit or a handful of fairy jewels—whatever it takes, Malcolm. But none of you is to try the cliff—understood? I can't worry about you. There just isn't any room left in my heart."

They all nodded, but she had her doubts. There was no more time to convince them as she looked to Sasha for the last time. "One hour, Sash. And keep an eye on Kyle."

"I know, Mama," Sasha said as Rainey slid out of sight into the cairn.

Emma gave Sasha a hug of encouragement as Malcolm hunkered down next to the cliff to keep an eye on the rope. It was far too early for a signal, but it made it easier on him to think he had a duty to perform.

"Yer not to worry, love," Emma said to Sasha kindly. She had hated to watch Rainey and Carrie disappear down that hole as if they were sliding into their own graves, but she wasn't about to let it show in front of Sasha. She and Sasha had been through more crises together than she cared to recall. She only hoped the magic was still there. "Our Rainey will find a way to solve all of this misery. You see if she doesn't, love. Now, we'd best do as yer mother said."

Sasha turned to Kyle, who sat beside the cliff's edge, his sight locked on the seals below. She walked over to him and sat down at his side, her eyes, too, on the seals. A part of her wished that she knew Norwegian so she could communicate with him in a comfortable way. But that was Carrie's department.

It was true that she alone had known what Carrie's name would be before Carrie was born. It had just come to her, as so many things did. But she was uncertain what Carrie's true kinship was with Kyle. Was it actually a bond with Kyle, the teaching assistant from modern-day Edinburgh? Or was it a kinship to some outcast Viking from centuries ago?

Perhaps the two elements of Carrie's soul could not be separated. Carrie was very young, but these spiritual pairings had nothing to do with chronological age. It was possible that Kyle and Carrie were meant to be together one day. She would not go where it might one day be Carrie's place to be.

This decided, she started to stand up. But the man beside her grabbed her sleeve and lightly pulled her down next to him again. She wasn't sure which man she saw as she looked into those eyes filled with anguish.

"Will you stay with me for a time?" he asked humbly.

She didn't know what he was asking her, but she shrugged and tucked her legs under herself. "I suppose I could keep you company for a while."

He nodded, satisfied with her answer, and looked out to the sea again, a frown of thought on his face. "The little one speaks the tongue of the Norse, but you do not. Why is this?"

He certainly looked like Kyle, but he sounded like someone else, a stranger to her. She shifted her position and hugged her knees to her chest. It was a defensive move, she realized after she had done it. "Norwegian. That's a good question," she said in a noncommittal fashion.

He turned to her with half a smile, all Viking. "Then you must give me a good answer to it."

Undaunted, she risked smiling back at him. "As a matter of fact, I don't imagine any explanation I could give would constitute a good answer to you. More to the point, I'm not sure why Carrie can speak your language so well. Papa knows it, but I don't think I ever heard him speak it. I know none of us speaks it, and she certainly never had any lessons. There are just some things that come to us, out of the blue, I guess you might say. Like the way I always knew Gaelic, that Celtic language you talk about. It was just there, from the time I first started talking in California."

His frown was back. "This California, it is where the glowing creatures live, the small witch's minions you converse with from time to time, the place my people call the Underworld?"

"Hell, you mean?" She stifled a laugh. "Well, I certainly had some monstrous moments there."

"Your women battle monsters in this California place. I can

see the value of leaving it. There were monsters in my home-land, too, though few of them had the courage to show themselves. My master was ruler of all. To offend him . . ." His troubles came back to him in a rush. "To offend my master was to beg for death on your knees." He scrubbed his eyes with the heels of his hands. "I failed my duties, even as my brother failed his. Perhaps it is in our blood. Perhaps this is why our parents were lost to us. Our father was bodyguard to the war-lord. He was killed protecting him in battle, but it was said he would have been of better service to his master if he had been deft enough on the field to stay alive."

"But that's ridiculous!" Sasha exclaimed, forgetting for the moment the peculiar nature of their conversation. "I mean, his whole job was to protect the warlord. Your father did his job. He kept the man alive, but they still weren't satisfied?" She remembered Kyle's story about how the Norsemen disposed of children they considered "unworthy." Was the whole race crazy?

"My father was not dishonored," he said without enthusiasm. "There was some talk, though, and perhaps our blood was tainted."

Sasha didn't want to dwell on this one. It only made her angry to think of some man who had given his all in the line of duty, only to be maligned in death. "What about your mother?"

"She died giving birth to me," he replied without feeling. "She should have been strong for her children. But she had lost seven sons in between the birth of Olgar and me. Two sons, when there could have been nine—she was a disappointment to many." He shrugged. "I never knew her. They say she was beautiful. But what is great beauty if you cannot bear your man strong, healthy sons?"

She rolled her eyes and had to look away from him. "I'll have to give that one some thought, Viking."

"Like you, for example, California," he said matter-of-factly.

Her head snapped around. "Just what are you saying?"

"You are beautiful. As beautiful as your mother, as beautiful as the Celtic witch. Of course, you are long in years to fool a man into thinking you are a virgin." He was surprised to see her offended reaction. "Well, it is a fact. But, assume I was blinded by this beauty of yours and I took you to wife."

"Assume you are way out of line, Viking."

"Do not speak out of turn, woman, or my point will not be well taken."

She had the perfect comeback for that one, but she couldn't wait to see where this little speech of his was leading.

"So, say for example, after a year of my throwing you on your back at every opportunity, you still insult us both by failing in your duty as a wife. I am obliged to feed you and keep a roof over your head in the hope that you will one day produce favorable results. What if that day never comes? In the meantime, aside from your cooking, cleaning, chopping the firewood, tending the livestock, and the heat of your body beside me for the long winter nights, you are nothing more than a constant drain on my money and an embarrassment to me and my family. Where is the justice in this, I ask you?"

She wanted to laugh at his logic. He had just listed enough menial chores to justify anyone's room and board and then some. "I honestly have to say I don't see justice in any of it, Viking."

"Well, there you see, then, why my mother did not live up to expectations. I wish her a place in Valhalla, for I am told her heart was kind. But her belly was sadly lacking in determination."

"She managed to bring you and your brother into the world, didn't she?"

He considered this. "*Ja,* you speak the truth in this. But you see what became of us. My brother had a weakness. He was bewitched by the spells of a foreigner. It made him into a traitor to his master and his people. And I could find no way to stop him short of putting him to my sword. The witch was to blame, but my brother and I both acted as fools. Had our mother's will been made of stronger stuff, perhaps things would have turned out differently for us all."

Sasha picked up one of the dried roots the Viking found so fascinating. "I've had a few psychology courses, and I know that blaming your mother for things that happen to you is pretty classic, according to the textbooks. But I think you take the cake, Viking."

He squared his shoulders pridefully. "You are accusing me of thievery, California?"

"What? Oh, right, 'take the cake.' No, I'm not accusing you of thievery. I'm just saying that you're not like anybody else I've ever met. And for the record, my name is Sasha, not California."

He nodded sagely. "Very well, woman, call yourself what you will. You do not belong to me, so you are free to call yourself whatever name your father chose for you. Sasha. I do not disapprove. And my name is not simply Viking, but . . . I am called . . ." After all his great declaration and pronouncements, all at once he was at a loss. He glanced at her out of the corner of his eye, confused and flustered. "It would be better for now if you address me as you have been. It would be unseemly for you to be too familiar."

"Fine! Sit here all by yourself. I don't know what I'm going to do right now, but at least I know it's going to be a lot more worthwhile than trying to talk to you!"

Again he grabbed her sleeve as she started to go. There was something akin to fear in his eyes, and he cast them down quickly. "Please . . . please, Sasha. You must help me. It is a foolish thing, but I cannot seem to remember my name. Do you know it? It will not be improprietous of you to say it under these circumstances. I need to hear the sound of it in my head, and I cannot seem to do it for myself."

She didn't know whether to laugh or cry. For all his macho posturing and archaic opinions, here was a man in serious distress. He couldn't help who he was. But as she started to say she didn't know his name, he held up his hand to stop her. His eyes locked with hers.

"Before you answer, I have another, more important question."

"What is it?"

"Do you sleep?"

There was some question in her mind about whether he meant did she "sleep around." But one look at his face told her differently. "On a daily basis, you mean?"

He pressed his fingers to his temples. "I remember it as being one of life's pleasures. And yet I cannot remember what it feels like. I long for it, this sleep. But it does not happen for me. Why do you think that is? Do you think maybe the witch has cast a spell on me as well as my brother?"

"I can't say."

The seals barked below, and the Viking sprang to his feet, his lethargy at an end.

"My brother calls to me!" he said excitedly. "He tells me my name is Haakon, and he is right. I will go to him now."

Before Sasha could stop him, he yanked the hearing aid from his ear and tossed it to the ground. "I have no need of it," he said simply as he sprinted to the rope that hung over the cliff's edge. He winked at her and called, *"Jeg vil hjem. Jeg er lei meg, vi kommer ikke hit igjen."* Then he remembered she did not speak his native tongue. It disappointed him. "I am going home, California. I am sorry, but my brother and I are not coming here again. May you be wedded to a brave and sturdy man who will put many fine sons in you. Sons who can be proud of their mother."

Before she could respond, he grabbed the rope and threw himself over the side, scaling the sheer cliff with absolute ease.

"Kyle!" she shouted after him as she leaned perilously close to the edge. But he did not respond to the name, and then the ledge of rock between them made it so she could no longer see him.

Malcolm tested the tension on the rope, and she was grateful to see there still was some.

"He canna hear yer shoutin', Sasha. His hearin' aid's there on the ground by yer feet, remember? If he's no made a noose of the other end, lassie, there's hope he's still on his way down."

Sasha watched below, but there was no sign, one way or the other.

Over the din of the disgruntled birdlife, she shouted down the face of the cliff. "If you haven't killed yourself by pulling this ridiculous stunt, Kyle Maclennan, I'm going to kill you with my bare hands. Do you hear me?" There was no reply. She picked up his precious hearing aid and folded her fingers over it protectively. "You don't hear me at all, do you, Edinburgh?"

Emma sighed and leaned her head against Malcolm's shoulder. "Not precisely *Romeo and Juliet,* I suppose," she said. "I've seen better-organized balcony scenes and slightly more poetic examples. But I'll grant ye, never a more dramatic one. Ain't love grand, Malcolm, m'dear?"

Malcolm hurried to the cliff's edge to grab Sasha's ankle before she let her anger take her over the side. He gave Emma a telling look over his shoulder. "Love, it's the death of us all, one way or another, and well ye know it, Em."

Emma folded her arms across her chest as Sasha continued to yell over the side. "Oh, aye, but there are worse ways to go, eh?"

* * *

Carrie had disappeared. Frantic with worry, Rainey flashed the light in every direction inside the musty chamber. What little air there was in the enclosure was stifling with the smell of dirt, mold, and lichen. Here and there, she got glimpses of design that told her this portion of the structure had been open to air circulation at one time. But now it wasn't a place intended for the living, not of the human variety, at any rate.

The room was empty of whatever treasure and artifacts it may have once contained. Grave robbing was hardly exclusive to this millennium. But the smaller chambers that opened off the main room were also empty, as far as she could see. It left the unsettling question of what had become of Carrie.

"Carrie, where are you?" she called. The thudding echo her voice produced was like the sound of calling down a well. It was self-contained, restricted by the walls around her.

She heard a faint call in return. The echo of it bounced off the walls, confusing her. It sounded as if it had come from beneath the floor at one corner of the west wall. The lack of oxygen was making her light-headed, and she prayed she wouldn't tumble down some flight of stairs that she came upon by accident.

Carrie called her again, more distant this time. It was nightmarish to hear her and yet not know where she was and not be able to get to her. Rainey pressed her cheek against the west wall in hopes of hearing Carrie better. To her surprise, the wall began to turn. A portion of it had been constructed between upright supports of flat stone so that it could be turned smoothly on a central axis. With a gentle push, it gave easily beneath her hands. When she flashed the light beyond the door, she saw a steep, narrow stairway that had been carved through the solid rock of the cliff.

How many years must it have taken to construct such a feat

of winding engineering? she wondered. This time when Carrie called to her, the sound echoed strongly from the twisting stairs below. Carrie had no flashlight to guide her. How she was finding her way through the total darkness was a mystery—although it was true that there were only two possible directions to go, up or down.

"Wait for me, Care!" Rainey called cautiously.

Mines caved in as a result of loud noises, she knew. There was no reason to take any needless chances here. Though made of stone, the steps were worn down in the middle from centuries of use. The stairwell was no wider than the breadth of her arms, and if she had thought the main chamber lacking in air, it was an open field of sunshine and daisies compared to this place. She doubted the caretakers of old would have had the luxury of bringing along a torch of any kind, since the flame would have stolen all their meager supply of oxygen. It was not a situation that allowed for a leisurely pace.

As she hurried down the steps, trying to catch up to Carrie, she noticed that at regular intervals there were simple instructions of some kind, messages scratched in vertical, sticklike symbols. She had glanced over Matt's shoulder one time as he was deep in study to see a written language such as this. The messages on the wall differed in length and complexity. She could only hope they weren't curses and promises of harm directed at trespassers from other centuries. She and her family had no need of any further misfortune. She was about to call out to Carrie again when, all at once, she was there, standing on the stairs several yards below her.

"Carrie! Thank God! You scared me half to death. Don't ever run off like that again, sweetheart. You could have broken your neck, or gotten me to break mine."

Carrie didn't give her mother her characteristic smile as they continued down the steps. "I couldn't wait for you, Mama, be-cause if you told me I couldn't come to the cove, things would have gone very badly for everyone. There are so many good-byes to be said. I have to be there, Mama. Can you understand?"

Rainey felt a fresh set of carvings slide beneath her fingertips as she followed Carrie. "So many good-byes, Care?" She prayed she didn't mean a final farewell to her father.

"They've been waiting for a very long time. We just *can't* make them wait any longer."

Carrie quickened her pace, and Rainey had to struggle to keep up. The thin air was getting to her. She couldn't catch her breath.

"Do you have any idea how much further it is, Care?" she asked.

"Three more to go, Mama."

Rainey was about to ask three more what when her nostrils were teased with the faint scent of salt. The air was cooling and there was more of it. She was tempted to run the rest of the way. Her pulse began to race and a surge of hope rose inside her.

If they were wrong about the cove, not only would it be the biggest disappointment of her life, it might also seal Matt's fate. There was no time to search elsewhere today, and another night in the cold would almost surely kill him. This *had* to be right. As a faint hint of gray light appeared on the steps below them, she focused all of her heart, her energy, and her faith on the safe deliverance of Matthew Macinnes.

"Tha an chridhe toileach adhbhar-iongnaidh," she said to herself over and over again. It was a saying Matt often used. He had said it at Carrie's birth, and he was fond of saying it as they shared their marriage bed. It meant, "The willing heart is a source of wonder." As they raced down these steps that had en-dured the life spans of so many human generations, she called

upon the power of this amazing place and the power of the spirit she knew as Macha to give her back the man she loved. What she would have to offer in return if her wish was granted was more than she could think about at the moment.

Chapter 12

His hallucinations were becoming far more sophisticated, Matt decided. This one seemed incredibly real. It was the size of a full-grown man.

There was a vague familiarity about the newcomer, though he couldn't quite place the fellow. Like so many of the visions he had, most probably as the result of fever, this one struck him as being from a bygone time, whether earlier in this life or from some other existence he supposed he may have had. He no longer bothered to speculate.

There seemed little point in trying to sort it all out, any more than he could figure out how the silver necklace had gotten off his neck and back into the palm of his hand. He had no recollection of how it had happened, but he was glad he hadn't lost possession of the piece in the process. The one drawback was that he had not seen his little kittiwake for a while. He missed her.

The hallucination man had descended on him from above by way of a rope. A strange technique for a fever dream to use to materialize, it struck him. He contemplated the man's rope, which dangled a few feet away. He should have seen it as a means of escape, a means to scale the cliff to safety. Once perhaps. Now it was only a laughable bit of irony. He was too weak to pull himself over to it, much less make use of the thing to any solid purpose. If he had had the energy to dwell on it, the situation might have depressed him. As it was, he hardly gave it any more thought.

The hallucination had seen him where he sat next to his precious water source. It had even spoken a curt greeting to him in one of the strange tongues that had been whirling around inside his head since he had first found himself washed up in the cove. But he hadn't been able to put together the words to answer the hallucination's greeting, so the man had chosen to ignore him in favor of calling to the two seals who kept watch a few yards offshore.

Now and then, the hallucination tried to wave the seals in to the rocks, to what purpose Matt could not say. Each time the seals did not comply, the man would turn to him and make one gesture of frustration or another. This particular hallucination had a short fuse, from the look of him.

Matt saw no problem with this, since it was all a vision he had conjured up strictly for his own amusement, a figment of his deteriorating imagination. Such bits of showmanship helped to distract him from the biting cold and the fact that he was losing all the feeling in his extremities. He closed his weary eyes, wondering if the hallucination would still be there when he opened them again.

His mind wandered back to that peat fire he had dreamed about what seemed like a very long ago. He pictured the little girl and the dark-haired woman. It occurred to him that this lovely woman was twice familiar to him. Yes, he had seen her before as she was beside the fire. But he had also seen her standing at the top of a very high waterfall, a vision he had had not long ago.

Above the falls, she had been wearing a shining crown, a crown of stars. She had smiled down on him. Her name was

Sirona. Compelling, like the lady herself. He didn't know how he knew it, but he was absolutely sure of her name.

He said it to himself again, intrigued by the sound of it, like silk, that name. Sirona. And as he said it, the silver necklace warmed in his hand once more. It must have been very warm indeed for him to still be able to feel it. He wanted to hear her say his name, this Sirona of his visions. What peace it would bring him to know his name had graced her lips! He could face whatever blackness lay beyond this life if he could have that one simple gift.

It came to him as if it were flying in from across the sea like his little kittiwake, faint and distant at first, but growing in strength. In his head, he put the sound of his name together with the woman at the top of the falls. It was natural to do so. Like music, sensuous and sweet. He could float on it if he tried. He wondered if he could float *away* on it. Surely such a glorious sound had been sent from heaven. When it returned to its source, perhaps he could go with it. The idea made a kind of sense. He could almost be content with the notion.

But the voice was changing. As it drew nearer, it lost its angelic, melodic nature. It was demanding, until in the end, the sound of his own name became a stern and relentless command. The loss of the beauty of it angered and disappointed him. He had been ready to abandon his struggle for life.

The voice had been there to show him the way into oblivion. Now it called him back to the cold rocks and the endless pain. He was broken in so many ways. He had no desire to return his conscious mind to the misery of the cove.

There was no shame in being defeated when God and all of nature had decided your time was at an end. He had gotten a large portion of his heart to accept this. That stubborn leftover bit that still clung to the notion of rescue was too worn and tired to last much longer. Better just to slip away. A kindness really. A gift.

"Matt!"

Really! The woman's voice was becoming a nuisance. If he thought it would do any good, he would cover his ears against it. But since the voice was of necessity inside his head, there was no point in trying that solution.

"Matt! Open your eyes! For the love of God, Matt, come back to us!"

She was playing tricks on him now, this beautiful, cruel-hearted hallucination. If he opened his eyes, he would see nothing but his own worthless body and the gray sea. No, he was not going to fall for that again. He couldn't bear the raw disappointment of it. It occurred to him that he might like to see his little kittiwake nurse one more time, and the seals. Yes, the selkies. He loved them. But it would be wiser just to remember them in his head.

"Papa? Papa, please, you have to wake up! We need you. You have to wake up!"

Papa? There were two harpies now? Someone was shaking his shoulder. His head was pounding in rhythm to the jostling.

A soothing hand touched his brow. That was good. He was quite fond of that. Then something harsh and stinging was wiped across his head wound, and he howled in pain.

"Oh, God, I'm sorry, Matt, but I can't tell you how wonderful it is to hear you yell at me again," he heard the older harpy say in a trembling voice.

So it was true. They had been sent to torment him. Perhaps he had descended into hell while his eyes were closed. That would explain why the visions he treasured most were now causing him such terrible pain. Well, he decided, if hell had been his destination, he supposed he would be wise to get the lay of the land. He opened his eyes with a genuine sense of dread.

The cliff still loomed above him. His dread had been well founded. But leaning over him were two angels with tears in their eyes. No, not angels. His vision.

"Sirona," he said as best he could. "This belongs to you." He tried to lift his hand to give her the necklace, but his muscles would not respond, so he turned his head to where the silver chain lay tangled in his stiff fingers. She took the necklace from his hand and fastened it around her neck. It looked very right there, nestled among her dark curls. The little girl smiled with approval, and the woman brushed his lips with her own. Her lips were warm against his, and he decided that perhaps she was flesh and blood after all. He prayed she was.

"We're going to take you home, Matt," she said, as if he were of great value to her.

It sounded like a dream come true. He was convinced the woman and the girl were real. And whatever "home" they meant to carry him off to, he was more than willing to go. But then something extraordinary happened, and he was just as sure that they were indeed hallucinations.

The mists had closed in tightly around the cove, preventing sight of the open sea beyond. And in his fevered state, he heard the bark of a selkie transform into the sound of a woman singing a hauntingly beautiful song. The dark-haired woman rose from him without a word and walked toward the water.

"Gaelic," he said softly. He comprehended every word of the melancholy song of profound loss clearly.

"That's right, Papa," the little girl whispered in his ear. "You remember." She sat down beside him and supported his head against her knees so he could see what was taking place.

The man who had come by rope was standing in the water up to his knees. The cold waves crashed hard against him, but he seemed unaware of them. Now the woman joined him in the surf. Their eyes were trained on the two selkies who circled them swiftly as the lilting Gaelic song rose to the heavens. The cliff dwellers left their nests to follow its upward journey in a timeless circular ballet.

The female selkie paused before the dark-haired woman, and the woman knelt down into the water to embrace her. Matt had to rub his eyes to believe what he was seeing. The selkie rose out of the water, now a woman dressed in the ancient garb of the old Celtic tribes. Clearly, the two women had the look of mother and daughter as they held each other in joyous, tearful reunion.

But this wonderful sight had a very different effect on the man in the water. He looked upon the two women with rage and hatred.

"Macha! You are the heart of all that is evil, witch!" he shouted as he started toward the women, his fist raised.

Matt tried to rise. "He will harm them! We must do something to warn them, child!"

He was pitiably weak, and the girl was able to hold him back easily. "It's all right, Papa. Just wait. You'll see. All will be well."

Even as he doubted her words, the second selkie, the large male, swam between the man and the women, putting the full force of his weight and his will in the man's way. The man was angry beyond reason, but the selkie would give him no quarter.

Try as he would, the man could get nowhere within reach of the women. In fact, the women paid him little mind, so confident were they in the male selkie's strength and so taken were they with this rare opportunity to reunite.

In time, the man grew weary and breathless from fighting the selkie's interference and the constant pounding of the waves against his body. He sat down in the water, his eyes cast down, his head barely above the tide.

"I can fight you no longer," he said as he spat the salt water from his mouth.

"I am glad to hear you say this thing," a new male voice said.

The man looked up to find not the male selkie but a Viking in full battle regalia.

"Olgar! My brother!" he said in awe.

"You have changed little, Haakon," Olgar replied. He smoothed his bright-red beard with a real pride of ownership. "Always did you doubt what you could not squeeze in your hand." He laughed wholeheartedly at the ribald nature of his own statement, then reached down and dragged Haakon to his feet.

The two men embraced as brothers after the passage of more centuries than either of them could remember. They both turned to where the women stood among the waves, and Olgar clapped his brother on the back.

Haakon gave a sigh of defeat. "So you have been with the witch all this time, my brother."

"She is no witch as you mean it, little brother, nor was she ever." He snorted at Haakon's look of disbelief. "She possesses the sacred ways of the Celt women, I grant you. And her songs have a magic to them no man can resist. But her only wish was to return to her own people. It was all she ever wanted. I could not give it to her until this very day when she could be brought together with her daughter, Sirona. She still pines for her Celt husband. I know this. She must go to him in their strange heaven. Her kindness toward me has earned her an honored place at the table of her gods. I can keep her no longer."

He looked to the mists behind him. "Now, see here, my brother, her husband comes for her. I have had her all these centuries while he has known only emptiness and the sorrow of loss as he sat with his gods. My time with her was generous beyond what I deserved. Among her people, her husband was a king. He must no longer be denied his queen."

The figure of a mighty Celtic warrior shone brightly against the wall of mists. The two women smiled in greeting, and as their spirits of old rose toward the heavens, the dark-haired woman from beside the peat fire remained behind, waving her farewell to the heaven-bound family.

"I wish you peace!" she called to them.

Sirona and her father continued their journey, but Macha remained, a look of concern marring her happiness.

"Tend to your husband quickly, now, dear Rainey. Return the silver necklace to its rightful place at Glomach for the sake of all who have suffered beneath Thor's Hammer."

She paused and looked toward the heavens as if she heard a voice speaking to her from that source. "You are a gift to Sirona and to me, Rainey. When the time comes, if we are able, we will be a gift to you."

She smiled with a touch of sadness when she saw Sasha watching from the top of the cliff while Rainey stood below. Even so small a separation between a mother and daughter brought her sorrow. As she rose to join her husband and Sirona, Macha laid her hands over her heart.

"Take strength from those who love you, Sasha, for the trials to come are many and difficult. You must prevail. You have no choice. Seek counsel from Mar a' Ghealach, and I shall watch over you from the place beyond."

Sasha nodded her solemn thanks, and in the blink of an eye, Macha and her family were gone from sight. Rainey turned back to where Matt and Carrie watched from the shore.

Matt watched her walk toward them through the waves. "Rainey." He said her name as if it were a prayer. "I remember."

She knelt beside him, shivering in her wet clothing. "Some people will do anything for attention, Stanford," she said as she grinned at him through her chattering teeth.

He made his arm respond so he could reach up and touch her cheek. "You're real," he said in amazement.

As she kissed the back of his cold hand to verify his conclusion, Carrie tugged at her sleeve.

"Look, Mama." She pointed to the two Vikings.

Olgar had his arm wrapped firmly and companionably around Haakon's shoulders. They had no more need of Kyle's body as they rose on the mists to enter their paradise. Kyle stood shivering in the waves, witnessing this event, struck with awe and confusion as he tried to take inventory of himself.

Olgar could be heard to say, "There is much to be said for this second life I have led, brother. Never did I want for food to hunt. Never did I spend a lonely day with my beloved Macha at my side. What joy it gave me to hear her songs today after so long a time. I thought never to have them dance upon my old ears again." He sighed with a hint of wistfulness. "But you and I, little brother, are long overdue in Valhalla." He smiled down at Haakon's look of amazement. "Even though I should give you a good thrashing first for killing me, eh?" He rubbed his fist against the top of Haakon's head.

"Ah, but you laid me low as well, Olgar. At least, for the most part," Haakon countered. He tried to break away from Olgar's iron grip, but even now he was no match for his older brother.

Olgar's laugh rang out against the cliff. "You were the aggressor, remember, my brother? I wanted nothing to do with your self-righteous anger. If I had wanted you dead, nothing could have saved you. As it was, it was through Macha's good graces that you were spared. She could not bear the thought of your death, knowing what you meant to me. So she tempered the warlord's anger, reducing it from what would have meant a death sentence to a simple beating."

"Do you mean to say the witch did me this favor?"

"I have told you she was no witch. But in answer to your question, yes, it was she who helped you in this way."

Haakon gave this some serious consideration. His brother had never lied to him. And there was no reason for him to do so now. "Then I shall sing her praises in Valhalla, Olgar."

"So shall we both. But you must remember, I have grown accustomed to a pleasing singing voice, Haakon, so I must ask you to sing her praises softly."

Haakon was like a puppy at his brother's heels. "So be it. Do you know the way, Olgar? Do you know how to get us to Valhalla?"

Olgar gave him a sly wink. "It has never been a secret, little brother. The gods are satisfied with us now. Valhalla waits above us. You have only to look and you will see it there."

"I do see it, brother! We are on our way to Paradise."

They rose and disappeared within the mists.

Rainey scribbled a quick note and attached it to the end of the rope. When she tugged on it, the message traveled slowly toward the top of the cliff, and she returned her attention to Matt. She glanced down at his injured leg, so crudely bound, and felt his anguish as she looked into his tired eyes.

"It seems a little silly to say now, but we always knew you were alive and that we would find you. Are you in much pain?" she asked gently. He closed his eyes, and she was afraid he might lose consciousness. But he returned his sight to her, his eyes filled with wonder that she was still at his side.

"What pain there may be makes no difference to me anymore, *mo chridhe*," he said with a valiant attempt at a smile.

Rainey smoothed the blood-caked hair from his forehead as a tear slid down her cheek. He had used his favorite term of endearment for her. Whatever pieces were missing from his memory, this one pivotal phrase renewed her faith in the future as nothing else could.

He sighed from deep in his soul and turned his eyes toward Carrie. "Tell me about my home, sweetheart. Your name is so near to my mind. I want to bring it back. With your help, it will come to me."

Carrie folded her arms across her chest, pleased to take on the cherished role of storyteller. There was a distant bark from the top of the cliffs. "First of all, there's Angus," she said confidently, despite her mother's dubious look.

"Angus. Does that mean I have a son?"

Carrie gave a little laugh. But when she caught her mother's eye, she did her best to return to a pious expression. "No sons, Papa, not yet."

Rainey gave her a searching look. "And just what does that mean, young lady?"

"Please, Mama, it's Papa's turn," Carrie said with a scolding frown.

Kyle reached them. He stood staring at Matt with a very subdued look on his face.

"Professor Mac, it's grand to see ye, sir," he said humbly. "Ye've led us quite a merry chase."

Matt turned to Rainey for help this time. "No sons. Is this Angus, then?" he asked, shifting his eyes toward Kyle. He was tired and hardly up to a game of Twenty Questions. But he didn't want to miss a single word of anything that was said. He was ravenous for any information about his life, no matter how trivial. Now that he was certain Rainey's love for him had endured, he feared nothing about the past.

"No, silly, that's Kyle. I'll give you a clue," Carrie provided. "Angus lives with Emma and Malcolm. Now do you know?"

Two more unknowns into the question. It hardly helped. "I'm sorry." The notion of sleep was becoming almost irresistible as he struggled to make his weary brain work.

Rainey gave Carrie a look of warning.

"Okay, I guess I have to make this really easy for you," Carrie said in disappointment. "We live beside a loch. You do remember what a loch is, don't you, Papa?"

He tried to get the rusty wheels in his head to move. He knew this one! "Fishing," he said, inordinately proud of himself. And there was more. "I used to go fishing on the shores of the loch."

"With . . . ?"

His eyes lit with excitement. "I used to go fishing on the loch with Malcolm!" he said in a rush of joy. "Malcolm. Malcolm." Just the sound of the familiar name of his lifelong friend filled his head with childhood memories. It was an incredibly rich beginning, and it made him voracious for more.

"Now we're getting somewhere," Carrie said with satisfaction. "And Malcolm is married to . . . ?"

"Wait, ye said it earlier," Matt said as he pressed trembling fingers to his temple. "If I can just picture them together." The light of revelation shone on his face. "Emma, by God! Malcolm is married to Emma." Now came the trump card. "And they have a wee Scots terrier named Angus, who dearly loves sausages and playing with the daughters of Clan Macinnes." He closed his eyes and smiled, reveling in the return of identity, the return of loving family and friends.

When he opened his eyes again, he was looking at Kyle. "But you? Kyle, isn't it? I still can't seem to place ye. Are ye kin, then?"

The color rose in Kyle's cheeks, but he returned Matt's gaze squarely. "Forgive me, sir, for I know yer askin' somethin' of me. But I cannot hear yer words, and the device I normally wear to help the problem seems to be elsewhere. I apologize. If ye'd care to write yer questions down, I'll do my best to oblige ye."

Rainey and Carrie exchanged a look. While Kyle had shared Haakon's spirit, his hearing had not been impaired. Now, with Haakon's departure, the deafness was even more profound. The brief miracle was at an end, making the harsh reality of loss all the more cruel. Rainey motioned for Kyle to come and sit with them. There was hardly any other place for him to sit while they waited for help from the others.

But he politely declined the offer and chose to stand away from them at the water's edge, his eyes focused on the rolling mists above him. He had been given no lasting gifts from heaven.

Matt saw the sorrow in his demeanor. "Who is he, Rainey? Has he always been this way?"

"He's from the university at Edinburgh. He was a teaching assistant for a Professor Cameron. You knew them both from the language and archaeology departments."

He considered the young man. "There are still so many holes in my memory. I remember much of Edinburgh, certainly, and Cameron. He was . . . on the plane with me, although he was in the habit of traveling first class while I settled for coach." He withdrew from them at the dark memory. Without looking at Rainey, he asked, "Any word of other survivors?"

"At last report, they were saying *no* survivors. We found you, Matt, so it's not impossible that someone else made it." His face was so pale, she wanted to change the subject without further discussion.

There would be a world of time to come to terms with the crash. But avoiding the mention of the disaster might be just as harmful to his psychologial well-being. There was no way to know.

"But this Kyle," Matt pursued, "my recollection of him is rather different from what you have told me. I suppose one could say he was a teaching assistant. He helped with research and the like, but for the love of the subject matter, not for much in the way of a paycheck. Although he probably could have used an extra bit of cash. Cameron confided in me that the lad was on a charity scholarship. Lots of gumption, but not a soul in the world."

Rainey glanced at Kyle while he stood forlornly at the edge of the tide. They knew so little about him. Then she leaned down and kissed Matt tenderly. In the middle of so much trouble, it was Kyle's welfare that concerned him. Here was something else about Matthew Macinnes that would never change.

"Do you have any idea how much I love you, Stanford?" she asked with a smile that promised him treasure beyond his wildest dreams once he was able to take advantage of the offer.

He looked into her eyes and saw not only his past but his future as well. "I suppose ye'll have to remind me now and again, Harvard, just to keep my memory fresh, ye ken?"

She rejoiced that he was beginning to sound like his old self again. There were so many prayers of thanks to be said, she didn't know where to begin.

"The others will be here soon, Matt. I'm not sure how we're going to get this done, but we're going to get you out of here just as quickly as we can." She looked down at that miserable break in his leg and felt the contents of her stomach begin to rise.

When their eyes met again, he read her pain, and it brought the horror of his leg into fresh, terrible focus. His nerve endings began to throb and tingle, and he made the mistake of trying to shift his weight slightly to steady the flow of blood to the injury. The strength and adrenaline drained from him as bone splinter scraped against bone splinter in hard contact. He gritted his teeth and groaned against the agony of it. But he couldn't shift it back, and he could gain no control over it. It was chewing him up with a massive set of teeth, and his sight began to telescope into blackness.

"Not dyin'," he whispered to reassure himself as much as the others. "Blackin' out. Up the . . . cliff . . . while I'm out cold, please God." He collapsed against Rainey's side.

"Carrie!" she said urgently. "There's no more time, sweetheart. We have to get him up the steps before he regains consciousness. Get Kyle's attention. We'll need his help. And hopefully, we'll run into the others on the way. We're going to need everybody to get him up to the truck. I just pray he doesn't have any internal injuries we're not aware of." She looked down at what terrible shape he was in. "It's so risky to move him. There's no telling what harm we may do in the process. But it has to happen right now. We have bandages and iodine, but we have nothing in the way of painkillers. If he comes around halfway up the stairs, I may have to slug him on the jaw for his own good." Carrie looked properly scandalized. "And somebody may have to knock me out, too, because I can't bear to see him in so much pain."

They pieced their sweaters and jackets into a makeshift hammock, and between the three of them, they managed to get Matt around the turn in the cove's wall to the cavelike structure of the staircase. The opening was very narrow, and invisible from the water. If the tide had not been out, it would have been under the waves. Only one obstacle stood in their way—a small gray-and-white gull.

Rainey sent Carrie to shoo it away while she and Kyle supported Matt's weight. But the kittiwake would not budge, no matter what Carrie tried. It was absolutely resolute in its determination not to let them pass. There was intelligence in the bird's bright eyes, and none of them had the heart to throw something at it. But time was of the essence.

Kyle took note of the bird's demeanor. "This is her place. She wants us to pay a toll to pass," he said, fascinated by the kittiwake's resourcefulness.

"A toll?" Rainey exclaimed. "You've got to be kidding! What do we do, hand her a pound note?"

Her words were lost on Kyle, but he called Carrie over and

unfastened his watch. It was a cheap drugstore variety. But in spite of all the salt water and rock climbing, the mechanism was still ticking away merrily, and the shiny metal band still held its silver finish, for the time being. Carrie gave him a smile of understanding as she took the watch from his hand.

"Place it over there on the rock with all the droppin's, if ye will, Carrie," he said to her as she started to walk away. "Make it grand so she'll know we understand she's the queen of this place, ye ken?"

Carrie nodded. She went over to the smooth rock Kyle had indicated and set the watch down with great ceremony.

The kittiwake cocked her head, first to one side, then the other, as she considered this shiny new offering. It wasn't the object the woman now wore around her neck. That would take some adjustment. But the new object would be easier to hold in her bill, and it was making a lovely noise, like a hundred tiny mussel shells cracking on the rocks, one at a time. It was like the sound of food.

There could be no doubt that it was a worthy prize, like nothing else she had ever seen. And from the look of things, these upright members of the Creature's peculiar species were giving it to her without a fight. A far easier proposition than the necklace.

She cocked her head toward the skies above. Others were already eyeing her prize. If she hesitated, someone else would get it. She was the one who had earned it by giving the Creature the best fresh herring she could catch and even sharing her precious source of fresh water. She shared her water source with no one else.

With a slow, regal gait, she waddled over to the rock for a closer look. It was a good bargain, she decided. Yes, she would let them pass. Presumptuous species that they were, when she looked back toward the opening to the stair cave, she saw that the trespassers were already gone. It was a mild insult, but one she could get over. After all, they were a pretty stupid breed.

Next year, if she was not too busy with her nest, she would watch for the Creature on the rocks again. Perhaps he was the migratory sort. Hopefully, he would not bring her any aluminum foil. She had to admit she still had a shameful weakness for the stuff.

Chapter 13

Making their way down the cliff stairs had been challenge enough. Getting back up them in the dark with Matt was a punishment. They met Sasha, Emma, and Malcolm coming down from above, but the stairway was so narrow, the advent of so many bodies in one place only robbed them of what little air there was.

Without a word, Kyle somehow squeezed past them all, grabbing Malcolm on the way up the stairs. Shortly thereafter, the two men returned with a piece of plywood from the truck's bed and a hefty quantity of rope.

They eased Matt onto the board cautiously. The stairs were extremely steep, so it still took some doing to keep him steady. But now they could concentrate on hauling him to the top more efficiently and without as much risk of injuring him further.

When they reached the light and air above, they all dropped to the ground in exhaustion. But there was no time to rest.

Rainey's clothes were soaked with seawater and sweat, and she shivered as the wind cut through to her skin. She was utterly miserable after only a short while. It struck her that Matt had endured this kind of wet misery for days.

"Come on!" she said as she tried to catch her breath. "We have to get him to a hospital. There's no more time!" She struggled to her feet, and the others did the same.

Once Matt was under the woolen blankets in the back of the ambulance, everyone breathed a sigh of relief. He needed real medical attention, but they had done all they could for him for the moment. All that was left was to huddle around him to lend their added warmth.

Rainey kissed Matt's forehead lovingly. He alternated between fever and chills, and she had to pray they hadn't done him any serious harm by moving him. If they had stayed where they were to wait for help, darkness and the weather would have closed in on them. Faced with another frigid night on the beach, Matt might well have been lost to them. She shuddered and tucked the blankets more securely around his shoulders.

He groaned, and it looked as though he might regain consciousness before they reached help. But if he did approach wakefulness, the pain from being moved must have proved overwhelming, because he slipped away from them again.

Rainey looked at Emma with concern. "He's so pale. On the one hand, I'm grateful he's so out of it. On the other hand, when he's like this, I can't tell how he really is."

Emma gave her a guarded smile. "There's little more we can do, one way or the other, love, until we reach civilization. For now, it's best that he can't feel each bump and stone beneath the wheels. It's a torture no man should have to bear."

As she smoothed the hair back from his face, Rainey tried to picture him at home, standing beside the loch with the fresh spring breezes off the heather blowing sunlight across his face. More than anything else on earth, she wanted to make that vision a reality. It was going to happen, no matter the cost.

She caressed his cheek. The old scar there felt hot to her

touch, as if it just been burned into his flesh. There were so many scars, old and new. He had suffered enough for now. It was time for their lives to take a turn for the better.

"I swear to you, we're all going home to the Highlands, Stanford. I'll make it happen," she whispered in his ear. He didn't stir, but she would have sworn his breathing came a little easier.

Kyle sat in silence next to Sasha, his teeth chattering from the cold dampness of his clothing. He hadn't protested when Malcolm climbed into the driver's seat.

The return to deafness had taken him down at the knees. Whatever brief light of optimism he had experienced while communing with Haakon's spirit had been extinguished into total darkness. The adrenaline mustered to bring Matt up the cliff was wearing off now. It meant thoughts of himself had time to creep into his consciousness. They were unwelcome thoughts.

He was back in his old world. And without the hearing aid that he had tossed aside so casually on the cliff, he was more closed off than ever. He dared not speak, for fear his voice would be overly loud or shrill. It was very difficult to gauge these things.

His teeth felt like they would crack from their chattering. He couldn't tell how loud they were being. Perhaps he was rattling the walls with the noise. There was no way for him to know, unless someone gave him a telling look. He couldn't trust himself.

It was tearing him apart to sit so near Sasha and be powerless to communicate with her. He needed a piece of paper and a pen. But it would be too humiliating to scribble out his thoughts and hopes for everyone to see.

There were so many things, large and small, he wanted to say to her. Silly things. Profound things. And yet he could say nothing at all, because to do so would make him look like a fool.

Sasha wrapped her extra sweater across Kyle's knees. It was

the only thing she could think to do to get past the barriers he had put up around himself. She could deal with his hearing loss. That was a physical thing, a *small* thing as far as she was concerned. It was a part of who he was, to be sure. But there was much more going on with him right now. His inability to hear was just the most visible symptom of all that was truly in turmoil inside him.

The incident on the beach had affected him profoundly. She knew that. How could it *not* shake his world to its foundation to have the spirit of another person from centuries ago take possession of his mind and heart? Some might never recover from such an experience. But it was more his own problems from the here and now that were plaguing him at the moment, Sasha decided.

The question was whether all that stubborn pride of his would ever permit him to accept help from someone who was determined to love him in spite of himself. He certainly didn't own the patent on stubborn. She came from a long line of stubborn, and as far as she was concerned, he might just as well surrender right now.

Kyle nodded his thanks for the sweater, but took it and laid it across Matt's chest instead. Sasha smiled at his generosity, then reached into the pocket of her jeans. She took Kyle's hand and pressed the hearing aid into his palm. She had seen to its safety.

He looked at the device with very mixed emotions. It was his curse and it was his salvation. For a brief time today, for the first time in memory, he hadn't needed it. He had experienced the miracle of sound that the rest of the world took for granted. He wanted that miracle back!

Didn't he deserve it as much as anyone else? A thin, small voice in the back of his head, a voice from his childhood, told him that he didn't, that he was no one. Perhaps if he had been worthy of anyone's love, he would have been given what everyone else had been granted freely.

This wasn't the voice of a rational, adult perspective. He fully recognized that. But it was a voice that had been his constant companion for so many years, he never questioned it. The voice knew him for what he was—abandoned, disconnected, slow-witted, handicapped.

The neat plastic device in his hand was a symbol of his inadequacy, his inferiority, for the whole of Creation to see and recognize as the badge of his shortcomings. He was not a man who permitted himself bouts of self-pity. It wasn't in his nature. And he hated himself all the more for indulging in it now, of all times, when so vital a man as Matthew Macinnes's life hung in the balance.

But all the years of neglect and abuse had taken their toll, the years of being hit in the head for not paying attention, of being told to step aside so that the children with all five senses in good working order could pass him by for adoption. He stared at the hearing aid until it felt like he was boring a hole through it with his eyes.

Then, to his surprise, Sasha took the device from his hand and pressed it gently into his ear. Whether she was aware of it or not, it was an extremely intimate move, one he would have cherished earlier in the day. Now it struck him as an ugly, piteous act, and he couldn't bring himself to look at her, no less thank her.

There was a bit of static, then the reliable little device started to do its job. His hearing was no better than it had been before his encounter with Haakon. It was also no worse.

He leaned his head back against the side of the ambulance and closed his eyes as they bumped over yet another jagged rock. Somewhere in his heart he was grateful to Sasha for saving the hearing aid. Somewhere else in his heart, he wished he could have gone to Valhalla with Haakon and Olgar, so at least in that heavenly setting, he might have heard them sing Macha's praises. But Valhalla was not his heaven. If there *was* a possibility of heaven waiting for him at the end of his journey through this life, he wondered if he could ever find a place there.

When he opened his eyes again, he found Rainey's perceptive blue eyes watching him closely. It made him want to curse his own weakness. She sensed his beaten state of mind so strongly, it was distracting her from her primary concern for her husband.

The marriage she and Professor Macinnes shared was the stuff of legend in so many ways. He would have felt blessed to his soul to know a fraction of such love for a single day, no less a lifetime. But his turmoil must have shown on his face. It made him feel selfish for distracting her. Worse still, her slow, sad smile only reminded him of Sasha, and he turned away, only to be met by Sasha's gaze. He was surrounded by these extraordinary women. There was no escape.

He had every reason to believe they would float through his dreams, even if he put a thousand miles between himself and their glorious presence. Out of self-defense, he looked at Emma. But she could see right through him as easily as the others.

"Go on, lad," Emma said kindly, "ye must have questions about what happened. Out with 'em."

At first he was tempted to say he had no questions, since he didn't know where to begin. But looking at the faces around him, he was quite sure they wouldn't let him get away with such a tactic. And, besides, what did he have to lose? He leaned forward, his eyes focused on Rainey in the hope that she would lend him strength.

"What the hell happened to me on that beach back there,

missus? Am I losin' my mind? Because if I am, are ye all losin'
it with me? I mean to say, I find myself sittin' neck-deep in the
North Sea, arguin' with seals and huggin' imaginary Vikings."
He raked his hand through his hair. "Now, maybe such like is
everyday lunch for you folks, but I for one am a bit puzzled
by the whole business. I mean, am I goin' to be givin' a classroom lecture one day and suddenly start spoutin' Norwegian
and swingin' an invisible war club over my head? I need to
know the answer, or I'm packin' for Bedlam."

Rainey gave Sasha a look that told her she could field this
one. Sasha started to reach for Kyle's hand, but thought better
of it for the moment. He was clearly on edge, and she didn't
want to push him any more than he had already been pushed.

"I don't think you have to worry, Kyle," she began. "You see,
when these things happen, it's most often linked to a particular
place or thing, like the beach, for example, or the necklace."
She stared at the silver necklace at her mother's throat. The
piece struck a very strong chord with her. "I don't know how far
you wish me to go with this, the fact of the matter is, you were
needed there on those godforsaken rocks. Haakon needed you.
He had been waiting for centuries to be reunited with his
brother. He could not have found peace without your help. So,
even though it wasn't something you were given a chance to
volunteer for or something you even understood, it was very
important to us all that you were there. There was a reason we
needed you more than anyone else in the world. We owe you an
enormous debt of thanks."

He turned to her at last, and she blushed as she tucked a dark
curl behind her ear, a habit she had learned from her mother.

"So what yer tellin' me, Sasha, is that the rest of ye don't
really understand why these things happen to ye any more than
I do." In a way, it was a relief to him. In another way, it only
made it all more mysterious and perplexing.

Sasha touched his sleeve. "What I'm saying, Edinburgh, is that when these things happen, it's always for a reason, a very important reason. And when we've accomplished what we must, some sense of how we have helped make things right in the greater scheme of things is revealed to us. We may never understand all of it. But we know in our hearts that everything we do for the sake of those who lived so long ago contributes to the balance of our world here and now.

"These things must be done from time to time. Now and again, they must be done through us." She looked so deeply into his eyes, there was no space for him to back away. "And it happens through you, too, it seems, Kyle. At times, it feels like a curse, I know. But at other times, as my father would say, it's a gift."

Kyle leaned his head back again. "A gift."

Sasha gave him a dazzling smile. "Just as we are all a gift to one another."

An innocent statement. For Kyle, she might as well have said, "Take me now!" for the response his heart and body had to her words. She was telling him that because of all his trials back on the beach, and perhaps because of something more, he was now to be a permanent fixture in her world, whether he liked it or not. And he liked it to his soul, fool that he was. She didn't know him. Wasn't he a stranger in their midst?

Or had this family known him for centuries, and he simply had no memory of it? Here was the offer of the sense of belonging he had craved all his born days. And yet, it was all so strange. He closed his eyes and tried to train his thoughts on something real, something concrete, like the fine points of the sport of rugby. But Sasha sighed wistfully beside him, and he knew he would gladly lay down his life for her, if it suited her fancy. She didn't even need to ask. She could wear his heart for all to see, or wear it for shoe leather. Just so long as she wore it.

What ragged thoughts of rugby he could dredge up didn't work worth a damn. He was a man possessed. Possessed by total strangers from the distant past and utterly possessed by the woman beside him.

When the little house next to Noltland Castle came into view, Rainey wasn't sure what to expect. There was a pickup truck parked there now, which meant the owners were probably back and sorely aware of their missing vehicle. Whether they would meet the weary rescuers with concern or a shotgun had yet to be seen.

As they pulled up to the garage, a gray-haired couple in their late seventies stood in the doorway to the house. Though there was no sign of artillery, the man frowned at the road-worn condition of his favorite collectible.

The couple approached the truck cautiously, but when little Carrie was the first one to jump out of the back, they relaxed visibly. As the man walked up to the cab, the woman ventured a peek into the back. One look at Matt and her whole demeanor changed.

"Howard!" she called. "Incoming!"

Howard had his hand on the cab door. He hadn't said a word to Malcolm in the driver's seat, but it was clear he wasn't a happy man. At the sound of his wife's call, however, he let go of the handle and hurried to where she was already folding down the tailgate.

"Head injury, possible internals, possible trauma. Don't move him, Liz," Howard said firmly. He grabbed Kyle by the sleeve and rushed toward the house, all other business set aside for now. When they returned, Howard was carrying a canvas stretcher and Kyle had a box of medical supplies. While the stretcher was vintage World War II, the supplies were quite new.

Liz was already checking Matt's vital signs with professional skill. Howard climbed into the truck with surprising agility, considering his years, and set about a thorough examination.

Rainey sat with Matt's head cradled in her lap. The couple ignored her completely as she stroked his hair. These two efficient strangers went about their work with the utter confidence of decades of experience. They compared diagnoses with each other as they worked, going down a mental checklist cooperatively as if it were something they did a hundred times each day. In no time, they had stabilized Matt's bad leg and seen to all of his external injuries.

Liz acknowledged Rainey at last. "We can't make any guarantees about internal damage, ye understand." She raised her clear blue eyes. "How did this happen?"

"He was in a plane crash. Maybe you heard about it on the news." The couple exchanged a look of surprise. Apparently they had heard about the crash. Rainey extended her hand. "My name is Rainey Macinnes. This is my husband, Matt. We can't thank you enough for your help. And I'm sorry we got your wonderful ambulance so dirty."

She had held up through it all, forcing her fears back into that dark little hole in her heart. She had been a trooper. But now, as these kind strangers looked at her expectantly, the tears streamed down her face and the knot in her throat made it impossible to speak. She could only stare at them, the days of pain and uncertainty written clearly in her eyes.

Liz laid her hand on Rainey's arm comfortingly. "Steady, love. I'm Elizabeth Henderson, and this is my husband, Howard. I think we have matters well in hand." She looked down at Matt. "Your husband is a very determined man. Not many could pull through what he must have endured. But I think Howard would agree with me, once he's been to hospital to have that leg tended to properly, there's a good chance he'll be right as rain."

Rainey smiled her thanks. It was all she could manage for the moment.

Matt began to stir, and Howard reached inside his box of supplies. "Does yer mister have allergies or adverse reactions to any drugs, Mrs. Macinnes?"

"Not that I know of. It's never come up before."

Howard nodded his understanding. "I'm goin' to ask him a question or two, then I'm goin' to give him a bit of painkiller. I'm of the opinion that if he had serious internals, we would have lost him by now. But if he can give us any additional information about where it hurts, it'll be a reassurance."

"I don't want him to suffer, Dr. Henderson."

Howard cleared his throat. "I thank ye for the compliment, Mrs. Macinnes, but I'm not a doctor. Liz and I were medics durin' the war. We served in the same unit. Then we did a number of years with the Red Cross and the local Search and Rescue. And just between you and me, as a team, Liz and I were a sharper pair of tacks than a lot of those pampered white coats with their fancy sheepskins." He gave his wife a flirtatious wink. "But, please, call me Howard, since we're all friends now."

Everyone was lined up across the back of the ambulance, waiting for any news on Matt's condition. Rainey smiled and nodded to them, and they let go a collective sigh of relief. She had never loved this ragtag crew more.

Matt stirred again and called out her name. He opened his eyes slowly and looked up at her as if she were a vision from heaven. But the pain quickly clouded his eyes, and once Howard had asked the questions about the extent and location of all the injuries, it was a blessing to see Matt drift into the welcome oblivion induced by the painkiller.

Rainey felt a new sense of urgency. "We have to get him to a hospital as soon as possible. You've both been so kind. We can't impose on your hospitality any further. Is there a local ambulance service we can call, some way to get him to civilization?" As much as she was grateful for all that the old ambulance had helped them to accomplish, she was ready for a little modern speed.

Liz and Howard exchanged a look. "Well, Mrs. Macinnes, the fact of the matter is, yer transportation is already on its way."

"You're kidding! But how did you know when we would be here?"

Liz pressed her lips together and gave her husband a telling look. "When we got back with our supplies, the winds had blown yer note a ways from the house. We found it about an hour ago, of course. But when Howard discovered that the Ritz was gone, he called the authorities straight off. That old warhorse is his pride and joy, ye see, and the merest thought that it had gone missin' sent him into quite a tizzy. It's not easy to find a bit of privacy on the front, mind ye. Durin' the war, this old thing is where the two of us spent the nearest thing we had to a honeymoon. That's why we call it the Ritz."

Howard cleared his throat to the point of pain. "Aye, well, what was I to think? She's quite a prize to the collectors these days. No tellin' what she's worth on the open market." He gathered his medical supplies and started to climb out of the truck. "We'll leave yer mister where he is, Mrs. Macinnes. No point jostling him about for no reason."

Liz leaned closer to Rainey and said for her ears only, "We could be livin' on kelp in one of those tide caves down by the beach and that man would never so much as consider sellin' a tire off this old buggy." She patted the floor lovingly. "Ye'd never know it," she said raising her voice for Howard's benefit, "but he's a sentimental old softie in his dotage. Daft as ye please." She smiled in the face of his censuring look.

"So, the police are on their way?" Rainey asked with a note of tension. "I mean, I'll be happy to answer their questions and pay for any damages we have caused. It was never our intention to commit a crime. But we can't have any more delays in getting Matt to a hospital."

Liz handed her a pristine linen handkerchief. "There, now, lass, clean yerself up. We're hardly goin' to press charges. After all, ye were on a genuine mission of mercy, the kind of thing this old truck was built for. I know my Howard. He couldn't be prouder that the Ritz still has it in her. Ye know how men are. If she's still got it, he's still got it, ye ken. Why, I'd be willin' to bet he won't even wash the mud off her till he's had a chance to show her off to his card-playin' mates down the road."

The sound of a helicopter beating its way northward made them all turn as one. Kyle was the first to announce that the vehicle was one they had seen before.

Rainey's legs were stiff from sitting so long as she climbed out of the ambulance just in time to see Jerry's unsmiling face behind the controls. It didn't take a lip-reader to make out the string of curses he shouted to himself at the sight of so many familiar faces.

Once everyone was settled in the chopper and the thank-yous were said to the Hendersons, Rainey turned to Jerry with a smile. "We're very glad to see you, Jerry."

"I wish I could say the same, mum. But ye found yer husband, at least."

"We did indeed. Has there been any more word of survivors?"

"No, mum. The searches have been called off till the first of the week. I don't suppose there'll be much point by then." He surveyed the rugged terrain beneath them. "Yer husband's a lucky man, mum. *Bloody* lucky."

Rainey glanced over her shoulder to all the loving faces gathered around Matt. "I'd say we're all pretty lucky, Jerry."

Chapter 14

He was dreaming about his kittiwake nurse. She was giving him a stern look for his laziness. Well deserved, he supposed.

It occurred to him that she was his only concern. For whatever reason, the cold was no longer a problem. Nor was the pain. Perhaps he had finally crossed that final threshold he had been eluding for so long.

The scent of lavender and lemon teased his nostrils, a memory of home. In his dream, the kittiwake ruffled her pristine feathers as if to be done with him, or maybe as a kind of good-bye. Sounds of a crackling fire distracted him. Was he returning to the vision of the peat fire?

Hushed voices—female. Selkies? But, no, the selkies were gone. Where? They had found their way to heaven. Lucky selkies.

He considered the risky proposition of stretching his sore muscles. It would bring him dangerously close to wakefulness and send him into a cycle of pain he might never be able to conquer. But the urge to move was irresistible. The scent of lavender again—it gave him courage.

With utmost care, he flexed the muscles in his hands. Not suffering the cold was a tremendous help. This much was doable.

He took a long, deep breath. The ache of exposure in his lungs was not nearly as strong. When he flexed his arms, he realized he was covered with something light and deliciously soft.

There had been a lot of noise before. He couldn't say how long ago. But it was quiet now, except for the comforting snap and hiss of the fire. It didn't sound like a hospital. Nor did it sound anything like the cove. *It sounded like home.*

With the potential for profound disappointment hovering at his shoulder, he opened his eyes. Perhaps he had gone to heaven after all. He was home in the safety of his own bedroom. The hearth was there with its carved double swans symbol from *The Book of Kells*. He recognized its outline even though his eyes were none too clever in their focus. His exquisite wife leaned down and kissed him adoringly on the cheek.

"Rainey. *Mo chridhe.*" It was salvation to say her name.

Apparently he was not as close to death as he had suspected because that simple, sisterly kiss of hers brought on a parade of lusty possibilities that would most probably put him into a coma and have them barring the Gates of Heaven.

"Hello, sleepyhead," she said softly. Her warm smile made that parade in his head a far more crowded place.

He smiled back. "So, there's a need to talk to me as if I'm three years old, is there? Is the brain damage permanent, then?"

She sighed luxuriously and teased the stubble along his jaw with her fingertips. "Your brain is just like it always was, Macinnes, stubborn, inquisitive, and full to the brim with stuff nobody cares about but you."

"Ever the sweet talker," he said with a smile. "Have a care, woman, or such flattery will land you on yer back in my bed."

Rainey gave him a sly, sideward glance. "You mean this bed? The bed I have to make each day, whose sheets I wash and hang out to dry just for your pleasure?" she asked with a hint of mischief.

"Aye, the same. I've always had a fondness for upstairs maids. They're so grateful for the slightest bit of attention, banished as they are to the loftier climes."

"Is that right?" she replied evenly. "I would have thought you'd be more partial to scullery maids, considering your usual appetites."

"Speaking of which, I'm famished. Is there any food about the house?"

She smoothed the sheets lovingly. "What sounds good to you?"

"Anything. Everything! That is, everything but herring. I'd prefer to stay clear of herring for a while."

Rainey shrugged at his preference. "How about hot tea and toast with some of Emma's strawberry preserves for a start?"

" *'S math sin!* Bring it on, love! It's the stuff of dreams come true, I promise ye." He relaxed and stretched his lower body out of reflex, before he had time to prepare himself for the pain. He braced himself quickly, but the pain in his leg was only somewhere in the medium range. Compared to how it had been before, it was nothing. Here was a true gift from God. But it also made him suspicious. He took Rainey's hand into his own. "Am I cruisin' on morphine, then?"

She sat down lightly on the edge of the bed and stroked his hair back from his worried brow. "Don't flatter yourself, mister. Morphine has to go to our fighting boys at the Front." His look of total confusion was priceless, but she took pity on him. "They used morphine at the start when we got you back to civilization. Once we got you up those miserable stairs in the cliff . . ."

He looked at her in surprise. "Yer tellin' me there were *stairs* to the top, *mo chridhe*? Christ, I had no idea." He shook his head at this amazing revelation.

"Carrie knew about them. She led us right to them. She feels a very strong kinship to that place. She and Kyle are both drawn to it. The two of them have been spouting Norwegian at each other like long-lost friends."

"Norwegian, ye say? And our Carrie has the language?" He shifted restlessly, trying to make his brain home in on all that he was being told.

Rainey smoothed his covers in maternal fashion. "She does indeed, Matt. It's like she was born with it, thanks to Kyle. Quite an amazing thing."

Matt's head was starting to ache, but he was determined to focus on the puzzle at hand. "Maclennan. Maclennan. Ah, yes, brilliant lad. A bit shy at times because of the hearin' aid, but all in all, not a bad sort. Wait. I seem to remember . . . That's the connection! The young man who was conversin' with the seals. The Norwegian. Och, but he wasn't Norwegian after all. I'm afraid my brain's in quite a state of disrepair, love. He came with you all to Orkney, then, in search of Cameron?"

Rainey toyed with a loose bit of thread on the bed quilt. "Well, I'm sure he had Professor Cameron's welfare in mind." She wasn't certain how to approach the fact that Kyle had come along with them primarily out of a wish to be near Sasha. Perhaps this wasn't the best time to address the subject. "But, my God, Matt, those stairs were so steep! It was a blessing for everybody that you managed to stay unconscious during that exhausting feat of strength. I've never been so tired in all my life."

Matt saw that in addition to the gold locket he had given her, she was wearing the silver necklace around her throat. It brought the kittiwake back into his thoughts. How that wee bird had coveted the shining silver! But memories of the kittiwake also brought on a fresh flood of unwanted images. His eyes misted as he thought of all those who had lost their lives in the crash.

He was here, now, in the safety and security of the home he

had known all his life. The mending had begun, and he was loved beyond measure. How was it that he deserved such riches when so many had been robbed of everything, including life itself?

He took Rainey's hand into his own, his jubilation over his own survival tempered by the reality of how much sacrifice had taken place. He couldn't bring himself to meet her gaze.

"So many innocent lives, *mo chridhe,*" he said, his voice rough with emotion. "Where is the justice in so many dyin'? Was it solely to bring me to that godforsaken strip of rocks?"

"In that bloody instant before the crash, I felt like I knew each and every one of them, Rainey! How can I live with the knowledge that I alone survived?"

His words tugged at Rainey's heart. She had wondered about it, too, why it had taken so severe a method to bring the necklace back to the Highlands. Certainly, they had all risked their own lives to return Sirona's crown to its rightful place years ago. And other lives had been lost then in the name of justice. But this was on a far larger scale than anything else they had encountered.

But deep within her heart, past the sorrow of so many lost lives, past the guilt and regret, there dwelled a stubborn sense of hope. The question was, after all he had been through, would she be able to convey that feeling of hope to Matt? She brought his hand to rest against her heart and pressed it to her.

"That storm out of the north that took your plane down was from another time and place, well beyond all those people on the plane, beyond you and me, beyond Macha and Olgar and Haakon, and yet targeted at us all. All those centuries of separation, all the tearing apart of families and friends—the time of reconciliation couldn't wait any longer. I wish to God it could have been different." Matt shook his head slowly.

"When I look back on it now," she said reverently, "I know

Alan's death was a forerunner to all of this, just as Sasha's knowledge of Gaelic as a child was a clue that none of us recognized or understood. It all seemed to come from out of nowhere, then, like an arrow to the heart. But it was only the start of all that was to come.

"I know Alan's death served a definite purpose. It was essential that you and I come together." Her eyes misted. It had taken so much tragedy to bring them to where they were now. "We had to join forces to bring about the end of those killer storms from out of the north. We had to bring peace to all those lost souls."

Her voice failed her, and Matt squeezed her hand for support. He wanted her to continue, to help him make sense of so much tragedy and loss. "Tell me, Rainey, tell me what you think it all means. Make sense of it for me. I need to hear it."

Rainey swallowed hard on the knot of emotion caught in her throat. Until now, she hadn't really been able to put all that had happened to them into perspective. She had been so consumed with Matt's rescue that the rest of it had been secondary. But he was right. How could the return of the necklace and Macha's consequent freedom justify so much human suffering?

In asking herself this question, she suddenly grew very calm. This new sense of serenity stemmed from a wisdom far greater than her own. And she knew as she spoke that the answers she had been given were not usually shared with those whose lives were still indebted to solid ground.

"There is another kind of freedom that comes after death," she said with conviction. "I believe this with all my heart. It's much better than anything you and I can know in this life. It comes when a soul is at peace, when all that must be done on earth has been accomplished, and the call of the next world becomes stronger than the ties of this one.

"It wasn't your time, Matt. There is so much more for you to

do here. Your life was spared. For all those other souls, the time
had come to journey on to the next world. I can't offer you an
explanation of why it was time for each of them. But I know
their deaths were not without purpose or reward." She smoothed
the furrows from his brow with her fingertips.

"The injustice done to Macha all those years ago resulted in
the loss of so many innocent lives. And all those horrific storms
of ancient retribution out of the north each year brought about
more suffering on a grand scale. One of them contributed to the
loss of your parents' lives and nearly the loss of your own. They
had to be stopped, regardless of the cost." She leaned down and
kissed his scarred cheek. A single tear from her eye splashed
against his skin, but she smiled to reassure him.

"Macha is reunited with her family now. Just as Haakon is reunited with his brother. All is forgiven. The time of sorrow is
over. The storms that were so driven by the imbalances these
separations caused are at an end. And when the necklace is returned to the falls, the circle will be complete. It's the best gift
we can give them. It's the best gift we can give each other." She
searched his eyes. "Can you accept it, Matt? Can you live with
what I've told you?"

He reached up and tucked her hair behind her ear as he had
done for all the years they had been together. "Aye, *mo chridhe,*
I believe I can, so long as yer by my side to remind me of the
greater purpose to all that happens. Yer the keeper of my faith,
Rainey. *Carraig mo meairt.* Rock of my strength. I only pray
that one day our daughters will know for themselves what you
and I share."

She snuggled up beside him, a smile on her lips. They had to
move on now. The sorrows of the past would never be forgotten, but the present demanded their energy.

"And since you're in such a receptive mood, Stanford," Rainey
offered, "perhaps I should tell you that your older daughter has

managed to fall head over heels in love in the last couple of days."

He would have sat bolt upright if she hadn't kept a restraining hand on him.

"In love? Whatever are ye talkin' about, woman? Why, Sasha's no more than a child! She couldn't be more than . . . More than . . ."

"Try eighteen for size," she informed him evenly. "Our 'little Sasha' is a woman. And God help her, she's set her sights on a university type."

Matt frowned in thought. "This Maclennan fella?"

Rainey nodded.

He stroked his chin, considering this development. "Well, she'll outgrow it, I imagine. It's only because the two of them were thrown together under adverse circumstances. They're both still wet behind the ears, for the love o' God. I'd wager they'll be off in their separate directions before the week is out." None of this removed the frown of paternal worry from his brow.

"We'll see," Rainey said noncommittally. She decided it would be wisest to change the subject, so she patted his cast beneath the blankets. "They did quite a job on that leg of yours, you know. Do you remember any of it?"

Matt rubbed his forehead as shredded bits of memory returned to him. "Aye, I remember groups of strangers in white coats peerin' at me in between all the noise and rumblin' about. Silly as it seems now, I though I was bein' processed through some kind of final judgment. I suppose all those medical types were angels of a sort. It's all a haze."

She fluffed his pillows. "You can be grateful for that haze, my love. They called in three separate groups of medical students to witness the setting of that leg of yours. I don't think those folks use the word 'miracle' lightly. But I heard it used more than once with regard to you, Macinnes. There was no reason on earth that you should have survived all those hours in the cove, to say nothing of the crash itself. I told them it was just because you were such a damned hardheaded Scot. They used every modern innovation in the book, including that reinforced fiberglass cast you've got. They said it weighs about a third of what the old ones weigh."

Matt threw back the covers and gave the cast a good look. It was true. There was hardly any weight to it.

"And it's basically waterproof," Rainey added.

"Indeed?" He looked at it with a new respect.

"More good news—they say you suffered a concussion, but there shouldn't be any lasting problems from it as long as you get some rest and some peace and quiet."

There was a single quick knock on the heavy bedroom door, then it flew open as Carrie burst into the room. She froze when she suddenly remembered the strict orders she had been given earlier about keeping the house quiet.

"Sorry!" she whispered. "But . . ."

Sasha appeared in the doorway. Her eyes misted with relief when she saw that Matt was awake.

"Sasha," he said with absolute joy. It was the first time he had seen her clearly since before his ill-fated trip. She raced across the room and threw her arms around him.

"I'm so glad you're okay, Papa," she said softly. "I don't know what we'd do without you."

He put her to arm's length so he could get a good look at her. "Three strong Highland women? Ye'd tip the world on its ear, love. Yer hardly in need of me."

She had somehow become a woman in the brief days he had been gone. He resolved not to mourn the passing of her childhood.

"Oh, but we *are* in need of you, Papa. Promise me you won't go on those crazy business trips of yours for a very long time. Promise me."

Her plea was in earnest, and he didn't have the heart to joke her out of her worries. "I think I've had enough of business trips to last me a very long time, Sash. If anybody needs to consult with me, I'll refer them to you and tell them yer my business secretary. That way, ye can keep a close watch over the mileage. What do ye say, is it a bargain?"

Sasha smiled with a touch of melancholy. "It's a bargain," she said as she hugged him to her again.

"That's grand, love." He turned to Rainey. "So what is on yer agenda for today, besides tendin' the wounded?"

Rainey glanced at Sasha and Carrie. Sasha pressed her lips together at the volatile subject matter. "The girls and I are going to the falls today to return Macha's necklace to its rightful place."

Matt's expression changed to one of concern. "Can't it wait until I'm able to help ye with the climb, Rainey? It's been hundreds of years. What difference could a few more days make?"

Rainey touched a kiss to his forehead. "We've made that climb before, Stanford. And I don't think I'll be able to sleep until the necklace is back where it belongs. It's the last piece to the puzzle. Besides, we'll have Kyle along to help us."

Sasha walked to the end of the bed. "I wouldn't count on Kyle, Mama."

"Why is that, Sash?"

Carrie jumped in front of her mother. "Because he's leaving! That's what I was trying to tell you. He's going away."

Rainey turned to Sasha. "What's up, Sash?"

Sasha frowned at her mother's question as she ran her fingertip along the twisted wood of the four-poster's upright. She was clearly reluctant to touch on the subject matter.

"He's going back to the university?" Rainey pursued.

Sasha shrugged. "He says . . . He says he can't go back there."

Matt and Rainey exchanged a look at this.

"Why not, Sasha?" Matt asked.

Her eyes were filled with the prospect of loss. "I don't know, Papa. He won't talk to me about it. And now he's leaving."

He beckoned Sasha to him. "Will ye do me the favor of bringin' the man to me, Sasha? Tell him only that I wish to thank him for his help in the rescue."

"I suppose," she said with doubt. "But he's so *stubborn*! Sometimes I just want to punch him for the way he acts. I mean, one minute he's all sensitive and caring. The next minute he's brooding over God knows what and walking out of your life forever. I can't make heads or tails of him. A person shouldn't have to put up with this kind of schizophrenic behavior. Am I wrong here?" She stormed out the door, presumably in search of her lunatic.

Matt looked at Rainey, his mouth hanging open in shock. "Good God, I had no idea."

Rainey nodded solemnly. "I'm afraid so. Your little Queen of the Woodland Fairies has got it pretty bad. It was quite sudden, actually. She wouldn't give him the time of day. You know, always angry at him for one tiny reason or another. They argued over politics, over whether it was warm or cold, day or night. The next thing you know, her young heart is right in her hand for all the world to see."

"And does our Mr. Maclennan see it there in her hand?"

"I haven't a clue. And you'd be wise to tread very gently around the subject, 'Papa,' or your name is going to be mud around here till the end of time."

Matt shifted restlessly. "Perhaps I should have gotten another hour or two of sleep. I'd be wiser to work up to this kind of fancy diplomacy."

She patted him on the shoulder. "Sorry, Stanford, your vacation break is over."

"Vacation, bah! Yer a hard woman, Rainey Macinnes."

She ran her hand lightly across his chest. "And you, husband of mine, have been known to be quite a hard man." He grabbed her hand with amazing speed and brought it to his lips.

There was the sound of someone clearing his throat in the doorway, and their attention turned in that direction. Kyle stood quietly in the doorway, his cheeks burning from the intimate scene before him.

Rainey brushed Matt's lips with her own and whispered, "You're on."

Her smile didn't comfort him much. She was very well aware of that fact as she hustled Carrie out of the room under protest.

Once the women were well on their way downstairs, Kyle walked into the room. "It's good to see ye more yer old self again, Professor Mac. Ye wanted to see me, then?" He pressed his hearing aid into his ear more securely. Clearly, his nerves were on edge.

"I wanted to thank ye for helpin' my family in their hour of need, Kyle," Matt said in all sincerity. "And I know we're all still in hopes that Professor Cameron will be found safe."

Kyle lowered his eyes. "I don't see there's much chance of that, sir. But then, findin' yerself was somethin' of a gamble in and of itself. Although I know yer family and friends there never doubted for a minute we'd find ye. I'm not a very religious man, sir, ye ken? But I have to say I wasn't above sayin' a prayer for the lot of us a time or two."

"Aye, well, ye've my thanks, Kyle, and the thanks of my family as well for yer services."

Kyle looked around the richly appointed old room and shifted his jacket from one arm to the other. "Och, sir, it was

nothin'. As ye know, I've always been a great admirer of yer
work. It was an honor to help yer ladies."

Matt smiled. "Ah, yes, my ladies." He spied Sasha listening
just outside the door. "I'm told ye have no plans to return to
the university, Kyle. Would ye care to explain to me just why
that is?"

The color rose in Kyle's cheeks. This was not an issue he had
wanted made known. He squared his shoulders and looked
Matt in the eye. "The fact of the matter is, sir, I've outlived my
usefulness there. Professor Cameron was kind enough to permit me to study with him, but my scholarships ran out last term.
I've been tutorin' and workin' in a bookstore to earn my room
and board. It's honest work, and I'm glad of it. But my studies
are at an end for a time. It was always a possibility."

Matt sighed. "Have ye no one, Kyle, no family at all?"

Kyle raised his chin a notch. "It was never my intention to
elicit sympathy from ye, nor from anyone, Professor Macinnes.
I'm quite able to tend to my own needs, thank ye. Now, if ye'll
excuse me, I'm certain ye could use a wee bit of rest, and I must
be goin'." He turned on his heel and started for the door.

"Kyle?"

He stopped midstride. "Aye, sir."

"I'm afraid I must ask one more favor of ye."

Kyle's shoulders slumped. He looked back over his shoulder
with genuine disappointment that he had not been able to make
a clean getaway. "What might that be, sir?"

Matt folded his arms across his chest, very much the captain
of this ship. "My ladies, as ye so aptly put it, have another expedition ahead of them. There's a waterfall not far to the north of
here. Their plan is to go there today. They're familiar with the
way and the terrain, and our good friend Malcolm will be ac-
companyin' them. But they need another steady hand.

"Normally, I would go along as reinforcement. But, as ye

well know, I'm not prepared to take such a journey just yet. If it's all the same to ye, I'd deem it a very large favor if ye would offer yer support to the women. It shouldn't take but a couple of hours, and at the end we'll get Malcolm to give ye a lift down to Fort William. Of course, I'll gladly pay whatever expenses ye may have as a result of all this."

Matt could see it in Kyle's eyes, how desperately he wanted to leave. He wanted to run back to whatever tightly boxed existence he had cut out for himself. The symptoms were very familiar to Matt because he had suffered from the same isolating disease himself in the old days, the days before Rainey and Sasha had come into his life. They had been a lifeline for him, his salvation and his sanctuary. He didn't know what Kyle's story was. He didn't have to know the specifics. But if Maclennan was half the man Matt thought he was, he was deserving of a chance at a lifeline of his own.

Kyle took a deep breath. "I'll do as ye ask, Professor Macinnes. But other than the lift to town, there's no need to compensate me for what I've been perfectly willin' to do."

Matt wished to God he could climb out of bed and walk over to shake the man's hand. He didn't take kindly to helplessness. "It's agreed, then."

"Aye. I'd best go and see if I can be of help with the preparations." Once again, he started for the door.

"Oh, and one thing more, Maclennan."

"What is it, sir?" He was waiting for the other shoe to drop.

"Consider this, if ye will, as yer fightin' with the climb up to the falls. I'm not goin' to be up to speed for a while because of my injuries. It would be of substantial help to me to have the assistance of someone knowledgeable in my fields of study. I know Professor Cameron's focus was more on Iron Age investigations. But if ye feel it could be of use to ye to delve into the

Celtic tribes more specifically for a time, I'd much rather be payin' you than someone else for the help.

"Of course, ye'd be stuck here at the house. And I'll be frank with ye, the place is fair overrun with females. Malcolm and I have to duck for cover half the time. But havin' ye here might help to shift the balance of power, ye ken." He reminded himself that if he was ever in a game of chance with Kyle Maclennan, the man's face was an open book. At the moment, it appeared to be Christmas morning in Kyle's life.

"Aye, sir, I'll consider it. I thank ye for such a generous offer. I'll most definitely consider it."

He nearly knocked Sasha to the ground as he sped around the corner in delight. He grabbed her by the shoulders, and then he kissed her firmly on the mouth. She looked at him in shock and amazement.

"Sorry, California!" he said quickly. Then he kissed her a second time before she had time to work up the steam to slug him a good one. He grinned at her like the Cheshire Cat and said, "Not sorry!" as he rushed down the stairs, to do what, Sasha could not guess.

Sasha walked into the bedroom in a daze. "He called me California. What did I tell you, Papa? The man's a raving lunatic! And he's going to drive the rest of us nuts if you keep him around here." She set her fists on her hips and shook her head as she stared at the door.

"Sasha?"

It took her a moment to focus on the fact that Matt had called for her attention. When it registered, she turned to him in embarrassment. He motioned for her to come closer, and she took her time crossing the room. When she stood beside him, he took her hand into his own.

"If Kyle is a problem to you, Sash, ye have only to say the word, and I'll send him packin', ye ken?" She lowered her eyes and frowned. "You and Carrie and yer mother are first and foremost my priorities. Everythin' else goes by the wayside. Pure fact.

"I asked the lad for his help only because I have my family's welfare to consider here. I know it's a small matter to ye that he has no family, but in light of the fact that we're in need of assistance and Kyle has proven his worth to us, I was obliged to ask if he would stay for a while. But I trust yer instincts far more than I trust my own, love. I have from the very start. And if yer feelin' is that the man is a risk to ye or to any of us, then ye must make yer opinion known to me right now. Speak yer piece."

Sasha considered her words carefully. "He just makes me so nervous, Papa. I never know what he's going to do or say. Half the time, he won't let me get a word in edgewise. The other half, he just sits there, listening to my every word like I have the wisdom of the ages, or something, even though I'm sure he's thinking I'm an idiot. I just never know what to expect. But I suppose, if you say we need him for a while, I can work on trying to ignore him. I mean, I don't think he's evil or anything."

Matt gave her a smile that was touched with commiseration. "I understand, Sasha. Just remember that I'm here for ye, love. And I thank every god who ever boasted of a heaven for the blessin' of bein' able to say that to yer lovely face."

She toyed with the comforter's edge, just as her mother had done. "Do you think I'm the crazy one, Papa? I mean, I always thought I was pretty levelheaded, all things considered. But now, with this Kyle business, I'm beginning to wonder."

He wanted to say it straight to her face, that she was no more crazy than anyone else who had fallen in love for the first time. But, fortunately for them both, he had more sense than to do such a thing. She was going to have to work this one out for herself, with all the joy and pain that went along with the tricky territory. He wanted to weep for her, having suffered from the same malady with regard to her dear mother. Instead, he adopted a businesslike manner.

"I am of the opinion, Sasha, that with what's happened in the last few days, we're all in a state of chaos. Don't judge yerself harshly, sweetheart. Things will sort themselves out, all in good time. If yer able, just ride with it for now. Most likely, young Maclennan will be too busy to be much of a bother to ye. If ye see he has too much in the way of free time, give me the high sign and I'll put him to cleanin' the gutters."

That brought a smile to her face. She brushed his cheek with a kiss. "Have I mentioned to you lately how much I love you, Papa?"

He gave her a comical scowl. "Hm, my memory is a bit like Swiss cheese at the moment. Tell me, do ye harbor enough regard for me to fetch yer mother to this poor man's sickbed?"

She tapped her finger against her chin. "I think I can manage that. But then I'm paid up till supper, right?"

His wink at her was one of admiration. "Said like a true Scot, m'love. Now, hop to it, lass. Off with ye, and send yer mother runnin' to me. Ah, but I love the sound of that."

She walked toward the door at her own leisurely pace, but he could hear her hustle down the stairs in search of Rainey. He didn't want to admit to himself that he was exhausted. After all, he had hardly moved an inch. But he had a full and complete dream before he sensed Rainey lying beside him on the top of the covers.

She was watching him as he slept, he realized. A gloriously comforting thought. His dream had been of the falls, that extraordinary and holy place where you had only to believe to see the magic dance before your eyes. He wanted to go with them on their journey to return Macha's necklace to its rightful place.

He ran his fingertips along the smooth line of the silver at her throat. "I want to come with you."

She rubbed the stubble on his chin. "You will be with us, Matt, every step of the way."

"Och, that 'in spirit' crap, is it? Well, it's not good enough, ye ken?" She was on his healthy side, and as she snuggled closer to rest her head on his shoulder, he knew he was a man in trouble. A very tempting tray of tea and toast with jam awaited his pleasure on the nightstand beside him. He wanted it. But he wanted the lady who had delivered it far more. "None of that gentle persuasion now, woman," he admonished with a comical scowl. "I will not be charmed out of my bad mood, understood?"

"Umhmm." She dipped her finger in the homemade strawberry jam and brushed it along his lower lip.

He took her finger lightly between his teeth and savored the tantalizing mixture of the sweet jam and the subtle salt of her skin—lover, wife, salvation. She tsked at him scoldingly, then kissed his chest lightly through the obnoxious medical gown he still wore.

"Emma will be here to play nursemaid for you. You know she always spoils you rotten when you're sick. And little Angus will probably dance on his hind legs to entertain you. But you're determined to be stubborn and frustrated as only you can do so well. And nothing I do can sway you from your angry course."

"Correct." He knew perfectly well what she was up to. And he was enjoying every second of it. She slipped her hand beneath him and across his back, raising one eyebrow when she contacted skin. If he jumped or flinched, it was going to hurt, so he concentrated on relaxing and letting her have her way. The door was open, after all. She was fully clothed and not even under the comforter with him. How far could she get with the two of them on public display?

"My compliments to your tailor, Professor." She slid her hand down his back and gave one of his haunches a firm, provocative squeeze. The sharp breath he took in had nothing to do with pain. "I've missed you, you know. God, how I've missed you! And a woman does have her needs. A pity about your invalid state. Of course, there are certain forms of massage therapy, I've heard, that can speed a man's . . . recovery to a supersonic pace."

"Ah, but yer a wicked temptress, woman," he said as he let his eyes drift closed. "Remind me to give ye a sound thrashin' later in the day."

She knew precisely what pleasured him most, and he groaned as she let her fingers perform with tender cruelty in the darkness beneath the covers. As she pressed a breathy kiss to his ear, she whispered, "We'll see who thrashes whom when the time comes, hero of mine."

He kissed her soundly. "No contest, *mo chridhe*."

Chapter 15

"Uisge-bheatha," Kyle said under his breath. It meant "whiskey," and although he could have used a bracer as he stared up at the enormous waterfall, it struck him that the words in Gaelic also meant "water of life."

What he saw before him certainly looked deserving of such a grand title. He adjusted the volume level on his hearing aid to compensate for the incredible roar of so much water plunging hundreds of feet over a stark wall of rock. There was a deep ravine and a pool at the bottom, carved out by centuries of falling water.

The hike from where they had parked the Land Rover had been a challenge, to say the least. He had done his share of treks and working remote digs, but it was very clear to him now why this particular geographic feature was not pushed in the tourist brochures. Such a hike was a nightmare. The monstrous storm that had brought Matthew Macinnes's plane down had washed out large portions of the trail, a trail that could only be termed inhospitable under ideal conditions.

Carrie came up beside him and pointed to the falls. "Glomach," she said reverently.

"Aye, so I see. It's a big place, is it not?"

She looked up at him as she considered his friendship. "It's big," she allowed. "But we're used to it."

He smiled down at her. "I don't doubt that ye are." Carrie wasn't wearing her customary grin, and it gave him pause. Because of the special world these ladies inhabited from time to time, he was tempted to excuse himself from whatever was about to transpire. What he didn't know couldn't hurt him, or them, he decided.

He had very neatly come to the conclusion that the incident with the Vikings at the cove had just been the result of light-headedness brought on by the lack of a decent meal and the disorientation of being without his hearing aid. Anything more than that was beyond what he wanted to process just yet.

Rainey was deep in conversation with Sasha, so he held his tongue until the time offered itself for him to talk with the professor's wife alone, to see if she, for one, would prefer it if he busied himself down the trail, away from the falls. He didn't know what was expected of him, but the one thing he did know was that he didn't want to give Sasha yet another opportunity to laugh at his ignorance of their ways.

The fact of the matter was, he would gladly fracture the laws of God and man for one wee glimpse of approval from those miraculous, delving blue eyes of Sasha's. He still couldn't believe she had let him live after he had had the audacity to kiss her—on the mouth, by God—not once, but twice! Just how far out of his mind had he been to pull *that* move? Credit it to the element of surprise.

He supposed he should count his blessings that she hadn't spoken a word to him since. She probably could have changed him into a toad as easily as sneeze at him.

As if reading his thoughts, Sasha turned to regard him with that look of hers that neatly knocked against his backbone. He should have left when he'd had the chance, he told himself sternly. But Professor Mac had locked him into a narrow golden paddock with his job offer. How was it Yanks were so fond of putting it? An offer he couldn't refuse? Well, he might yet find the gumption to refuse it if he decided it had been made out of pity. He still wasn't sure.

It took a moment for it to register that Sasha was walking toward him, a frown on her lovely face. She was wearing worn jeans and a loose-fitting gray sweatshirt with a Stanford University logo on it. He had never seen a sexier set of clothing on the woman in his life. He would be slobbering at her feet in a minute if he didn't get a handle on himself.

If he couldn't deal with the simple fact that she was coming toward him, how was he going to manage living under the same roof with her on a daily basis, brushing past her in the hall, happening upon her in the kitchen? He was going to have to come to grips with this very large problem.

If he didn't find a way to curb his lust for her, both the physical and mental varieties, he would be forced to remove himself from her permanently. There were no other options. Anything less would be an act of cowardice and dishonesty.

He squared his shoulders. If he was going to take it on the chin for kissing her earlier, he would face it like a man. He was a head taller than she was, but somehow, it felt like they were always eye to eye.

"Can you hear me okay, Edinburgh?"

The opening volley. To his way of thinking, the question was one of impatience more than concern. "Aye, I hear ye." The one thing he would not tolerate was to have her treat him like he was somehow deficient because of his hearing loss. "Ye may shout at me if ye like. I know ye'd prefer it."

Her frown deepened. "I don't think that will be necessary.

But I'm not sure you understand how important all of this is."
She set her hands on her hips like a disgruntled drill sergeant.

His gaze softened. "For starters, I don't understand this
family's propensity for callin' people by the names of places. Is
it so difficult to call me by my true name, Miss Macinnes?"

She raised one eyebrow. There was a flicker of something in
her eyes. It could almost be taken for vulnerability.

"Is it so difficult to call me by mine, *Mr.* Maclennan?"

He folded his arms across his chest and tried not to let his true
feelings creep into his words. "Aye, it is difficult when it's been
made clear to me that ye loathe anythin' of a personal nature
from me. Perhaps one day, say in a decade or two, you'll find
me less offensive to yer taste. I much prefer kisses given as a
gift, *kjaereste,* to those that must be stolen."

It was hard to say what she would do next. He thought he was
prepared for any eventuality, including a prolonged hospital
stay. It wasn't as if her opinion of him had sweetened. On the
contrary—if anything, she looked more displeased with him
than ever.

Sasha reached out and took his hand, to the surprise of them
both. "Look . . . Kyle, truce, okay? These last few days have
been hell for everyone. I'm not the horrible person you think I
am. It's just that there's been so much going on, it's been hard
for me to focus on anything but getting my father home safely."

He tucked his finger under her chin to raise her eyes to his.
"I fully understand, Sasha. And believe it or not, I want to be
yer . . . friend. I want to learn about the elements that make up
yer world—all of them—from an academic standpoint." He saw
her defenses start to rise.

"Gently, lass. I'm willin' to be a foot soldier in this strange
army of yers. God, I've already been through the initiation cer-
emonies, have I not? I've got the saltwater stains on my trousers
to prove it. I must be deservin' of some faded claim to sainthood

for assistin' old Haakon with his climb to Valhalla, wouldn't ye say?"

"You remember it?"

"Aye, torn bits of it. But I have to say, I'm not anywhere near understandin' it."

She gave him a smile that he could only term mystical. "You ain't seen nothin' yet."

He bowed over her hand in knightly fashion. "Whatever the future holds, I'll do my best not to look the utter fool in yer eyes."

She patted his hand. "Don't get carried away with yourself, *friend*. I just might hold you to it."

Her hand was still in his, and resisting the temptation to press his lips to it was growing into a physical pain. "Ye may hold me to whatever ye like, *a ghra ` idh.*"

"You're the rookie. We'll be nice." The fact that he had used a term of endearment had not escaped her. There was more color than usual in her cheeks.

His hand firmly in hers, she led him over to where Rainey stood in conference with Malcolm. Malcolm was blustering protectively about their safety.

"Can ye not take care of the matter from down here, Rainey?" he asked with genuine concern.

Rainey secured Macha's necklace around her throat. Carrie nodded her approval. "No, Malcolm. You know me. I'm not big on climbing. But it has to be done right. We're definitely going to need your help, Kyle. Sasha and I are familiar with the terrain, but we really need a steady anchor for the safety rope. It's not as steep as it looks."

"Naw, it's nine times steeper," Malcolm interjected.

Rainey gave him a censuring look. "What do you think, Kyle? Is this something you're willing to help us with? We'll understand if it's not."

Kyle looked down at their sparse climbing equipment. "It's to the top, then, is it?"

"Yes." Rainey exchanged a look with Sasha. She noticed Sasha had not let go of Kyle's hand. A breakthrough in their relationship, or a security measure to keep him from marching back to the Land Rover?

Kyle gave Sasha's hand a reassuring squeeze, then let it go as he started to gather up the ropes. "Then we'd best have at it, ladies," he said firmly. The questions he had about what was going to happen once they reached the top had to be set aside for now. He gave them all a smart salute.

"Are we ready to conquer Everest, crew?"

Rainey picked up a coil of nylon rope and slung it over her shoulder. "I think this climb will be challenge enough, thanks."

Malcolm stayed below with Carrie in the hope that the two of them might be able to shout warnings to the climbers if there were any trouble spots more easily seen from below. He sat down on a large rock beside Carrie as they watched the other three take to the steep trail that led to the top of the falls.

"Och, and it's discrimination, I tell ye, lassie," Malcolm grumbled. "You and I are forever the ones left behind to preserve the watch."

Carrie patted his arm comfortingly. "That's okay, Malcolm. Our turn will come. And besides, they left us all the sandwiches." She started to rummage in the backpack that held their supplies.

Malcolm's mood brightened. "Left us in charge of the provisions, did they? Well, all this fresh air has put a terrible hunger on me at the moment, and I suppose we would be wise to keep our strength up in case we're required in an emergency, wouldn't ye say?"

She turned on her best Shirley Temple dimples. "You're

right, Malcolm." She promptly handed him a peanut butter and jelly sandwich, and he turned up his nose.

"Have ye nothin' of substance, Care? This here's not fit for a grown man's belly." He handed it back to her and dusted his hands clean of the offending crumbs.

"Okay, Malcolm, how about this instead?"

Malcolm had his sight trained on the climbers, so when he stuck out his hand for a fresh sandwich, it came as a surprise to feel a smooth skipping stone in place of a sandwich. He glanced at it suspiciously.

"What's the meanin' of this, then?"

Carrie shrugged, all wide-eyed innocence. "Well, we never got to finish our contest. I never got my turn. I'm even willing to give you a fresh try into the bargain."

"Hmph. Some bargain. Ye stacked the deck against me last time, ye wee scamp. I've no reason to suspect any different from ye now."

Carrie stuffed the last of her peanut butter sandwich into her mouth, chewing the wad with difficulty as she stood up and dusted off the seat of her jeans. "Okay, here's the deal. You can pick out my rock as well as your own." She swallowed hard. "That's fair, isn't it? I mean, how can you lose?"

"How, indeed." Malcolm lifted the top slice of bread off another sandwich, only to find peanut butter again. He slapped the bread down in disgust and looked to see how the climbers were progressing. All was going well.

"All right, lassie, we'll give it a go. But then it's back to business. No more tomfoolery. Understood?"

Carrie crossed her heart and raised her right hand in a solemn oath of obedience. She kept her face trained to seriousness, but there was a definite gleam in those brilliant blue-gray eyes.

There wasn't a doubt in Malcolm's mind that she was hoodwinking him again. But he knew her well enough to realize she wouldn't let the matter go until it had been resolved. He made a quick but thorough study of all the rock candidates in the vicinity, and came up with two that were almost identical. All things considered, it was an even match.

"You go first, Malcolm," Carrie said with a comical curtsey.

"Why?"

That wide-eyed innocence was back. "Why? Because I'm being polite."

"Not bloody likely," Malcolm replied under his breath as he drew his arm back, then let go of his rock. The waters of the pool were more turbulent than those of the loch near the Macinnes home, but Malcolm's stone skipped through the foam a total of eight times. A very respectable number under the prevailing conditions. Malcolm set his fists on his hips.

"Top that, if ye can, ye wee charletan," he said with pride.

Carrie set her jaw in determination as she pulled her arm back like a World Series pitcher. When she let the rock fly, what looked to be a group of dragonflies clustered around the stone and carried it bouncing over the frothy water, jumping it dozens of times before they turned it back in the direction from which it had come.

As they flew near, it could be seen that they were not dragonflies at all but tiny winged beings, residents of the falls. Their laughter rang out as they delivered Carrie's stone into Malcolm's hand. In the blinking of an eye, they disappeared into the rolling mists. It was as if they had never existed.

"Och, lass, callin' on the wee Glomach folk. Ye're not playin' fair."

Carrie grinned as Malcolm stared down at the wet rock in his hand. "You never said I *couldn't* use their help. Besides, they've given you a present, Malcolm. The good news is, now you have a rock that will skip better than any other rock in Scotland.

The bad news is, I won. Shovel duty is all yours. Make Angus proud."

Malcolm pressed his lips together, perturbed at her antics. He tossed the magical stone up lightly in his hand. "If memory serves, when ye lost the one toss not so long ago, ye stated that the rules of the game were, whoever loses may demand a rematch for best two out of three." He hefted the magic stone again meaningfully.

Carrie realized her ploy might be backfiring. "Those were the *old* rules." She wasn't too pleased with the smile on Malcolm's face.

"The old rules, is it?" he asked pointedly. "Well, I do recall a pinky swear the two of us made at the Winter Solstice, somethin' to the effect that we would take turns makin' up the rules. Now, usin' the wee folk was most assuredly a rule of yer makin', lassie. So, what remains to us now is my turn at the rule-makin'. And I say it's best two out of three." He turned the fairy-blessed stone over in his hand for her benefit. Carrie's mouth hung open at this revelation of the hole in her logic. Malcolm tucked a finger under her chin to close it for her. He gave her a sly smile. "Choose yer weapon, lassie."

"As always, yer a marvel to me, ladies," Kyle said as he surveyed the breathtaking view from the top of the falls. Miles of forest and rolling, heather-covered hills spread out before them. "Ye take that hellish climb as if it were a grand Sunday stroll through the park." He also saw how small Malcolm and Carrie looked nearly four hundred feet below. It was dizzying to see how far they had climbed.

Rainey came up beside him as she rewound the climbing rope. "Well, we've done this little jaunt a few times."

"So I take it."

Sasha lifted her hair off her neck and let it fall to cool herself from the climb. It was an unconscious gesture, but she realized Kyle was watching her, even as he spoke to her mother. It made her feel self-conscious. It also made her feel powerful. Apparently he liked it when she did that to her hair. With deliberate slowness, she performed the move again.

Kyle cleared his throat uncomfortably. "What now, ladies? Does a flying saucer appear to carry us off to the Mother Ship?" It was said only partially in jest.

Rainey unfastened Macha's necklace and held it in her hand. "You're not the first one to ask that question. To be honest with you, Kyle, I don't know what will happen next. This is as new to us as it is to you. I only know we are where we should be." She looked out over falls, reveling in the sheer majesty of water so driven to join the sea. It was more a home to her than any place on earth. "What do you think, Sash?"

Sasha closed her eyes. "I think everything is as it should be." She opened her eyes with a smile.

As he came up beside Sasha, Kyle chanced looking down to where Carrie and Malcolm sat. Carrie smiled and waved up at him cheerily, as if he had climbed nothing higher than an apple tree.

"I don't belong in all of this," he said, as much to himself as to Sasha and Rainey.

Sasha looked at him out of the corner of her eye. That cowlick of his was doing its thing. She considered it dirty pool. He was getting under her skin again, and she didn't have time to sort through her feelings for him right now. Still, all of this was new to him. She supposed he deserved some small reassurance.

"Listen," she said to him kindly, "you said something earlier, about not wanting to steal things from me."

He kept his sight trained on the horizon. "Aye, I remember the conversation and its subject matter." He was careful not to be more specific, for a number of reasons, not the smallest of which was the fact that her mother was standing right beside them.

"Well, I want to thank you for what you said and for coming up here with us. I know how hard all of this must be for you. But you do belong here with us. I can feel it in my heart. So whatever else happens from here on out, I want you to have this."

She threw her arms around his neck and kissed him soundly on the mouth. Even though it had been her plan, it took them both by surprise when she actually did it. The move was so spontaneous, so completely out of bounds, that Kyle had no time to construct his iron defenses. She was there, warm and immediate, pressed against him, flooding his senses to overload.

He heard a strange growling sound from somewhere and realized only then that *he* was making it. It was a sound of animal possession, a sound that bordered on a primitive demand to mate, and he tore himself away from her as if he had been burned.

He couldn't bear to look at her for fear she had decided he might well have the potential for rape. But worse yet, if he looked at her and saw any small hint that she was not totally offended by his ferocity, that she didn't detest him for his actions, he would be lost. He clasped his hands behind his back, presumably to punish them for their lack of control.

"I do beg your pardon, Mrs. Macinnes," he said in a rush. He bobbed his head, first to Rainey, then to Sasha. "I beg your pardon as well, Sasha. Perhaps it's the precariousness of our situation, but I must apologize for my rash and forward behavior."

Sasha shrugged. "Why? I kissed *you,* remember? If anyone should apologize, it should be me. And I have no intention of doing so." She noticed the color had drained from his face, and she had to wonder if the tremendous height was bothering him.

But he seemed to recover himself, so she made no comment. And the fact that she was feeling a bit dizzy herself probably had to do with the revelation that she wanted Kyle Maclennan to kiss her again, here, now, and every day for the rest of her life. It should have been disturbing, she supposed, but for some reason, she found it incredibly reassuring.

Sasha grinned to herself, then glanced at her mother. But Rainey seemed oblivious to her. "Where do we go from here, Mama?"

"Let's see if this works." Rainey placed Macha's silver necklace in the palm of her hand and held it out before her so that the cool mists from the falls danced across her skin.

Sasha smiled down at the necklace. She loved it as she loved the brooch Matt had given her when she was small. It was a tangible token of Macha's newly won freedom, of her homecoming, of making peace with the past.

"We must say something, Mama," she said reverently.

"You're right. I hope I can find the proper words." Rainey held the necklace up toward the mists swirling overhead.

"In the name of Sirona! In the name of Macha!" she called out. "I return this symbol of their spirits to this place that has always been and will always be their home! They dwell here for all time through those who love and remember them, through ties of blood and allegiance to the mystical ones who truly possess this land. No longer will we suffer destruction from the north as we have in centuries past. You are defeated, Viking! There is nothing more for you here. Return to whatever hell holds your eternity, and leave us in peace!"

She threw the necklace over the edge of the falls so that it might forever rest safely at the bottom of the deep pool below. It was a moment of triumph, of victory over all who would try to steal the freedom of another.

A slow smile crossed Kyle's face as he touched the velvet pouch Sasha had given him. His heart was still beating hard from their kiss. The brooch had become such a part of him, he had forgotten he still had it. As he laid his fingers on it, he said Macha's name. This moment belonged to her.

As the necklace shone and twisted in its long descent toward the churning waters below, a bright-winged falcon dove through the mists and caught the silver in her beak before the water could claim it. She rose on the updraft and circled above them all, a miracle of swift and agile grace. Then she came to rest beside them and laid the necklace at Sasha's feet, her dark eyes watchful and insistent.

"She's makin' ye a gift of it, Sasha," Kyle said in amazement. "I do believe she wants ye to have it."

But surprisingly, the falcon picked up the necklace and laid it at Kyle's feet this time.

Rainey smiled. "I think she wants *you* to give it to Sasha, Kyle. She wants to see the two of you . . . going steady, shall we say?"

Sasha and Kyle exchanged a bewildered look. This was no small gesture for either of them. They had had so little time to learn about each other, and such a pledge might well be binding far beyond the limits of this place.

The look in Sasha's eyes reflected the conflicts going on inside her. She knelt beside the falcon. There was no doubt in her mind that their visitor was Macha's spirit.

"Grandmother Macha," she said reverently to the little bird, "your wisdom is far beyond my own. I trust these gifts of knowledge you're giving me, but I don't understand them fully. I ask you to grant us a bit more time, so that whatever pledges we may make will be with full understanding and the openness of a truly loving and committed heart. Do we have your permission, my Grandmother Macha?"

The little falcon's eyes shone with wisdom as she regarded Kyle. He bowed before her, and she opened her wings, then folded them closed. She gazed at them all, including those who waited below. Then she spread her wings in flight. As she dove and soared above the falls, tears of joy fell from her eyes. Kyle stretched out his hand, and the tears collected as diamonds of every different size and shape in his palm. He looked at them in wonder as their dazzling facets shimmered and sparkled within his grasp. They were worth a fortune beyond calculation. But he felt Sasha's hand on his arm.

"They belong to the falls, Edinburgh," she said softly. "Let them go."

He stared at the brilliant stones, hypnotized by their beauty. Such stones would mean an end to his poverty, an end to uncertainty about the future. Here would be an easy answer to his problems.

But whatever else he was, he wasn't a thief.

This wasn't the first time temptation had been thrown into his path. The day might come when he could no longer resist such a sin—to preserve his own sanity, to risk making Sasha his own. But this was not that day. He let his hand fall to his side. The stones shot over the edge and were lost in the cascading waters.

"A pity," he said as he saw them splash into the blue-green waters below.

Sasha patted him on the back. "Hardly. You never have to put money into insuring them, and you always know right where they are."

He looked at her, his curiosity aroused. "Like the story I told all of ye around the campfire. I never dreamed . . . Just how many such stones are down there?"

She shrugged. "You're a college man. Impress me. What's the highest you've ever counted?"

When he looked into the deep waters, just for the blinking of an eye, he thought he saw a glowing mountain of brightly colored stones right beneath the turbulent surface. But when he looked again, he saw nothing but water. He heard Sasha laugh at him again. This time, it didn't bother him a bit.

But he had to wonder, deep in his heart, if he would ever again stand where he was now. A week from now, a month from now, where would he be? There was little doubt in his mind that he would have to put distance between himself and Sasha very soon.

He had already proved the weakness of his resolve to keep his distance from her. The sweet taste of her was still on his lips. But she had no notion his traitorous body had transformed her simple kiss into pure heat. She didn't know the scope of what she was playing with here, and she deserved far better. It was all new to him, and he would be a fool to try to convince himself he could control it. Even in broad daylight, he was helpless against her. What would his desire for her drive him to do in the hours of darkness? He loved her too much to risk finding out.

Chapter 16

When they returned home from the falls, they found Matt dressed and downstairs. He was sleeping in an overstuffed chair by the fire in the main hall. On his lap was a detailed list he had made of all the reference materials he would need from his office at the university and a birdwatcher's guide opened to pictures of kittiwakes. Except for the cast and the bandage above his eye, it looked for all the world as if he had never left the hearth. Sasha wrapped her arm around Rainey's shoulders.

"That's a beautiful sight, isn't it, Mama?"

There was a knot of emotion in Rainey's throat. She simply nodded.

The chilling mists had closed in over the loch, throwing a hush over all of nature for the night and giving everyone a hearty appetite. So, while the others followed the tantalizing aroma of Emma's home-cooked stew and buttermilk biscuits to the kitchen, Rainey settled at Matt's feet and laid her head against his knee.

She was exhausted from all that had happened over the last few days. But Matt was home safely. They were all safe. That was all that mattered. She fell asleep content.

She didn't know how long she had slept when she awoke to

the feel of Matt's hand caressing her hair. It was still a miracle to her that he was truly there, and she blinked at him, trying to focus on the reality of his being home.

"How are you?" she asked drowsily. "Shouldn't you be up-stairs in bed?"

He smiled down at her. "That bed holds little comfort when yer not around to share it, *mo chridhe*." He grew more serious. "There was a phone call I had to make to Dormach. It was a promise I made to the lady who was sitting next to me on the plane. As it happens, she was the mayor of that wee town."

Rainey laid her hand on his arm. "Oh, Matt, I'm so very sorry."

"Aye, she was a dear woman, and she'll be sorely missed by many, as will all those poor lost souls." He was starting to lose himself in horrific memories of the crash, so he summoned himself back to the joys of the present.

"On to brighter matters, then," he said quickly. "I'm not about to stay out of the thick of things any longer than is ab-solutely necessary. But yer dreams were troubled, love. How can there be anythin' but sweet dreams in yer head right now? Was there a problem at the falls, then?"

She tried to remember the nature of her dreams. "Everything went fine at the falls. I wish you could have been there, Matt. Just as I threw Macha's necklace over the falls, a bird, a fal-con, flew down out of nowhere and caught it before it hit the water. She was so incredibly strong and graceful. She flew up to where we were standing and laid the necklace first at Sasha's feet, then at Kyle's. It was a very definite message."

Matt picked up his glasses from the arm of the chair and set-tled them over the bridge of his nose. He had lost his best pair in the crash, so these were not his favorites. But he was grateful for a return of far better sight than he had had in the wild. He rubbed his chin in thought. "And do you remember what your dreams were about?"

Rainey was a bit perturbed that he wasn't more impressed with her tale of the falls. "I don't know. I was still searching for you, I think. I was wandering the Highlands, calling your name. Then you and I were calling Sasha's name together because she was the one who was lost.

"I imagine the dreams about you are just leftovers from before we found you. But I'm not sure about the ones with Sasha." She stood up and started to give Matt's shoulders a soothing rub.

"We're losin' her from the nest, Rainey," he said, giving a luxurious sigh as his sore muscles began to relax. "She's growin' up. I wasn't there, mind ye, but it sounds to me like the falcon's actions were Macha's message to us all that Sasha has found the man who will share her life, if she chooses to accept him."

Rainey paused in her massage. "Do you think that's possible, Matt? I mean, I like Kyle. He's really quite a guy. But Sasha's so young. She has years of college in front of her, and, well, it's a very big world out there. I just don't want her to rush into anything."

Matt smiled at her hesitancy to let her daughter grow up. "Time'll tell, Harvard. I'm just sayin' it the way I see it. No force known to man will ever make that amazin' young woman do anythin' that goes against the grain. She's been the queen of her own fate every day of her life, and I don't see that that's goin' to change anytime soon. Give her a chance to make her own way, love. She's smarter than the pair of us put together, more often than not. Besides which, don't go tellin' me yer all of a sudden prejudiced against university men who fill their days with ancient cultures and languages. A woman could do far worse, by God."

"Right, a woman could have *two* such lunatics in the family."

She gave his ear a playful nip from behind, and he grabbed her hand to pull her around in front of him.

"Look at it this way, *mo chridhe,* where you'll find one of us, you'll most likely find the other. It's a gift."

"Like taxes and root canals," she said with a teasing smile, as she looked down at the pages of the bird book. She ran her finger along the kittiwake's pristine wings.

"An old friend and benefactor," Matt said fondly.

"An old *girl*friend, if you ask me. She wasn't about to let you go without her proper due. We had to give her Kyle's watch to buy our way out of her jurisdiction."

"Yer jokin'! Well, I suppose it was a small price to pay, considerin' she and the selkies were the ones who kept me alive."

Rainey sighed. "Well, I guess if there has to be another female in your life, it's reassuring to know she took good care of you. And that she's of another species."

He drew her nearer. "No one could ever hold a candle to you, and well ye know it, Surfer Girl. Besides, there's only so much *sushi* a man can eat, no matter how hungry he may be. And, I got the distinct impression from time to time that dear wee bird was fattening me up to some other purpose. A man's thoughts wander to the extreme when he's got no one to talk to but spirits, beasts, birds, and the madman who dwells in his own head."

She pushed his glasses up the bridge of his nose. "I can't guarantee much relief from the spirits, but that madman has no place inside your head anymore, and the beasts and birds will just have to fend for themselves. You belong to us for a while, Matthew Macinnes—for a *long* while."

"Body and soul, Rainey, it all belongs to you. I'm at yer mercy. Do with me what ye will."

She gave him a devilish look and ran her hand along his thigh. "All in good time, professor. All in good time."

He was about to let her know in no uncertain terms that as far as he was concerned, there was no time like the present, when someone giggled in the doorway.

Sasha, Carrie, and Kyle were all standing there with embarrassed grins on their faces. Kyle was holding a tray of food, Sasha was carrying the tea service, and Carrie had the napkins and silverware in preparation for supper by the fire. Emma scooted between them, with little Angus trotting at her heels, and began giving orders to all involved. Malcolm was right behind her, his mouth already smeared with butter from a stolen biscuit.

"Come along, now, you lot," Emma insisted. "Don't be standin' about like sheep after shearin'. Have ye never seen a husband and wife sayin' hello to one another? Well, it's sustenance of another sort these two are needin' at the moment, and the rest of ye as well. Carrie, love, mind the good linen. Yer mother was determined that we use nothin' but the family's best to celebrate Matty Mac's homecomin'." She saw Rainey blush and gave her a wink.

Rainey took Kyle's tray, which was filled with bowls of piping hot stew and a mountain of biscuits and butter. She set it by the fire and started to pass out the goodies.

"I just think that any homecoming deserves our best," she was quick to explain. "And this homecoming in particular is one for the history books." Her eyes were bright with unshed tears of joy and relief as she handed Matt his bowl.

He gave her a smile that promised her every day of his life. "And speakin' of history books," Matt said, handing his lists of reference materials to Kyle, "if I might impose upon ye, Kyle, to heft these items home for me from the university at the earliest opportunity. I'm goin' to have need of them soon, and I suppose it's only fair to let the hierarchy know I'm not lecturin' the schools of fishes in the North Sea at the moment."

"And let them know that he won't be available to them for a while," Rainey was quick to add.

Kyle nodded. "I'd be honored to do whatever needs to be done, sir. Ye have only to give the orders, although I cannot guarantee I can be at it permanently. If I might beg the use of a vehicle, I could leave tomorrow."

"I'll come with you," Sasha blurted out. She looked at them all nervously. "I mean, I can help him find things. I've been to Papa's office before."

"Twice," Carrie said, wagging two fingers in her sister's direction.

Sasha glared at her. "More than twice, Carrie. But he's going to need help, don't you think?" She elbowed Kyle, and he gave her a confused look.

"I really couldn't say."

Rainey caught Matt's eye, and he inclined his head, signaling her that she should let them go. She pressed her lips together. "How long do you suppose the trip will take you?"

Kyle's eyes lit up as he glanced down the list of intriguing items that would soon be at his disposal also.

"Kyle?" Rainey asked again.

"What? Oh, yer pardon, mum. I was just a wee bit lost in the possibilities here. I shouldn't think it would take more than a day. We should be back the day after tomorrow."

Rainey set her biscuit down. "So you'd have to stay the night."

Kyle suddenly felt the need to loosen his collar. "Er, purely for the sake of safety. The roads can be treacherous at night, and far be it from me to put Sasha in any kind of danger. I want her safe above all else." He realized he might be saying too much about his feelings for Sasha and was quick to amend, "Just as you yerself want only her safety, mum. I cannot tell ye how much I respect ye in that regard."

Carrie giggled at his obvious discomfort, and Matt tried to ease the situation.

"Relax, lad, yer not on trial."

"Am I not?" Kyle said under his breath.

Malcolm cleared his throat gruffly. "If I may interject, perhaps it would be for the best if I went along to help with the drivin' and such."

They all turned to him as one, each with his or her own reaction to his suggestion. No one said a word as Emma poured a fresh round of tea.

"I think it's a brilliant idea, Malcolm," she said firmly. "And what's more, there are a few household items I'm in need of. I'll come along as well, purely for a lark. We'll make a jolly foursome of it. The work'll be done in jig time, and we can all have a lovely supper together in the city. What do ye say?"

Sasha looked as if she had been given a new puppy and it had just been taken away from her, while Rainey did her best not to look like the weight of the world had been lifted from her shoulders.

Kyle wasn't accustomed to all of these family political undercurrents, so he smoothed his moustache nervously and said, "I thank ye for yer help, Emma. The more the merrier, I suppose." At Sasha's pointed look, he could do little else but shrug.

"We'll all have a grand time, just you wait and see if we don't," Emma concluded for them all.

"Grand," Sasha said dismally into her biscuit.

As the meal progressed, Kyle took in the old hall, with its impressive parade of family portraits, some more ancient than the house itself, some more recent. There was a definite resemblance throughout the male side of the family. And there was a predomination of dark-haired women with extraordinary blue eyes among their wives.

"I envy ye so much family, Professor Mac," he said humbly. "It must give a man courage to know so well who he is."

Rainey laid her hand on Matt's knee. Kyle's pain at having no family was so near the surface. There was no way for him to realize the trials Matt had been through for the sake of family.

Out of old habit, Matt laid his finger along the scar on his cheek, as he always did at a reminder of the nightmarish storm in the North Sea that had robbed him of his parents so many years ago. "It can be a double-edged sword, my friend, havin' so many faces from the past judgin' yer every move. It can be a burden as well as a blessin'. And if by chance ye fall short of what's expected of ye, there are so many who must find it in their hearts to forgive.

"My parents are lost to me as well, Kyle. I'm an orphan as much as yourself. The difference is, you were too young to ever bear the blame for the loss of your parents. I, on the other hand, was there when my parents were killed and could do nothin' to save them. One hell, two different roads."

Kyle stared hard into his teacup. "My apologies, sir. I didn't realize yer loss. Ye have my heartfelt sympathy."

Matt smiled sadly. "I know, Kyle. You of all people would understand what it is to live without such an enormous piece of yer life. And since yer goin' to be hangin' around these premises, it's probably best ye know the score."

Kyle stood up and shook Matt's hand. Clearly, he was restless in the confines of the hall. "I thank ye for takin' me into the fold as ye have, sir, and for all yer gracious hospitality. You and yer lovely family." He bobbed his head toward Rainey. "We've a long day ahead of us tomorrow. If ye could be so kind as to point me in the direction of where I should sleep, mum, I'd be most appreciative."

Sasha jumped to her feet. "I'll show him to the guest bedroom, Mama. You stay here with Papa. I'll be right back."

Carrie was instantly at Kyle's side. "I can show him where it is, Sash," she offered, all wide-eyed innocence. "You're older. You're probably tired. Why don't you stay here and rest? Busy day tomorrow, remember?"

Rainey gave her younger daughter a telling look. "Excuse me, Carrie, but since you seem to have so much extra energy right now, I think Emma and I could really use your help in carrying all these dishes back into the kitchen."

The color rose in Kyle's cheeks. "Forgive me, Mrs. Macinnes. I should have been the first to volunteer to help with the cleanup."

Rainey waved away his concern. "Don't worry about it, Kyle. We'll get plenty of work out of you before we're done. Sasha, show him the way to the guest bedroom. We need this man well rested." She raised one eyebrow to emphasize her point.

"Okay, Mama, whatever you say," Sasha was quick to agree. She was tempted to stick her tongue out at Carrie for trying to horn in on her territory, but she decided it wouldn't be prudent.

When the good nights were said, Sasha guided Kyle to the stairway that led to the second-story bedrooms. The stairs were many and dark, and when Sasha didn't bother to turn on the light for their ascent, Kyle tugged at her sleeve halfway up the climb. He heard the breath catch in her throat. They were a safe distance from the others, with only the light of a scant, mist-shrouded moon shining down on them from the windows at the landing.

"Sit beside me for a moment, if ye will, Sasha," he said softly. He brought her down next to him on the stairs, but was careful to keep a distance between them.

"What's going on, Edinburgh?"

The way she said it made him want to kiss her to within an inch of her life. They were alone in the dark. There was little chance that anyone would disturb them—for a minute or two, at least. And as far as he knew, she wasn't mad at him for any particular reason. It was the kind of stuff his dreams had been full of since he had met her, schoolboy scenarios and ridiculous erotic fantasies.

But they were no longer thrown together by the immediacy and adrenaline of the search for her father. Now, he had been foolish enough to let himself be lured into a situation where he would be forever near her, but she would have no real need of him.

"I feel there are certain things we must discuss, Sasha," he said with as much formal reserve as he could muster, considering she was only inches away, and the scent of her was driving him mad—fresh Highland air and just a hint of jasmine and heather . . . He cleared his throat to the point of pain. "In working with your father, we'll probably be seein' a fair amount of each other about the house."

"Yes, I imagine we will."

She shifted his way slightly and she might as well have said, "Let's breed!" for the effect it had on him. He put another inch or two between them out of self-defense.

"This is quite difficult for me, Sasha." He was gripping his knees so tightly that only when her hand brushed his fingers in the darkness, did he realize he was shaking from the tension. When her hand came to rest over his, he was a ruined man.

"What's difficult for you, Kyle?"

He stood up so abruptly that he nearly went tumbling down the stairs. "You, Sasha! You are unbearably difficult for me!" he said in a harsh whisper. "You, your family, this phenomenal house, and a thousand ancestors, not just in this world, but in the spirit world as well, by God! You are what all of these elements have made you. And you deserve nothing less than what surrounds you at this very moment."

Her silence was so profound that out of habit, he checked to be sure his hearing aid was in service. It was, which only disturbed him all the more. He heard her stand up beside him, felt the air between them brush past as she moved.

"What if I told you that I don't care about any of it, Kyle?" she said very near his ear.

He laughed low in his throat at the irony of her words. "Then I would say that yer hardly the proper judge of such things, since ye've never actually had to do without them. I have, and I know what it's like to be nobody from nowhere. It's paralyzing, Sasha. It makes ye feel trampled underfoot. I've tried to overcome it, the orphanages where the heat's turned off each night in the dead of winter, the daily thrashin's for not payin' attention in school when I couldn't hear a word that was bein' said, and havin' no one to turn to, no one to say, 'There, there, lad, things'll get better, I'll see to it on yer behalf.' That's what it means to be a nobody, Sasha, no home of yer own, no family, nowhere to run.

"I'm doin' my damndest to make somethin' of myself. I should turn down yer father's generous offer. But it may well be my last chance to continue my studies. It's still a kind of charity, ye ken, however well intentioned, because that's what I am, a bloody charity case! And as much as I love ye to my soul, I won't bring ye down to the places where my heart lives. I could never be that cruel to ye." He grabbed her hand and pressed the green-velvet pouch into it.

"Kyle . . ."

It hadn't been his intention to pour forth his sorrows, and he didn't give her the opportunity to shower him with her pity or perhaps even her ridicule. He dashed down the stairs blindly and out into the cold night air. And as desperately as he wanted to keep going, to leave all the Macinneses behind and run back to his one-room existence and the anonymity of pennilessness, he knew it couldn't happen.

For one thing, he had no way to get himself back to Edinburgh before morning. For another, with Professor Cameron gone and the academic year at a close, he would be left to scrounge the city for part-time work.

But even that might be an easier sentence than having to spend his days and nights around Sasha with no hope of even holding her hand in good conscience. There was no future for them, and to ignore that fact would be a lie he wasn't willing to promote.

He could no longer blend into the city and the university community unscathed by knowing eyes. Sasha herself would be on the campus in a few months, and it was only a matter of time before her father was visiting the university on occasion. To think Professor Mac could stay away from that environment permanently was an illusion his wife was not going to be able to preserve for very long. He knew it, even if she wasn't prepared to accept it.

He wasn't sure how long he had been sitting on the big, flat rock beside the water when he sensed that he wasn't alone.

"Christ, just don't make it one of those dragonfly people," he muttered to himself.

"It's Rainey," a voice said softly from behind him. "That's Sasha's rock you're sitting on, you know. It's been her favorite spot since we moved here nine years ago." He started to get up, but she laid her hand on his shoulder, indicating that he should remain where he was.

"Sasha says you're having a problem justifying your stay with us, Kyle." She heard him stifle a groan, and she sat down with her back to his. "I don't think you're aware of this, but there was a time, before we met Professor Macinnes, when Sasha and I had nothing but each other. Sasha's biological father was lost to us, I was out of a job, and Child Welfare was fully prepared to take Sasha away from me because she would speak to no one, not even me.

"If it hadn't been for the help of a total stranger, one Professor Matthew Macinnes, our lives would have turned out very differently, I promise you. There's a lot to be said for that old business about the kindness of strangers."

"Professor Mac is the sort of person people turn to for help," Kyle said with genuine admiration. "The man's a rock, a pillar of the community with a pedigree a mile long to prove it."

Rainey snuggled deeper into her jacket against the cold dampness and listened to the gentle lapping of the waves along the shore. That steady rhythm had always had a reassuring effect on her.

She wasn't absolutely sure why she was doing this, except that she had seen the look of desolation on Sasha's face at the prospect of Kyle's leaving. As far as Rainey was concerned, a look like that one demanded action, even action against her own better judgment. She hoped this wasn't a mistake.

"Matt lost his parents in the North Sea when he wasn't much older than Sasha. Although he had no way of knowing it at the time, the ship he and his parents were on had been rigged to blow up by a madman who wanted to see that whole family wiped off the face of the earth."

"Good God, that's hard to imagine! If I may ask, why?"

"It's a long story. Sasha knows it quite well. Perhaps you could get her to tell you about it one day."

He didn't bother to dispute the possibility. "Was the blackguard ever caught?"

Rainey smiled grimly into the darkness. "Let's just say that justice was done. But not until many years after the crime. And in the intervening years, Matt held himself responsible for not being able to save his parents from drowning. The fact of the matter is, he did everything humanly possible to save them. But for a very long time, he was alone in the world, carrying a burden of guilt that should never have been his."

Kyle considered this. "Why are ye tellin' me this, Mrs. Macinnes?"

"That's Rainey, remember?"

"Aye, mum, as ye say."

Rainey hugged herself for warmth. "We have a policy in this family, Kyle."

"A policy."

"In this family, we judge people by their hearts, not by the blueness of their blood." She patted the rock beneath them affectionately.

"That's very kind of ye to say, Rainey, but—"

"I'll be the first to admit that we're a pretty tight-knit group, Kyle. It's always been that way of necessity. Because we're in large part a self-made family, we've always been very guarded about outsiders. I suppose it's a Highland thing, this closing of the ranks. But Matt has seen fit to draw you into our number. No small feat. And Sasha . . . Well, I'm not really at liberty to speak for her. Suffice it to say, she seems to have developed a fondness for you. I think I can say that. And if she comes to the conclusion that you're tearing for the hills because of something she's said or done—well, to put it mildly, we'll all be very aware of the problem."

"Aye, it's been my experience she's not one to bottle up her true feelin's."

"And to think there was a time when we would have done anything to get a word or two out of her."

"Sets the mind to reelin'!" He turned so that he was sitting beside her. This was very hard for him, but he thought the world of her, and she deserved the truth.

"I'm a simple man, Rainey. All my life, my needs and my goals have been very basic. I'll grant ye that every now and again, I daydream about better things—a family, a fine house, a career, to one day be half the man yer husband is. But I know my own limitations, what's possible and what isn't. And right now, Sasha is in the Not Possible column, ye ken? I won't fool her and I won't fool myself in that regard.

"I'm tryin' to be fair to us both here. Ye say the lass is fond of me in her way. Well, let's just say I'm fond times ten of her, which makes it all the more difficult for us both.

"I'd use the excuse that she's so very young, but the fact of the matter is, you and I both know she's got a heart full of wisdom that would put Methuselah to shame. Maybe one day I can make myself more worthy of her. But right now, today, I can give her nothin', and it's killin' me."

Rainey was quiet. The situation was a sticky one at best, but she found herself rooting for the young man beside her. She wanted to tell him to set aside all of his worries about money and social status, that happiness didn't depend on such things. But that would not have been the way for a good mother to react under the circumstances, she supposed. And it was true that having no money could create very real problems in a relationship. It was Kyle who was thinking like an adult here. And she had to be careful not to overplay her hand just now. It would be a disservice to everyone.

"I understand what you're saying, Kyle, I really do. But the two of you have only known each other for a few days, and that was under extremely stressful conditions. You need time to really get to know one another in more relaxed surroundings. You'll be here, but I promise you, my husband is planning to keep you extremely busy. There won't be time for much else. You and Sasha will be constantly surrounded by other people—most notably Carrie, I'm afraid. And Sasha will be getting ready to enter the university. I honestly don't see that it will be a problem."

Kyle rose and looked into the darkness across the loch before he spoke. He sighed from the depths of his soul.

"I fancy that one of the few things I possess in this world is the ability to speak honestly, mum. I appreciate all that ye've said, and I'll grant ye that the majority of it is true. But the unhappy fact of the matter is, I love yer daughter as a man loves the woman he chooses to take to wife. Ye have my sincerest apologies if I've given offense by confessin' this to ye. I don't suppose it's fittin' for someone like me to say I'm a proud man, but there ye have it.

"I admire ye greatly, Rainey, and I won't give ye anythin' less than the truth because these are words I can never say to Sasha herself. I thank ye for yer kindness, but polite hellos to yer daughter over the breakfast porridge and nothin' more will soon make a madman of me, ye ken?

"And when that day comes, it will be the end of it. So, I want to express my appreciation to ye now for yer faith in me and Professor Mac's, because one mornin' I'll most likely be gone from yer lives, and there'll be no opportunity for good-byes." He turned on his heel and melted into the darkness.

Rainey looked out over the loch as well. The mists separated briefly to display a pristine sliver of moon, which sent glimmers of silver light leaping across the black waters. "Well, Stanford," she said to herself, "I wonder if your famous kittiwake has the answers to this one."

Chapter 17

The drive to Edinburgh was proving to be uneventful in the extreme. The men sat in stoic silence in the front seat of the Land Rover, and all of Emma's attempts at sparkling conversation with Sasha, beside her in the backseat, were greeted with lackluster one-syllable answers or simply sighs. So Emma chose to redirect her comments to little Angus, who dozed blissfully on her lap.

"Angus, my love," she said brightly. The devoted Scottie's ears swiveled back toward her voice, even in his sleep. "Did I ever tell ye about the time I had lunch with that movie star fella, Sean Connery?"

Malcolm was driving, but he tilted his head toward the backseat. "007, Em? Go on with ye. Ye would have told me *that* one by now, surely. Ye know I'm ever a fan of the man's work."

Emma gave Sasha a covert wink, but Sasha's answering smile was a bland one at best. It was going to be a very long ride.

"Well, now, a woman has to have a few secrets left in her pocket for just such an occasion as this, does she not? Has the telly ruined us all for a good story?"

Kyle did his best to roust himself out of his gloom. "When was it, Emma, this movie star encounter of yers?"

Emma dove at the opportunity for conversation. "Och, well, it was in Edinburgh, as ye might imagine. The famous folk tend to cleave to the flocks in the big city. And to give ye a clue, the man had a head of hair to rival my Malcolm at the time."

Malcolm ran his hand through the thick shock of snowy-white hair on his head with a hint of vanity. "These days, James Bond must wear a hat for fear of catchin' cold," he added for emphasis.

"Aye, well, as may be, there are those among us who would still be willin' to find *other* ways to keep that man from takin' a chill." When Malcolm frowned into the rearview mirror, Emma blew him a kiss.

"Just be at yer story, Em. Goodness knows, we need somethin' to help us pass the time."

At his comment, Kyle and Sasha looked out their respective windows simultaneously. The way they were seated, each could see the other's reflection in the glass, and they both pulled their attention back to the Rover's interior to avoid the gauntlet of what they were truly feeling.

"Well, there I was," Emma told them dramatically, "mindin' my own business, as always, chattin' up some friends at a lovely cafe and nibblin' at me kippers. They were a bit dry for my taste."

"Yer friends or the kippers, woman?" Malcolm insisted impatiently.

Emma gave him a disgruntled look. "The kippers, of course. Don't be daft, Malcolm."

"Daft, indeed!"

"As I was sayin', we're all sittin' there, mindin' our own business, when my friend, Marjorie, says to me, 'Em, Em, yer not goin' to believe this, but Sean Connery's sittin' over there in the corner, and he's starin' at us, just as bold as ye please!' "

Malcolm rolled his eyes and said to Kyle under his breath, "They say the man's nearsighted as a mole." Kyle nodded sagely.

"He's nothin' of the kind, Malcolm Macpherson!" Emma countered. "And I'll thank ye not to make snide remarks durin' my story."

"Fine, fine, ye had 007 for lunch and he made ye his queen!" Malcolm snapped.

"I never said that. So there we are, my friends and I, tryin' to ignore the fact that a movie star is starin' at us with a hungry look in his eye."

"Of course he looked hungry. The man was waitin' for his lunch, Em," Malcolm interjected.

Emma sighed in exasperation. "Just ye wait till yer tellin' one of those borin' stories of yers about the fish that got away, Love of My Life. Three feet long, my eye! It's fortunate I know the truth about some of the other things men tend to boast about the size of."

"Em, mind the children in the car!" Malcolm blustered.

"I was referrin' to their *attention spans,* Malcolm," she said with a wink at Sasha. She leaned over and whispered in Sasha's ear, "The fact of the matter is, the illustrious Mr. Connery wanted to borrow the Worcestershire sauce we had at our table. He had a waiter come and fetch it."

Sasha feigned a gasp of shock. "Sean Connery did *that*?" she exclaimed. "Right there in a public place in front of the whole world? Emma, I'm amazed you didn't run off with the man!"

Emma nodded solemnly and raised her right hand. "He did everything, exactly as I told ye, dear child. I swear it."

"Wow."

Malcolm was staring so hard into the rearview mirror that he lost track of the road and sent a shower of loose rocks flying on the shoulder. He corrected the problem immediately, but cast a sideward glance at Kyle, who was sitting with his arms folded across his chest, struggling to keep a grin off his face.

"Ye mark my words, young Maclennan," Malcolm said sagely, "I'm an old-fashioned man, very old school and set in my ways. A military man, by God. But there are times—mind ye not many of them—but there are times when a man has to ponder the possible advantages of what they're callin' today yer Alternate Lifestyle." He pressed his lips together and narrowed his eyes at the road ahead.

Kyle caught Sasha's reflection in the glass again. He smiled at Emma and Malcolm's antics, and after a moment's hesitation, she smiled back.

By the time they reached their destination, it was as if Emma and Malcolm's little exchange had never happened. They were both looking forward to a day in the city, and it was decided that they would take care of their respective chores while Kyle and Sasha set about the business of retrieving the research material from Matt's office at the university.

The plan was that after they met for supper, they would drop Kyle off at his apartment, so that he could gather his own belongings. He made it very clear this second chore was something that would not require the help of others and that this would be where he would spend the night. In fact, it was only at Emma's unrelenting insistence that he agreed to join them for the evening meal. Being in Edinburgh was clearly bringing back a flood of reminders to him about the real state of his life.

When Sasha and Kyle reached Matt's office, Sasha drew in a sharp breath at the sight of the simple, black-ribboned wreath of condolence hanging on his door. There was a card on it, stating that it had been sent by members of the faculty. It was tastefully done and very well intentioned, but, thankfully, it had no place on Matthew Macinnes's door. Sasha was loathe to even touch it.

"Please, get rid of it, Kyle. Put it somewhere else. I can't bear the sight of it."

Kyle removed it quickly and set it around the corner, out of Sasha's sight. When he returned to her, her eyes were bright with unshed tears of thanks, and the temptation to take her into his arms and lend her comfort was a sharp reminder that he was beginning to let his guard down.

Out of self-protective instinct, he reached for the sound-level adjustment of his hearing aid. He wanted to shut her out. But she wasn't saying anything just now. She was just looking at him with those mystical blue eyes that so filled his dreams with euphoria and misery. There was no button he could push to remove those eyes from his world.

"Come on, then," he said gruffly, "there's a lot of work to be done, so we'd best be at it."

He handed her several pages of Matt's list, and she nodded dutifully. But they had difficulty pushing open the office door because of the mountain of sympathy notes behind it. They were of every size and variety, some gold-embossed and very formal, some handwritten with small decorations. They were there by the hundreds, and even as Sasha and Kyle stood in the sea of them, a heavyset young woman pushing a postal cart stopped in front of the door with a large bag of new deliveries. She handed the bag to Kyle with no small effort.

"I'm Sheila. These were in the professor's box at the administration office." She lost her official tone and sniffed. "I never missed a one of his lectures, ye know, even though I'm majoring in economics. I'm so sorry he's gone."

Sasha stepped over the letters and took the woman's hand. "It's okay," she said kindly. It struck her again what a blessing it was to be able to say the words. "We found him. I'm his daughter Sasha, and he's home right now, waiting for us to bring him some of his things so he can get back to work."

"H-he's safe? You're tellin' me he survived the wilderness, miss?"

Kyle patted her on the shoulder reassuringly. "Aye, that he did. And if ye'd be so kind, Sheila, it would be doin' us all a service if ye would let the rest of the world know about it as well."

Sheila beamed, overjoyed at the prospect of being the one to spread such good news. She started off, but stopped and turned back to them, her face beaming with hope. "And Professor Cameron? Was he found safe as well?"

They lost their smiles. Sasha glanced at Kyle. She could see the reminder of his lost friend was a painful one.

"We haven't gotten any news about Professor Cameron," Sasha explained. "Certainly, we're all hoping for another miracle."

Sheila looked down at her mailcart, her enthusiasm subdued. "Aye, well, at least there's been some good news come our way. I thank ye both for that." She wheeled her way down the hall.

Sasha laid her hand on Kyle's sleeve. "I'm sorry, Kyle. I know how hard this is for you."

He looked down at her hand. "I know ye think ye do, Sasha, but ye haven't a clue." He walked away from her and took a piece of typing paper and a marking pen from Matt's desk. As he handed the items to Sasha, he wouldn't look her in the eye. "Make a sign tellin' the world he's safe, if ye would, Sasha, so we can be on about our work."

She nodded and printed out in large letters: PROF. MACINNES HAS BEEN FOUND SAFE. HE AND HIS FAMILY SEND HEARTFELT THANKS. She glanced up at Kyle, but his back was to her as he started to sort through the books against the wall. In larger letters, she added, WE PRAY FOR THE RESCUE OF THOSE STILL MISSING.

When she had taped the sign to the outside, she pushed the door shut, so that they wouldn't be disturbed and without a word set about finding the items on her portion of the list. Matt hadn't used an assistant because his schedule made it unpredictable when he would be in his office. So the system, such as it was, most probably made perfect sense to him. But to the uninitiated, the words "random chaos" came to mind.

Kyle latched on to the rhythm of it somewhat as the afternoon wore on, but Sasha was forced to ask far more questions than she cared to, keeping them both on edge. Her few attempts at simple conversation were met with single-word responses and reminders that time was short. She stopped trying.

By five o'clock, they had piled most of the requested material on Matt's desk, but they were both weary from their searching and the tension in the room. Sasha flounced down in her father's desk chair and blew a stray wisp of hair out of her eyes. She was about to say she thought they had done a pretty good job under the circumstances, but before she could speak, Kyle opened the door, ready to leave.

"I feel I should go down to Professor Cameron's office and check on things," he said, his eyes on the stack of research material instead of her. He shifted restlessly, anxious to be gone. "Ye'd be best to stay here and rest. Emma and Malcolm will be here in another twenty minutes to wine and dine ye proper."

Sasha got to her feet. He didn't have to face this alone, and she was going to make that clear to him. "I'd like to come with you, if you don't mind. It still makes me kind of uncomfortable to be here when my father isn't."

He concentrated his sight on her directly now. "There's no point in yer comin', Sasha. Ye didn't know the man, and the place is of no interest to ye."

Undaunted, she squared her shoulders and came around the desk to stand in front of him. "That's where you're wrong, Edinburgh." She folded her arms across her chest in a show of defiance. "Cameron's office is where we met, remember? I fell on my backside, and you warned me about denting university property. I believe the question of the day was, Was I a freshman?"

She saw the warm memory flicker through his eyes. She had hit home, and she knew it. But she also knew it had been a low blow. It hurt when he didn't smile.

He turned on his heel. "Suit yerself."

He was angry, and his strides were longer than hers, so by the time she caught up to him, he already had the door to Cameron's office open. There was a wreath on it as well, the same as the other had been. Kyle didn't bother to take this one down. And there were messages of condolence, two dozen, perhaps. Nothing compared to what Matt had received. Kyle placed them on Cameron's ornate desk reverently, without opening them.

But one envelope had made its way under the bookshelf behind the door. Sasha spotted it and picked it up to add to the others. It was different from the rest. It was legal-sized, and instead of being addressed to Cameron's loved ones, it was addressed to Kyle.

Kyle was busy writing down the phone messages from Cameron's answering machine, so Sasha held on to the envelope for the time being. She reasoned there was no point in getting under his skin any more than she already had. But there was no denying that she was really curious to know what was inside that envelope. When he had finished with the messages, she set the envelope on top of the others on the desk, with his name visible.

"What's this?" he asked without emotion.

She shrugged. "It was on the floor. You missed it. Whatever it is, it was intended for you."

He opened it impatiently and skimmed over the enclosed business letter. He read it a second time. "What the bloody hell?"

"Did you win the lottery?"

His expression was one of concern and confusion. "It has to

do with Cameron. If I'm to believe this, the old man's solicitors want to see me. I suppose they want to know where he's hidden the key to the liquor closet. I've done nothing wrong. I can't imagine why they would even have my name, unless they need me to help them decipher Cameron's handwritin'. It was atrocious. I was the only one on campus who could ever make heads or tails of it. I can only suppose that's the meat of the problem." He seemed to be having trouble focusing on the page in front of him.

"They don't give you any clue what it's regarding?"

"Nil."

Sasha picked up the phone and handed it to him. He glanced at his wrist, forgetting that his watch was somewhere in Orkney.

"It's late. The office will be closed for the day."

Sasha grabbed the page from his hand and dialed the number of the law offices for him. No one was there but the receptionist, but he made arrangements to visit the offices at nine o'clock sharp the next morning. When he hung up, his eyes met Sasha's.

"I don't like the sound of this," he said grimly. "Something may have come up missin'. I'd be at the top of the list if somethin's been taken from this office." He glanced around the room, trying to focus on whether anything was out of place.

Sasha sat down on the edge of the desk and toyed with one of Cameron's mother-of-pearl fountain pens. Kyle snatched it from her hand and put it back precisely in its place.

"Ye mustn't touch things, Sasha," he said in a harsh whisper. "I don't have a clue what this is all about. We must get out of this office right now. I won't have you under suspicion of anythin'. It'll be hard enough to defend myself, for chrissakes." He rushed her through the door and slammed it shut. But she stopped in her tracks and turned to face him.

"Listen, Edinburgh, let me remind you that you haven't even been in this city for days, and you have plenty of people to vouch for that fact. You're not alone in all of this. You have friends now. People who will back you up. And you haven't done anything *wrong,* remember? It's going to be okay."

He laughed, a bitter sound that came from a very dark place in his soul. "Ye just don't get it, do ye? For all I know, Cameron may have been the one doin' the stealin', robbin' this place blind. I have no way of knowin'. And if he was, who are they goin' to blame, a man who owns a dozen houses and twice that many automobiles? A respected scholar? A pillar of the university and the world in general? Or the penniless man with no family at all, a handicapped charity case the noble fellow took in in a moment of naive pity?" He grabbed Sasha's arms. "I ask ye that, Sasha Macinnes? Who will they hold accountable now that the old man is no more? Who?"

There were tears in Sasha's eyes, but she blinked them back and stood her ground. His pain cut through to her heart, and she wanted to weep for him. But this was not the time for tears. It was the time for strength, strength for herself and strength for him.

"You're wrong, Kyle," she said with every ounce of conviction she could muster. "I don't know what this is all about. But maybe it *is* simple. Maybe it is about Cameron's handwriting. You can't assume the worst. You've done so much to turn your life around. And it's going to get even better, if you let it. Maybe Professor Cameron left behind some final words of wisdom for you. Don't you owe it to yourself and to him to find out?"

He let go of her and began to pace the width of the hallway. "I don't know what I owe anyone anymore!" he said with an anger that had lived inside him since he was a very small child, fighting off the world in bits and pieces. He gave her a look so filled with anguish that she reached out her hand to him. But he turned away from her and stalked back toward Matt's office without another word. When she reached the room, Kyle wasn't there. He had simply kept going.

Sasha toyed with her potato-leek soup. She had no appetite, but Emma had insisted that she order a full-course meal at Martin's, a favorite restaurant of Malcolm's.

Malcolm tapped his spoon on the edge of her bowl. "That's not out of a tin, ye know, love. Best eat it up before it goes cold on ye. We've still got the game hens and the trout ahead of us."

Emma picked up his hand and put the spoon back in his own bowl.

"Och, I'm just sayin'," he protested.

Emma smiled at Sasha with concern. "So, he went ahead to pack up his things, did he, Sash?"

Sasha nodded. In truth, for all she knew, that was exactly what he did. She didn't know. And because she had no clue where he lived, she had no way of finding out. She had already looked in the phone book. Either he was unlisted, or he didn't have a phone. She had tried to check with the university, but the information was not available to her, and anyone who might have been helpful had gone home for the night.

There was the very real possibility that she would never see him again. Each time that notion occurred to her, she had to swallow back her tears. She had been forced to tell Emma she suspected she was coming down with a cold to explain her infernal sniffles.

"So, he'll call us on the morrow to let us know he's ready and where to pick him up, I take it?" Emma offered.

Again, Sasha nodded.

"Well, then, I hope he's an early riser. It's a long drive home, and I don't want us caught in the evening mists."

Sasha set her spoon down. "Actually, I have a quick errand to run first thing in the morning. It has to do with my registration for next year, and the office doesn't open until nine. But I'm sure it will only take a minute. Then we can all be on our way."

"They can't send ye this information through the post, Sasha?" Malcolm inquired as he scraped the last of his soup from the bottom of the bowl.

"No! I mean, to get the best classes, you have to be one of the first ones to sign up. This is a marvelous opportunity, our being here like this. It could make all the difference. I know Papa could probably pull some strings for me, but I think it's important to take charge of it for myself. Very grown-up and responsible, don't you agree?"

Emma gave her a long look. "Aye, I suppose," she said with a definite element of doubt. "We'll see how things are goin' in the mornin', Sash."

"Thank God. I mean, thank God you're such an understanding friend, Emma. I don't know what we'd all do without you."

"Hm, sugarcoatin' to the flattery as well, is it?"

Sasha gave her a pleading look as Malcolm grew distracted on the next course. Emma let the matter go, with no small reservations. But it was enough to give Sasha back her appetite. She emptied her soup bowl so quickly, she nearly caught up to Malcolm.

Later that night, as she lay on her hotel bed in the darkness, listening to the comical symphony of Emma's and Malcolm's snores from the adjoining room, she tried to picture where Kyle was. What did it look like, the place where he had eaten and slept for the last several years?

Strangely, she found it difficult to picture him anywhere but at the loch. It seemed the natural place for him to be. But she knew that wasn't how it was tonight. She wondered if he was sleeping. Or if he had left Edinburgh altogether. Maybe he was somewhere on the road without even a thought to where he was going.

She wanted to go with him. Wherever he was going, whatever his future held, she wanted to share it. It was a frightening thought. But it was also a reassuring and exhilarating one. No way was he gone from her life. She knew it. Grandmother Macha knew it. The only one who had yet to admit it to himself was Kyle Maclennan.

Too restless to sleep, she got up and threw on her bathrobe. The room was chilly. Emma and Malcolm were Highland folk. They turned down the heat at night and snuggled up to one another to fight the cold. Sasha liked that custom, even though she had never tried it personally. But she could envision a circumstance where she might be willing to give it a try.

She walked over to the window and pulled back the curtain an inch or two. Little Angus rubbed against her leg and curled up at her feet. Emma knew every hotel from one end of Britain to the other where dogs were allowed.

It was late, but there were still lights shining around the base of Edinburgh Castle as it loomed in the distance. The castle spoke to her as so many ancient places did. It was a comfort to see something built of old stone and the mortar of human history. It rose high above the car exhaust and neon of the modern city. She could almost imagine it smiling sadly in the darkness, a prisoner of time and place, held fast by its own steadfast nature.

It was the perfect time for a power outage, Sasha mused. If the city were plunged into the kind of darkness it would have been in at this hour in bygone centuries, the shadow of the castle would have filled the night sky with its power and its sheer presence. There would have been a kind of fairness to such a thing. The world needed more fairness. Fairness to people like Kyle.

Angus sighed, and Sasha let the curtain fall back into place.

She sat down beside him, and when he curled up in her lap, she scratched his ears just the way he liked best. He leaned into her hand.

"He's out there, Angus, that stubborn Scot," she whispered in Angus's ear. "Well, if I can't sleep, he's not going to either. I'm going to think about him so hard, he'll fall out of bed if he even *tries* to sleep." Angus opened his eyes and his tongue lolled out, telling her he was in full agreement with her plan.

On the other side of town, in a walk-up flat within hiking distance of the university, Kyle lay atop his bare mattress, fully clothed, staring at the familiar pattern of plaster cracks and flashing neon lights that were a nightly show across his ceiling. He had already packed everything he owned, including his sheets. All of his worldly possessions had fit into his backpack, a single suitcase, and a plastic garbage bag. Once he had finished his packing, such as it was, he had paced the room for hours, plagued with indecision about Sasha, the next day, and the world in general.

His belly growled from hunger. He was exhausted to the bone, as he had been for most of his life. As he lay there in the chill of the night, in his right hand he clutched his hearing aid, so that in the event of disaster or if he awoke to the suspicion that he wasn't alone in the room, he wouldn't be forced to search for the mechanical device that might well save his life.

Some people required a scrap of blanket from childhood to sleep. For others, it was the glow of a light in the hallway, the ticking of a familiar clock, or a hug to an old stuffed toy. For him, it was far more basic. There had been no special blankets or stuffed toys in his youth. He had little reference for them.

For him, it was the feel of a small piece of warm plastic pressed securely in his fingers. It gave him comfort and a rare sense of stability. God help him if the thing ever gave out or became lost. He couldn't afford a new one.

His decisions had been made, for good or ill. He could see no other path to take. The question was, would he have the strength to follow through on his oh-so-noble resolve. He didn't know. And the only way to find out would cost him everything. Now, he could only pray for sleep.

He turned one way, then the other, until he could no longer bear the smell of the old mattress. Out of habit, he got up and walked over to the tiny window above the sink that had served as the major feature of his kitchen for so long. The one good thing about this dive was that if you leaned to the left far enough, you could get a glimpse of Edinburgh Castle, off in the distance.

It wasn't much, as views went, but it had often given him a lift to catch that mighty stone beast at sunrise, or just as the lights were coming on. The presence of it somehow made it possible to raise his spirits above everything else, just as the castle itself rose above the rest of the bustling city. He felt a very strong connection with it, and now he felt obliged to gaze at it one more time.

It made him think of Sasha.

He tore himself away from the window and threw himself down on the bed again. The worn springs creaked and groaned in protest, but he didn't hear them. One thing he didn't need tonight was more reminders of Sasha. As he lay on his back, he tried to think of *anything* else—how hungry he was, how tired he was, how no matter what he did tomorrow, he would probably be making the biggest mistakes of his life. Irreparable, heartbreaking mistakes.

He tried to think of poetry. He tried to *write* a poem in his head. It ended up being a sappy love sonnet, and he wanted to cauterize it from his brain. But it wouldn't anymore go away than she would.

He brought his arm up over his eyes to block out the room, to block out the world. There was silence. There was darkness. But there was no peace, and his sleeve was wet from his tears. He had no more strength left for the battle.

But just as his prayers were answered and he started to drift off into oblivion, Sasha's hauntingly beautiful face swam before his mind's eye. She smiled at him. He knew that smile. And the next thing he knew, he found himself facedown on the floor. He groaned against the worn floorboards.

"Christ, woman, have a wee bit of mercy. I get the message."

Chapter 18

Sasha pulled open the massive wooden door that led into the grand foyer of the law offices of Brannaugh, Melrose, and Ross, the source of the letter to Kyle. She had made a careful mental note of the office's address. Now, as she peered around the door, she was hoping Kyle wouldn't be staring back at her hostilely for intruding into his life. He had made it quite clear he didn't want her in his future.

She didn't see him. In fact, for all its tall white columns and parqueted marble floors, the wide, circular foyer was empty. Every small sound echoed to the domed skylight overhead. The place smelled of generations of wood polish, bookbinding glue, and leather furniture. Even the receptionist's desk was empty for the moment, so she seized the opportunity to slip in unnoticed.

There were a number of broad mahogany doors leading off the central room, each with an elaborately engraved brass name-plate that gave not only the officeholder's name, but his rank, title, and his family's tenure within the firm. The exception to this was the plate on Anderson Brannaugh's door. The door was open slightly, but she could see that this rectangle of polished brass was far larger than the others, and it had not been deemed necessary to state anything more than his name. Apparently, if you didn't already know he was the absolute ruler of this domain, you had no business pushing through the front door in the first place.

"My God, Kyle, what's this all about?" she whispered to herself as she self-consciously straightened the collar on her blouse and smoothed her hair. Even though the room was empty, she felt as though she was being watched by an army of unsmiling saints.

It hadn't been easy to persuade Emma and Malcolm to let her go on this pilgrimage alone. She was pretty sure she had convinced them she was going to the registrar's office at the university. In fact, they had driven her there and offered to wait with the motor running. Fortunately, she had been able to convince them that she might have to stand in line and talk to a counselor as part of the procedure, so they had agreed to meet her in front of the office in an hour and a half. She had been given strict orders not to "wander off."

To her dismay, then Emma and Malcolm had sat in the car, debating where they should go to pass the time, for what seemed like an eternity as she lurked just inside the administration building. By the time they left and her taxi arrived, a lot of precious time had been wasted. She knew Emma wouldn't hesitate to come into the building to hunt her down when her time was up, so she could only hope everything else would go quickly.

It had been hard enough to explain why Kyle hadn't called in the morning as she had said he would. Emma had made noises about getting in touch with the university and even the police, for fear he had run into a medical emergency or foul play. She had calmed some when Sasha promised to check on his whereabouts with university personnel and to look for him in Cameron's office.

It wouldn't satisfy Emma for long. If this little plan of hers didn't work out, Sasha mused, she was going to have a lot of fancy explaining to do. Knowing Emma, she knew that in the end, no explanation in the world would do but the truth. And the truth was, Kyle didn't want to be with them. It was all that could be said.

It was a foolish decision, and Emma would search him out to tell him so. It would be nasty for everyone concerned. If she could just find him first, Sasha told herself, reason with him somehow, no matter how *un*reasonable he was being, maybe things would work themselves out.

The question of the hour was, would Kyle actually come to this intimidating place voluntarily, convinced as he was that he would be accused of wrongs he hadn't committed? Or would he simply disappear from their lives, withdraw into his own small world where no one could find him?

She was willing to gamble that he wouldn't leave without saying his piece to this fancy lawyer, without putting the truth on record, for whatever that might be worth. It was the Kyle she knew in her heart. It was the Kyle she desperately hoped she would see through the crack between the door and the door-jamb when she peeked into Brannaugh's office.

There was a luxuriously appointed reception area inside. She could see only half the room from where she stood. Kyle was nowhere to be seen, but there was a slim, impeccably dressed young receptionist. On her desk was a lavish arrangement of fresh roses, peonies, and gladioli. From the way the desk was set up, chances were that such costly displays were a usual feature of her work area.

"I'll bet she earns those in her off hours," Sasha muttered to herself. She slapped her hand across his mouth when the receptionist looked up. The woman rose from her chair and walked smoothly toward the door. There wasn't time to hide, so Sasha stood up straight and presented herself in the doorway.

The receptionist gave her a silky professional smile. "How can we help you, miss?"

"Sasha? What the hell are you doin' here?"

Kyle appeared behind the receptionist. He didn't look at all glad to see her. In fact, he looked positively up in arms. And he was most definitely the handsomest man she had ever seen, all decked out in his wrinkled and out-of-style suit. If she was honest with herself, she had to admit that she had known this response might be a possibility. Certainly, she had hoped for better, but she could tell by the look of him that he hadn't slept well. He was pale, and there were lines of stress around his eyes. Obviously, he needed reinforcements, whether he was willing to admit it or not.

"Miss? Were you looking for someone in particular?" the receptionist asked again.

Sasha raised her chin a notch and looked Kyle straight in the eye. "Yes. I was looking for Mr. Maclennan here. We're . . . friends, and I wanted to . . . that is to say, I'm here to keep him company."

"Sasha, this isn't fittin'!" Kyle scolded her in a rough whisper as she walked past him and the receptionist motioned her to a seat.

"I would have to disagree with you, there, Edinburgh," she whispered back out of the corner of her mouth.

Before she could sit down, Kyle took her by the arm and started to escort her out of the room. They hadn't gotten more than two steps, when a light came on on the telephone board, and the receptionist cleared her throat to get their attention.

"Mr. Brannaugh will see you now, Mr. Maclennan," she said formally. "If you would prefer, your friend is welcome to wait for you here." She indicated the chair again.

Kyle gave Sasha a hard look, letting her know in no uncertain terms that it would go better for them both if she left. In reply,

Sasha gave him a slow, sultry smile that sent a highly inappropriate surge of desire coursing through his blood. They were in the middle of a prestigious law office, in the middle of the day, with one of the most influential legal minds in the world waiting impatiently, possibly intent on prosecution, and all he could think of was whether there would be enough room on the receptionist's desk, once that mountain of flowers was shoved to the floor, for him to make dizzying, mind-numbing love to her, right here, right now. The future be damned!

"Sasha, I'm beggin' ye," he pleaded in her ear. "Go home. Ye don't belong in the middle of all this. Get out of here while ye can, for the love of God!"

She turned to him and pulled her collar back just far enough for him to see that she was wearing the silver necklace. He groaned, and she kissed him lightly on the cheek. Her answer was simple.

"I'm staying."

"Christ, what am I to do with ye, woman?"

"I have a few thoughts on the matter," she said evenly, "but at the moment, we have more pressing matters to attend to, *Mr.* Maclennan." She started to walk toward Brannaugh's office, her head held high. There was little for him to do but to follow her in misery.

There was a sense of genuine antiquity about Brannaugh's personal office, with its dark wood-paneled walls and ceiling-high windows draped in maroon velvet. Three of the four walls were lined with matching sets of legal texts. It wouldn't have been too surprising to see the Ten Commandments tablets under glass in one corner or another. The place looked as if it had been occupied with the business of the law since the Reformation.

The receptionist introduced a rather stodgy-looking gentleman well into his eighties as Anderson Brannaugh. He was dressed in impeccable Scottish tweeds, and he sported an outrageous set of old-fashioned muttonchops down his cheeks. The fellow was the embodiment of every British drawing room comedy from the thirties.

"Master Maclennan, I take it?" He looked Kyle up and down as if he had met him before and was trying to place him in memory.

"Aye, sir, Kyle Maclennan." Kyle extended his hand. The older man took his hand and shook it with firm, well-practiced professionalism.

"I am the late Professor Cameron's personal solicitor, Mr. Maclennan."

"A pleasure to make yer acquaintance, Mr. Brannaugh." Sasha tugged at his sleeve. Kyle looked at her tensely. "And this, sir, is a friend, Sasha Macinnes."

Sasha took his hand and smiled. It was not the kind of smile any man would dismiss, and Brannaugh's mouth twitched in as close to a smile as he could manufacture during business hours. He raised one eyebrow in her direction.

"Macinnes, Macinnes. Any relation to Professor Matthew Macinnes, perchance?" he asked with interest.

"I'm his daughter, Mr. Brannaugh," Sasha provided. "Do you know him?"

Brannaugh cleared his throat uncomfortably. "Yes, yes, of course, a very accomplished man, your father. Terrible loss, miss. You have my deepest sympathies."

Sasha exchanged a look with Kyle.

"The professor is very much alive, Mr. Brannaugh," Kyle explained. "We have just returned from his rescue in Orkney. Certainly, it's our fervent hope that our mutual friend, Professor Cameron, will be found safely as well."

Brannaugh picked up a weathered pipe from his desk and lit it. "This pipe was a gift from Professor Cameron. We were old school chums at Oxford, you know." He breathed the fragrant smoke in deeply as he digested the information about Matt's return.

"I could not be more pleased to hear that your father has been found, Miss Macinnes. Matthew Macinnes is a great asset to the university. Unfortunately, such a happy fate is no longer possible for Professor Cameron." He gave Sasha a long look. "Perhaps you would prefer to take a stroll while we attend to our business, Miss Macinnes. I'm sure a celebration is in order for your family, and legal matters are seldom of interest to the ladies in their raw form. There are some shops down the way that my secretary seems to think are quite the thing."

Kyle looked at her hopefully, but the answer was very clear in her eyes.

"If it's all the same, sir, she'll stay."

Brannaugh shrugged. "As you wish, Mr. Maclennan. She is a very *close* friend, I trust. Because the information I am about to impart to you is of a highly confidential nature."

Kyle looked at Sasha out of the corner of his eye. "Let's say that she would probably get it out of me anyway, Mr. Brannaugh. She has a way about her."

Brannaugh exhaled a row of perfect smoke rings. "As do they all, Mr. Maclennan. Shall we proceed, then?"

"Aye."

Once they were seated, Brannaugh opened a folder that had been placed at the center of his desk. He took a pair of thick bifocals from his vest pocket and seemed to read the entire document over, word for word, as they waited. Perhaps he was still having trouble adjusting to the contents of the pages. Kyle and Sasha both jumped when he drew in a sharp breath and prepared to speak.

"Well, now, Mr. Maclennan, at this juncture I'm afraid I must ask to see some form of identification." Kyle showed him his driver's license and university identification card. Brannaugh was satisfied. "Just a precaution, you understand."

"Mr. Brannaugh, sir, at the risk of soundin' rude, I don't understand. Could ye be so kind as to tell me, please, why ye've called me here?"

"You worked with Professor Cameron over the years, I'm given to understand."

"Aye, sir."

"You were . . . well acquainted? Friends, as you might say?"

"I'd like to think so, sir. But what . . . ?"

Brannaugh made a pyramid of his fingers. He tapped his fingertips together in a kind of simple rhythm. "Professor Cameron's body has been found, Mr. Maclennan, one of the few that were recovered and identifiable."

Kyle sat back in his chair. "I'm truly sorry to hear that. He was a good man, and he always treated me fairly."

"I wouldn't be surprised if he did." He gave another glance at Sasha, to be sure she had not changed her mind about staying. She made no indication that she had any thoughts of leaving, and Brannaugh leaned forward, giving the conversation an air of secrecy.

"I'm going to be very frank with you, Mr. Maclennan. Some years ago, Professor Cameron attended another conference in Oslo, Norway. He participated in many such conferences. He was far from home, and in order to keep up with his workload, he hired a transcription secretary, a local from an Oslo temporary agency. Pretty thing, to hear the story told.

"Well, to make a long story short, Cameron had a very brief but torrid affair with this Norwegian woman. And, as luck would have it, she became pregnant with his child."

"Good Christ."

"As you say. Professor Cameron was a married man, you

understand. He married well, scads of money and influence, though there was never any issue from the relationship. I daresay, when we were alone and he was in his cups, old Cammie used to talk of his love for that Norwegian woman. Something about all that Viking mystique, I suppose." He dismissed the matter with a wave of his hand. "At any rate, with his fine standing in the academic community in the balance, there was no question of ever claiming the child as his own. The truth was, the mother died in childbirth, a tragic kind of poetic justice."

"Justice? How do ye figure?" Kyle asked coolly.

Sasha laid a staying hand on his arm.

"Yes, well, the child was born with a hearing defect, as it happens. With the mother gone and the father unable to claim responsibility, the child was quite naturally put into the care of an orphans' asylum. No more was heard of him."

"No more was heard . . ." Kyle's knuckles were white on the arms of his chair. "Get to the point!"

"The point is, dear boy, that from the moment you walked into Cameron's classroom, he knew you were his son. Who can say how a man knows such a thing? He hired private detectives to have your background researched to be certain of his suspicions, of course."

"Detectives?" Kyle said incredulously. "Ye mean there were people pokin' around in my life, and I didn't even know it?"

"Yes, well, it's standard in these cases. I know of several reputable firms. But the fact of the matter is, you turned out to be who he thought you were. The day he found out, the two of us had a rousing toast of celebration right here in this very office. He was quite proud of himself for what a fine young man you had become."

"Proud of himself? Aside from spillin' his seed into the woman, he had nothin' to do with it, by God! The man was hardly more than a stranger to me, aside from offerin' me the occasional cup of tea or two fingers of Scotch on a cold night. I realize now that I didn't know Cameron at all."

Brannaugh raised his finger to make a point. "Ah, well, the man's hands were tied, you see. His wife had since passed away, but there was no way for him to make up for all the time lost between you. He did the only thing he could do in the public eye. He took you under his wing, Maclennan, gave you opportunities you would not have had otherwise."

"He erased me from his life."

"Well, now, you see, old Cammie feared this kind of reaction. And with an unstable heart condition, he wasn't at all sure he could survive such a thing as loathing from you. Which is why he waited to reveal all of this to you in the form of his will."

"So what yer tellin' me is, he never had any intention of tellin' me the truth to my face. He knew how I lived, hand to mouth, while he wallowed in money. The detectives must have told him that much. Now, I'm supposed to be all grateful and happy that the bastard threw me a few crumbs to salve his own rottin' conscience? Ye'll forgive me, Mr. Brannaugh, if I have no tears to shed for him now. It would have been far better for everyone if ye'd left well enough alone.

"At least before, I could respect the man. As it is, ye've only put a familiar name on the devil I've hated all these years. Do ye know what a child goes through when he's abandoned, Mr. Brannaugh? Do ye have any small clue? When he's too little to fend for himself and handicapped to boot? When the only thing he can think of is that he did somethin' so wrong or that he's so stone stupid that his own parents cannot stand the sight of him?

"At first, ye make up stories to tell yerself and the others about how yer dad was a spy killed in the line of duty and yer mother was killed by the other side for tryin' to save him. But then ye hear that all the other orphans are tellin' that same sad lie, and ye can't even convince yerself of it anymore."

"Kyle . . ." Sasha tried to lay her hand on his, but he stood up abruptly and started to pace the room.

Brannaugh set down his pipe. "These situations are always unfortunate, Mr. Maclennan. I'm sure Professor Cameron was helpless to solve your plight. He was most probably not even aware of it."

His anger barely held in check, Kyle leaned over the desk so that he was eye to eye with Brannaugh. "Was he not?"

Brannaugh didn't flinch. "Bygones, Mr. Maclennan. Bygones. But the truth about your paternity was only one of the reasons you were asked here."

Sasha tugged on the hem of Kyle's jacket. "Please, Kyle, listen to what he has to say."

Kyle straightened. "I've heard enough. The old bastard humped the help, all of a long winter's night. She pays with her life, and he gets off without so much as a wag of the finger because he is who he is. Ye'll excuse me, but I feel the need of a place to vomit, and I don't suppose I've got the brass to pay for the mess." He turned on his heel to leave.

"On the contrary, my dear Mr. Maclennan. You own this building. Vomit to your heart's content, my boy. Put us all knee-deep, if it suits you. You won't hear me raise a fuss." Brannaugh leaned back in his high-backed leather chair, a smile teasing at the corner of his mouth.

Kyle froze. He toyed with his hearing aid, but it was in good working order. When he turned back toward Brannaugh, his face was a portrait of anger, hope, and disbelief.

"I'm in no jokin' mood, Mr. Brannaugh."

Brannaugh turned the file around so that Kyle could see the

long list of enormous sums of money. "It's no joke, Mr. Maclennan, I promise you, it's as real as the Crown Jewels."

Kyle stared at all those numbers, but he couldn't make his
eyes focus on them. This was all a dream—or one very elabo-
rate hoax. He turned slowly and looked at Sasha. "This is all a
lie, is it not, Sasha? It's some fantastical illusion, a product of
yer bloody magic to deceive me into thinkin' we'll be able to be
together. But it'll all melt beneath the surface of the water, just
like before," he said in a daze. "Is it yer life's ambition to break
my heart, woman? I cannot forgive ye for this trickery. It's just
another reason I must get ye out of my life."

Sasha rose from her chair at his accusations. "You're wrong,
Kyle. I had nothing to do with this. If you were thinking
straight, you'd know I'd never do anything to hurt you this
way."

She saw the raw pain in his eyes, but he was unswayed by her
words as he addressed Brannaugh.

"What's the bottom line, Mr. Brannaugh? In plain language,
if ye will."

"In plain language, everything is yours, the estates, the commercial real estate, the cars, the stocks, the deeds of trust, the
goldfish in the fountains. It all belongs to you. The taxes have
been provided for in perpetuity. It's yours free and clear. But let
me make one thing very clear, Mr. Maclennan, or should I say
Mr. Cameron?"

"Maclennan will do nicely."

"You might want to think twice about that, lad. The Maclennan name means nothing. It's little more than an alias, a name
picked at random, if you will. Cameron is where your blood
lies. It's your past and your future, my boy."

Kyle stood up slowly. "With all due respect, Mr. Brannaugh,
I am not yer *boy*. I'm not certain how I came by the name

Maclennan. It hardly matters. But it is who I have been all these years. It's how I think of myself. And for now, I see no reason to change it. Perhaps if Professor Cameron had come to me personally, I would be of a different opinion."

"Yes, well, these properties are not to be seen as an apology, Mr. Maclennan, though perhaps there are some schools of thought that might conclude you are due one. These goods are meant as an inheritance from father to son. Cameron was very adamant on that count."

"Father to son."

Sasha stared out the office window at the bustling traffic. He wasn't about to let her into his life. What was worse, he hated her now.

"Oh, yes, one more small detail I was told to pass on to you," Brannaugh said as he glanced at his gold wristwatch. "The mother mentioned a name preference if her child was a boy. She had chosen the name Haakon. Peculiar Norwegian thing, I'm led to believe. A family name, perhaps. Obviously, her request could not be honored. No one on this side of civilization could be expected to know how to spell such a name. Cameron wished for you to know this much about your mother, however. Apparently it was important to her."

Something snapped in Kyle. He would never see so much as a photo of his mother. Before, he had adjusted to it in a way, because she had always been a totally nebulous person to him. Now, he had some concept of what she had gone through to bring him into the world. She had had a name chosen for him, by God!

He shoved the folder to the floor. "I don't want it! I don't want any of his bloody houses and cars!" He stormed toward the door.

"Kyle!" He stopped at the sound of Sasha's voice, but they

all knew he wouldn't stay long. She directed him over into a corner of the room, away from Brannaugh.

"What is it, for godsakes?" he demanded. "Is it the money ye want, Sasha? Do ye think for a minute it would make things right for you and me? It's tainted with my mother's blood, ye ken? Christ, I still don't even know her name! And Cameron? He sentenced his own son to a living hell. That money doesn't belong to me any more than it should have belonged to him. I want no part of this deal with the devil. Can ye not understand what this is doin' to me, Sasha?"

She took his face between her hands. "Listen to me, Edinburgh. If you don't take all of this, the government will. If you take it, you can sell it. You can put the money toward helping kids with hearing disabilities and kids stuck in orphanages with no hope of parole. You can complete your education and maybe go on to teach at the university. Something good can come out of all this, Kyle, something very good."

"How can you ask me to do this, Sasha?"

"I'm not asking it of you, Kyle. I loved you an hour ago, when you thought you had nothing. I love you now, whether you take the money or not. I'll love you thirty years from now, if we're sleeping in army surplus. All I'm saying is, you might be able to save so many kids from what you've had to go through. I know it's hard for you to think of it this way, but you can bring about a kind of justice. You'll be a better man for it, I promise."

He looked at her hard. "And it's not just so the two of us can afford to be together, Sasha?" He saw the tears well up in her eyes and wanted to throw himself off the nearest cliff. Had he been thinking clearly, he would have known better than to ask such a thing. But he felt hunted and betrayed, and he couldn't focus on how far the treachery might have reached down into his life.

Sasha reached up and unfastened the silver necklace at her throat. She handed it to Kyle, and he stared down at it in his trembling fingers. "I was more than willing to be at your side when you had nothing, Kyle. I put Grandma Macha's necklace on to show you that I was ready to face a life together, no matter what the future held. But I see now that you don't want that to happen.

"You're so busy building those precious walls of yours for the sole purpose of keeping me out that you never once realized I was already on the inside. But you know what? I'm not so sure that's where I want to be right now. Maybe one day you'll find it in your heart to trust me. If that day ever comes, you know where to find me. I can't promise you how long I'll wait. I guess we'll have to find that out together." She brushed his cheek with her lips, then left the room without looking back.

Kyle wanted nothing more than to run after her and bring her back. He clutched the necklace so tightly it cut into his hand. But for that one instant, he was still unsure whether he could ever truly be worthy of her, and by the time he reached the main entrance, she was gone.

The wisdom of her words sank in. There was very real pain to be dealt with, but she was right. Perhaps something good could come out of this twisted hell. He couldn't go back and fix the damage that had already been done. The memories of being beaten regularly for being "slow" would always be with him. Such treatment probably contributed to the severity of his hearing loss. He had been told he was deaf so many times as a very small child, what was to say that his brain hadn't obliged him? How many others were living such torture right now?

He heard Brannaugh laugh low in his throat as he walked back into the office.

"She wants the money, does she, my boy?" The file was back

on the table. "Well, the gentler sex often has more sense than we do about these things. No such obstacles as a man's pride to get in the way, you see. They want their comfort and security, and who can blame them? The girl comes from quite a prestigious family, your little Sasha. A nest egg like this just might sway the good professor to let you have her. A father always wants what's best for his children, after all. It's only natural."

Brannaugh's thoughtless words struck Kyle like a kick to the midsection. The old misery of helplessness and worthlessness hovered around his heart, threatening to rob him of the strengths he had built up within himself over the years. He knew that wealth in and of itself wasn't the answer. But he also knew that the use of the money to make positive changes in children's lives might be a substantial step in the right direction.

The rest of the answer rested in the fact that a moment ago, for one shining moment, he had felt truly loved. With utmost care, he had managed to crush the moment, to be certain it neatly matched all the other elements of his life. Now, he was as alone as he had always thought himself to be. Sasha had walked out of his life, and with very good reason. All the other times when he had deemed himself unworthy of her paled in comparison to this one.

If he refused Cameron's money, the world would judge him a lunatic, and he would live his life of solitary poverty always wondering if Sasha might have been his had he taken the other course. If he accepted the money, his future would be changed forever. He would in essence be forgiving Cameron for all that he had done or, more properly, failed to do. The abandoned child in him could not let go of the pain so quickly. In its own way, either alternative would be a kind of death.

There was madness in his head as he unfolded his fingers and looked down at the silver necklace. It was still warm from

Sasha's skin, and he had been holding on to it so tightly, a trail of blood slid down his hand. There could be only one answer. But another question still remained. Had his decision come too late? If it had, he was twice damned.

Chapter 19

"Fem, seks, sju. A naoi, a tre deug." To pass the time, Carrie counted the skips the stones made across the surface of the loch in Norwegian and Gaelic. The last one had jumped thirteen times, a record for the day, but her heart wasn't up for celebration.

Emma and Malcolm were busy catching up on the chores at their own little house on the other side of the property, so she didn't even have Angus to keep her company. Her parents were so busy staring into each other's eyes and being madly in love that they hardly had a word to say to her. And Sasha? Well, Sasha had been an absolute hermit in her room for the three days since they had all come back from Edinburgh—without Kyle.

"Mama and Papa never let *me* get away with such sulking fits," Carrie muttered to herself as she tossed a stone for distance. "Sasha's just spoiled rotten. That's why they're letting her get away with acting like such a brat. Just because she's the oldest and Mama says she has a broken heart. A broken heart . . . Sasha's the one who did the breaking. She just wants all the attention. I'd be punished clear till Christmas if I tried to pull a dumb stunt like that."

Carrie tossed the next stone hard, without a care for how many times it skipped. She didn't know what Sasha had done to make it so Kyle didn't want to come back to the loch, but-whatever it was, she was not about to forgive her for it. Kyle was *her* friend, too. A flock of geese flew overhead, and Carrie talked to them as if they were her lifelong confidantes.

"Sasha had no right to send him packing out of everyone's lives," she informed the geese. She had to shout because her impatient audience was flying away at a very rapid clip. "Just because she's too stupid to see what a nice person Kyle is is no reason to make him go away. It's not fair, and sooner or later, I'm going to find out what she did that was so mean, because I want Kyle to come back! Do you hear me? I want Kyle back here right now!"

"Aye, lassie, I'm deaf as a post, but I'll wager I could've heard ye on the east side of Inverness."

Carrie heard the stone fly past her ear before she saw it. It skipped so many times across the top of the water, she couldn't count them all. When it finally dropped beneath the surface, she turned and stood on her tiptoes to throw her arms around Kyle's neck. She laid her head against his chest and smiled.

"I'm sorry Sasha was so mean to you, Kyle." She looked up into his eyes. "If she'd ever come out of her room, I'd tell her what I think of her."

The air hissed between his teeth as he looked back toward the house. "So, she's playin' Rapunzel, is she? Seems a wee bit out of character, don't ye think?"

Carrie shrugged noncommittally. "I don't know. With Sasha, you never know."

"Aye, that's the truth," he said with a touch of wistfulness. "I suppose that's one of the things I love about her most."

At these unsavory words, Carrie drew back a step. "But she was mean to you. That's why you didn't come back."

Kyle picked up another stone and threw it. Carrie's eyes were wide with admiration as he skipped it two dozen times with no effort at all. He was every inch her idol.

"The fact of the matter is, Carrie, *I* was mean to *her*. She did everything she could to try and persuade me to come back here, but I'd have none of it."

All of Carrie's suspicions were beginning to go up in smoke. "She tried to make you come back? So why didn't you want to? Are you mad at me? Did I do something wrong?"

Kyle tucked his finger under her chin and brought her eyes up to his. "You? The Queen of All Orkney? I hardly think so, *engel*."

The fact that he had called her angel in Norwegian only made her heart ache all the more. She wanted Kyle to wish he could always be with her, not Sasha. It wasn't her fault she had been born too late, and she didn't see why it should make such a difference.

But even now, she knew her cause was lost. She could tell she didn't have a chance, just by the way Kyle kept glancing up at the house in the hope of catching a glimpse of Sasha. A single tear slid down her cheek. It was breaking her heart.

Kyle had never fancied himself much of a genius with the female of the species, but he knew disaster in the making when he saw it. He sat down on a large rock, being careful not to sit on Sasha's customary stone of choice.

"Vil du sette deg here?" he asked, inquiring in Norwegian if she would sit down with him.

Carrie was reluctant at first, and it looked as though she might run off. But when he smiled at her, she relented and sat down, a skipping rock held securely in her hand. He picked up a stone, too, and hefted it confidently in his hand.

"Yer sister's not an easy problem, Creideamh," he said with a thoughtful frown.

Carrie sat very straight. She was pleased with his use of her real name, but she was not pleased with the subject of their conversation. "To tell you the truth, she can be a real pain sometimes, Kyle," she said sagely.

"Aye, that she can. But one thing's certain, we're stuck with her, you and I." He glanced at Carrie out of the corner of his eye. It was hard to tell if the ice was melting. "And the fact of the matter is, I'm in serious need of yer help with her just now."

Carrie turned the stone over in her hand, staring at it hard. "You don't need my help, Kyle. All you have to do is walk up to the house, and she'll be all over you like a stupid bug or something."

Kyle dropped his stone and picked up a fresh one. "Well, I'm not sure on that account, Carrie. Ye see, while we were in Edinburgh, we found out that in one regard I had not been an orphan all these years."

She laid her hand on his sleeve. "You mean you have a family? But that's great! Isn't it?" He certainly didn't look very happy about it.

Kyle ran his hand through his hair. "It's a long story, Care, but the short of it is, my mother died givin' birth to me, and the professor I worked for at the university was my father."

"And he never told you so? You didn't know it?"

"No, for a number of reasons, I never knew. Not until the man died. He was killed in the same plane crash that nearly took yer father from ye. That's why I know the truth now. Once he had left this world, he was willin' to admit I was blood to him."

Carrie frowned as she looked out across the loch. "How could he do that, Kyle? How could he know you were his son and not say anything? It doesn't make any sense."

Kyle tousled her hair affectionately. "Certainly not in yer world, *engel*. But to make up for not bein' there for me for all those hard years, the professor left me everythin' he owned when he passed on."

Carrie raised an eyebrow with interest. "Did he own a lot of stuff?"

"Oh, aye, great mountains of it."

"Well, then, what's the problem? You didn't have much stuff before. Now you've got a bunch of it. Isn't that a good thing?"

Kyle stood up and started to pace restlessly. "This may be hard for ye to understand, lass, but there's no mansion, no fancy car or skyscraper on earth that could ever make up for what that man did to me by simply puttin' me out of his mind. I'm a pretty easygoin' fella on most counts, but somehow, acceptin' all that money and real estate lets that old man off the hook for what he did to me. He's dead and gone. I know that. There's no changin' the past. But I'm not so sure I'm ready to forgive him just yet, ye ken?"

"So you decided not to take the professor's stuff?"

He stopped in front of her. "Aye. But then Sasha told me I should take it and put it to use toward causes I hold dear, finish my degree, find ways to help children who are orphaned or hearin'-impaired. I could see the logic of what she was sayin' so very clearly, but my heart was withered by the news of the professor forsakin' me in such a way. I couldn't turn the pain around so fast and make myself sign the papers. We had words, Sasha and I, and she left.

"Watchin' that woman walk out of my life made the rest of my troubles seem very small by comparison. I wanted desperately to go runnin' after her. But I had nothin' to offer her unless I accepted Cameron's money. She deserves the better things in life, ye ken, the things she's used to." He glanced toward the house again, narrowing his eyes as he searched for any small sign of Sasha.

"And for that reason, if for no other, in the end, I signed those bloody papers, Carrie. It's all mine now. But I don't know what to do with any of it. I want Sasha to spend it for me. I want her to find proper uses for it, because it's goin' to be very difficult for me to ever touch a penny, except to make her happy."

Carrie tried to put all of this into perspective. "So you got the money and the houses and the cars. All that stuff."

"Aye, I'm afraid so."

"But Sasha doesn't know that yet, right?"

"True enough."

She tapped her chin in thought. "And she's mad at you, but you aren't really mad at her, even though you took the money because of her?"

"No, I have no quarrel with Sasha. She was right to say the things she said. But I acted like a fool, Carrie. I even asked her if she had conjured up the inheritance with her magical ways, just so we could be together without the problem of bein' poor."

Carrie was properly surprised at this. "You mean, you asked her if it was a mean trick she was playing on you?"

"Somethin' of that sort. But ye must understand, after the trip to the falls, lass, I had my doubts. Ye remember how I held a fortune worth of diamonds in my hand for a minute there? And those precious stones materialized from the tears of a bird, for godsakes. I was bound to wonder if this was another short-lived windfall pulled out of the air. But it was hardly the time or place to confront her about such matters. I put my foot squarely in my mouth. Again, I'm afraid. And I threw away the most miraculous thing in the world. I threw away yer dear sister's love."

"Maybe not, Kyle. I mean, you ended up doing what Sasha wanted you to do, even if she doesn't know it yet. And you're here. I'm pretty sure she'll give you another chance. She drives me crazy sometimes, but she's not *stupid*."

"No, she is most definitely not stupid, except perhaps in her choice of men."

He watched as a family of ducks waddled their way up onto the shore a short distance away. It was a very contented domestic scene, and it tugged at his heart. When he spoke, his words held the weight of a thousand lonely nights.

"Life has a way of removin' the good things sometimes, *engel,* just so ye'll have a true appreciation of what ye no longer have. And it's been my experience that love is one of the first things to go."

For Carrie, there had never been a day in her life when she had not felt loved. True, today was not one of her more shining days, but she knew in her heart that her family loved her fiercely, that Emma and Malcolm loved her. And that little Angus *adored* her.

Even Kyle loved her in his way. He didn't love her as she wanted him to, but the idea of still having him around to talk to now and then was certainly far better than not having him around at all. Besides which, they could talk to each other in Norwegian. It would take Sasha a while to catch up with them on that account. Kyle's pacing had picked up speed.

"I'll see what I can do to help you with her, Kyle," Carrie said with a sigh of resignation. "But just remember, this was all your idea, not mine."

"Kan du tilgi meg?" he said, asking her if she could forgive him.

She tossed her stone. Twenty skips, a new all-time record for her. She laid her small hand on top of his. *"Ja. Velkommen tilbake."*

She welcomed him back, and he was tempted to give her a hug to seal his return. But her mood was fragile, and he had enough good sense to think twice about such a tactless move.

Besides which, there was still one very large hurdle to be faced before he could truly accept good wishes for this unusual kind of homecoming. He squared his shoulders.

"So, my wee general, what is our plan of attack?"

Carrie braided a short, thick strand of her hair as she formulated their plan. When Kyle saw the impish smile that came across her lovely face, the word "angel" in any language evaporated from his mind. She grabbed his hand and started to pull him in a wide berth around the house, toward the deep forest of ancient oaks at the back.

"Am I allowed to ask where yer takin' me, Carrie?" he asked as he hurried along beside her.

"No."

He was grateful that he still had his small suitcase and garbage bag full of possessions stashed in the bushes. There was a strong possibility that he might yet be spending the night curled up by the side of the road.

Sasha crumpled the letter she had been writing and tossed it to the floor with a dozen of its brethren. After days of stewing over her last exchanges with Kyle, she had come to the conclusion that writing down her confused thoughts about him might help to clear her head. It hadn't helped so far.

In fact, it had only made matters worse, because now the whole of her concentration was more focused on him than ever. And the truth was, she wouldn't know where to send a letter to him, anyway. He had rejected Brannaugh's offer out of hand. She had seen him do it. So she couldn't resort to contacting Kyle through those channels. And he had broken off his ties with the university. Something told her he wasn't even in Edinburgh anymore. He was gone, lost to her.

But even recognizing that she didn't have a clue where he might be, she felt astonishingly close to him. It made no sense to her, but it was as if he were there, standing behind her at this moment. She lifted the long curls off her neck as she had done at the falls. He had liked it when she did that. Feeling foolish, she let her hair fall. For all she knew, he could be on the other side of the world by now, and here she was, still trying to please him. She wanted to scream in frustration.

In no way was she pleasant company. And with her mother and Matt so very wrapped up in their reunited love for each other, she didn't have the heart to mope about the house. She was desperate to get over it. Being miserable over Kyle was a tremendous drain on her energy, and she resented him, herself, and the world in general for the fact that she couldn't make herself stop and get on with her life.

Another piece of crumpled writing paper hit the floor. Then, realizing the clutter she had created, she scooped up all of her rejects and tossed them into her wastebasket. The room felt like a prison, and she went to her window in the hope of watching Carrie toss her skipping stones for a while. But Carrie was no longer beside the loch. Even that lackluster diversion wasn't available to her. She flung herself down on her bed and stared at the ceiling.

Enough was enough. She had to get out into the fresh air, or she would suffocate from this self-imposed confinement. Carrie wasn't by the loch. She would go hunt her down. It was the kind of thing big sisters were supposed to do, and it gave her a good excuse to wander around outside for a while. Maybe that would cure her of her mood. She grabbed her sweater, then slipped down the stairs and out the kitchen door unnoticed.

It was good to feel the soft, cool air of early evening on her face. The scent of deep water nearby mixed with heather and the fragrance of the season's first roses made her feel a bit light-headed and almost euphoric, despite her troubles.

Carrie was nowhere in sight. Sasha was tempted to set her search aside and simply meander through the gardens. But she felt the need to walk further away from the gentle confines of home. She needed to stretch her legs and have a change of scene, so she took the path that led into the oaks behind the house. The route was so familiar to her that she didn't really pay attention to how far she was going. All that mattered was that for the first time in days, she felt like she could truly breathe.

The oaks were lush with new growth, and at either side of the path, lily of the valley and wild iris peeked out between the thick fern and bracken. It lifted her spirits tremendously to be out among nature's happy prosperity. It was exactly what she had needed. And yet, the one overriding feeling in her heart was the wish that Kyle were there to share the green splendor with her. It was too lovely not to be gloried over with another person who could appreciate such wild treasures.

She had been walking for a long time, lost in her own thoughts, when it dawned on her where she was. A clearing stretched out before her. At its center was an enormous oak tree. This was the place she loved most in the world.

It took only the blinking of an eye for her to see the flurry of activity going on high in the branches. She was a strong believer, and the residents of the tree had no reason to hide from her. Everywhere, there was rustling among the leaves as great clouds of sparkling colored dust rose into the air.

"Tag," Sasha said to herself with a smile. The rustling stopped, and a tiny face peered out from between the highest leaves. Merry green eyes smiled at her from beneath an acorn cap.

"You're being naughty again, aren't you, Sium Mhaith?" she proposed to the little fellow. His name meant "Pretty Penny" because of his fondness for other people's coin. He gave her a wink, then disappeared back into the tree. The game instantly picked up where it had left off.

At the heart of the tree, where it divided in two separate directions, stood a silver chair, no larger than Sasha's palm. Below it, set deep into the wood, was a symbol, a complex pattern of interwoven curves and knots from the time of the ancient Celts. It was the same pattern borne on the silver brooch Matt had given her so long ago. She had been too taken up with the twists and turns of her own life lately to visit this place. But it was as important to her as the air she breathed.

As she drew nearer, a feminine resident of the tree descended out of the branches on iridescent wings and took her seat on the silver chair. Her auburn curls reached to her waist, and she wore a crowning wreath of tiny violets. Her eyes were the color of spring moss, and her gown was of shiny green rose leaves, sashed at the waist with lily of the valley blossoms. There was a sense of infinite wisdom about her. All the other residents of the oak floated down out of the branches and bowed before her. Sasha bowed as well. For now, the games were set aside in deference to their queen and their visitor.

Sasha walked up to the tree and bowed again. "Mar a' Ghealach, it's wonderful to see you." When she raised her eyes, she saw Sium Mhaith make a funny face at her from behind Mar a' Ghealach's throne. She was tempted to make a face back at him, which was, no doubt, his plan. But they were in royal company, and she resisted the temptation.

The fairy queen was very well aware of what was going on behind her back. With a simple lifting of her delicate hand, Sium Mhaith came skidding and tumbling down the tree branch until he lay on his belly before her. The multitude in the branches overhead burst into laughter, sending clouds of shining dust heavenward as their wings fluttered about. But when Mar a' Ghealach turned slowly to regard them, the laughter faded into the occasional titter.

Without a word, the queen directed Sium Mhaith to sit silently beside her chair and behave himself. The little fairy was quick to obey, and Mar a' Ghealach returned her attention to Sasha. She spoke in the ancient language of the Celts, a language very familiar to Sasha.

"We are all very pleased that you have come to visit us, Sasha," the fairy queen said smoothly. "We have missed you." She indicated the leaf-and-blossom-clad throng above them. They all waved and nodded.

Sasha waved back at the hundreds of familiar faces. She could name each and every one of them. "I'm sorry I haven't been coming to see you, but things have been so . . . complicated lately." She started to twist the button on her sweater. "You have the heartfelt thanks of my whole family, Mar a' Ghealach, for your aid in my father's rescue. I can't tell you how wonderful it is to have him home again."

Mar a' Ghealach rose from her throne, and with a light fluttering of her wings, she came down to Sasha's extended hand. The fairy's weight was no more than a breath as her rose-petal slippers touched the center of Sasha's palm. Mar a' Ghealach settled herself down and wrapped her arms around her knees, her dark-green eyes only on Sasha.

"Helping Matthew was our privilege, Sasha, just as it has always been. Just as helping you is a privilege." Her wings opened and closed slowly in the cool late-afternoon breeze. "You and your family have done so much to help us in the past, we are only too happy to be of service to you."

"Thank you, Mar a' Ghealach."

Never one to stay in one place for very long, the fairy queen spread her wings and rose until she was at eye level with Sasha. There was an air of secrecy to her smile.

"You must persuade your young man to let himself believe, Sasha," she whispered. "If you can do that, nothing will stand

in your way." She rose into the branches, and the rest of her sub-
jects ducked out of sight and remained very still.

Sasha watched them disappear with a puzzled look on her
face. "What? I don't understand."

"Sasha?"

The breath caught in her throat at the sound of Kyle's voice
from behind her. She turned to find him standing at the edge of
the clearing, wearing Carrie's sweater rolled up across his eyes
as a blindfold. Carrie grinned at his side and mouthed the word
"Surprise!" The temptation was to run to his arms and forget all
else. But they were in a sacred place, and there were still some
stubborn issues between them. At least, stubborn on *his* part,
she reminded herself. Carrie led him forward into the clearing.

"I'm here, Kyle," she said evenly. "The question is, why are
you here?"

It looked as though he was ready to say something, then
thought twice about it. "I'm here because yer sister brought me
here. I don't even know where *here* is." He laid his hand over
Carrie's on his sleeve. "Has the time come for me to take this
thing off my eyes, *engel*?"

Carrie looked at Sasha. Sasha nodded slowly.

"Okay, Kyle you may take it off. But just remember all the
things I told you."

"Aye, a bloody encyclopedia worth."

Carrie tugged at his sleeve. "Keep your voice down! You're
not going to remember any of it, are you?"

"Sorry!" he said in a whisper. He untied the sweater and
blinked his eyes back into working order. There was no hiding
the joy he felt at seeing Sasha again. But as he glanced around
the clearing, his expression became one of reverence. "This is a
wondrous place, Carrie, just as ye said. I've never seen such an
amazin' tree."

He walked over next to Sasha and laid his hand on the oak's rough bark. At first, he saw only a supreme accomplishment of nature, nothing else. But when Sasha laid her slim hand on top of his, the transformation began. As Kyle looked up into the dense branches, first one small face, then another, and another appeared until the tree was alive with wings and smiles of greeting. Kyle gazed up at them in astonishment.

"Good God, the dragonfly people! And so many! Tell me, am I dreamin' or just drunk far beyond logical thought?"

Carrie laughed. "Neither one, silly. They're always there. But you can't see them if you don't believe in them."

Sasha smiled at him. "You want logic, Edinburgh? You wouldn't be seeing them right now if you didn't already believe in them. Therefore . . . You're a card-carrying believer, whether you know it or not. They're willing to trust you. Are you willing to trust them?"

Mar a' Ghealach's elegant face beamed down on him from above, and out of purest instinct, he bowed before her. She drifted down to them both.

"Kyle Maclennan, I'd like you to meet Mar a' Ghealach," Sasha said formally. "She is queen here."

He bowed again. "Yer majesty, it's an honor to make yer acquaintance."

She floated nearer to him and ran her tiny hand along the edge of his deafer ear. "We have known you a very long time, young sir. We are very glad to be able to speak with you openly at last."

Kyle looked to Sasha at this revelation that he had long been known to the residents of the tree. She shrugged and gave him an enigmatic look, so he turned his attention back to Mar a' Ghealach.

"If I may be so bold, yer majesty, might a man ask just how long I've been known to ye?"

Her gentle laughter of delight was like silver bells on the breeze. "Since the time of the Old Ones." She whirled and tickled his nose with her wings. When he sneezed, she quickly scooted herself up out of harm's way.

Carrie tugged on his jacket pocket. "That's what happens every time anybody sneezes," she said sagely. "People who think they sneeze because they have allergies have just been nonbelievers for too long." Sasha withdrew her hand from Kyle's, proving to him that what he was seeing was his own doing, not hers.

Kyle watched Mar a' Ghealach hover above them effortlessly. "Incredible."

"Sit down, please, Kyle, Sasha," she instructed them, with a nod to Carrie that she was welcome to stay also.

The fairy queen settled herself on Kyle's shoulder, and the throng above them drew nearer, until they, too were seated on the mossy ground at the base of the tree. It was an act of faith for them to come down out of the branches to sit beside Kyle. He realized this and smiled his thanks.

Sium Mhaith was about to jump into his pocket, but Sasha spied him at his old antics and shook a warning finger at him. The little fairy doffed his acorn hat with a shamefaced grin and settled back among the crowd. All eyes turned to Mar a' Ghealach.

"My people," she said regally, "this man and our Sasha have been brought here together for a reason."

Sasha glanced over her shoulder at Carrie for some clue about where this was heading. But Carrie ducked her eyes and busied herself with the study of a bit of twisted twig.

The fairy queen leaned forward and gave Sasha a knowing smile. "I have seen the future of these two for a long while. This man who has known no father during this life will, in turn, be the loving father of three children of his own. This man who has known no mother in this life, will see motherhood worn like a shining crown by our dear Sasha as she nurtures his family."

Kyle started to open his mouth, but one glance at Mar a' Ghealach told him he must wait until the end of her speech. He looked at Sasha, but she was sitting very still, her eyes closed, her face serene.

"As those of us who dwell here know, this marriage reaches far beyond the world of material needs. Such matters are of no consequence and should be set aside as such. Their union will help to secure our future, the future of this place and the safety of the sacred falls. The time of loneliness, the time of separation and misunderstanding is at an end. These things have been known to us for a very long time. All that remains is the need for their honest declarations before this gathering of hearts." She tugged on Kyle's cowlick.

Sasha's eyes were open now, but when he looked at her lovely face, Kyle couldn't find the right words to say.

Carrie cleared her throat. "He took the money for your sake, Sash," she whispered.

Sasha drew in a sharp breath. "You took the inheritance, Kyle?"

"Aye. But I want no part of it, Sasha, unless ye'll spend it for me. Everythin' ye said in Brannaugh's office was true. That money must be put to proper use. It's the only way I can live with all that's gone before. And if we can spare even one child from goin' through what I had to go through, it'll all be worthwhile."

Mindless of their audience, Sasha threw her arms around Kyle's neck and hugged him for dear life. And with a quick glance at Mar a' Ghealach for permission to reciprocate, Kyle wrapped Sasha in his arms as if he might never let her go.

"Can ye forgive me for all the foolish things I said, Sasha?

Can ye find it in yer heart to give me another chance to be some small portion of the man ye deserve?"

Sasha hugged him all the tighter. "There's nothing to forgive, Kyle. It was all too much for either of us to comprehend so quickly. Can you forgive me for pushing you like that, for not understanding how the pain you had carried around for all those years would color your whole world?"

He kissed the top of her head. "Ye said it yerself, Sasha, there's nothin' to forgive. I'm only askin' if yer willin' to help me work through all of this madness. It's a lot to ask, far more than either one of us realizes, I expect."

Sasha looked up into his eyes. "I'm more than willing, Edinburgh. And I get the distinct impression you and I are going to be a force to be reckoned with." She took the green-velvet pouch containing the silver brooch from her sweater pocket and slipped it into his hand.

He smiled at last. "Aye, movers of heaven and earth, wouldn't ye say?"

Her lips were very near to his as she whispered, "Aye."

As Sasha and Kyle made their promises to one another, Mar a' Ghealach fluttered over to Carrie and sat down on her knee. "This good deed will not be forgotten, Creideamh," she said with a smile.

Carrie looked away from Sasha and Kyle and focused her attention on a small female fairy who was sitting a short distance away from the others. She was dressed in dark-green violet leaves, but her dress was torn in places and the ring of marguerites and willow leaves she wore in her hair was wilted. Carrie felt a kinship with her.

"I thought Kyle was mine," Carrie said for Mar a' Ghealach's ears only. "I was wrong."

The fairy queen followed the line of Carrie's sight to where the bedraggled little fairy sat, staring up into the tree. "No, there is another waiting for you, my dear Creideamh. In some ways, he has much in common with your sister's choice. But in other very important ways, he is far different, just as you are different from your sister. You, whose name means 'faith,' will have your work cut out for you. But it will be a task worth doing. This much I can promise you." Carrie still looked doubtful. "Would you like to know two things about him?"

Carrie brightened, and Mar a' Ghealach summoned the sad little fairy to them. The fairy tried to straighten her appearance, but had only limited success.

"Carrie, this is Seileach," the queen said. "She has visited the man in your future. As you can see by her appearance, he is not doing well at the moment, and she is staying away from him until he is in a better mood. But she has permission to tell you two things about him. She cannot tell you his name or where he is at any given time. But if you choose your questions thoughtfully, there is much to be learned."

"He's stubborn!" Seileach blurted out.

Mar a' Ghealach raised her hand. "She is allowed but two questions, Seileach. Let her ask them, if you please."

Carrie and Seileach sized each other up with friendly curiosity as Mar a' Ghealach returned to Sasha and Kyle. They were smiling now, and looking into each other's eyes as humans did when they would soon be lovers. The fairy noticed that Sasha was wearing the silver necklace that had once belonged to another woman native to these woods. She was glad. In her heart, she could already see the children these two would have. There would be many turns in the road for them, many challenges, but they would be worthy of the journey.

She noticed a telltale motion in the pocket of Sasha's sweater.

"Sium Mhaith!" The motion stopped abruptly and a tiny red-cheeked face peered out of the top of the pocket. There was the sound of a coin clinking against another coin as he dropped the evidence. His shrug of feigned innocence got him nowhere with his queen. "A word with you, Sium Mhaith, if you please."

Chapter 20

It didn't concern Sasha when Carrie decided to run ahead of them on the path that led home. Her little sister was more familiar with the intricacies of these woods than anyone else in the family. That was saying a great deal. And it would soon be suppertime, which meant Angus would be around.

Sasha smiled to herself, happy beyond measure that they were finally returning to regular family life. But more than that, she was glad that Kyle was going to be around to share their refuge in the Highlands.

They hadn't gone very far from the clearing when Kyle touched her shoulder to stop her. She hoped he was going to kiss her again, now that they were away from family of the usual and the fairy sort. Of course, these woods were alive with observant eyes. But she still felt a strong sense of intimacy here on the path that she had traveled since she was younger than Carrie. When she turned to Kyle, that silly, happy smile was still on her face. She didn't see any point in hiding it. But his expression was deadly serious.

"I'm goin' away, Sasha."

She did the first thing that came to her mind. She laughed. "No, you're not, Edinburgh. You just got here. And my father needs you. You agreed to help him." He was looking at her with such intensity, she knew he wasn't joking and that he would be gone by morning. "Where are you going?"

"Oslo."

She had come to hate the word. It signified death and disaster.

"For godsakes, why, Kyle?"

He took her hand and brought it to his cheek. "I know who my father was now. That's goin' to take a hell of a lot of gettin' used to, I promise ye. But I don't even know what my mother's name was.

"She died bringin' me into the world, and I don't have a clue what color her hair was or if she had a favorite flower. For all I know, she may have had other children." His eyes misted. "I may yet have family, Sasha. I know ye cannot imagine how important that possibility is to me."

She kissed him lightly. "You'll never be without family again, Kyle."

He smiled at her sadly. "Aye, I know that somewhere in my heart. But after so many years of havin' it all be so very far away, I'm close now. Brannaugh knows my mother's name. I'm sure of it. And I'm goin' to lean on him till he tells me.

"I have money now, by God. I can find out what I need to know. No one can keep me from the truth anymore. It cannot possibly hurt any more than the lies.

"Yer father is goin' to need a week or two to get his strength back. He has the research material he needs for the time bein'. If he cannot understand why I have to do this, then he's not the man I think he is. I'll be there for him. I'll be there for you as well. I give ye my word. But first, I must do this. Can ye understand, Sasha?"

She moved away from him and knelt at a gathering of wild violets beside the path. She saw Mar a' Ghealach's glorious green eyes watching her from their depths. The little fairy made no move that might sway her decision one way or the other. She only kept a watchful eye on her favorite human.

Sasha stood up and walked over to Kyle, who waited in misery for what she might say. She tucked a fresh violet into the button of his shirt.

"You have to go, Kyle. I know that. But I won't let you go alone. I'm coming along to keep you company."

It was one of the things he had dreaded hearing from her. "I can't let ye, Sasha. After what yer parents have just been through, after what we've all been through, I can't let ye tell them we're flyin' to Oslo. I'm beginnin' to know yer mother well enough to know she'd take a broadsword to my head or sic the dragonfly people on me. I don't know which would destroy me faster."

"You're probably right," Sasha conceded. "So, we just won't tell them we're going to Oslo. We'll tell them . . . we'll tell them we're going to Edinburgh to look at all your pretty new real estate."

"Christ, don't remind me. Just lookin' at that list of property makes my head spin. I think I'll chuck the lot of it, except for the lodge in the Grampians."

She looked at him sideways. "You have a lodge in the Grampian Mountains?"

"Aye, I double-checked. It's there on that bloody list. I think it was the one thing old Cameron actually loved in this life. He used to talk about it no end. It was his hiding place from a cold marriage, his bloody, goddamned, rich-bastard sanctuary."

"Have you ever seen it, Kyle?" Sasha asked with interest.

"Never. It wasn't the kind of place you took the hired help."

"And now you own it."

"Aye."

"We have to go there, Kyle. I want to see it."

"All in good time, love. At the moment, other things are more pressin'."

"Then we'll leave first thing in the morning. I'll be ready whenever you are."

He knew by the look in her eye that it was pointless to argue with her. And the fact of the matter was, he'd love to have her at his side for this. His perspective on things had taken too many blows in the last few days, and she was undeniably a steadying factor.

But Matt and Rainey Macinnes were good parents, and they were no fools. Even if they bought the notion that he was taking her to Edinburgh only to help him tally his new holdings, he wasn't sure they would let her go unchaperoned. If Emma and Malcolm were assigned to accompany them for the trip, their little conspiracy would be at an end before it started. Worse yet, if anything happened to Sasha on the trip, no matter how small, he would never be able to look her parents in the eye. They would never trust him with her safety again. The risk was far too great.

As he looked down into her fathomless blue eyes, the unqualified love he saw there nearly melted his resolve. Except for his need to know who he was, he wanted her more than he wanted anything on earth. And because he wanted her to his soul, he was going to have to leave her behind.

She would curse his name. *All* of his names, he had no doubt. But by the time her anger cooled, he would be back with all the information he needed to set his heart to rest. He would be back for good, if she would still have him.

Sasha rose on her tiptoes and touched her lips to his. It was an innocent, almost shy move, very out of character for her. It was the kind of kiss a wife might give her husband, and it set his blood on fire. He was about to say good-bye to her. Just for a little while. She would be none the wiser that he was going to leave her behind until after he was gone. But the merest thought of separation from her made him wrap her in his arms as if to save the pair of them from drowning.

The feel of her, warm and willing in his arms, that was what he truly wanted from life. The strength of his embrace didn't give her pause. In fact, she pressed him closer and raised her eyes to his in a silent request for more. He answered her with a kiss that promised her his heart for all time.

"I worry about it, Sasha," he whispered against her ear.

"What now, Edinburgh, the price of eggs?"

He put her back to arm's length. "The deafness. I lay awake nights worryin' about the deafness. Not for myself, but for whatever life you and I might make for ourselves. What if it's genetic?"

She gave it some thought. "Have they ever told you that it was?"

"No. But ye must understand, because I've only ever been treated through public clinics, I've never gotten much information about my condition. I can only conclude that it was a birth defect of some sort. But if my hearin' degenerates, if it's somethin' that can be passed on to a future generation . . ."

"Then we'll deal with it, Kyle. It's not a problem for me."

He kissed the top of her head. "Spoken like a woman who hasn't a clue what she's lettin' herself in for. I don't deserve ye, Sasha Macinnes."

"You may be saying that in a whole different way before we're done, you know?" She ran her fingers down his cheek. "I don't know what I can do to convince you that we can get past all these things if we just trust each other. I'm willing, Kyle. I don't know how I can say it any plainer than that."

It was Sasha who led them off the path to the lush patch of new spring moss beyond the sight of the path, beyond the sight of all the world. They sat there together, listening to the breezes of late evening play among the branches of the ancient oaks. There was a lifetime of things to be said between them, but they spoke not a word.

Sasha felt the knot of tension at the back of Kyle's neck as she rubbed his tired muscles. It was something she had seen her mother do for Matt at the end of a difficult day. She knew it worked.

Kyle closed his eyes slowly as he began to relax against her hand. This was all new to her, and yet it was so natural, it felt as if she had been extending doing this simple gesture of affection to him all her life.

"What do you suppose she was really like, Kyle, your mother?"

"I don't know, Sasha. I honestly don't know."

She rose on her knees behind him and started to rub his shoulders. "I mean, we know she worked for a living."

He snorted at the notion. "Aye, but what *kind* of work? She called herself a part-time secretary of sorts, from what I can gather. But I have to wonder if she slept with all her employers. Just because she told Old Wallie he was the father doesn't make it true. She might have just latched on to the richest possibility of the lot, ye ken. Accordin' to Brannaugh, Cameron was a fool for the woman. She might have figured she had a shot at the easy life."

Sasha considered this. "Or, she may have simply been a woman in love with a man she couldn't have. Maybe she knew he had no children, but that he desperately wanted a child. As rich as he was, maybe that was the only gift she could give him to show how much she loved him."

Kyle opened his eyes and took Sasha's hand from his shoulder. He persuaded her around so that she was sitting on his lap.

It was a move that tantalized them both. She laughed with delight and wrapped her arms around his neck playfully as she laid her head on his shoulder.

He wagged his finger at her like a stern teacher. "You, Sasha Macinnes, are what we in the academic world term a Hopeless Romantic. Yer a very dangerous breed."

She toyed with the little violet she had tucked into his buttonhole. "Are you telling me you're a coward, Edinburgh? Because if you are, I just may have to cure you of it."

She laid her hand over his heart and felt its pace quicken. Then, in a bold move, she took his hand and pressed it against her own heart. He drew in a sharp breath and started to pull his hand away. But she would have none of it. She returned it to its place and held it there.

Kyle groaned. "Do ye have any vague notion how much I want ye, Sasha?" he asked.

It was as if he hadn't really intended to speak the words aloud. But she had most definitely heard them, and she shifted herself so that she was on her knees in front of him. He couldn't look her in the eye for fear he would totally lose control over his passion for her. Every breath she took, every small sound and move she made intensified his need for her.

She caressed his cheek and brought his gaze up to meet hers. "I know I can trust you, Kyle."

She might as well have shot him through the heart. For her to say those particular words twisted the desire inside him. He could have dealt with most anything from her—hatred, disappointment, rejection. He could not deal with this, and as she leaned into him and her lips parted beneath his, he knew he was a lost man.

Their separation would be for only a few days, he told himself. But somewhere in a dark corner of his heart, that thin little voice kept telling him this might be the end for them. Love was always the first thing to be surgically removed from his life. And if there was even the remotest possibility that he was about to lose her love, how could he endure the rest of his life never having tasted of her as she was demanding him to do at this moment? He had every intention of returning to her within a week. And when he did, he was going to ask her to marry him. It was a legitimate request, now that he was no longer a pauper. She claimed she could live with his deafness. What if he were minding the baby one day and failed to hear its cries? He pushed the notion out of his mind. He would feel the baby's calls through his skin if necessary, he promised himself.

Their kisses deepened, and he leaned her back into the soft bed of moss. She smiled up at him tenderly as he caressed her breast. The smooth cotton of her blouse only made him yearn for the silken feel of her skin. If they went much further, he wasn't sure he would be able to protect her from the magnitude of his own lust. He was only human, and this had been on his mind for so very long.

"Ye don't know what yer askin' of me, Sasha," he whispered into her ear. The scent of her hair was like paradise.

She pulled him down to her for yet another kiss. "I'm not afraid, Kyle."

He shook his head slowly. "Then yer a fool, love."

When she unbuttoned her blouse, he couldn't resist pressing his lips between her breasts, just once. Such a kiss was sweeter than he could have ever imagined, and he was sorely tempted to try it once more. But to do so would most likely seal both their fates, and he had just enough brain left to know better. His fingers trembled as he struggled to rebutton her. She pushed his hand away and sat up so that her breasts teased him just behind the opening.

"So, what are you saying to me, Kyle, that you don't find me attractive?"

The question was asked in all sincerity and with an unmistakable edge of hurt. He would have dearly loved to demonstrate how wrong her conclusion was. It would have been better to wait until after he returned from Oslo for this, but the words were burning his tongue. As he stood up and straightened his clothing, he had to turn away from her slightly to cover his obvious arousal.

"What I'm sayin', you exquisitely lovely idiot, is that I want to marry ye, damn it!"

One plentiful breast fell free as she propped her elbow on her knee and frowned at him. "You want to marry me, damn it? Now who's the Hopeless Romantic?"

He gawked at her anatomy like a twelve-year-old. "Please, Sasha, I beg of ye, cover yerself!"

She made no move to do so. "Now I want to be sure I have this straight," she said, fully aware of where his attention was hopelessly locked. "If you'll remember, I was fully prepared to love you before we knew anything about your background, right?"

A trickle of perspiration traced down his temple. "Aye, ye were. That's true."

"So now, I need some assurance from you that if you discover that your birth mother was not a saint, or that she had one leg shorter than the other, you're not going to back out on this marriage proposal of yours because the poor woman wasn't perfect. I know you, Edinburgh, and I'm not going to tolerate that kind of thinking from any fiancé of mine. Understood?"

She had nailed him squarely, and he knew it. He might well judge himself to be unworthy of her if his mother turned out to have a history of mental illness, for example. Such things were by no means impossible. He hadn't even been aware of the excuses he was already manufacturing in the back of his mind if he found himself to be unworthy of her because of a defect in his mother's pedigree. She was going to hold him to this rash offer of marriage, and he knew that when she made up her mind about something, she was not a woman to be trifled with.

"And just what sort of assurances would ye need to seal the bargain, Miss Macinnes? I'll gladly sign over all my property to ye."

She shrugged, which only shed a more delicious light on her exposed breast. "You've already admitted the property means nothing to you." With the timing of a Paris stripper, she undid the bottom button on her blouse and peeled the garment off entirely. "No, I'd say if you're serious about this marriage thing, the only way I'll be able to believe you is if you take my virginity."

"Yer daft, woman!" The sweat was finding its way down his backbone as well now. "Ye mustn't say such things!"

To his shock, she stood up and proceded to unzip her jeans. With his next ragged breath, she was standing before him as he had seen her in that foolish dream of his, where she had been dancing among the oaks, every inch of her skin as smooth as porcelain and glowing before his eyes. She was angel, goddess, and soul-stealing temptress, all in one gloriously tantalizing body.

When she reached up and lifted the hair off the back of her neck, she gave him an unhindered view of the full curve of her breast before she let the dark curls fall. His gaze lowered. She was earth. She was pure erotica. She was salvation for the taking.

No more perfect woman had ever stood before a man. He was beyond speech, and she smiled at him as Eve must have smiled at Adam as she extended the fateful apple to his lips. She shifted her weight to the right, then back again.

"What do you say, Edinburgh? How's your courage holding up? Because mine is doing just fine. Do we have a bargain?"

* * *

The house was dark and quiet as Matt and Rainey kissed beneath the covers. The fire on the hearth was down to a warm glow, and shadows danced across the double swan emblem on the mantel. Carrie had informed them that Kyle was back and that he and Sasha were walking in the woods together, although they had yet to see either of them.

"So, do you think those two are going to be all right?" she asked.

"Those two? There was never a doubt, *mo chridhe*. Don't ye read the daily news? They've been written in stone since the grand openin' of Stonehenge."

"I suppose you're right. I just can't help wondering if Sasha is serious about a commitment to him."

Matt smiled at her adoringly. "When the time comes, she's goin' to hit that poor lad like a ton of bricks, my love. Believe me, he won't stand a chance, so whisht yer frettin'."

Rainey stretched from fingertips to toes. The time had come for a true reunion of the hearts. She and Matt had been husband and wife for a long time. The simple scent of each other was enough to inspire a tantalizing mixture of remembered pleasures and heated fantasy.

"How are you feeling, dear husband? If you're tired, I could go busy myself elsewhere." Her smile was a tantalizing one.

He laid a possessive hand across her arm. "Stay right where ye are, woman. I think I require a bit of massage therapy."

As she stroked Matt's flank with a practiced hand, Rainey was pleased to feel the gooseflesh rise. She laughed low in her throat and brushed her palm over his nipple. It was already hard as a pebble, just as her own were. Her fingers slid down the flat of his belly, and he drew in a sharp breath.

"So, since I'm no longer allowed to worry about my oldest, and I no longer have to worry about you, Mr. Dances with Selkies, how ever am I going to fill my days, pray tell?"

Matt tucked a stray curl behind her ear for her, as he had been doing for as long as he had known her. "Might I remind ye, yer younger daughter is comin' into her own faster than either of us is ready to admit. I don't fancy ye'll find yerself with idle time, love. Of course, if ye were to ask me, yer current activities suit ye just fine."

She gave him a provocative grin. "Ah, so for the next twenty years, you see me as a full-time . . . How can I say this delicately? Courtesan?" She teased the hair on his chest.

It was his turn to grin. "How *I* see ye? How I see ye is standin' at the top of the Falls of Glomach, twistin' all of heaven and earth to yer dainty heels as ye declare yerself queen of all ye survey, includin' the royal, outright possession of my humble heart. That's how I will always see ye, *mo chridhe.*"

She replied with a kiss that quickly wiped away all else around them. It renewed the vows of the past and hinted strongly at new promises about to be made. Rainey snuggled closer, her skin radiant in the soft firelight.

"So tell me, Stanford, when you were out there on those rocks with nothing but selkies and kittiwakes to keep you company—female ones, from all I can gather—did you ever give a thought to me?"

She caressed the ready length of him and gave him a bold squeeze. In reply, he rolled her over and pressed her beneath him with a lusty grin. What pain there was, was forgotten as he rubbed her nipple gently between his thumb and forefinger. She groaned and arched herself against his pelvis.

"I saw ye beside a peat fire, *mo chridhe,* you and Care. I wanted nothin' more in the world than to be able to sit there with the two of ye till my dyin' day. Just as, now, there is nothin' I want more than to feel myself beatin' inside ye. And to feel ye hold me fast, like ye'll never let me go. I want to climb inside ye and stand at the very top so I can feel it all pour down into that deep pool where our children wait for their time. I want to drench myself in the glory of those miraculous waters till I'm like to drown."

"God, how I missed you, Matt!" she whispered. "I can't get enough of you. If anything ever happened to tear us apart again . . ."

"I'm here, Rainey, I'm here beside ye." He leaned down and pulled her nipple into his mouth, kissing it tenderly, then gave it a gentle tug of ownership with his teeth. He began a trail of kisses that started at her solar plexus and traveled down her middle till he paused at the triangle of dark curls that covered her from his sight. The scent of her arousal flooded his nostrils, and once again he was a starving man. "Let me in, my love, take me out of the cold."

She parted herself and welcomed his hunger. He held nothing back, and it spurred her need for him to the very edge of her resistance. She grabbed his hair with both hands and held him to his task until she could bear the tension no longer. She drew him up to her mouth and kissed him as they shared the salt-sweet essence of her desire for him.

Their passion was a desperate thing, born of the knowledge of what the loss of it would have meant. Born of a knowledge that each day, each joining, each breath was a precious gift to be seized and held on to tightly, for there were no guarantees about the future beyond the reality of their timeless ties to one another, their undying love, and their absolute commitment to their children's happiness.

"I can't bear the emptiness," Matt. You've been away too long," she said breathlessly. "Please . . . inside me, now!"

As he slid his warm fingers inside her firmly, he felt her powerful climax begin to pulse downward, a climax meant to carry his seed closer to her heart. He withdrew his hand and drove the hard strength of himself deep inside her. She cried out in welcome and celebration as she clasped his haunches, driving him deeper still. No caution, no compromise, only the fusion of body and soul as the torrent rose inside him and flooded her warm, fertile waters. Once again, he had given her his heart. The pledges between them had been renewed.

They trembled with the impact of what had passed between them. This had been no simple reunion, but a powerful, driven act of creation. Their lives were about to take another turn as Rainey's inner muscles pulsed, holding fast to the promise of new life within her. Here was yet another miracle, another story waiting to be told. It was what their lives were about. The past and the future would once again find an understanding sanctuary in the present.

"A son," she breathed joyously against Matt's ear.

"Aye, my sweet Rainey, a son. Are ye game?"

ONYX

LYNN HANNA

A child in peril....A journey through ancient Scotland....A timeless destiny.

STARRY CHILD

Rainy Nielson is desperately worried about her daughter. Since the tragic death of her father, eight-year-old Sasha has not spoken a word. And sometimes, especially in bad thunderstorms, her behavior is strange and inexplicable. Rainey has taken Sasha to medical doctors, to child psychologists, to speech therapists. All the experts are baffled.

Matt Macinnes, a brilliant young linguist at Stanford University, recognizes that little Sasha's babblings are not her own invented gibberish—she is actually speaking in fluent Gaelic. Matt's understanding of Sasha opens a door to her secret world. At last someone can communicate with her, but what he discovers is both exhilarating and terrifying.....Could a modern American girl really carry within her the soul of a long-ago Scottish princess?

❑ 0-451-40838-1/$5.99